PATHS TO THE STARS

TWENTY-TWO FANTASTICAL TALES OF IMAGINATION

EDWARD WILLETT

SHADOWPAW
PRESS

ISBN 978-1-9993827-0-4

Cover art by Tithi Luadthong

Order From:
SHADOWPAW PRESS
303 - 2333 Scarth Street
Regina, Saskatchewan, Canada

orders@shadowpawpress.com
www.shadowpawpress.com

This book is dedicated to all the writers whose books I loved as a child, who inspired me to tell my own stories, in the hope I could move and entertain readers as much as I have been moved and entertained.

INTRODUCTION

IT'S HARD TO SAY when I first began reading science fiction. My two older brothers, Jim and Dwight, both read the stuff, and thus I was exposed to it at an early age.

What I do know is that for many years I probably read more science fiction short stories than novels: short stories by Asimov and Heinlein, collections of short stories, anthologies of the year's best, single-author collections—I loved short stories, and so it wasn't too surprising that when I first started writing science fiction, I began with the short form.

(Besides, I thought that was the generally agreed-upon path to science-fiction writerdom: you wrote short stories, you got them published in magazines, you got noticed for your brilliance, and only then did you move on to novels.)

My very first fiction sale, in 1982, was a short story (although, not being science fiction, it's not in this book). "The Storm," about two kids caught in a prairie blizzard, sold to *Western People*, the magazine supplement of *The Western Producer* (an agricultural newspaper), which would later also publish my short story "Strange Harvest" (which *is* in this book, and is quite possibly the *only* science fiction story *Western People* ever published). I was in

Zurich, Switzerland, of all places, touring with the Harding University A Cappella Chorus (I'd graduated three years earlier but did two European tours with the chorus as an alumnus), when I received an aerogram from my mother: a letter from the magazine had arrived in the mail, and, with my previously granted permission, she'd opened it, discovering the good news.

And yet…over the years, I really haven't written that much short fiction. See, despite my love of short stories, I soon found that I personally had trouble with the "short." Inside many of my short stories were novels trying to get out. "The Minstrel," which starts this collection, expanded into *Star Song*, the first novel I tried seriously to sell. (There were three high-school novels before that, *The Golden Sword*, *Ship from the Unknown*, and *Slavers of Thok*, my Grade 12 *magnum opus*.) "Lost in Translation," a longish short story published in *TransVersions*, became *Lost in Translation*, my first adult SF novel, first published in hardcover by FiveStar, and then brought out in mass-market paperback by DAW Books. "Sins of the Father" was never published as a short story, but became *Marseguro*, my second novel from DAW, and winner of the 2009 Aurora Award for best Canadian science fiction novel (well, technically, Best Long-Form Work in English).

But despite my predilection for novels, every once in a while, I do write and (Lord willing) sell a short story. And I've also kept tucked away on my hard drive a few unpublished stories that I think deserve to see the light of day, even if I've never found a home for them. (At the very least, you may find it interesting to compare some of these very early efforts to my latest ones. Be kind.) As a result, I've often thought of publishing a collection. Trouble is, a short-story collection by an author who isn't exactly known as a short-story writer seemed like it would be a hard sell for any traditional publisher…so I never acted on that thought.

Until now. I like my stories (obviously), and am egotistical enough (hey, I'm a writer) to think that perhaps other people might like them, too. And so, at last, I *have* collected my short stories—almost all the published ones, plus a few unpublished ones—into the book you now hold in your hands, whether in ink-on-paper or pixels-on-screen format.

I hope you enjoy them.

Edward Willett
Regina, Saskatchewan
February 2018

THE MINSTREL

I chose this as the first story to present because its central image, of a youngster gazing longingly at the silver spires of starships, aching to ride them into space, is a metaphor for the way I reacted to science fiction as a young reader. The stories of Heinlein and Asimov and Clarke and Norton and Silverberg and Simak and many, many others were, in a very real sense, my shining starships—my paths to the stars. Kriss's longing in "The Minstrel" was, and is, my longing. It's no wonder this was one of the first science fiction stories I wrote, and one of the first I sold. It appeared in the long-defunct teen magazine JAM, sometime in the early 1980s.

~

THE MUSIC SANG OF THE INFINITE DARK and the suns that burn within it. It shimmered like starlight on alien seas, and whispered with the voices of strange winds.

~

Kriss stopped playing, and as the last chord died slowly away, sat

1

quietly with his head bowed, cradling his touchlyre in his arms. The orange glow of the oil lamps gleamed on the instrument's polished black wood and burnished copper.

One by one those in the smoky bar, mostly offworlders, rose from their tables and came to the low platform where Kriss sat, to drop coins into the wooden bowl at his feet. The murmur of their conversation was slow to resume.

When the last had come and gone Kriss stood, bowed, and left the stage. He divided the money with the innkeeper, then slipped the touchlyre into its soft leather case and went out into the chill night air.

In the cobblestoned street he stopped and looked up at the stars blazing in the night sky, as he did every evening when he finished playing, burning into his mind's eye the goal for which he had striven, it seemed, forever.

Two local men staggered by. One poked the other with his elbow and nodded toward Kriss. "Uppity offworlder," he whispered loudly. His companion made an obscene gesture, then, laughing, they weaved on down the street.

Kriss clenched his fists, then spun and strode in the opposite direction.

Where the cobblestones ended and concrete began, artificial lights banished the night. At the sight of them, Kriss forgot the drunks' insults and broke into a run. In a moment he reached the tall wire fence that surrounded the spaceport, and pressed his face against the cold mesh, peering through it at the starships, silver spires that seemed to soar skyward even though standing still. The lights glittered on their mirrored sides.

There lay his path to the stars, away from this hated planet where he didn't belong, couldn't belong, though he had been raised on it. The drunks had known; they had seen his height and his blonde hair and had *known* he came from the stars.

Somewhere out there must be his true home; somewhere out

there he had to have a family. His parents were dead, but they had to have had parents of their own, brothers, sisters...

He blinked away tears, and, disgusted with his own self-pity, turned away from the fence and set out along a dark, garbage-strewn alley for his barren lodging, a tiny attic room above a seamstress's shop. He was fooling himself if he thought he would ever leave Farr's World, he thought bitterly. The spacecrews called him "worldhugger"; neither Union nor Family, and without contacts in either of those spacefaring groups, he could never gain a berth as a crewmember, and he could entertain in spaceport bars for the rest of his life without raising enough money to buy passage into orbit, much less to another world.

Lost in dark thoughts, he didn't realize he was being followed until a hand touched his shoulder.

He instinctively spun away from that touch and pressed his back against a rough stone wall, his heart pounding, his arms wrapped protectively around the touchlyre.

"I mean you no harm," said the man who faced him. Shadows hid his features. "I only want to talk."

Kriss did not relax. "Then talk."

"What is your name?"

Kriss said nothing.

"Perhaps if you knew mine...? I am Carl Vorlick, a dealer in alien curiosities." He waited.

"My name's Kriss Lemarc," Kriss said finally. "Why?"

Vorlick ignored the question. "And how old are you?"

"Fifteen, standard."

"That would be just about right." Vorlick's eyes glinted faintly in the starlight. "I heard you play in Andru's—remarkable. Almost as though you projected emotion, not just sound."

Pleased despite himself, Kriss shrugged. "My instrument is...special."

"Indeed it is. And very beautiful. May I...?" Vorlick held out his hand.

Kriss looked up and down the alley, but saw no hope of rescue. Slowly he unfolded the leather covering and took out the touchlyre. The copper fingerplates and strings shone even in that dark corner.

Vorlick took a handlight from his pocket and played the beam over the instrument. Kriss caught a quick glimpse of a lean face with thin lips and ice-blue eyes before the light switched off. "Lovely," the man murmured. "How does it work?"

Kriss hesitated. "I hear music in my mind, and the touchlyre plays it," he said finally. "I can't explain any better than that."

"Touchlyre?"

"That's what I call it. I don't know what its real name is."

"Where did it come from?"

"It belonged to my parents. But I don't even remember them."

"Your parents, yes." Vorlick paused for a long moment, then said, "You desire to leave this world, don't you?"

Kriss said nothing. This stranger knew too much. Once again he glanced up and down the alley. He would have welcomed even the two drunks who had insulted him earlier—but there was no one.

But Vorlick took his silence as consent. "I own a ship."

Kriss stiffened. "What do you want from me?" he demanded; but inside he already knew.

"The price is small: your instrument. Give the touchlyre to me, and I will take you into space."

Kriss looked down at the touchlyre. "It's that valuable?"

"To the right person, everything is valuable. Your music spoke of your longing for the stars—some of those hardened spacefarers in Andru's were near tears. You value the stars, I value your instrument. A fair exchange."

"A musician once told me there isn't another instrument like this one in the galaxy."

"But there are other instruments. You could choose from those

4

of a thousand worlds. Surely one construction of wood and metal is not so different from another?"

To go to the stars, Kriss thought. *To cross the great Dark, to breathe the air of alien worlds, to perhaps touch Mother Earth herself...*

...to find a family...

Almost unconsciously, his arms loosened from the touchlyre. He looked up again at the stars, drank in their light with his eyes —and made up his mind. "Agreed."

Vorlick rubbed his hands together. "Excellent! Come to the spaceport gate at dawn. Bring the instrument." He turned and vanished into the darkness.

Kriss listened to his footsteps fade, then turned and walked slowly on toward his room. He climbed the familiar, rickety wooden stairs on the outside of the old brick building, past the dingy window through which shone a faint yellow light from the seamstress's lantern, unlocked his door, and went in. Lighting his single candle, he looked around the tiny chamber. The ceiling, with its small square skylight, was simply the underside of the roof, and so low on one side he had to stoop to get to his bed, the only furniture aside from a rough-hewn table and rusty metal chair. *I won't miss this,* he thought. *I won't miss anything on this planet.*

But he didn't feel euphoric, as he had always expected to feel when he finally found a way to fulfill his dream. Instead he felt— numb? No, not numb—depressed.

Why? he asked himself. *I'm going to the stars—all my dreams are coming true!* But the feeling persisted.

As always when his spirits needed lifting, Kriss took out the touchlyre. Playing it was cathartic; he could lose himself in music as so many others on this impoverished planet did in wine. He held the instrument in his lap for a moment, running his fingers over the sinuous curves of its velvety, unvarnished wood. Then he raised it and placed his hands on the copper plates.

The strings screamed: discordant, angry, ear-shattering. Kriss snatched his hands away. The touchlyre had never made a sound like that before! Had he broken it? He touched the plates again, cautiously, and again the instrument howled.

Disgusted, he tossed it on the table. If it was broken, he was well rid of it. He'd find himself another instrument, from one of those thousand worlds of which Vorlick had spoken. He undressed, blew out the candle, and crawled into bed.

Just before sleep claimed him, he thought he heard the instrument's strings softly humming; but of course that was impossible, with no one touching the plates.

He dreamed.

He was performing in Andru's, as he had done so many times, playing of his longing for the stars. That longing filled him with almost physical pain, but pain he could bear as long as he kept playing.

But suddenly the touchlyre disappeared, and he stood on an alien planet, strange and beautiful. Then another new world surrounded him, and another, and another, flashing past faster and faster, but no matter how exotic, how wonderful, they did not satisfy his longing, and the ache grew ever more acute.

And then he came to a world where dwelt a man who, he somehow knew, was his father's brother. His uncle rose to greet him, laughing, and hugged him, welcoming him to his family...

...but still the longing burned within Kriss, stronger than ever, so strong he suddenly knew it could never be quenched, and he broke away and screamed and screamed and—

—woke, gasping, bathed in sweat, his blanket a tangled heap on the floor, the scream echoing in his ears.

His scream? Or...?

He glanced sharply at the touchlyre, barely visible in the faint illumination from the skylight. It seemed to him he could hear the strings vibrating down to stillness, as though a mighty chord had just been wrung from them.

Nonsense, he told himself. He retrieved his blanket. No dreams troubled him the rest of the night.

In the morning he rose very early, put the touchlyre and the few clothes he owned into a backpack, and headed down the stairs and through a thin morning mist to the spaceport. The mountains towering above the city still hid the sun, but light filled the sky.

Vorlick waited at the spaceport gate. "Did you bring it?" he asked at once.

"Yes," Kriss said, startled by the blunt question.

"Take it out. I want to see it in the daylight."

Nonplused, Kriss did as he was told. But as he took the touchlyre from its case it hummed to life in his hands, and from it crashed a single explosive chord that echoed through the silent streets. Vorlick stumbled back as though slapped. "What—"

Kriss didn't hear him. The chord had sent the whole dream of the night before flashing through his mind, and it suddenly made perfect sense to him. His longing wasn't so much to see the stars, or even to find his family, but to find himself. He was doing that, bit by bit, through the touchlyre, journeying into his own soul to find out what kind of person he was, healing the wound made when he was orphaned on Farr's World.

Without the touchlyre, he could never finish that healing process. Wandering around the stars with the touchlyre lost to him forever would only hurt him worse; and even if he found a family, he would have lost something just as important.

Kriss's eyes suddenly focused on Vorlick. "No."

"No?"

"I've changed my mind. I'll keep the touchlyre. I'll find my own way into space." He started to turn away.

Vorlick reached into his pocket with his right hand, and pulled out something metallic. "Stand still," he said, his voice as cold as space. "That's not one of your options." He pointed the object at Kriss, who froze as he recognized the deadly form of a hyper-needler. "You don't even know what you have, but I do. It's a working artifact from an ancient, alien civilization, uncovered by two archaeologists on a planet we may never find again. They fled here with it when they realized someone knew they had it and was out to get it." He smiled humourlessly. "Me, of course. It was almost fifteen standard years ago. I tracked them here, only to find they had died in an aircar crash. I assumed the artifact was destroyed with them.

"But then, just a few months ago, a spy on this world told me of a strange instrument in the hands of a boy—an instrument unlike any other.

"I did some checking. I found that the archaeologists had an infant son shortly after they arrived here, a son who was not in the aircar when it crashed—a baby who has become a young man —the minstrel with the unique instrument.

"So now, Kriss Lemarc, though I must withdraw my offer of placing you in a ship's crew, I give you your parents: Jon and Memory Lemarc, archaeologists. And I also give you knowledge of what your 'touchlyre' is: the only relic of an ancient alien culture, and worth a fortune you cannot imagine.

"In exchange for that information, you will now give me this instrument." Vorlick put his left hand on it. "Or I will kill you."

Kriss tore the touchlyre away from him. "No!"

His cry of defiance woke a matching cry from the strings of the touchlyre, a crashing chord that exploded outward with a force that surpassed sound. Kriss felt all his violent emotions, fear, awe, defiance, hatred, pouring through his hands into the touchlyre, adding to the force it hurled at Vorlick like a weapon. The power coursed through Kriss like a cleansing tide—and he knew he couldn't stop it if he wanted to.

Vorlick's face paled and slackened, and his eyes glazed, then closed. The gun dropped from his nerveless hand as his legs buckled, and he fell to his knees, and then to the ground.

Finally it ended. Kriss felt, not empty of emotion, but as if he now had room to truly experience and understand his emotions for the first time, as though a gritty residue clogging his mind had been washed away.

He looked down at Vorlick and pitied him. The man lay unconscious, and Kriss knew he had nothing more to fear from him.

Then he raised the touchlyre, silent again, and held it at arm's length, studying it in the first rays of the sun, streaming like searchlights through a cleft in the mountains behind him. The orange beams made the wood and copper glow, reflecting the power hidden inside the ancient artifact. Just what that power was, and where it came from, he might never know: but he knew it was on his side.

He let his gaze travel to the tall starships beyond the gate, stark against the brightening sky. Above the tallest a single star still outshone the dawn light.

Someday, Kriss thought. *Someday I'll make that journey.*

That dream was still his: but now he knew the real journey lay within him. He turned his back on the spaceport and walked back to his attic room.

In a bar called Andru's, near the only spaceport of an obscure planet, starship crewmembers come to sit quietly and listen to a boy play a strange instrument of space-black wood and burnished copper.

His music sings of the infinite Dark and the suns that burn within it. It shimmers like starlight on alien seas, and whispers with the voices of strange winds.

A LITTLE SPACE MUSIC

*T*his story, which was published in the Spring 2012 issue of On Spec, *you have to blame on my friend Robert Ursan, brilliant composer, amazing accompanist, musical-theatre director* par excellence, *and very funny man. He occasionally refers to* The Sound of Music *as* The Sound of Mucus. *And for some reason I thought, "The Squill are alive with the sound of mucus"...and this story was born. (Did I mention I'm an actor and singer with a long history of appearing in musical theatre? Though never any productions quite like these...)*

DRIPPING VISCOUS GREEN SLIME onto the brushed-steel plates of the recreation room floor, the pulsating blue slug reared until it towered a full meter above my head. Three eyes the colour of old blood reared up on black stalks, somehow remaining focused on me even as they weaved like demented cobras in thrall to acid jazz played by a drunken snake charmer. Its mouth peeled open like a gaping wound.

Then came the ultimate horror.

It began to sing.

"Midnight..."

Oh, no. No!

"Touch me..."

That which does not kill me makes me stronger, I reminded myself. I felt very strong indeed by the time Lloyd Webber's oft-abused "classic" ground to its inevitable conclusion.

"Thank you, Mr...Urkh(cough)lisssss(choke). That was very...interesting. We'll be letting...people...know in about a shipday."

The slug grunted something that might have been "Thank you," or might have just been a correction of my pronunciation of his—I checked the information sheet—oops, *its*—name, and slithered out, leaving a trail of green goop a meter wide in its wake. A cleaning robot scurried after it on clicking insectile legs, its elephant-like nose-hose swinging back and forth, slurping up the surplus mucus for recycling in the galley.

Groaning, I rested my aching head in my hands, twitched my jaw sideways three times to activate my implanted commbug, and croaked, "Next!"

This nightmare had begun the moment I boarded the *LSS Mendel*, rushing down the loading ramp as though the hounds of hell were after me—not far from the truth, considering Governor Fexeldub's minions sported long black fur, long blue teeth, and bioluminescent eyes that radiated heavily in the longer wavelengths of visible light.

One thing neither of the two possessed, however, was a boarding pass for the *Mendel*. The security tanglefield stopped them in their tracks at the top of the ramp. My elation evaporated two seconds later when, at the bottom of the ramp, the tanglefield likewise wrapped me in molasses, and hardened to amber. Immobilized, I watched the ship's security hatch open, revealing a stocky, auburn-haired-and-bearded man wearing a bright-red uniform liberally adorned with gold buttons and braid. He looked like he'd just stepped offstage from playing the Major General in *The Pirates of Penzance*. "Professor Peak, I presume?" he said.

I found myself rather breathless, though probably due more to the tanglefield's compression of my lungs than the sudden outbreak of alliteration. "You have...the advantage...of me...sir."

"Forgive me. Robert Robespierre Robinson, Captain of the multi-species-capable luxury liner *LSS Mendel*, pride of the Blue Nebula Line, at your service." The Captain inclined his head slightly. "My friends call me Redbeard. You can call me Captain. Or 'sir.'" He looked back at the security hatch and made a cutting-his-own-throat gesture, which alarmed me until the tanglefield suddenly shut off and I realized it hadn't been a signal for summary execution. I staggered. The Captain caught me and straightened me up, then released me.

I took a couple of deep breaths. "I'm honoured you felt it necessary to greet me in person...sir."

"I'm sure." The Captain looked up the ramp. Fexeldub's hell-hounds snarled at him. He turned on his heel. "Come with me, 'Professor.' We have matters to discuss."

Relieved but alarmed, I followed the Captain, through corridors panelled with pearl and carpeted in pink, to his spacious stateroom. From the platinum-floored foyer he led me into an office, and pointed me to a grey blob of pseudoleather facing a desk of black metal, topped with glass. He eased himself down on the identical grey blob on the other side of the desk; it swelled and puffed into a comfortable-looking armchair. I sat down on my blob, and it instantly sprang into a rigid, straight-backed shape with all the give of a block of steel. *Okay, then*, I thought. *At least I know where I stand...er, sit.*

The Captain steepled his fingers under his chin and looked at me. "You're a wanted man, Professor. And not just by your friends on the loading dock." He tapped the desktop, and the faint glow of a holodisplay, indecipherable from where I sat, sprang into existence above the desk. "There are outstanding warrants for your apprehension on half a dozen different planets."

I cleared my throat. "Cultural misunderstandings. I'm a businessman trying to make an honest living, that's all."

Captain Robinson barked a laugh. "You're a con man. 'Professor Peter Peak' is not your real name. Too alliterative, for one thing."

I felt my left eyebrow lift. The Captain noticed. "I never said Robert Robespierre 'Redbeard' Robinson was my real name either, did I? But we're discussing your past, not mine."

"With all due respect, I'd rather talk about my future."

"In good time." The Captain tapped the desktop again. "Before you became Professor Peter Peak, purveyor of programmable paramours, you went by the name Aristotle Atkinson, and sold life-long subscriptions to *Encyclopedia Galactica*...until someone realized there's no such thing. Before that, you were Dr. Schroeder Petering, sole authorized human sales agent for life-extension nanomachines from Tofuni Secundus...quite a feat, since Tofuni has no planets."

"An unfortunate accident involving a planet-eating nanoswarm," I said. "Hardly *my* fault. As I explained."

"And yet, your customers tried to lynch you just the same. People can be *so* unreasonable." He shook his head. "But never mind. The version of you *I'm* interested in is the original."

I stiffened.

"Jerry Smith," he said (and the sound of my birth name made my heart skip a beat), "this is your life." He tapped, and the holodisplay suddenly became visible to me, revealing all the sordid details of my past, including birthplace (Moose Jaw, Saskatchewan), birthdate (much longer ago than I liked to admit), parents, and education. But what terrified me was something I had thought long-since lost in the mists of decaying data storage: a head-and-shoulders shot of a much-younger me. The Captain pointed at it, and the computer began reading the text of a press release: "Persephone Theatre is pleased to announce that Saskatchewan's own Jerry Smith will be playing the leading role of Bobby in this fall's production of Stephen Sondheim's *Company*. Smith, originally from Moose Jaw—"

Captain Robinson pointed again, and the computer's voice cut off. "You're not just a con man," the Captain said. "You're an actor, singer, and dancer—in short, a musical theatre performer. A triple threat, in fact." He made it sound like a sentence of execution...and I knew it very well could be.

But I couldn't argue with the evidence. "*Was.* For about eight years. You know the difference between a stage actor and a pizza?"

"A pizza can feed a family of four. Yes, I've heard the joke." He leaned forward, like a cat tensing to leap at a mouse. "But that was on Earth, 'Professor.' You're not in Kansas anymore."

"Actually, I've never been to—"

"Here on the *LSS Mendel*, you *can* make enough money to feed a family of four. Not as an actor, perhaps, but certainly as...a director."

Uh-oh. "Contrary to cliché, all I've ever really wanted to do is *avoid* directing."

The Captain pointed at the holodisplay. "You've directed at least five shows."

"That résumé is twenty years out of date."

"It's like riding a bicycle."

"I can't ride a bike."

The Captain sighed. "Professor Peak, I really don't have time for this. You've been in space a long time. You know as well as I do that of all the culture Earth has produced, all the artwork, all the novels, all the symphonies, only one thing holds the slightest interest for any of our alien neighbours."

I decided to try playing dumb. "You tell me."

"Musical theatre, Professor." The Captain tapped the desktop, and on every wall, previously opaque screens suddenly displayed...theatre posters. *Oklahoma. Oliver! The Sound of Music. Sweeney Todd. My Fair Lady. The Most Happy Fella. Candide. West Side Story. Chicago. Cats. Starlight Express,* for God's sake. *Wicked. The Light in the Piazza. Avenue Q. Passion. Hamilton. Dear Evan Hansen. Thunder in the Night. What the Cat Dragged In. Jimi! Apollo 13: The Musical.* The posters kept changing; by the time I'd looked through them once, there was a new batch on display.

"I collect them," said the Captain. "I have a poster from every musical that ran on Broadway from *Show Boat* in 1927 to *The Singularity* in 2024, the last new Broadway musical produced..."

Suddenly furious, I forgot about playing dumb. "Yeah, because a Squill spaceship the size of Yankee Stadium appeared over Times Square one Saturday night and mysteriously vanished the casts of every show," I snarled. "And because over the next week, any actor who dared to step out on stage and burst into song vanished, too. Which is why Jerry Smith disappeared, too—into a different line of work."

"A criminal line of work."

"I was an actor. I wasn't suited for honest work."

"My Squill passengers are hungry for musical theatre, Professor Peak." He gestured at the walls. "As am I."

"Squill!" My voice actually squeaked. "You have *Squill* on board?"

He had the nerve to smile. "Didn't you know? Most of the vessel is currently occupied by Squill on a...pilgrimage, I suppose you'd call it...to their homeworld."

Worse and worse. "We're going to Squill Primus?" I hadn't had time, what with hellhounds after me, to check exactly *where* the only ship in port would take me. "And you want me to direct *musical theatre?*"

"I told you, my passengers are hungry for it."

"*Maybe literally!* We still don't know where all those actors went. Maybe the Squill are serving up ham sandwiches—*with bits of real ham!*—on their homeworld right now."

"They don't eat people, they eat algae and the occasional sulphurous rock," the Captain said. "And anyway, they said they were sorry. *And* they gave us the spacetime drive by way of reparation. If not for Broadway, we'd still be stuck puttering around the Earth and Moon, Professor. We owe musical theatre a huge debt of gratitude."

"You're welcome." I stood up. "Now, if that's all you wanted—"

"I want you to direct a musical, Professor," the Captain said. "The first live musical to hit the boards since the sad but profitable demise of Broadway. And I want you to cast my passengers."

My knees buckled and I hit the pseudoleather hard. "Oh, God. You want me to direct Squill." No, it was worse than that. "*Amateur* Squill!"

"Squill this time. But next time..." He spread his hands. "Who knows? It could be Hellhounds. Skitterings. Even humans. And as for being amateurs...well, Professor, remember that amateurs are those who do something because they love it. Presumably *you* first went into theatre because you loved it, Professor. Reach down deep into your heart, if you still have one, and..." His grin widened. "Feel the love."

"Scripts...orchestra...stagehands..." Like a drowning man, I grasped at straws.

"Scripts are in the ship's database. The computer will provide the accompaniment. And I'm sure, in time-honoured community theatre tradition, that those not cast for roles will be happy to serve as stagehands."

"I'm not the only performer in hiding," I said. "There must be others with more directing experience. Why me?"

"You're here. And you..." He waved at the holodisplay. "...have an incentive they do not."

"This is blackmail."

"Of course it is! Feel free to complain to the local constabulary." He flicked a finger, and the holodisplay showed a sudden close-up of the red-eyed, slavering visage of one of Fexeldub's hellhounds. "Oh, look! There's a peace officer now."

I knew when I was beaten. "How long do I have?"

"It's four weeks, ship-time, to Squill Primus. I'm looking forward to seeing your production on the penultimate evening of our voyage. It will be a wonderful treat for our passengers on the eve of their big festival."

"Festival?" I couldn't imagine Squill partying. "What kind of Festival do giant slugs gather for?"

"It's a religious festival, Professor. I told you they were on pilgrimage."

I groaned. Not just Squill, but *religious* Squill. "We apologize for the action of our religionists," had been the message from the *second* giant spaceship, which had entered Earth orbit shortly after the performer-eating one had departed. "We offer reparations."

For a moment I seriously considered taking my chances with the hellhounds...but only for a moment. I doubted I'd still be in one piece two minutes after they dragged me out of sight.

I glared at the Captain. "I hope, when I'm spirited away by Squill fanatics, you'll at least have the grace to feel guilty."

"Should that happen, I'll do my best."

I sighed. "When do we start auditions?"

Captain Robinson had been very sure of himself, I thought sourly, as I read the in-ship newsfeed, *The Mendelian Factor*, in my cabin an hour later. Before I'd even run down the ramp into the tanglefield, early arrivals on the ship had been reading, "Auditions for *The Sound of Music*, the premiere production of the *Mendel* Amateur Musical Entertainment Society (MAMES), will be held in Multipurpose Recreation Space 7 tonight beginning at 1900. MAMES is pleased to announce that Professor Peter Peak, a musical theatre professional from Earth itself, will direct. Bring a song that shows off your voice; computer accompaniment will be provided."

Auditions were every bit as horrifying as I'd anticipated. The "Memory"-warbler was perhaps the worst...but perhaps not. "I'm Just A Girl Who Cain't Say No" sung by an elderly female Squill with bladder—or something—control problems sticks in my mind as well. And the less said about "On the Good Ship Lollipop," the better.

Unable to cast by appearance, I could only go by vocal skills. Fortunately, some of the Squill actually had some. I chose the best as my leads, relegated most of the rest to chorus, and suggested that a few hopeless cases join the stage crew—which they seemed thrilled to do.

In fact, all the Squill seemed permanently thrilled about every-thing. As the *Mendel* left orbit on its four-week-subjective journey to Squill Primus, I felt pretty good about the show's prospects—assuming the cast didn't eat the director.

Staging was simplified by the complete absence of dancing ability—or legs—among the cast, and by the fact that humans can't read the emotional content of a Squill's "face." (Indeed, the computer informed me, "some scientists believe the colour of a Squill's mucus is a better indicator of emotional state. When asked, the Squill change the subject.") With choreography impos-sible, I only had to come up with simple blocking. And my being unable to read my actors' expressions meant that if they were acting badly, I couldn't tell—so I just pretended they were acting well.

Memorization was no problem; all of them had their music and dialogue note- and word-perfect at the first rehearsal. The movement, limited though it was, posed more of a challenge. I had to modify the set after the first on-stage rehearsal of "So Long, Farewell," when my entire group of "children" ended up in sickbay with nasty fluorescent bruises. Squill don't do stairs, apparently. Who knew?

Squill don't wear clothes, either, so our only costumes were hats—wimples, Nazi caps, sailor hats—and a couple of wigs. Maria looked terrifying in a long brown one; Gretl looked cute, in a nightmarish sort of way, in blonde pigtails.

After the first few days, my fear of sudden disintegration began to fade. No Squill ever threatened me or was anything but friendly...which was more than I could say of all the *human* actors I'd worked with.

And I began to learn more about my cast—and just how badly I had miscast some of them. The Squill playing the Mother Superior turned out to be an elderly "it" (the Squill have three sexes that we know of). The "children" were mostly twice as old as me (three times as old, in the case of Gretl).

They were all very curious about my acting past, and we took to meeting in the main lounge after rehearsal for drinks. (The Squill drink a lot; their prodigious mucus production requires constant replenishment of fluids. Their staterooms looked more like indoor swamps, with thick black mud on the floor and a constant spray of fine mist in the air.) There I would regale them with the traditional actor-stories of forgotten lines, collapsing sets, drunks, hecklers, and wardrobe malfunctions.

It was at one of those get-togethers, four days from our opening (and closing) performance, that the matter I'd been very careful not to mention suddenly came up.

I was sitting with "Captain Von Trapp," "Maria," "Liesl," and "Rolf," and had just told a joke about a producer, a director, a writer, and an actor walking into a bar, when Rolf, the youngest member of the cast at 65 Earth years (he'd only recently been released from his mandatory adolescent confinement), put down his third glass of what I privately called Smoking Green Goo, burped, and slurred, "Prophet Matthew Broderick tellsh that shtory better, Professhor."

Sudden, absolute silence as the babble of Squill and human voices from all around us abruptly ceased...even though I could still see mouths moving. I glanced down. Von Trapp had hurriedly slapped down on the table a little golden egg (exactly where he had had it hidden, in the absence of clothes, I preferred not to think about). A sound-dampener, presumably.

My heart jumped, then raced. Rolf blundered on. "Hash lecture at the sheminary lasht year was the besht thing I ever..." his voice trailed off at last. All three of his eyes widened, and his mouth slapped shut so suddenly gobs of mucus spattered the table. The slime oozing from his flanks took on a pinkish hue.

I looked around at the others. They were all staring at Rolf; but then, one by one, they looked at me.

My blood ran cold. But I couldn't pretend I hadn't heard. And we knew Squill "religionists" had stolen musical theatre. It wasn't really a secret...

What had happened to all the actors, though, had been.

Until now?

Heart still pounding, I said, as casually as I could, "Matthew Broderick? Wasn't he playing Henry in *Old Fool*, that awful musical version of *On Golden Pond*, back when...um..." My voice failed.

I winced as high-pitched squealing erupted around me. Squills talking their own language sound like seagulls on helium being tortured in an echo chamber.

The sound cut off as suddenly as it had begun. "We would like to tell you something," Von Trapp said. "We had discussed doing so earlier, but had not made up our minds. Now, however...," two of his eyes swivelled toward Rolf, whose eyestalks drooped in response, "...the matter has been settled for us."

"Don't tell me anything I shouldn't know!" I said. (*Squeaked*, if we're being perfectly honest.) "Much as I'd like to meet some of the great old Broadway performers in the flesh, I'm not that keen..."

"Only a Rapturer—a priest of the Order of Religious Insight Collection—would or could transport you," Maria said. "It is unlikely any of them are aboard."

"*How* unlikely?"

"Reasonably," Liesl said. "They do sometimes travel incognito."

"Knowing the truth does not make it any more likely you will be raptured," said Von Trapp. "If a Rapturer is on board, you are already marked simply because you are a prophet."

"A prophet?"

"Of musical theatre."

A prophet of musical theatre? Musical-theatre actors had been called many things over the decades, but *prophets?* I didn't like the sound of it.

I drained my beer and called for another...to no effect. *Damn sound-dampener.* For a moment I eyed the remnants of Rolf's Smoking Green Goo, but I wasn't that desperate...yet. I sighed, and met Von Trapp's disconcerting gaze. "I'm all ears."

Two hours later I staggered back to my cabin (having made up for the initial lack of drink several times over once the Squill departed). I fell into bed, looked up at the slowly spinning ceiling, and didn't know whether to laugh or cry or throw up.

The decision was suddenly made for me. I staggered into the bathroom and vomited up everything I had eaten for the last twenty-four hours or so—but not, alas, everything I had drunk.

Discretion being the better part of valour, I decided to spend the next hour or so on the bathroom floor. I had little else to do in that position but reflect on what I had heard.

The Squill religionists, it seemed, had "raptured" Broadway in order to get closer to God.

In view of how far from God, in my experience, most people in the acting profession considered themselves (an opinion shared by most of those in the God-bothering business), the irony was rich. But if you could wrap your head around the Squill point of view, it almost made sense.

The Squill Church, unlike its human counterparts, did not pretend to *know* the Truth about God and/or the gods, or how to best please/serve/placate/worship He/She/It/Them. Instead, the Church's purpose was to *seek* the Truth. It did so by conducting a cosmic opinion poll: it gathered various "Truths" from all over the galaxy to see what could be gleaned from them.

Along the way, the Church had spawned innumerable sub-cults, as various factions decided that the latest "Truth" was THE TRUTH, and stopped searching. But the Great Church Fluorescent and Iridescent (really, that's how Von Trapp translated it) carried on, collecting bits of alien cultures from all over the galaxy.

The secular government of Squill Primus, while condemning the practice, made no move to stop it. Instead, its ships trailed the Church's Rapture ships at a respectable distance, apologizing to and reimbursing the affected planets...and, in the process, opening up lucrative trade routes. It seemed a recipe for disaster if the Squill ever met their technological match. But so far they hadn't, and probably even the Great Church Fluorescent and Iridescent had enough sense of self-preservation not to rapture members of a technologically superior race.

The Rapturers, being essentially pollsters, sought a random sample of religious insights—and used a very broad definition of religious that boiled down to "activities that draw crowds." On Earth, the "winner" had been musical theatre (with professional hockey a close second).

But something had happened with musical theatre that had never happened before: the Great Church Fluorescent and Irides-cent had declared, after watching the actors perform their shows, that there would be no further collecting of religious insight—musical theatre provided THE TRUTH.

The musical theatre performers raptured from Earth, Von Trapp had told me, though prohibited from leaving Squill or contacting their human counterparts, now formed a thriving, pampered human colony, a kind of Vatican City, on Squill. Not only did they produce incredible musicals—the special effects alone, thanks to Squill technology, were literally out of this world —but they sent "missionaries" around the planet, instructing everyone in the newly discovered Great White Way.

Which meant that *The Sound of Music*—*my* Sound of Music— was, for the Squill, a worship service.

It made a strange sort of sense, I thought as the bathroom's spinning finally slowed. Like religions, most musicals present neat little packages of supposed insight, wrapped up in pleasing tunes and eye-candy. To coin a phrase, they're the "spoonful of sugar to help the medicine go down."

Nothing had come up for a while. I crawled back to my bed and climbed into it. But as darkness descended, I felt a faint *frisson* of fear as I recalled being told it was "unlikely" I would be raptured.

"How unlikely?" I asked the dark, but got no answer.

I was not at my best for dress rehearsal the next day. But the Squill were, and if you closed your eyes and ignored the multi-coloured trails of slime all over the stage (the cleaner 'bots just couldn't keep up), you could imagine you were hearing, if not a Broadway show, at least a good-quality regional production.

The next day we entered orbit around Squill Primus. After a one-Squill-day (29-hour) quarantine, the pilgrims would disembark to worship at the feet of the Broadway Prophets, Original Cast.

And that meant it was show time.

I gave the traditional Pre-Opening Pep Talk. "You're ready," I informed the cast. "You're good. I admit I had my doubts going in, especially with such a short rehearsal time, but you've all done a terrific job. I'm proud of you all. And if Rogers and Hammerstein were here—" *And not busy spinning in their graves...* "they'd be proud of you, too. Break a..." I hesitated, looking at the sea of slugs before me. "Um, good luck."

The stage manager's voice squealed over the monitor. I still couldn't understand Squill, but I knew what he had just said: "Places."

I made my way out front. The audience of humans, non-performing Squill, and one or two non-Squill aliens quieted as the lights went down. *"Dixit Dominus Domino meo, sede a dextris meis,"* sang eight Squill in wimples as they slithered up the aisle onto the stage, and we were off. Scene followed scene, and if "I Am Sixteen Going on Seventeen" looked more like a nature documentary about the mating of garden slugs than a touching musical tribute to young love in troubled times, no one seemed to care. The audience watched raptly, completely caught up in a tale whose historical elements must have been incomprehensible to most of them. By the time the family slithered off, leaving a rainbow of slime behind them, to "Climb Every Mountain," there wasn't a dry...well, much of anything, considering the preponderance of Squill...in the house.

Squill don't applaud; if they see something they like, they pay it the honour of being silent, while their slime turns bright blue. Our audience paid us the greatest compliment of all: a Silent Blue Departure.

Like they're leaving church, I thought.

The ear-splitting cast party more than made up for the audience's silence. Enormous quantities of Smoking Green Goo disappeared down gaping maws, and even larger quantities of squirming blobs of shapeless protoplasm, the Squill equivalent of potato chips.

Still a little alcohol-shy, I confined myself to a glass of the champagne sent to my dressing room by Captain Robinson. I was just finishing it when "Redbeard" himself appeared. He seized my free hand and pumped it. "Fabulous! Bravo! Bravissimo! I admit I had my doubts about you when you first came aboard, but you've proven them groundless."

I looked around. The Squill had congregated in the furthest corner of the large banquet room, watching a holorecording of "The Lonely Goatherd." For some reason, puppets fascinated them.

"Thank you for the champagne, Captain," I said. "Can I pour you a glass?"

"I'd be honoured."

I filled one for him, and decided to risk a second one for myself. "Tell me, Captain," I said casually as I handed him his drink, "have you ever heard of the Rapturers?"

Did his glass hesitate, ever-so-slightly, on its way to his lips? He took a sip, lowered the glass, and said, "What an...odd question. Why do you ask?"

The Squill were still engrossed, but I lowered my voice anyway. "Someone in the cast let it slip. Captain, I know what happened to Broadway!"

"Really? What?" He took another sip of champagne, sharp blue eyes focused on me over the rim of the flute.

I recounted what Von Trapp and the others had told me. He said nothing until I was finished, then set down his now-empty glass. "Interesting. Well, Professor, I must prepare for disembarkation..."

"Interesting!" I grabbed his arm. "Didn't you hear what I said, Captain? There are humans being held prisoner on Squill! Shouldn't you...tell someone? Shouldn't there be government protests? A rescue, even?"

The Captain removed my hand from his arm as though lifting damp garbage from a pristine floor. "Professor, I run a liner, not a battleship. I suggest you make a report to the human authorities at our next port of call after Squill Primus." He gave me a cold smile. "For now, enjoy your success."

I poured a third glass of champagne. I seemed to have regained my taste for alcohol.

~

In the morning, not *quite* hung over, I went to the shuttle bay to say goodbye to my cast. Captain Robinson was already there; he nodded to me, then stood at ease, watching the line of departing slugs.

Von Trapp was the last of my performers to board the shuttle. "Farewell, Professor," he said. "We are most grateful for the insights you have shared with us. The cast has asked me to give you a token of our appreciation."

He extruded a manipulator tentacle from...somewhere. It held an egg-shaped, multifaceted crystal, fiery as a diamond, but with a pulsing spark of blue fire deep within. The bits of green slime clinging to it couldn't dim its beauty...well, not much.

"Thank you," I said...

...and Captain Robinson's hand snaked out and seized Von Trapp's manipulator. I stared at him; I'd never seen a human willingly touch a Squill before. All three of Von Trapp's eyes whipped around: they focused first on Robinson's hand, then on his face. "Explain yourself!" he barked.

"*You* explain yourself," Robinson said. "On what authority do you do this?"

Authority? I looked back and forth from Von Trapp to Robinson like a spectator at a tennis match—except I had the distinct feeling I was the ball.

Von Trapp hissed, spattering mucus. "The Director commanded—"

"The Director?" Robinson let go of Von Trapp's tentacle and

straightened. "Don't speak to me of the Director. *I am the Producer!*"

Von Trapp goggled at him, his eyes forming the points of an equilateral triangle, every stalk stiff. "The Producer? Himself?"

"The same."

Von Trapp's slime went grey. "There are theological disagreements over the role of the Producer. The Director claims—"

Robinson pointed at me. "*He* is also a Director. *A* Director. One of *several* possible Directors. But I am the Producer. I *choose* Directors. I hire and fire Directors. Would you challenge *my* authority?"

Von Trapp's maw opened and shut a couple of time slowly, strings of mucus looping from it. "The Director must decide this," he said finally. "It is beyond me. But for the moment—*for the moment* —we will leave matters as they are." His mouth snapped shut, the crystal egg went back into whatever orifice he had taken it from, and he slithered aboard the shuttle, his slime trail now an inky black. Captain Robinson made a chopping motion at a crewman standing by the door controls, and the door slid shut, clunking and hissing as it sealed. A moment later the ship shuddered as the shuttle disconnected and began its descent to the planet, and cleaner 'bots moved in to hoover up the accumulated Squill mucus.

Captain Robinson turned to me. "I think perhaps we should have a talk, Professor."

I licked dry lips, and nodded.

"Let's adjourn to my office."

Once there, Robinson tapped his desktop to light up his collection of Broadway posters, then tapped it again; a panel slid open beneath a poster from the original production of *Follies*, revealing a wet bar. "Drink?"

"Scotch." Beer just didn't seem up to the task of preparing me to face whatever might be coming...though I already had my suspicions.

"I have some information related to the...concerns...you voiced last night," Robinson said, pouring me a double of...I squinted. *Oban? Nice!* "Ice?"

"No thanks."

Robinson handed me the drink, then sat down at his desk. "I believe the time has come to tell you the truth," he said.

"You were a Broadway producer," I said.

He inclined his head. "Myron Summerfeld, at your service."

I gaped at him. "You produced *The Singularity*. I almost auditioned for that show..."

"I made the mistake of hanging around backstage during that...final performance. When the rapture came, right in the middle of the big 'Exponential Existentialism' dance number at the top of Act 2, there was a flash of light. We thought someone had sneaked a flash photograph. It wasn't until the holographic theatre they had transported us to vanished that we discovered we —and the cast of every other show then on Broadway—were actually on an alien spaceship populated by giant slugs.

"Some people reacted badly, but I've always prided myself on being a quick thinker. Somebody needed to take charge, and who better than a producer? The actors were happy to let me do the talking to the Squill priests. So..."

"...so when the Church Fluorescent and Iridescent decided it had finally found Ultimate Truth in musical theatre, you were the Pope."

"Something like that." Robinson shrugged. "The Church is led by a three-Squill supreme council. They're now calling themselves the Production Manager, the Stage Manager—and the Director. But for the moment at least, I'm still the only Producer. Lucky for you, or I never would have gotten around Von Trapp like that."

"What would they have done with me?" I asked.

"Oh, nothing bad. The Squill have been very good to everyone. First-class digs. Fabulous food. And Squill Prime is heaven for actors and directors: no budget or technical constraints, freedom to perform any musical ever written, and audiences that literally worship you. Matthew Broderick is head of the new seminary, you know. And if the insights on offer seem banal to us—'Always leave them wanting more,' 'Never act with children or animals,' 'Dying is easy, comedy is hard,'—they seem to be new to the Squill."

"So why aren't you down there right now?" I demanded.

"I'm a producer," Robinson said. "Once the Church signed on to the whole Musical Theatre is the Ultimate Truth thing, there wasn't much for me to do. The Church's hierarchy does all the stuff I'd normally be responsible for. And there's no chance of producing anything new: the Musical Canon has hardened into dogma, and woe betide he who shall alter a jot or a tittle of it." Captain Robinson sipped his Scotch, then set it down on the desk. "So I made a proposal. I pointed out that now that the Church has discovered Ultimate Truth, it needed to share that truth with other races."

I took a largish gulp of Scotch, and had to overcome a fit of coughing before I could choke out, "You made them evangelical!"

He shrugged. "Proselytizing had never occurred to them before, but they quite liked the idea. So...they gave me this ship, and sent me out into the galaxy. I told them the first thing I needed to find was a director." He pointed at me. "They already knew about you, Professor. If I hadn't made sure Governor Fexeldub herded you—"

"Herded me!"

"—to my ship, the Rapturers would have taken you. But the deal was, if I succeeded in getting you on my ship—Von Trapp had no business—" Robinson bit off what he was going to say. "Never mind. I'll take that up with the Director itself, when I see it.

"Now you have to make a decision, Professor. Will you stay here and continue directing for the Mendel Amateur Musical Entertainment Society, or..." He reached out of my sight behind the desk, and pulled out an egg-shaped, blue-pulsing crystal identical to the one Von Trapp had offered me. "...will you join your counterparts on Squill Primus?"

"You want me to be a missionary!"

"Why not? You've been everything else. What better way to make your living than spreading the joy of musical theatre around the galaxy? And remember, Professor, I don't just transport Squill. You'll get to work with all kinds of aliens...maybe even humans."

I looked deep into my Scotch glass, thinking. A life spent directing musicals featuring amateur casts with uncertain vocal abilities and a varying array of body parts...or a life spent surrounded by aging Broadway actors whose egos were constantly fed by seas of worshipping slugs.

Put that way, it was no decision at all.

I looked up at Robinson. "What's our next show, Mr. Producer?"

So here I am, halfway between Squill Primus and Arbus Tertius, trying to teach six-legged felinoids to dance.

The show? *Cats*, of course.

We're saving a fortune on makeup.

STRANGE HARVEST

*his was an early sale of mine, appearing in 1988 in an
unlikely market:* Western People, *the magazine supplement
of the* Western Producer *agricultural newspaper.* On Spec *magazine
reprinted "Strange Harvest" in 1998, and in 2005 it was recorded for
CBC Radio, broadcast nationally as part of "Six Impossible Things," a
two-week tour of Canadian speculative fiction hosted by Nalo
Hopkinson for CBC's* Between the Covers. *The inspiration came from
my years as a reporter, and then news editor, of the weekly* Weyburn
Review. *Every spring, people would bring in funny vegetables: tomatoes
with noses, potatoes that looked like John G. Diefenbaker, embarrass-
ingly shaped cucumbers. We'd photograph them and run them as a photo
feature which, one year, I titled "Strange Harvest"—a headline I liked so
much, I wrote this story.*

THE TOMATO ROLLED ACROSS my coffee-spattered notes
from the previous night's school board meeting and fetched up
against my Garfield cup with a "clink!". I stared at the fruit, then
tapped it with the end of my pen.

Yes, definitely a "clink!".

I looked up at the elderly woman who had brought me this unsolicited gift, and winced—she wore a yellow-and-red floral-print dress under a man's bright-blue nylon ski jacket. "What can I do for you, Mrs. Annaweis?"

"I want you to take a picture of my tomato and put it in the paper."

I had already guessed as much. As editor of the Drinkwell, Saskatchewan, *Herald* (circulation 1,100) for three years, ever since I graduated from journalism school, I had seen enough four-pound potatoes, heart-shaped tomatoes, foot-long cucumbers, and two-headed stalks of wheat to last any sane or insane man a lifetime. Every autumn these bizarre bits of vegetation were delivered in triumph to the *Herald* office by an unending procession of proud gardeners and farmers like Mrs. Annaweis, now glaring at me through her bifocals. I call it "funny vegetable season," and here it was starting again—if in a bizarre manner. "Mrs. Annaweis, this is a lovely bit of ceramic, but..."

"Young man, it grew like that."

I bit my lip. Mrs. Annaweis's stern face defied disbelief. I opted for stalling. "Really?"

"Mr. Harkness, I am not crazy. I picked that tomato and a bushel more just like it from my garden this morning."

"Of course you did, Mrs. Annaweis," I said soothingly, while thinking sad thoughts about senility. I played my ace-in-the-hole. "It's just that I don't think it would photograph well, so..."

Mrs. Annaweis snatched up the tomato. "I'll prove it. Outside."

"What?"

"Outside!" She marched away with such authority I had no choice but to follow, shrugging at my bemused receptionist on the way out.

The lot adjacent to the *Herald*'s ancient brick building was given over to Drinkwell Community Park, an acre of patchy grass and scraggly trees equipped with four red picnic tables, a single blackened barbecue, and a rusting baseball backstop. "Watch," commanded Mrs. Annaweis, and tossed the tomato at the barbecue.

It exploded with a sound like a shotgun blast, spraying barbecue, tables, and grass with blackened pulp. A cloud of greasy brown smoke mushroomed skyward.

I found I was holding Mrs. Annaweis's hand. "See?" she said smugly.

I released her. "Uh—yes, ma'am."

"Good. Get your camera."

"Yes, ma'am." Numb, I did as I was told, photographing Mrs. Annaweis standing with proprietary glee next to the mess on the grass. Then I went back inside and stared at the phone.

I had a contact in the University of Saskatchewan's College of Agriculture, but couldn't quite bring myself to call her. Somehow I didn't fancy telling a university professor someone had just brought me a fresh-picked hand grenade.

Finally I decided to run the story and photo without comment, like a UFO sighting, or Phil Nutterworth's annual report of Bigfoot raiding his chicken coop. "Freak mutation," I muttered as I typed it up. "Pollution. Toxic waste. Ozone depletion."

The next day was Wednesday, paper day, and as usual my morning was devoted to frantically laying out the last few pages while the pressman glared at me over folded, ink-blackened arms, and the advertising manager and his assistant sat at the coffee table and told jokes at my expense. In the afternoon I went home and went to bed. The tomato was momentarily forgotten.

But Thursday morning, as I sat yawning at my desk, leafing gingerly through the paper in expectation of finding some horrible typographical error, the story caught my eye: "Local woman gets bang out of tomatoes." I chuckled.

I chuckled again when Art Kapusianyk brought in the radishes

—until he cut one open, and I had to waste a cup of coffee to douse my burning blotter.

And Art was only the first of half-a-dozen people stirred by Mrs. Annaweis's fleeting fame. Three more exploding tomatoes, two acid-filled cucumbers, and a glow-in-the-dark electric potato followed. The parade of peculiar produce was only ended by the onion someone tossed through the open window above my desk. It took us the rest of the afternoon to clear the gas out of the office, and my eyes were still bloodshot and burning when I drove home.

"It's gotta be a hoax," I muttered, then coughed, and restricted myself to silent black thoughts. Someone was trying to make me look like a fool—that had to be it. Maybe it was an elaborate attempt to discredit the newspaper.

But by whom? That town councillor arrested for growing marijuana in his greenhouse? The used car dealer caught rolling back the odometers? Abigail Runne, irate because her last name was spelled "Runny" in her daughter's wedding write-up?

None of them seemed likely candidates for high-tech humour of this kind. But somebody was behind it, and I intended to find out who.

After gnawing a half-thawed TV dinner, I spread a map of the Rural Municipality of Drinkwell on my kitchen table and began marking the farms of the people who had brought me violent vegetables.

A pattern emerged at once. All six farms abutted on a seventh, belonging to a Nelson Roysum. "What did I ever do to you, Mr. Roysum?" I muttered, reaching for the phone.

"Hello?" said a voice creaky as a rusty gate.

"Mr. Nelson Roysum?"

"Yes?"

"This is Steven Harkness, the editor of the Drinkwell Herald."

"You don't say?"

"Mr. Roysum, we've had reports of some—um, strange vegetables grown by your neighbours. I was wondering if you've noticed anything."

"Strange vegetables?" Roysum sounded puzzled. "Well, no, but then, I don't keep a garden. Just my field crops."

I had a sudden vision of kernels of wheat popping like firecrackers. "Mr. Roysum, may I come out tomorrow and take a look around?"

"Well, sure, young man, if you like. Be my guest."

"Thank you, Mr. Roysum. I'll be out first thing."

That proved to be slightly imprecise, since to reach Roysum's farm I had to first follow one of the grid roads that crisscross Saskatchewan in geometric fashion, then find precisely the right turnoff, and finally keep the oil pan of my 10-year-old Toyota intact over ruts apparently made by the kind of pickups you see crushing cars on TV.

But at last I drove into Roysum's yard, which was surrounded on three sides by the ubiquitous poplar windbreaks of the prairies, in an advanced stage of autumnal yellowing. The old-fashioned farmhouse, tall and narrow, might have once been painted blue; behind it stood a sagging, weather-beaten barn, possibly painted red at the same time as the house. In the yard a thirty-five-year-old swather leaned for support against an even older tractor. Four slope-roofed sheds and three shabby granaries completed the farm assets. No one was in sight.

A knock on the door of the house brought no answer, nor did repeated calls of "Mr. Roysum! Mr. Roysum?", so I set off across the farmyard to see what evidence I could find that Roysum was involved in terrorist truck farming. After hearing his Will Geer voice on the phone, I no longer thought he had done it deliberately, but I still had some vague notion of an illegal dump of pesticide containers leaking mutagens into the water table.

I went first into the barn, permeated with the odour of dust, moldy grain, and old hay peculiar to its species. The sunlight streaming through holes in the old walls cast narrow beams of dancing motes through the darkness.

In one corner were a couple of horse stalls, *sans* horses. But something moved, shuffling into the light from the doorway—and resolving into a bent old man in dirty overalls, the prerequisite baseball cap of the Saskatchewan farmer perched precariously on his grizzled head. He squinted at me. "Who are you?"

"Steven Harkness, from the *Drinkwell Herald*." I held out my hand, and he crushed my fingers for me. I revised my mental estimate of his frailty. "Nelson Roysum, I presume?"

"That's right."

"Mr. Roysum, are you all alone out here?"

"Never saw much use for a wife—"

"I mean, do you have any farmhands?"

"Never saw much use for them, either. Been farming this land sixty years on my own. Why, you looking for work?"

I sighed. "No, Mr. Roysum. I'm the editor of the *Herald*, remember?"

"'Course I remember. Ain't lost my memory yet. Just thought you might be ready for a real job." He guffawed, revealing yellowing teeth.

I managed a small smile. "Ha, ha."

"Now, what was it you were looking for...?"

"Strange vegetables, Mr. Roysum."

He squinted at me. "Are you sure you're not looking for honest work, son?"

"Mr. Roysum—"

"Poke around all you like. Have fun. But you won't find anything strange on this farm." He shuffled out.

"I already have," I muttered, and followed him. He disappeared into the house, while I continued my search, with depressingly consistent results—all negative. The sheds and granaries were as innocent-looking and empty as the barn. A fruitless hour later I stood at the edge of the farmyard, beyond the windbreak, staring across the acres of ripe wheat that glowed in the morning sunshine like a quilt of pale gold, broken only by the winding, bush-lined path of a creek, and the bump of a large haystack alongside it.

Roysum's tractor had been on and off all through my search, as he tinkered with the engine. For the past few minutes it had been idling; now it died again, and in the sudden silence I could hear the cool wind whispering in the trees behind me and hissing, with a more high-pitched, urgent note, through the wheat. It was a beautiful, crisp, absolutely ordinary Saskatchewan autumn day.

I was about to turn away from the field when I glimpsed movement among the bushes along the creek. *A deer?* I thought, then saw it again. *Not unless Mr. Roysum likes to spray-paint wildlife bright green.* "Some green venison with your exploding tomatoes?" I muttered. Feeling like I'd wandered into a Dr. Seuss book, I set off toward the haystack, about half a mile away, aiming to intercept whatever-it-was.

The wheat was tall and strong, the best I'd seen in the region, though it had been dry all summer. Almost reaching my waist, it rustled normally as I pushed through it: no exploding heads, tear gas, fires, smoke, or electric shocks. But something was wrong, and it took me only a moment to realize what: there wasn't a grasshopper in sight, though the splattered front of my car bore witness to their numbers elsewhere. *That's it!* I thought, with the smugness of every journalist who thinks he's solved a mystery. *Roysum has sprayed so heavily he's polluted his neighbours' land.*

Of course, that still didn't explain the green thing in the bushes, but I was confident my theory would have a place for it— once I knew what it was.

I was halfway to the haystack before it occurred to me to wonder why Roysum had one, when he had no cows or horses. I frowned, but only for a moment. I was on a roll. "Of course!" I said out loud. "He's using the hay to cover the pesticide containers!" Pleased with myself, I redoubled my pace. This could be big news. It might even bump the Saturday night bridge club results from their time-honoured front-page spot.

Then the glowing potato whizzed by my ear and struck the ground behind me with a miniature thunderclap. I stared at the black, scorched wheat where it had landed, then whipped around just in time to see a tomato heading for my head. I ducked in a panic, and it exploded nearby, with enough force to knock me down. Red, pulpy matter dripped from the back of my neck as I raised myself up. *I'm dying!* I thought; then, crazily, *Blood really does look just like ketchup.* Then I saw the seeds in it. It *was* ketchup —or, more precisely, tomato paste. I scrambled to my feet, dazed but unhurt.

Both potato and tomato had been bigger than anything brought to the office. I wondered what kind of fertilizer Roysum used.

Another tomato soared overhead, but exploded harmlessly several yards away. This time I marked where it came from— further up the creek, near the haystack—and dashed toward it, urging myself to remember Ernie Pyle.

My unseen assailant fortunately seemed to be short of both tomatoes and potatoes, but a barrage of round, white objects hurtled toward me, trailing blue smoke. *Onions!* I gulped air and held it—but there were too many of the vile vegetables. I had to breathe before I made it through the pall of gas, and dropped to my knees, coughing and choking, still twenty yards from the haystack.

Or rather, where the haystack had been.

Doubled over, gasping for breath, I saw, through streaming eyes, an enormous green oval, pulsing with light. From an irregular opening in the side a tongue-like brown ramp extended, and up it scampered something the size and shape of a small Christmas tree, bright green, upright, with a dozen white, wriggling feet like animated roots, and four upper limbs ending in splayed, twig-like fingers. A leafy canopy spread from its pointed top, and six glowing red circles on its body glared at me for a long moment before it ducked inside. Then the ramp disappeared with a wet, sucking sound, the opening closed, and the green oval blasted skyward in a whirlwind of loose hay.

And me? Well, I staggered back to the farmyard, bid an incoherent farewell to Roysum, somehow drove home without killing myself—and never told a soul until now. I have a journalistic reputation to maintain, after all, and the *Herald* is not the *National Enquirer*. As for the strange vegetables—people took them in stride, and wrote them off like they did that substitute schoolteacher once seen dancing naked under the full moon to the music of the Four Tops, or the ghostly figure Eddie Macoun swears he saw flitting around the United Grain Growers elevator last July.

But now I know I can't keep quiet any longer.

Try this for an explanation: a wandering, intelligent being discovers Earth—a being which is not an animal, but a plant. What does it find here? A world where plants are completely subjugated to animals, that's what.

Being a green-blooded patriot, naturally it decides to help. It does a little genetic tampering, adding genes that code for an unstable compound here, an increased mineral content there. When it is discovered, it flees. The end.

But I kept asking myself, why exploding tomatoes and electric potatoes? Why create what are essentially weapons when there's no one around to use them? And why didn't the creature do anything to Roysum's wheat?

Then last week I ran into him at the Co-op, and he told me he had the best harvest in all his sixty years, which, he said, was good news not only for him but for a lot of other people—because Roysum grows registered seed.

That means that next spring, hundreds of farmers across the prairie are going to be planting what grew in his field this summer.

When do you need weapons? When you have to outfit an army, of course.

I hope I'm wrong—but next year may be the funny vegetable season to end all funny vegetable seasons.

Watch your weekly newspaper.

WATERLILIES

Originally published in the Summer 2010 issue of Space and Time *magazine, "Waterlilies" was my take on the dangers of runaway nanotechnology. Why, it occurred to me, did the goo have to be grey...?*

"HERE, MONKEY, MONKEY, MONKEY!"

Danny eased a step closer to the black-leather couch. The rhesus macaque balanced on the armrest bared its teeth. Danny snarled back, then lunged. All he came up with was a handful of fur; the monkey, chattering, scampered to the farthest armrest.

Just beyond rose a meter-and-a-half-tall column of purple glass, lit from within and topped by a 25-centimetre nude woman. Molded of synthiflesh over a robotic armature, lifelike in colour and texture, correct in every anatomical detail, she was the only piece from Danny's breakthrough one-man show *Fembots* that he had kept for himself. Her name was *Fembot 21*, and as her motion sensors registered the monkey's presence, her programming activated. She stood on tiptoes, spread her arms wide, and—

The monkey leaped to the top of the pedestal. *Fembot 21* bounced off the wall and thudded in pieces into the burnt-orange Neo70s Revival shag carpet, where she lay on her back, one leg sticking straight up, the other lying some distance away. The monkey stared down at her and howled triumphantly.

"Shit!" Danny started around the couch. The monkey screeched, leaped down, and vanished into the hallway. It emerged like a jack-in-the-box, shrieking even louder, dashed over Danny's shoes before he could grab it, dribbling pee as it went, and disappeared into the kitchen.

Helga emerged hard on the monkey's heels. A head taller than Danny and twice as muscular, a former member of Germany's Olympic waterpolo team, she carried a huge suitcase in one hand as easily as though it were a briefcase, and with the other wielded her electrobrolly like a Teutonic sword. Blue sparks crackled and popped along the 'brolly's length as its water-repellant static charge reacted to the dust and monkey fur in the room's air. Helga's eyes, as they locked on Danny, were the exact same colour as the sparks.

She lowered the 'brolly and stepped close, forcing him to either crane his neck or talk to her breasts. She had turned on her recently acquired Medusa-'Do, and like clouds scudding above a skyscraper, the tendrils of hair weaving snakelike patterns above her forehead made him feel a little queasy.

"Is over," Helga said, her voice a booming contralto. "Over! No more model. No more sex. No more nothing. You promise me Orbital Hilton. You go out to buy tickets, make reservations. You come back with monkey!"

Glass shattered in the kitchen, but Danny didn't dare turn around.

"Helga, sweetheart, you don't understand," he said in his best wheedling voice. "That monkey is going to win me—*us*, I mean—the Stanislaw Prize for Avant-Garde Art!"

"The Stanislaw?" Besides enormous prestige, the Stanislaw

carried a $500,000 prize. Danny could almost see Helga translating that into euros as she stepped back a pace. "Explain."

More crashing in the kitchen; it sounded like the monkey was throwing teacups against the walls. Danny kept his eyes on Helga. "Androids make money, but they'll never win the prize, love, no matter what I do with them. My *Fembots* are *passé*; the artistic statement I made with them has been heard and assimilated into the *milieu*. 'Just as robots are programmed by their creators and masters,'" he quoted from the exhibition catalogue, "'so we are programmed by *our* creators (our parents and teachers and) and *our* masters: the corporate conglomerates that determine what we see, feel, and think. Like the *Fembots*, we are all robots under the skin.'"

"You are boring me," Helga said. "Answer question!"

From the kitchen came a sound like fingernails on a blackboard. What the *hell* was that monkey up to? "So, honeybunch, it's time to rethink!" Danny said. "To be relevant, art must argue with itself. To win the Stanislaw, I will argue, not with other artists, but with myself, with my own earlier work: how much more avantgarde can you get? I will argue that rather than being robots under the skin, as I said before, we are..." He paused for effect. "Animals!"

As if on cue, the monkey screeched; and outside, where the skies had been leaden all day, lightning flashed. The ensuing clap of thunder coincided with the sound of something heavy falling over in the kitchen.

A thundercloud seemed to have descended on Helga's face, as well. Her lips pressed together, her eyes narrowed, the Medusa-'Do writhed, and the 'brolly came up again, flashing sparks like the magic sword from *Final Fantasy XXI*. "You—want—to—put—*my*—body—on—a—*monkey?*" Helga shouted, emphasizing each word with a poke—and a fat electric spark—from the 'brolly. "*Nein! Nein, nein, nein!*" Four more pokes, each sharper than the last, then Helga swept by him, flung open the front door, and stalked down the front steps into the rain, the 'brolly popping up and open in an explosion of sparks. The monkey burst from the kitchen, crossed the living room in a brown, furry blur, and dashed after her.

Danny ran after both of them, but at the end of the front walk, Helga turned right, heading for the tube station—and the monkey turned left, toward the towers of downtown. Danny stopped, looked after Helga, looked after the monkey, did a quick mental comparison of the cost of the monkey versus the cost of hiring a new model—and followed the monkey.

Three hours later, soaked, chilled, and seriously pissed at all primates, Danny stood at the mouth of a downtown dead-end alley. He hadn't seen the monkey for half an hour, but he'd long since figured out its destination. He'd have been here two minutes after that if he'd been able to find a cab, but cabs, it seemed, were avoiding long-haired bearded sandal-wearing coatless artist-types tonight.

A single blue light illuminated a rust-red door at the alley's far end and the black letters stencilled on it: "Honest Art's Avant-Garde Art Supplies." Smaller letters beneath the main sign added, "And Surplus Store."

The door opened before he got there, revealing a short, brawny figure, silhouetted against the bright interior light. "Well, well, well," it said. "First a wet monkey, then a drowned rat."

"Hello to you too, Art," Danny said. "Are you going to let me in or make fun of me?"

"Both, probably," Art said, but moved to one side and gestured Danny in.

Danny stepped gratefully into the warmth and stood dripping on the store's tile floor. Art handed him a towel. Danny took it and began drying his hair. "You always keep a towel handy?"

"Didn't you ever read *A Hitchhiker's Guide to the Galaxy*? Besides, once the monkey showed up, I figured you'd be close behind." Art headed toward the back of the store. "Come back to my office when you're dry."

Danny and Art had known each other forever; they'd grown up as next-door neighbours in the Assiniboia Arms Apartments. Danny had been into art and music and drama, Art was more interested in science, computers, and blowing things up—but somehow, they'd maintained their friendship right through high school.

Then Danny had enrolled in art school, and Art had vanished —just dropped out of sight like a black hole had swallowed him up. For eight years Danny hadn't heard a word from him; then, just a couple of years ago, he'd suddenly popped up again, looking fit, muscular, and tanned. Pretty soon it was like they'd never lost touch, but Art never told Danny where he'd been. "Traveling," was the most Danny ever got out of him. Every once in a while, Art would disappear again for a couple of weeks, but he always came back.

He'd opened the store after hearing Danny lamenting the lack of a local source of the supplies needed by truly serious artists. Danny had just started working on the *Fembots*, and the cost of shipping in synthiflesh and microgears from out of town was eating up his grant money so fast he was afraid he wouldn't be able to build the complete series. Art had listened, questioned him extensively about what kind of supplies were needed, and then vanished.

A month later, he'd called Danny to invite him to the grand opening of Honest Art's Avant-Garde Art Supplies and Surplus Store.

Danny hung the towel on the coat rack by the door, then started toward Art's office. But as always, he was distracted by the store's amazing contents. Here was a pattern for a dress made entirely out of flank steak, next to a freezer full of the steak you would need to make it. Next to it, a variety of cutting tools "ideal for dismembering small animals," plus hooks and chains for hanging and stretching the body parts—although he personally found artistic putrefaction *so* 20th century.

Sensitive to the limited budgets of grant-dependent artists, thanks to Danny's input, most of Art's high-tech hardware was used. Danny passed a rack of last-generation VR goggles, shelves of discontinued digividcorders and clunky old table-top genesplicers, and a whole selection of Geiger counters so beat up they looked like they'd doubled as prospecting hammers.

He paused at the selection of pigments made with diseased blood, each tube marked with a biohazard sticker detailing the virus that infected it. "West Nile Vermilion? I know someone who would kill for a tube!"

"The price isn't *quite* that high," Art said, materializing at his left elbow. "Forget all this stuff. I've got something special to show you."

"All I want is my monkey," Danny said, following Art to the back of the store, where several small animals scampered around large cages, transparent from the outside, that Danny knew provided their occupants with endless natural vistas. His rhesus was happily ensconced in one, eating monkey nuts. Danny paused, but Art kept walking.

"Forget him," Art said. "He's not going to win you the Stanislaw." He stopped at his office door. "I sold my only other monkey just this morning."

Danny's heart skipped a beat. Two Stanislaw entries making use of monkeys, no matter how differently, would render each other non-unique—grounds for automatic disqualification.

That was it, then. He couldn't use the monkey. And that meant...the thought hit him like a fist. *Helga!* He'd let Helga leave, had let her walk away without trying to stop her, for nothing.

Danny had feigned existential despair often enough in interviews with critics, judges, and granting agencies; this time he felt it for real.

"Chin up, Danny," Art said. "What you need is obviously an entirely new approach."

Danny massaged his forehead. "How about 'Portrait of the Artist as a Young Suicide?'" he muttered.

Art chuckled. "I don't think you need to go that far. Instead...well, let me show you. Something so new no one is using it yet. It's military. Experimental. Cutting-edge. Interested?"

Military? What did the military know about art?

On the other hand...turning weapons into art...he could call it *Swords into Ploughshares*, or something like that...what did he have to lose? "I'm interested."

Art nodded, and opened the door into his office. As always, Danny was struck by the contrast between the shop's dim-lit clutter and this room's bright-lit, perfect order.

Two computers flickered and clicked to themselves on two separate desks, their screens portraying an endless flow of gibberish; Danny couldn't tell if they were doing serious work or if Art was running his antique *Matrix* screensaver again. Tools ranging from a rack of screwdrivers to a series of callipers gleamed on the wall above a workbench whose centrepiece was a miniature scanning electron microscope.

It was *not* the office of an art dealer. Not for the first time, Danny wondered what exactly the "Surplus Store" portion of Art's business entailed.

Art took a pair of insulated gloves from a hook next to the callipers, and walked to the far end of the room, where he had installed a walk-in vault. He tapped a long sequence into a keypad on the vault door; then, as the door hummed and clanked, pulled on the gloves.

The door swung open automatically, revealing a room half again as big as the office, packed with crates and lined with what looked like safety-deposit boxes. At the back of the vault was a smaller door; Art went to it, slipped a keycard on a silver chain out from under his shirt, slid the card through a scanner, and then tugged the door open. As ice fog tumbled out around his feet, he pulled on the gloves, then reached in and slid out a gleaming, golden metal cylinder about ten centimetres in diameter and maybe twenty-five centimetres long. He closed the freezer door and exited the vault, and the vault door shut noiselessly behind him before locking with a metallic clank.

Art placed the tube on the workbench and took off the gloves. *"This,"* he said, "will win you the Stanislaw Prize." He pressed the end of the cylinder, and it split down the middle and popped open, revealing a dozen crystal vials nestled in red padding. He lifted one out; silvery liquid, like mercury but less viscous, sloshed inside it.

Danny took a step back. He'd seen too many movies where terrorists pulled out just such a vial before announcing their plans to unleash a plague that would wipe out humanity. "What is it?"

Instead of replying, Art took the vial turned to one of his computers, to which was attached something that looked like a battery charger. He dropped the vial into the hole on top.

"Something simple," he said. "Mondrian."

"What?"

Art ran his fingers over the computer's touchpad for a few moments, occasionally clicking a button with his right thumb. Nothing seemed to happen. He removed the vial and unscrewed the lid, walked toward the vault, and, without the slightest warning, splashed the vial's contents against the metal door.

Danny gasped, but Art laughed. "It's harmless," he said. "Watch!"

A complex pattern of lines and boxes filled with primary colours covered a portion of the door; within two minutes it covered the entire surface of the metal. Art glanced at the computer. "Any second now..."

The wall's outline suddenly blurred behind a veil of shimmering dust, and the pattern vanished.

Danny stared at Art. "What the *hell?*"

"It's called nanopaint," Art said. "You can program it to cover any surface with any pattern you want. Great for camouflage. Also good for bridges and other large structures."

"But the scaling problem—it would pixilate—"

"Fractals," Art said, as though that explained everything. "Never mind that. What you need to think about are the artistic possibilities. What you have here is a self-replicating, completely programmable pigment. The silvery stuff is made up of assembler nanomites. They build the pigmented nanomites out of whatever raw materials are available on the surface on which they're placed —dust, old paint, it really doesn't matter. Then those pigmented nanomites make more pigmented nanomites, and so on, and so on, and so on."

"It didn't last very long."

"You set its lifespan to whatever you want," Art said. "And watch this." He set the vial on the floor. A stream of silver coalesced out of nowhere and flowed into it. "Only the second-generation nanomites have a limited lifespan; the initial assembler nanomites are permanent. The vial contains a transmitter they home on, so you can always get them back; then you can reprogram them and use them again."

Danny looked at the tube. "Wow." The Stanislaw Prize was as good as his. Paint that made its own paintings! Intelligent pigment that could crank out fake Picassos, ersatz Pollacks, phoney Miros, then vanish into dust. Who was the artist? *Was* there an artist? Was it art or artifice?

"Forget the monkey!" he said. "I'll take it." Then he hesitated. "How much?"

"It's yours," Art said.

Danny stared at him in astonishment. Friend or not, Art had

never given him art supplies for free before. "Why?" he said, unable to keep the suspicion out of his voice.

Art shrugged. "Advertising. You win the Stanislaw, I won't be able to keep this stuff on the shelf."

"You said it was military surplus," Danny said slowly. "I'm not going to get in trouble, am I?"

"Danny!" Art looked hurt. "Of course not! I own this stuff fair and square. Got it at government auction. Got all the documentation, too—well, most of it; there were some blacked-out chunks, and there's so much of it I haven't finished reading it yet. But I got the gist of it. The army canned the program, and sold off the equipment."

"But if it works..."

"Obviously it doesn't—not for military purposes. Maybe it falls off tanks when they're hit by machine gun fire. Maybe it isn't waterproof. My guess is, it just isn't permanent enough. Anyway, what do you care?"

Good question, Danny thought. He didn't have to know how the stuff worked; he didn't understand the science behind synthiflesh or threedee recorders, either, and he used them all the time. This wasn't Renaissance Italy; he didn't have to mix his own pigments. That kind of thing was for the post-postmodern fundamentalists, not the avant-gardistes.

Art gave Danny the tube of pigment he'd just demonstrated, and packed it into a chilled, insulated tube for him, then packaged up the programming interface, its cable, and a datastick. "It takes energy to make new nanomites," he explained as he worked. "So don't get any on your hands; you do, and you're looking at minor frostbite at least. Worst-case scenario, I figure, is that your fingers break off like so many Popsicles. When you're not using it, keep it in your freezer. The assembler nanomites were designed to stay quiescent at about -10 Celsius."

Danny was feeling uneasy again. "What if I do get some on me?" he said. "What should I do?"

"Pray," Art said solemnly. Danny stared at him wide-eyed, and after a moment Art's grave expression crumpled into a grin. "Rubbing alcohol," he said. "Kills 'em dead. Or you could try a blowtorch—they can't assimilate that much heat all at once—but that's a rather drastic form of first aid."

Uneasy but eager, Danny said good-bye to Art and took a cab home. By the time he got there he had his work that would win him the Stanislaw firmly fixed in his head.

It would consist of three gilded, old-fashioned frames, all hung on a wall within a larger frame—a simple black square delineating the edges of the work, with his signature in the lower right corner.

Within each of the smaller frames would be a layer of the nanopaint, programmed to create a particular classic style of painting: pre-Raphaelite, Abstract Expressionist, Impressionist, Neo-Classical, Cubist. But every few minutes, each painting would change to a different style. No human would touch the canvases, yet scores of original paintings would appear, tease the eye for a few minutes, then vanish, never to be seen again.

How could any avant-garde jury resist a work that had so much to say about the mechanization of art, the dehumanization of the creative process, the transience of genius?

It was almost midnight when he got home. He went into the kitchen, turned on the light, and gasped. Table on its side, cabinet doors swinging open, broken glass everywhere, his best Scotch puddled on the floor...*damn* that monkey!

Well, he'd clean it up tomorrow. He put the cylinder in the freezer compartment of his refrigerator, then went into his office, connected the programming interface Art had given him, and installed the software, feeling only a slight uneasiness as the first screen warned him this program was CLASSIFIED and PROPERTY OF THE UNITED STATES ARMY and said something ominous about FEDERAL PROSECUTION. *Art said he bought the stuff fair and square*, he reassured himself.

A lengthy text file popped up first, plastered with more WARNINGS and CAUTIONS, but Danny closed it without looking at it. He preferred the intuitive approach.

There were a lot of options for programming the paint, but Danny ignored everything except for the FAMOUS PAINTINGS menu. He picked something at random—Monet's *Waterlilies*—and clicked PROGRAM.

A warning box popped up on the screen, empty except for an exclamation point and the words, WRITE WARNING TEXT HERE. Impatiently Danny closed the box and was rewarded with a new one: INSERT PIGMENT INTO INTERFACE.

"All right!" Whistling, Danny made a quick trip to the freezer; a few seconds later, he was slipping a vial of nanomite assemblers into the "battery charger."

Almost at once, the computer beeped. PROGRAMMING COMPLETED, it said. He closed the software, pulled out the tube of pigment, and went down the stairs to his basement workshop.

In between serious pieces, Danny liked to paint oil landscapes, so he already had a couple of prepared canvasses. He set one up on an easel, opened the vial, and dribbled half of its contents on the canvas. Almost at once, colour appeared, spreading slowly, faint and amorphous at first, but soon vividly, unmistakably, one of Monet's famous paintings of waterlilies.

Yet it seemed...thin, somehow, like watery gruel. Danny frowned at it, thinking. Of course, *Waterlilies* was far more complex, visually, than the Mondrian that Art had demonstrated; and Art had said something about fractals...didn't that mean almost endless levels of complexity? That would obviously take time.

Danny yawned. He was eager to start on the frames, but he didn't do his best work when he was tired. Maybe a few hours' sleep wouldn't be a bad idea. Screwing shut the vial, still half-full of programmed nanomites, he climbed back up the stairs, returned the vial to the tube and the tube to the freezer, then went to bed.

It felt cold and empty without Helga, but Danny was confident it was only temporary. She'd be back. Once he won the Stanislaw...yeah, she'd be back. Or someone else would take her place...he slipped into a pleasantly erotic dream.

The phone rang. Groggily, Danny rolled over and looked at its glowing screen. *Art's Avant Garde Art Supplies*, he read; and, *3:27 a.m.*

He punched the speakerphone button. "Art, what the hell are you doing calling me this time of night?"

"Danny, listen carefully." It was Art, all right, but he sounded odd—breathless and frightened. "Danny, whatever you do, don't use the paint."

"What?" Danny yawned hugely. "Art, is this some kind of a joke?"

"Danny, I'm not joking. *Don't use the paint.*"

Danny rubbed his eyes, trying to come awake. "It's too—" he yawned again. "Too late," he finished. "I've already started my project. You were right, Art; it's going to win me the Stanislaw."

Dead silence for a very long moment. "You've opened it?" Art finally said, barely whispering.

"It's making me a Monet," Danny said.

When Art spoke again, he sounded half-strangled. "Did you..." He cleared his throat. "Danny, did you fill in *all* the specifications when you programmed it?"

"Huh?"

"Did you tell it, very specifically, what kind of surface to paint, and most importantly—did you program in a lifespan?"

"No."

"Oh, God," Art said, and if Danny hadn't known Art was an atheist, he'd have sworn he meant it as a prayer.

"Art, what's wrong?"

"I finished reading the documentation, Danny. You've got to destroy that paint. Now. Have you got any alcohol? A blowtorch?"

"There's a bottle of alcohol in the medicine cabinet—"

"That's not enough. Look, Danny, I'm on my way. I'll bring a drum of alcohol and a spray pump. Maybe we can still stop it."

"Stop what?" But all Danny heard in response was a clatter, as though the receiver had been dropped. "Art? Art?" Was that the sound of a door slamming?

Very odd. Danny yawned. He tried to roll over and go back to sleep, but Art's call niggled at him until finally he muttered, "Shit," and got up.

Naked except for his slippers—protection against all the broken glass the monkey had left behind—he padded down to the kitchen, opened the freezer compartment door—

—and slammed it shut again in an instant.

Either everything in there had gone spectacularly bad all at once, exploding and covering the inside of the fridge with multi-coloured mold, or he had a problem.

He opened the door again, just enough to turn on the inside light.

It wasn't mold. Everything, from shelves to walls to containers to a loaf of bread, bore a fine representation of Monet's waterlilies.

He ran to the basement door, opened it, took one look, and slammed it closed.

Every goddamn thing in the basement was covered with Monet's waterlilies, too. Another step, and he'd have drowned in them.

He looked back at the refrigerator. Waterlilies were starting to creep around the edges of the refrigerator door.

Alcohol. Art had said alcohol would kill them. Danny spun around to run to the bathroom medicine cabinet, but his slipper twisted under his foot and he stumbled and almost fell, catching himself with one hand on the refrigerator.

Icy cold bit at him and he jerked himself upright again, staring in horror at the faint colour on his fingertips; almost instantly it began to spread, running up his fingers toward his knuckles. "Shit!" he screamed, and ran for the bathroom. There he flung open the medicine cabinet and jerked out the bottle of rubbing alcohol. He twisted the cap off with his teeth and splashed the alcohol over his hand, now as numb and cold as though he'd been cycling in January without a glove. To his relief, the colour faded, and when he wiped his fingers clean on the towel, nothing bloomed on it.

So the little bastards weren't invulnerable. But his rubbing alcohol wouldn't go very far, and that damn monkey had smashed every bottle of whiskey he had in the house. Art was on his way, but even a tank of the stuff might not be enough...how far had they spread?

Danny ran back to the kitchen, to discover waterlilies creeping across the kitchen floor, avoiding the puddles of spilled whisky. They covered the kitchen counter, and the refrigerator wore a complete mantel of Impressionism.

Something popped downstairs and all the lights went out. With an audible hiss, the pigments spilling out across the kitchen floor, now barely visible in the glow of a streetlight outside the kitchen window, accelerated their growth, reaching hungrily toward Danny's feet. He jumped onto a chair. The temperature plummeted. His naked body erupted in goose bumps and he could see his breath.

The damn nanomites must be doubling their numbers every few minutes. In no time they would engulf the house, then the block, then the city...eventually, maybe the world.

He suddenly envisioned Earth covered with Monet's *Waterlilies*, a stunning Impressionist painting hanging in space— beautiful, and quite, quite dead.

He had to stop the nanomites there and then, and if he couldn't do it with alcohol, he'd have to do it with fire.

But first, he had to get off his chair; nanomites were running up its legs. Fortunately he was close to the arch into the living room, where the nanomites had so far been stymied by the thick shag rug. He took a deep breath, and jumped.

He landed on the now-motionless *Fembot 21*, twisting his ankle and falling into the purple glass pillar, which went over with a crash. Swearing, he staggered up and limped out the front door, hobbling as fast as he could around back yard to the gardening shed, where he fumbled frantically with the combination lock. It took him three tries to get it open. By the time he emerged with the gasoline can, waterlilies covered the kitchen windows like exquisite stained glass.

He dashed around the house, splashing gasoline on everything he could reach. He must have been making too much noise; a window slid open in the next-door house, and a little boy's voice shrieked, "Mommy, he's not wearing any clothes!" Danny shot one frantic glance around in time to see Mommy take one long appraising look at him, then disappear with the child. A few seconds later he could hear her yelling to the 911 operator.

Danny threw aside the can—and realized he didn't have any matches.

Back to the shed for the butane lighter he used for his barbecue. By the time he got back to the house, he could hear sirens in the distance, drawing closer.

He stuck the lighter against the siding and pulled the trigger.

The old wooden-frame building went up like a torch, the flames licking hungrily across the clapboard, racing across the roof, dancing around the chimney. The kitchen seemed to resist burning at first, and he could imagine the nanomites trying to suck up all the extra heat energy surrounding them, but there weren't enough of them, thank God, and soon the kitchen, and the pigments, and all of Monet's waterlilies were burning merrily.

By the time Art, the police, and the fire trucks all arrived, flames roared a hundred feet into the sky, and the whole neighbourhood was on hand to watch Danny, a blanket thrown around his shoulders, being handcuffed and led away.

Art had the decency to look guilt-stricken as Danny passed him. "Don't worry," Art said. "I'll bail you out."

Danny said nothing. A deep sense of relief made him almost giddy. He looked up with satisfaction at the tower of black smoke billowing into and merging with the overcast sky.

Then, as he slid inside the police cruiser, it started to rain.

Relief gave way to numbness as he watched the raindrops hit the ground. In a way, he supposed, it was his finest work, definitely worthy of the Stanislaw. Instead of society devouring and debasing art, as it usually did, this time art would devour society. From the Orbital Hilton, no doubt, it would be spectacular.

He wished he was going to live long enough to travel there and see it, but he doubted that he would…because everywhere a raindrop fell, waterlilies bloomed.

SINS OF THE FATHER

*A*t *9:15 a.m. on September 20, 2005, in a class on writing science fiction taught by Robert J. Sawyer in the Writing With Style program at the Banff Centre, I wrote the following opening lines, the exercise Rob set for us that morning:*

> **Emily streaked through the phosphorescent sea, her wake a comettail of pale green light, her close-cropped turquoise hair surrounded by a glowing pink aurora. The water racing through her gill-slits smelled of blood.**

My classmates thought it sounded interesting, so, as the week progressed, I turned that opening into this short story, "Sins of the Father." However, I never submitted it anywhere. Before I got around to it, DAW picked up my novel Lost in Translation, *originally published by Five Star, for a mass-market-paperback release, and Ethan Ellenberg agreed to be my agent. Needing something to propose to DAW for my next book, I took the seeds I had planted in "Sins of the Father" and let them sprout into the synopsis for what became* Marseguro, *my second novel published by DAW (and my first written for them), and winner of the 2009 Aurora Award (honouring*

Canadian science fiction and fantasy) for Best Long-Form Work in English.

The sequel, Terra Insegura, *followed. (The two were later published under one cover in an omnibus edition,* The Helix War.*) As of this writing, I'm looking forward to publication of my ninth novel for DAW Books,* Worldshaper, *in September 2018.*

Here, published for the first time, is the short story that became my first book from a major publisher. Those who have read Marseguro *will see a lot of elements here that made it into the final book. Those who haven't read* Marseguro...should.

AS HIS HOVERBOAT BURST INTO FLAMES, Richard Hansen plunged into the water. Thanks to the envirosuit, he felt no shock of cold, no sensation of pressure, as he let himself sink into the darkness. But he was shocked and under pressure all the same.

The hunterbot had fired on him!

By God, I'll have someone disfellowshipped for this when I get back to Safehaven, he thought.

He looked up at the bottom of the hoverboat's hull, outlined by the red glow of the fire consuming it. If *I ever get back,* he amended. Something cold wound its way down his spine, and for a moment he thought his envirosuit had sprung a leak. But then he recognized the sensation for what it really was:

Fear.

Without the hoverboat, the only way he was going to get back to Safehaven was to swim. He hadn't come more than twenty kilometres or so since he'd left the harbour that morning, so it wasn't impossible—but it wouldn't be quick, or easy. Especially not for him. He might be a Superior Deacon in the Office of Developing Omniscience, but he normally worked surrounded by dataspheres and holodisplays, not out in the field. He wasn't exactly fat, but he wasn't exactly fit, either.

Well, he'd do what he had to. One problem at a time, and his first concern was the hunterbot.

He needed information. "Jihad Revelation," he said, and his faceplate lit with the head-up display for his Indweller, the nanoputer implanted at the base of his neck. "Display Safehaven Purification briefing material relevant to term 'hunterbots.'"

Words appeared, apparently floating in the black water. "Despite the best efforts of the Holy Warriors, it is inevitable that some of the merpeople will escape; we have no technology on board capable of blocking the five-kilometre-wide mouth of the harbour. It is imperative that these escapees not be permitted to reach and warn other merpeople pods currently at sea or in other communities.

"In addition to warriors in hoverboats tasked with searching for and destroying any survivors, we will deploy a large number of hunterbots, programmed to detect, track and destroy merpeople, which they can locate through a variety of means, including infrared signature, visual recognition, and DNA traces. To ensure maximum effectiveness, a positive ID through any one of these means will be sufficient to trigger an attack."

It must have been the envirosuit, Hansen thought. *It made me look like a merman to that stupid 'bot, never mind the fact I was driving an OHD hoverboat.*

A stolen one, another part of his mind insisted on adding, but he argued it down. *It all belongs to the Church of Humanity Purified, and I am a servant of the Church.*

The argument would have held more water if he had bothered to tell the servants of the church responsible for the hoverboat that he was going to "borrow" it.

"Page," he said, and another screen of text appeared. "Hunterbots come in a variety of specialized forms. Aerial 'bots will identify targets and attack those that they can. Targets which cannot be attacked by the aerial 'bots will be tracked and attacked by submariner 'bots as soon as they can intercept."

"Jehovallah preserve me!" Hansen whispered.

How close would the submariner 'bot be?

No way of knowing, but it wouldn't be far away, not if it was meant to support the aerial 'bot. It could arrive any minute.

He needed shelter. "Light!" he snapped, and his headlamp came on; it showed nothing but drifting white specks, thick as falling snow.

It might also show the aerial 'bot or the probably incoming submariner 'bot exactly where he was, he realized.

"Light off!" It wasn't doing him any good anyway.

"Sonar!" he said instead. It would give him away even more surely than the light, but it was his only hope of locating any hiding places that might—please Jehovallah, *did*—exist among the rocks of the nearby cliff or the seafloor blow.

His display lit with a sonar-generated image of the surrounding five hundred metres or so. His heart almost stopped when he thought he saw a moving blip, but it vanished before he was even sure he had seen it. If it had been a submariner 'bot, it wasn't homing on him yet.

Probably just some local wildlife, he thought. *I've got bigger fish to fry.*

"Analyze," he told his nanoputer. "Identify possible caves."

Instantly, the display showed him two bright-green spots. One was far below his current depth, but the other was above him— right at the water level. *Perfect,* he thought. The deep one was designated 1 and the higher one 2. "Guide me to Target 2," he said, and a spot of red light appeared in his faceplate, well off to the left. He turned until it was centred in the display, and swam toward it.

He kept the sonar sweep active—no point trying to hide now, he suspected—so he could see how close he was getting to his target. He was about twenty metres from it, and the red dot had grown into a ragged, red, almost-circular opening sketched against the blackness, when the nanoputer beeped at him.

"Moving target acquired," its uninflected male voice murmured inside his head. A red blip appeared on his display, tagged, "Submariner Hunterbot Mark III." Numbers below that told Hansen the target had been acquired at 465 metres and was closing at 5.2 metres per second, and would intercept him in...

Less than two minutes.

Hansen said a frantic prayer, but he said it silently: he needed all his breath for flight. He kicked as hard as he could, forcing his way through water that only pushed back more the faster he tried to go, as though doing its best to hold him up for the hunterbot to catch.

The mouth of the cavern became visible in his helmet lamp—and at the same instant a red gleam like a single baleful eye appeared in the water behind him.

He hadn't thought to read far enough in the briefing material to find out what weapons the submariner hunterbot was armed with. Instead, he found out the hard way. Just as he swam in through the cavern opening and dared to think he might yet escape, the first torpedo caught up with him. Only the fact he had turned abruptly upward, following the path of the cavern entrance, saved him. The torpedo impacted on one of the rocks outside the cave mouth.

The blast hit him like a hammer blow, hurling him upward in a welter of bubbles and mud, spinning over and over, out of control. Dazed, he felt himself slam into a rock, then another—a knife-like pain stabbed him in the chest—he collided with something else, this time more yielding—and then he erupted into open air, tossed up in a fountain of water and foam like a leaf.

He splashed back down, went under, then rose to the surface and floated, face down, dazed, consciousness fading.

In the last instant before he blacked out, he saw the face of a young girl, eyes closed, drift upward into the light of his helmet lamp.

～

An insistent beeping roused him, an indeterminate time later.

He opened his eyes. He was floating on his back. His helmet lamp reflected off a wet rock ceiling, just a metre or two above his head. He hurt all over, but the worst pains seemed to be coming from his chest—he must have broken a rib—and his shoulder, which he thought he must have dislocated. "Revelation Jihad," he whispered.

Nothing happened.

"Revelation Jihad," he said louder.

Still nothing.

The shockwave must have disabled my nanoputer, he thought, and felt the first budding of panic.

Those buds blossomed into full-fledged terror when a girl suddenly erupted out of the water beside him and stared down into his face.

He screamed, and her eyes widened and she screamed back, then disappeared under the water again. That didn't reassure him; she must be underneath him, and he knew what she was:

A mergirl. There could be no mistaking that strange face, with eyes the size of an old-Earth anime character, a nose whose nostrils were sealed tight into almost invisible slits, a mouth filled with sharp, triangular teeth—and the triple-frilled gill flaps on each side of her shapely neck.

She was one of the very abominations he had brought the *SS Simon the Zealot* to this planet to destroy, and if she found that out...

He was hurt. He was unarmed. The merfolk were much stronger than ordinary humans, and they could breathe underwater. All she had to do was open his faceplate and drag him under, and she could finish the work of the hunterbots.

Maybe the hunterbots weren't after me after all, he thought. *Maybe they were really chasing her, and I was just in the wrong place at the wrong time.*

That might explain the sub-bot, but it didn't begin to explain the air-bot.

He couldn't stand the thought that she might be sneaking up on him from underwater, so he rolled over. The envirosuit, having gotten him to the surface (even if that surface was inside a cave) had no intention of letting him go under again without a fight. The buoyancy it had established made it possible for him to recline comfortably on top of the water; it also made what he intended to be a swift, decisive move into a clumsy, floundering, splashing struggle.

At the end of it, he was pointing face down...and there was the face again, looking up at him. Underwater, it looked less alien than it had in the air, more as if it belonged. The gill slits were open, pulsating gently as the frills weaved a slow, silent wave. The eyes glowed in his helmet lamp. A halo of close-cropped, green-tinged hair surrounded her skull.

He could see her body now, too, naked except for a silvery smooth belt around her hips. Her hands and feet were out of proportion to her body, bigger than they should have been. Her toes were almost as long as her fingers, and webbed; her fingers were also webbed. But the rest of her was disturbingly human—disturbing, because the sight of her nakedness woke in Hansen a sexual urge that shamed him. *It would be like mounting a sheep!* he thought, deeply disgusted at his own weakness. *She may look human, but she's an animal.*

And then the "animal" spoke. "Who are you?" she said.

The sound was high-pitched and inhuman—whatever method she used for producing it obviously didn't involve moving air over her vocal cords, since she didn't breathe air—but perfectly clear in his ears.

Don't answer, a wary part of him insisted, but, "Richard Hansen," he heard himself saying. *I'm trapped in here with her,* he defended himself to himself. (He wanted to think of her as an "it," but she was all-too-obviously female.) *I can't very well ignore her.* He didn't give his title, though. She probably had no idea who had attacked her colony, or why—but some part of him, remembering those sharp teeth, seeing her sleek, muscular form, so at home in the water, thought it the better part of valour not to give her immediate reason to connect him to the slaughter of her friends and family.

"My name is Emily," she said. She paused, as though having her own second thoughts, then finished, "Emily Hansen."

Richard felt as though he'd been punched in the stomach. "We have...the same last name?" he finally managed to squeeze out through his constricted voice.

"I am a descendant of the Shaper," Emily said. Her voice didn't change—or if it did, he lacked the skill to interpret it—but her face showed pride. "Direct in line from his grandson, the First."

Richard felt sick. His great-great-grandfather had not only polluted the human genestream, he had modified the gametes of his own son—Richard's great-great-uncle—and his wife so that they gave birth to the first of these monsters.

He swallowed, hard. Throwing up in an envirosuit was a really bad idea. "How old are you?" he asked instead, trying to regain his mental balance.

"Fifteen."

For a moment Richard was startled, and doubly ashamed of his lustful urges. She was only a child...

Then he remembered that one Safehaven year equaled 1.42 Earth years. That made her...it took him a few moments—he'd gotten used to having his nanoputer calculate things for him...

Twenty-one. A young woman, but an adult.

No. She was not a woman at all. She was a monster—a young monster, perhaps, but a monster. And among monsters, she might very well already be a mother many times over. Maybe they gave birth to whole litters before they were ten and another one every year thereafter. He must not think of her as a human being...

...not when everyone she had ever known was being turned into bite-sized bits of fish food back in the harbour.

She watched him closely, obviously wondering if he was going to say anything about her age. When he didn't, she said, "Why do you wear that thing? How can you breathe?"

She doesn't know, he thought. *She doesn't know who or what I am.*

"It's a...protection," he said. "Things here are different from my...home waters. This keeps me from...getting sick."

"Would it protect you from the machine thing outside?" she said, her voice going even higher. Eagerness? Fear? He couldn't tell. "Could you help me get past it? I have to get back home. My mother will be worried."

She doesn't know, he thought again. *She doesn't know what has happened!*

"Why were you out here?" he asked.

"Allie and I were camping," Emily said. "Down in the Featherbed Fish Canyon. It's a protected area, no large predators. My church has a cave down there. Allie and I are prayer buddies."

Richard heard the words, but couldn't believe he was hearing them. Didn't *want* to believe he was hearing them. "Church?" he said. "Prayer?"

"Are you all right?" Emily sounded concerned.

No. No, I'm not.

Animals don't go to church.

Animals don't pray.

Animals...

"Where's your friend? Allie?"

Emily blinked rapidly. For the first time, Richard saw that she had a nictitating membrane that slid rom side to side across her oversized eyes. "I don't know," she said. "I'm so worried. When the machine thing came into the canyon we got separated...the machine went after her, first...I swam the other way. I was trying to get home, to get help, but the machine..." her voice trailed off.

Allie was almost certainly dead. Richard knew it, and suspected Emily knew it, too, but wasn't allowing herself to think it, yet.

"The machine chased you, too," Emily said then. "What were you doing out here?"

"I was just...arriving. From my trip. My hoverboat—"

Suddenly remembering she thought he was a merman, he broke off, but she'd already noticed.

"Hoverboat?" She stared at him. "Oh! You're an air-breather! Why didn't you say so?"

"You're not...frightened by that?" he asked, taken off guard. Of course they had known there were surface dwellers here as well as the abominations, but they'd assumed the two groups had nothing to do with each other...

"Why should I be? I have many air-breathing friends."

There will be a great deal of work to be done in Purifying the land community, too, then, Richard thought, but did not say.

"I didn't know how you would react," he said truthfully. "I'm from...very far away."

"Do you know what those machines are?"

Tread carefully, Richard thought. *She's still dangerous—and amoral.*

"I think they came...from another place. Another...planet." Would that mean anything to her?

"You mean one of the other worlds settled by the Ten Thousand Ships?" she said, her eyes widening. "But why would they attack us? We're all of Old Earth."

Once again, she caught him off-guard. She knew so much. He'd always assumed the merfolk would be simple barbarians, barely able to speak—more like glorified dolphins than anything else.

She has as much of Joseph Hansen's DNA as you do, his inner voice reminded him. *Maybe more.*

Modified *DNA,* he snarled silently back.

"I think...they came from Earth itself," he said out loud.

"But Earth was destroyed!"

"No...we..." He thought quickly. "Where I live, we recently were visited by a space trader. He said he had run into a ship from Old Earth. It seems there was a..." *Miracle? No.* "...an extraordinary bit of luck. Another asteroid collided with the Killer before it struck. It hit the moon instead of the Earth."

"But..." Emily looked bewildered, insofar as he could interpret her strange features. "But why would Earth send machines to kill us? What have we done? Earth was our home..."

Not your *home,* Richard thought. *Never the home of people like you.*

He realized he had just thought of her as a person instead of a thing, and felt confusion again.

What to tell her?

Tell her the truth, he thought. *See how she reacts. Valuable information for further Purification efforts.*

He almost convinced himself.

"After the Ten Thousand Ships left...we were told...many of those left behind were convinced that the Killer was an act of God, a punishment for the wickedness and licentiousness that had descended on the planet." He had heard this story so many times he could tell it in his sleep. "And so it came to pass that they rose up against the irreligious, the irreverent, the immoral and the ignorant; rose up and Purified the Earth with blood and fire, and the smoke of the burning cities had a sweet savour in the nostrils of Jehovallah, and he repented of his decision to destroy mankind. He sent the Saviour, the second asteroid, to strike the Killer. But as a warning, he sent the Killer into the moon, where it destroyed Apollo City, a haven of sinfulness, the place where many of the abominations of the bio-meddlers had fled the Purification of the

Earth. And so was the Third Covenant sealed. God would withhold punishment so that mankind might have one more chance to Purify itself. And if we succeed, then Earth will never again be threatened with destruction, and Jehovallah will bless his Chosen People, Humanity Purified, through all of space and all of time, forever and ever, amen."

As he came to the end of the lesson, he realized what he had just done, but by then it was too late. Emily might be an abomination, but she was no fool, as she had already shown.

"My God," she said, and he knew it was not *his* God she referenced. "You're one of them. You're from Earth. You brought those machines!"

"No," he said. "But...I arrived with them." *And I found your planet in the first place and told those with the machines where to bring them*, he thought. *And your family is dead, and you don't know it yet, and I brought the Holy Warriors who killed them...*

He felt his heart pounding in his chest.

"How many of them are there?" she demanded. "Are they all over the planet? Are they in Safehaven?"

"I don't know."

"You're lying," Emily said flatly. "I can hear your heart pounding, hear the tension in your voice. You airbreathers have no control."

Think fast. "All right," he said. "It's true. They're in Safehaven. But they're not all over the planet." *Not yet.* "The Holy Warriors are attacking one community at a time."

"Holy Warriors? Is that the name of the machines?"

"No...there are humans, too. Soldiers."

Her reaction wasn't what he expected. She blinked. "Soldiers. Unmodified human soldiers?"

"Yes."

"Are they all wearing envirosuits?"

What an odd question. "No...the air here is breathable."

She suddenly flipped over and swam out of range of his light,

69

then back again. "What have they done to the settlement?" she said. "If the machines attack on sight—what have these Earthlings done?"

Richard said nothing.

"Answer me!" she demanded, and then, faster than he would have thought possible, she darted forward and seized the suit's air hose. "I can rip this out and you will *drown*. What have these Earthlings done?"

Richard swallowed. "They have Purified the village," he said.

"Purified?" Her face was suddenly pressed against his face-plate. "Killed?" she shrieked, the sound so loud, so high, that he tried to clap his hands over his ears, even though it was pointless inside the suit. "My parents? My brother? My friends? They killed them all?"

"I don't know for sure..." Richard began, but she squeezed the air hose closed and his next breath failed. "Yes! Yes!" he choked out.

She released the hose and vanished again. "Jehovallah preserve me," he whispered under his breath. "Jehovallah preserve me as you preserved the Earth. I am pure, oh Lord, preserve me. I obey you, oh Lord, preserve me. I—"

Emily was back, fluttering her hands and feet, agitated. "Who is this Jehovallah?"

"The Creator. The Lawgiver," Richard said.

"Jehovah? Allah?"

Richard recoiled. "Those names are forbidden. They reflect an imperfect understanding. The Church of Humanity Purified worships the One True God behind the false gods of the past, the one they saw through a glass darkly, but we now see clearly: Jehovallah."

"I worshipped God," Emily said. "We have..." she grimaced. "Had...a large congregation. We are Christians here."

"That would not have saved you, even had we known," Richard said. "Christianity is anathema. Along with Islam, and Judaism, and all other religions from before the Miracle. If you were air-breathing humans, you would still have been Purified."

"You would have slaughtered non-modified humans the way you slaughtered my people? What kind of monsters are you?"

You're the monster, Richard wanted to say, but he didn't dare. "They would not have been slaughtered," he said. "They would have been detained and re-educated, taught the error of their ways."

"But because we breathe water instead of air, we're fair game?"

Richard swallowed. "Yes."

Emily shook her head, a human gesture beyond doubt. "Great-great-grandfather was wiser than we knew," she said. "He warned us all. We didn't listen."

That got Richard's attention; her great-great-grandfather, after all, was also his. "Warned you? How?"

"He said that the rest of humanity might not understand what he had done here, that just as the Ten Thousand Ships fled the Earth to try to ensure humanity would endure among the stars, so his creation of the merfolk would help ensure humanity's survival by opening up entirely new worlds for us to inhabit. He said some humans might not be able to see that. And so he made sure that even the airbreathers of Safehaven were not unmodified humans. They all, every one of them, underwent a minor modification that has been passed down successfully since."

Richard shook his head. "I don't understand." Not just the words, but how this non-human abomination could speak so intelligently.

Emily swam close. "Great-great-grandfather also modified a local microbe. He made it lethal. And then, after everyone on the planet had the modification that made them immune, he had it spread around the planet—everywhere, from the seas to the air to highest mountain peaks. It is ubiquitous. It is deadly. Symptoms don't appear for about 36 hours. When they do, the progress of the disease is rapid. Most victims die within 12 hours of the onset of symptoms. And there is no treatment."

Richard swallowed. "I don't believe you."

"Wait a few hours." Emily swam even closer. "There is only one way to save you or any other human who has breathed the air of our planet. You must undergo massive genetic modification."

"You're lying!"

Emily's face was now only inches from his own, though separated by glass and water. "Am I? How are you feeling? Take stock, Richard Hansen. Are your lungs a little thick? Does your head ache, just a little? Are your joints feeling sore?"

In fact, all those things were true, Richard thought, with something approaching panic. *The power of suggestion!* he told himself. "No," he lied.

"Then you may have a little longer. But the infection, and the outcome, is certain." She flipped on her back and swam out of his headlight.

"Come back!" he yelled. He suddenly didn't want to be alone.

But she remained out of sight.

He swallowed. His throat hurt. There was a dull ache behind his left eye, an ache that had surely spread since he first noticed it. He took a deep breath, and felt a strange resistance in his chest.

She's telling the truth, he thought. *Oh God, she's telling the truth!*

He had to get out of the cave. Had to...

Had to what? He was many hours' swim from the harbour. *Most victims die within 12 hours of the onset of symptoms*, Emily had said. And he would most likely be too sick to swim within far less time.

And if she spoke the truth, if he did make it to the harbour, what would he find there? Dead and dying Deacons.

And on the ship...?

There had been constant traffic between the ship and surface since they had arrived, with no decontamination procedures—

after all, they knew humans lived on the planet successfully, so there couldn't be anything here that could harm them, right?

We were fools, he thought. *I was a fool.*

Soon to be a dead fool.

Unless Emily's offer...

No! He recoiled from the thought. How could he accept genetic modification? How could he join the abomination?

The Christian scriptures were forbidden, but those in the Church hierarchy had studied them to know the heresies they must combat. He remembered something that was not forbidden, something that had made the transition to the Pure Book, the scripture of the Church of Humanity Purified: "What shall it profit a man if he gain the whole world, but lose his soul?"

If he saved his life by accepting the mergirl's offer, he would lose his soul. He would no longer be Pure, and he would be cast out of God's Kingdom.

He swallowed, hard. It hurt.

Great-great-grandfather Joseph must be laughing his head off in hell, Richard thought bitterly. *He has had his revenge.*

Emily reappeared in his helmet-lamp light so suddenly he gasped, which triggered a fit of coughing. When it subsided, he felt substantially weaker.

"So it begins," said Emily. "I came to tell you the machine has left. I cannot hear it within swimming distance."

"That...doesn't make sense," Richard said. But he felt cold. It did make sense...if the Deacons of Holy Destruction had realized something was wrong, if they were falling ill, and had already withdrawn from the planet.

No one would look for him, if that were the case. He was on his own.

"Nevertheless, it is true," Emily said. She swam up until her face was once again just centimetres from his. "There is still time for genetic therapy to give you a fighting chance for survival," she said. "I can take you back to Safehaven. But you must decide now.

If you wait much longer to begin treatment, nothing can save you."

And there it was. The martyr's choice. Die for what you believe in, or live—and kill the part of you that believes, or else live with guilt and the knowledge of certain damnation.

Lord, I believe, help thou my unbelief, was another line from Christian scripture.

"Leave me to die," he said.

"As you wish," Emily replied. She flipped on her stomach and disappeared into darkness.

Almost Richard called out to her, begged her to come back...but he bit his lip, held in the cowardly cry, until he was certain she had left the cave and could no longer hear him.

Then he took a deep, painful and constricted breath, and followed her.

When he emerged into the open water, he tried his nanoputer again. It still wouldn't activate.

Well, he didn't need it to find his way back to the harbour. All he had to do was follow the coast north.

He set off.

He managed to swim fairly strongly for the first hour. But each breath and each stroke was incrementally more painful than the last.

The second hour, he moved much more slowly, and the pain increased.

The third hour, his forward progress slowed to a crawl, and every movement seemed torture. His breath crawled in and out through slime-choked channels in his lungs. Ground glass seemed to have been injected into his joints. Occasionally, his vision blacked around the edges.

Sometime in the fourth hour, he came to, to find himself simply floating, face up, three or four metres beneath the sun-dappled surface of the water. His breathing seemed less painful, but he felt no desire to move. He watched the play of light and water until it blurred and faded and finally went black.

When he woke again, he was no longer wearing the enviro-suit...or anything else.

He lay naked beneath a thick white blanket, staring up at a white ceiling. Air moved easily in and out of his lungs. There was a faint discomfort in his left wrist, which after a moment he realized must be caused by an IV line, which explained the bottle of clear liquid hung on a shiny metal stand to his left.

With difficulty—he felt as weak as a kitten—he turned his head in that direction. Through a window, he could see purplish leaves and a cloud-flecked blue sky.

He turned his head the other way. He was in a plain white room. Aside from the IV, the bed, and a table beside the bed, there was nothing in it except a simple wooden chair...and in the chair, a woman he had never seen before.

He frowned. Or had he? Her face looked...familiar.

She rose when she saw his head turn toward her. She wore a white lab coat and simple blue shoes. She walked over to him and stared down at him. She didn't smile. "So, you're awake."

He licked his lips, tried to speak, failed, and tried again. "Where...where am I?" His voice was little more than a croak.

"Pinkshore Hospital," the woman said.

"Pinkshore...? " The name was familiar; after a moment Richard's brain, which seemed to be spinning up to speed with agonizing slowness, managed to attach additional information to it. "I'm still on the merpeople's world?"

"You are," said the woman.

"But...I'm alive."

"Brilliant deduction."

"But..." Many things came back to him. "You didn't—Emily didn't—I haven't been...modified, have I?"

"You have not," said the woman, her voice hard.

"But Emily said..."

75

"Emily," the woman corrected, "told you the truth. Every one of the murderers you brought to our planet is dead in orbit above us. But you survived."

"I don't—"

"I'll let her tell you herself," said the woman. "I don't want to talk to you anymore."

She went out without another word.

Richard's mind raced. Everyone else was dead? Was that true? She could be lying to him...after all, he was alive. Maybe the plague wasn't as fatal as they claimed. They might just be sick up on the ship. If he could get to a radio...

The woman—nurse? guard?—reappeared, pushing a cart with a vidscreen atop it. She positioned it at the foot of the bed. "Emily will be with you in a moment," she said, and went out again.

Richard stared at the screen. Nothing happened for several seconds, then it suddenly lit with the face he had last seen just centimetres from his own on the other side of the envirosuit faceplate.

"I did not save you," the mergirl said, without preamble. "I was more than willing to give you your wish, Richard Hansen. If you wanted to die, I wasn't going to stop you."

"Then why am I still alive?" Richard said hoarsely.

She didn't answer right away. "A patrol from Pinkshore, sent to investigate what had happened at Safehaven, found you and pulled you from the water. By then you were too ill to treat genetically. They took you back to the hospital and waited for you to die...but you didn't. And you won't."

"I guess your plague isn't as perfect as you thought," Richard said. "I think I see God's hand in that."

"Do you, Richard Hansen?" Emily smiled, showing sharp white teeth that reminded Richard of a shark. "Then God has a strange sense of humour. You lived, Richard Hansen, because you *already* have the genetic modification that protects you from the plague."

He felt cold. "You're lying."

"You are always telling me that, but you are always wrong. You became sick because you haven't grown up with the virus, like we have, but you are every bit as much genetically modified as every other human on this planet. Great-grandfather Hansen modified all his children, Richard Hansen...not just the one who came with him here. You are not, and never have been, a Pure Human. You are, in your way of thinking, an abomination.

"You've come home, Richard Hansen. You've come home...and for the rest of your life, you will live here, among the people you despised, among the people whose friends and family were slaughtered because of you, because they were modified just as you have been, because they bear the same genes you did...because, in fact, they are of your own blood."

And then her shark-smile faded. "And here's the difference between us, Richard Hansen, between what we abominations believe and what you Pure Humans believe.

"We forgive you. You will walk out of that hospital a free man. Your identity will be known to only a few of us. You may tell people what you wish, or nothing at all.

"We forgive you. Whether you can forgive yourself, or whether your God can forgive you...only time will tell."

The screen went blank.

And Richard Hansen...wept.

THE PATH OF SOULS

F or several years, Globe Theatre, here in Regina, ran an
event called Lanterns on the Lake, *during which people
paraded around Wascana Lake, in the heart of the city, carrying paper
lanterns of every colour, size, and shape. The visual effect was ethereal
and otherworldly...and inspired this story, published in* Tesseracts
Seventeen: Speculating Canada from Coast to Coast, *edited by Colleen Anderson and Steve Vernon.*

HELLO, TRAVELER. HOW MAY I HELP YOU?

It's true I am not Andillan. Nor are you, obviously. Not
enough fur.

Ah, you're curious. You are wondering what a human woman
is doing on such a strange, remote world.

Are you a journalist, perhaps? An academic? No? Just a
traveler?

I do not share my story, as a rule. Others have come, and
asked the questions you ask, and always I have turned them
away. But tonight...tonight, fortune smiles on you. Tonight, I am

in the mood to answer questions. It is, after all, my final opportunity.

First, let me welcome you to the City of Light and Death. That is what the Andillan name means in this tongue you and I share, a tongue I use rarely these days.

The answer to your first question, why I am here, is simple. I tend the lanterns. I have tended them for twenty years. I suppose I should say, for twenty years, local, but I will never leave this world, so what use have I for the turnings of another planet about its sun?

Your pardon. Of course I understood your true intent. Not why I am here on this street, moving the lanterns from post to post in their long, long journey to the sea, but why I am *here*, on this planet, when I was once like you.

Oh, yes, young sir, more like you than you might think. I once wore a uniform not unlike yours, though from another ship...a ship that has never returned since the day I chose to remain here.

A drink? No...no. I do not drink alcohol. Not for twenty years. But a glass of water...thank you, sir.

The city is beautiful, is it not? The Andillans have toiled lovingly over it for centuries. They know that, in the end, they all come here.

See how the towers catch the sun as it sets into the sea? They might almost be on fire, so brightly do their windows gleam. And here below, the lamps are beginning to show their colours...so many colours, so many shades of blue and orange, of green and yellow, of violet and red. So many lamps, marching in rows on the grey weathered posts that line this street and many others, marching down to the sea, where tonight ten thousand will enter the waves...one lamp for every Andillan who died twenty years ago.

That is how long the journey takes, this final journey of this planet's people. Twenty years, because that is how long it takes the Star of Life—that one, the bright one just above the horizon—to make its circuit through the constellations. It is not a star at all, of course, but a planet, swinging far out in the coldest reaches of this solar system, but the name goes back a long, long time, long before the Andillans dreamed of other worlds—or of strange creatures like you and me.

When the Star of Life is in the same constellation as it was the year an Andillan died, the soul-lantern of that Andillan reaches the sea. The waves will be aflame tonight. The lanterns will move out over the sea, taken by a current that curls against the shore at the bottom of the Path of Souls. You can see them for hours, growing smaller and dimmer...and when you can't see them anymore, that's when the miracle happens.

You don't believe in miracles? Neither did I, when I first came here. Maybe I still don't. But twenty years isn't much of one's life to give for the chance to witness one, is it?

I'm sorry. I'm not making sense. I can see it in your eyes, the way they shifted away just then. But I assure you, I am quite sane.

I'll tell you the whole story. As I said, I've never done that before. But tonight...tonight the story comes to an end. Or maybe to a beginning.

Twenty years ago. A ship. A crew, much like your crew; men, women, each with his or her own reason for sailing the Dark between the stars. My reason? Nothing special; a love affair gone bad, a place I never wanted to see again, a planet suddenly too small...and a childhood spent looking at the stars and wondering what lay among them.

I thought I was running *away* from something; I never expected to run *to* something, but so I did. I met a man on the ship...Piotr. A man with his own reasons for sailing infinity, reasons I never heard. They didn't matter to me, and my reasons didn't matter to him.

We'd been together for six months of ship-time when we landed here. We completed each other, he and I. In my happiness, in my contentment, I thought I could see the future. I was wrong.

We didn't come here for the Festival, of course. We came for cargo. I don't know what it was; anonymous pressure containers bound for the next system along the Arm, where we'd exchange them for more anonymous containers bound back the other way. The loading went well and we were due shore leave...and so we left the ship and crossed the bridge and passed through the Gate—just as you did, on a night just like this—and were swept up in the crowds of Festival.

We came first to this very inn. It has been here much longer than twenty years. Many a mourner has drowned his sorrows within its walls. We had no sorrows, so we drank instead to our happiness. We drank...

You're done? Then come. I will finish my story in the street. As I tell you what happened I will show you where it happened. What I cannot tell you is *why*.

This way...here. Through this archway. This is where we first emerged onto the Path of Souls. And turned this way and....

It is breathtaking, is it not? The long, straight sweep of the Path. The lanterns, so many lanterns, so many colours, gleaming off the mother-of-pearl pavement. A river of light, leading down, down to the sea.

Like you, we were enchanted. We began to walk, down the Path...this way...then to run, drunkenly, staggering. Down, down...

Here, Piotr began to weave from one side to the other, grabbing the lantern posts, swinging around one, hurtling across the road to grab another and swing around...

You've stopped. What do you see?

They're caretakers, like myself. See how carefully they handle the lanterns, as though the globes are made of eggshell? They're not, of course. Nor are they glass. They're of a substance woven by tiny worms that feed on vines from the hot, sunny hillsides above this city. Like silk, I suppose, but also unlike, for woven into cloth, bound onto a wooden frame, and left to dry in the sun, it hardens into those beautiful shells.

They look fragile. They aren't, really. They're very difficult to break. Difficult...but not impossible.

Not impossible at all, when a heavy post gives way, and falls directly onto the shell.

Here. After twenty years, it's beginning to look like all the others, but see how this post is slightly paler; weathered, but not quite as weathered as its neighbours?

Piotr, laughing, ran from that post—the one by the statue of the Unknown God—to this post, swung himself around it...I heard a crack, saw the post start to fall, screamed Piotr's name...

The post missed him, but it did not miss the lantern. It shattered. The light went out. And something...escaped. Something swept through me, an emotion, or a sensation—both, or neither. The taste of twilight, the sound of salt, a silvery light that rang in my mind like a clear, distant bell...there are no words for it. In twenty years, I've never found the words.

Tears filled my eyes, spilled down my cheeks. I thought it was only a reaction to Piotr's close call—the post would surely have shattered his skull as easily as it did the lantern, had it hit him— but now...I'm not so sure.

I ran to him. He hugged me tight, shaking but also laughing, telling me everything was all right, would always be all right...and then we heard running footsteps all around us and then...

I looked up to see caretakers surrounding us, their gold-flecked eyes fixed on Piotr.

Piotr stopped laughing. He held up his hands. "I'm sorry," he said.

That was all he had time to say. Someone grabbed me, pulled me out of the circle. I screamed, struggled, but the Andillans are so strong, I couldn't get away...

The circle closed around Piotr. I saw a six-fingered fur-covered hand come up, holding a long knife—the only weapon I've ever seen on Andilla. It flashed all the colours of the rainbow as it rose, reflecting the lights of the lanterns, then flashed again as it descended, and...

I'm sorry. Twenty years have not dimmed that memory.

Thank you. I'm all right now.

The circle moved back. Piotr lay still, eyes staring blankly at the stars, dark blood, almost black in the dim light, beginning to flow slowly down the glistening pavement toward the sea. I was screaming, screaming at the top of my lungs, but in my memory I can't hear myself, I can't hear anything...only the most dreadful silence...

A single caretaker remained over Piotr's body. In one hand he held the still-dripping knife. In the other...

I thought it was a candle at first, as much as I could think anything. But he held it cradled in his hand more as if it were a butterfly, and though it looked like flame, flickering and guttering, it didn't go out, and it didn't seem to burn him. He looked up at me. I couldn't read his face, I knew nothing about Andillan expressions then, but when those wide golden eyes met mine, I stopped screaming.

This is the way they took me then. This narrow side path, almost hidden. An altogether different kind of path. No lanterns, no gleaming pavement—just black, dull rock.

It was much darker then, for the sun had long set. The only light was that which spilled from the lead caretaker's hand.

Here, at this corner, I looked back, and saw them lifting Piotr's body. I never saw it again.

I suppose I was in shock. I walked this path numb and silent, not thinking, not feeling. It seemed endless, but as you can see, it wasn't, for here is the end now...

A dead end? So I thought...the dead end of all my hopes and dreams. But I was wrong. There is a door here, hidden somehow, for we moved through this wall into a room...a chamber...

A round chamber, made of black stone. A single lantern burned high up, hung from the domed ceiling, casting little light.

On shelves along the walls lay other lanterns, endless lanterns...all dark. In the centre of the room rose a pillar of black stone, waist-high, so smoothly polished it looked wet. *Wet with blood*, I thought when I saw it. *Wet with Piotr's blood.* Atop the pillar rested another dark lantern, its door standing open.

The caretaker handed the knife to someone else, who took it away. No words were spoken; no words had been spoken since Piotr's last. The caretaker held up the light in his hand. It had no source that I could see, and no form...it was only a diffuse ball, like a will-o-the-wisp, and still it flickered as though it would go out.

But suddenly the lantern under the dome waxed stronger. Every time the light in the caretaker's hand guttered, a brighter flash came from the lantern far above, filling in the darkness. With each flash the light burned brighter and steadier, until at last it didn't flicker at all.

Then the caretaker placed it into the lantern, and closed the door. The lantern came alight. He picked up the lantern...and gave it to me.

And then he told me what I had to do.

And so I have done it. For twenty years, I have cared for the lantern the Andillans believe contains the soul of the man I loved...and the soul of the Andillan whose lantern Piotr broke.

When a lantern is broken, the caretaker told me on that night, as I stood so cold and numb, the soul within it must find a body, or become a...ghost, I suppose is our closest word for it, a wandering, tormented spirit. Breaking a lantern is thus a terrible crime...but that was not the only reason they killed Piotr. They killed him because they believed that the soul from the lantern must have entered his body, mingled with his own. He had to die so that the soul from the lantern could complete its journey alongside his own.

I can't blame you for that look. There is not much room on human worlds or in human spaceships for talk of souls. No doubt, you are thinking, the glowing sphere the caretaker placed into the lantern was only some naturally occurring luminescent mineral. No doubt the lantern in the ceiling, the mystical light the caretaker told me came to the shores of this city a hundred centuries ago, floating against the current that takes all other lanterns out to sea, flashed through some simple chemical process designed to awe the gullible.

No doubt.

But...

Piotr seemed unchanged, still drunk and laughing, in the few moments he lived after he broke the lantern. Whereas I felt...whatever it was that I felt.

I could not help thinking, on that shock- and grief-filled night, that the soul from the broken lantern entered *me*, not Piotr; that *I* should have died, not him.

I still cannot help thinking that.

And so I stayed and cared for his lantern for the debt I owed him, for the love I'd felt for him, and in memory of the life we might have had together.

And tonight...

Come. Let us walk to the sea.

Here it is. Piotr's lantern. To you it may look the same as all the others, but to my eye it shines differently...a little brighter, a little more redly.

In an hour's time, I will take Piotr's lantern from this final post, and with all the other lanterns I and the other caretakers have shepherded down the Path of Souls, will send it out to sea. Somewhere, far out of sight of land, the lanterns will release the souls they carry...and tonight, the Andillans say, new stars will blossom across the universe.

The lanterns on the water are a glorious sight, traveler. A sight worth crossing the galaxy to see.

I have seen it twenty times, but tonight will be the last. Tonight Piotr's journey ends.

Tomorrow, mine begins.

Thank you for hearing my tale. Take it with you...and on the next world you visit, look up at the stars, and think of Piotr, though you never knew him.

And in twenty years, traveler, if you still live, look up at the stars again...and think of me.

FOLLOW A SONG

This is the oldest story in the book, written while I was a student at Harding University in Searcy, Arkansas. It won (or at least placed in—I can't quite remember anymore) the annual creative writing contest. I was nineteen. Be kind.

TELAR, PERCHED ON THE BOTTOM BRANCH of the dead tree, stared sheepishly down at his father, who glared up at him. "Telar," said Annuin with some heat, "I am a blacksmith, but I cannot make a living as one when I must leave my forge cold to search for you. Why are you not at the war-hall practicing your swordplay as you should be?"

Telar climbed down from the tree, but hung his head and said nothing, hearing exasperation in Annuin's voice as he continued, "It has been three months since the First Rite, boy. What's wrong with you? For two months you were the most promising firstling, when Master Nimarl was teaching you the history of the kingdom. Yet now he tells me you are spending more and more time away from your instruction—now, when you have left behind the dull classroom and gone on to the war-arts, your true study. Nimarl tells me you are far behind the others in swordplay, archery, and spearwork. Yet when you should be practicing, I find you sitting in a tree, playing the harp and singing!" His voice rose almost to a shout.

Telar flushed. He fingered the carved and polished wood of his harp, and ran his fingers over the silver strings. The instrument breathed a faint chord. He dared to raise his head slightly, peering up at his father through his eyelashes.

Annuin's jaw clenched. "You are my youngest son, Telar. Your three brothers are all warriors; Kerpal is even now recovering from the honourable wounds he received defending the King at Sazaran. Where have I gone wrong with you?"

Telar looked down again. He loved his father, but it hurt to know Annuin considered him a failure. In his younger days Annuin had been a King's Guard, and could not understand why a healthy, strapping youth of Telar's years, bearing the scar across his chest of the coming-of-age ceremony known as the First Rite, would want to waste his time in reading and, worse, music.

But Telar detested all the trappings of war the firstlings were taught: the clashing swords, the bloodthirsty shouts, the weight of a shield, the awkwardness of a scabbard, the dust and sweat of the practice court. He hated—

He suddenly became aware of an expectant silence. He glanced up. "What did you say, father?"

"Go to your lessons, boy," Annuin said wearily, and turned away.

Telar watched him go, then looked at the sun and sighed. His father had found him too soon. There would be a lot of daylight for swordplay yet, and he didn't dare stay away now his father had come looking for him. Slinging his harp over his shoulder, he waded through the tall grass to the narrow path leading down to the village.

He could hear the crack of wooden swords and the cries of his fellow firstlings as he approached the gate of the War Hall, but silence fell as he entered the courtyard. Every face turned toward him, then looked expectantly at Master Nimarl, a burly, middle-aged man, just beginning to turn grey, who pushed through the boys until he stood glaring down at Telar. "Well?"

"I'm sorry, master—"

"Sorry? You're not sorry. Twice before you have been so late you missed sword practice altogether. You have also missed spearwork three times and archery at least once."

The other firstlings snickered, and Telar looked at the ground. "Yes, master."

"You must be punished, Telar."

Telar's head jerked up. "Punished?" The only punishment until now had been the lectures on the importance of the war-arts that Nimarl would deliver to anyone at the slightest provocation.

"Unless you can demonstrate that your skills in the war-arts are such you can afford to miss practices."

"But, master, I'm the best reader, I spend more time than is required on geography, history, calculating—"

"Enough!" Nimarl roared. "Such things are important only in better suiting you for battle. Without the war-arts, they are meaningless, suited only to women and old men!"

Telar's face grew hot. "Meaningless? They're our noblest achievements!"

The courtyard rang with Nimarl's scornful laughter. "Women's words! Here, boy." He tossed a javelin to Telar. "Now we'll find out how much of a *man* you are!"

The rest of the afternoon was a nightmare. Telar's javelin missed the target by the width of a doorway, and in spear-and-shield sparring he received, almost at once, a blow to the stomach that doubled him over, gasping. "What good is reading now, boy?" Nimarl taunted him.

In archery he fared little better. Though he hit the target, his arrow was so near the edge the wood splintered and the shaft fell to the ground.

Then came swordplay. His first bout was with one-handed swords and shields; he lasted no more than ten seconds before his opponent's wooden blade cracked him on the wrist so hard he dropped his weapon. Then came two-handed swords; almost before he could blink something smashed across his head and he found himself flat on his back in the dirt, looking up into the sneering face of the other boy.

Telar sat up, gingerly feeling the bump on his head, then got a little shakily to his feet and faced Nimarl. "All right!" he said defiantly. "You've proved I'm a poor fighter, master. How will you punish me?"

Nimarl looked from him to the contemptuous faces of his fellow firstlings, and shrugged. "I think your punishment is already sufficient." He turned his back and clapped his hands. "Enough standing around, lads!"

Telar heard the taunts thrown at him as the firstlings returned to their own weapons, and realized what Nimarl had done. Furiously he snatched up his harp and left the courtyard.

He climbed back up to the tree where his father had found him, slammed his fist against it, then leaned his forehead against its rough bark and kicked at the ground with his foot. No doubt his father had known Nimarl intended to make a fool of him, and had approved it as suitable "punishment." That made him even angrier. He knew his father didn't think very highly of him, but to agree to his humiliation...

But he was just as angry with himself. What was wrong with him? Why didn't he like the war-arts? He was sure he was the only firstling the village had ever produced that was not dying to go into battle.

He turned his back on the tree, unslung his harp, and slammed his fingers across the strings, crashing through a raw, sorrowful tune and ending with a harsh discord that summed up his feelings very accurately.

A voice behind him said, "A poor note on which to end a performance, don't you think? It might spoil your host's appetite, and that could easily spoil your own."

Telar spun to see a tall, broad-shouldered man with greying hair and beard. He wore a longsword on the belt of his blue tunic, but he also carried a harp, and Telar's eyes went to it immediately. "Your pardon, my lord—"

The man laughed. "Kailar is my name, and my only title. I come from a fishing family; hardly noble heritage. Now, however, I am a bard, as you seem to be yourself. I see there is no great house at which to play in this village, so if you could direct me to the inn—unless, of course, you already have the only business here, in which case I shall certainly leave it to you and move on."

"I am not a bard, my lord."

"Kailar. What are you, then?"

Telar grimaced. "Only a firstling, and a poor one. As for our inn, unless you sing of war, you won't find much welcome there."

Kailar shrugged. "I can sing songs of war if of war I must sing." He looked at Telar thoughtfully. "You deny you are a bard, but I heard you playing as I came up—and playing well, though, in truth, the tune was not much to my liking."

"Nor mine. But little is. The things I want to learn are despised by my teachers. Most of our time is spent in the 'glorious' pursuit of learning to kill."

Kailar raised an eyebrow. "Traditional firstling instruction disagrees with you?"

"I hate it!" Telar burst out, and, instinctively feeling Kailar would understand, poured out the story of his embarrassment that afternoon. "History—geography—the things that *matter*, he dismissed as meaningless! You're a bard, Kailar, a learned man—is what I feel wrong?"

Kailar said nothing for a moment, looking down at the town.

"I think I will come to your house, Telar," he said finally. "You said your father was in the Guard—he will surely welcome me for my news, if not for my music. Then tomorrow I will try to help you with your problem."

Joyfully Telar agreed and started down the hill at a gallop. "Come on!" he called over his shoulder. "It's almost suppertime!"

Kailar followed more slowly, smiling.

~

Annuin was more than a little surprised when Telar arrived with a guest, but made Kailar welcome, as the custom of hospitality demanded. "Your name, my lord?" he said, taking the bard's cloak.

"Kailar, son of Gerra, originally of Rhys." Kailar took off his sword and leaned it against the wall by the front door. "My father was a fisherman, but I am a bard—and in your debt."

Annuin laughed. "A bard. I might have known. Well, you are welcome, Kailar. Take a place at our table." As Kailar bowed and sat down, Annuin turned to his son. "And you, firstling. Did you go to your practice as I commanded?"

"Yes. And what you knew would happen, happened," Telar said sullenly.

"What?"

"You knew Nimarl planned to humiliate me in front of the other firstlings!" Telar burst out. "You must have! You probably arranged for it. But it won't work, father! I will not learn the war-arts. I—I'll go with Kailar, and be a bard!" The last was a flash of inspiration.

His father's face reddened. "You will hold your tongue, Telar," he growled. "I will not have you being disrespectful to me before a guest—a bard, at that! Would you shame me before the entire country? Sit at table!"

Telar banged down on the bench beside Kailar, shooting a glance at the man with whom he had just allied himself. But

Kailar seemed oblivious. His eyes were closed, and his lips moved silently.

Thus he remained until Telar's mother, Hella, brought in the meal. She retired at once to the kitchen to eat her portion; it would not have been seemly for her to dine at table with a strange man. As his plate was set before him, Kailar opened his eyes, smiled at Hella, and reached for his spoon. "What were you doing?" Telar asked.

"Working on a new song," Kailar replied. "Part of it will be finished tomorrow."

"Will you sing it for me?"

"Perhaps. If all goes as it should." He would say no more about it. Instead he began talking to Annuin, and soon the two men were deep in discussion of the latest news of the King and his court. Telar marvelled at Kailar's memory—he seemed to know everyone in the kingdom by name *and* everything they had done for the past ten years.

When the meal was over, they settled in chairs around the fire and Hella rejoined them. Then Kailar sang for them, mostly the great old songs of the ancient heroes and the world as it had been before the Scattering. Telar admired the bard's skill, but the songs were war-songs. He stirred impatiently.

Perhaps Kailar noticed; abruptly his playing changed to a minor key, and his voice filled with longing:

> Tree and leaf and wood and plain,
> Snow and wind and sun and rain;
> Day by day they come and go,
> And pass forever by.
>
> Deeds of peace and deeds of war,
> King and warrior, rich and poor;
> One by one they rise and fall,
> And pass forever by.

Day to night and night to day
I go my ever-restless way:
No home, no hearth, no kith, no kin—
They've passed forever by.

Infant, child, youth, and man;
The months and years like seconds ran.
My life, my songs; like winter wind,
They pass forever by.

But flowers blossom, rivers run;
Each day beneath the springtime sun
New life, new hope, new joy appears
That never will pass by.

And so I play, and so I sing,
To bring my wintry soul its spring,
And new souls, too, my legacy
To pass forever—on."

For a moment after the last chord died away only the crackling of the fire on the hearth broke the silence. Then Annuin stirred and said gruffly, "You've travelled far today and must be tired. Telar will show you to your room."

Kailar rose and bowed. "I thank you, sir and lady. May you sleep well." Taking up his pack, Telar led him to the room they would share. He offered the bard his bed, but Kailar laughed and said he was as used to sleeping on the ground as on a mattress. He took blankets from his pack and spread them on the wooden floor.

Telar sat on the bed and watched him. "Kailar..." he said finally.

The bard glanced at him. "Yes?"

"That last song. It's...I...I would like to learn it," he finished lamely.

"It touched you, then? I thought it would. I wrote it a year or so ago, after—well, after a painful time. Certainly I will teach it to you—if you will return the favour and teach me some of the songs you know."

"I know nothing you would want to hear!"

"But you do, lad, you do. We each learn songs in our day-to-day lives that no one else knows. I try to share mine; won't you return the favour?"

"I have written one or two," Telar admitted shyly. "If you really want to hear them—"

"I would. But," he continued, lying down on his blankets, "I think it should wait until tomorrow. I've walked my legs to the bone today, and you should rest as well. Tomorrow I will come with you to the War Hall."

Telar looked down. "I—I almost wish you wouldn't."

"Why not?"

"I—well, I know what Nimarl and the others think of me for not wanting to be a warrior. I don't want them to think that of you."

"But, Telar, that's exactly why I'm going—to show them, if I can, that to be a bard and not a warrior does not make a man any less a man."

"They won't listen."

"Perhaps they will, if I use the right language. Now will you please go to bed and douse the candles so we can both sleep?"

Telar said nothing more, but though he undressed and lay beneath the blankets, it was a long time before he slept.

The next day dawned clear and cold; autumn was giving way to winter. Telar dreaded what was to come; he doubted he would be allowed near the library, after slipping off the day before. He would have to spend the whole day at the war-arts. Nimarl might never let him read again.

"And I have read only half of *The Book of the Great,* up to the passage where Shirra meets Gharus on Mount Nyngal to decide in single combat the fate of the kingdom," he told Kailar at breakfast.

Kailar looked at him with the amused expression Telar was beginning to find familiar. "*The Book of the Great?* Isn't that a rather war-filled book for someone who hates the thought of war as much as you do?"

"It's different in legends," Telar said defensively. "It means something. Here-and-now, all it is is killing other people. Can that ever be right?"

Kailar chewed and swallowed thoughtfully, then said, "Do you see nothing noble in war, then?"

"Nothing!"

"Nothing? Is it not noble for a man to give his life to save another's? Or to give it to save his family—or even the lives of an entire race? Is there nothing noble in such acts of heroism?"

Telar frowned. "Well—perhaps there can be noble acts in war. But war itself is evil!"

Kailar shrugged. "There are many evil things in the world, Telar. We try to avoid them, but we don't always succeed." Then he grinned. "Come, enough philosophy for early morning. Eat, then lead me to your War Hall. I am eager to meet your teacher."

Telar finished his bread and cheese in thoughtful silence. Kailar had a way of making people examine their assumptions more closely than they were used to. Telar found it a not-entirely comfortable experience.

The War Hall courtyard, full of laughing firstlings strapping on practice armour and swords, fell silent when Telar entered with Kailar. Nimarl came forward to greet them. "Telar, you're late again—" he rumbled.

Kailar interrupted. "It's more my fault than his, Master Nimarl." He bowed. "I am Kailar, a wandering bard. I have accompanied my friend Telar to watch your instruction of firstlings."

Nimarl laughed. "I might have known our little harp-plucker would bring us a bard. Well, sir, you are welcome. But since you have given up the manly art of war, I don't know that you will find much here to interest you."

Kailar raised an eyebrow. "You consider barding unmanly?"

"Nay, sir! It is as manly as any occupation can be for someone who can no longer be a warrior. No doubt you were wounded or weakened by illness—I'm sure you were a mighty warrior in your youth."

Telar winced. He knew what was coming.

Kailar gave Nimarl an innocent look. "Master Nimarl, I have never been a warrior—only a bard, since my First Rite, trained in it by the great Theros of Gharwen."

Nimarl snorted. "Then I'm quite *certain* there is no point in your remaining here. We do not waste our time on such matters. Since you have no knowledge of the war-arts—"

"I didn't say that, Master Nimarl. I said I was trained as a bard."

"Sir, a bard is not a warrior."

"I bear a sword."

"Even Telar can bear a sword—though he has been known to trip on it!" Telar flushed. "But only a man can wield one—and all true men do!"

Telar's stomach lurched. He expected Kailar to leave in anger, but instead the bard astonished him by quoting a section of a song Telar knew:

> "The minds of men do differ ever;
> what's dull to one, to another's clever."

Then he said, "I propose a wager, Master Nimarl. I wager I can defeat your best warrior—yourself, no doubt—in archery, spear-work, and swordplay, just as Telar was tested yesterday."

Nimarl laughed. "And what would you risk on such a hopeless contest?"

"Name my stake yourself."

The firstling master considered. "Very well, then! If I win, you will proclaim to the firstlings that I am right, and you are no true man. Then you will spend the winter here, and amuse us at meals. If you win—"

Kailar raised his hand. "Nay, Master Nimarl, this part of the wager is mine. If I win, you will release Telar from his firstling instruction, and send his father a recommendation, as is your right, that he be apprenticed to me."

Excitement filled Telar. He straightened his shoulders. "There's nothing I would like more, Kailar!"

Nimarl shook his head. "You set a small stake. It would be little loss to me or the village were Telar gone. But, so, the wager is set. Shall we begin?"

"By all means," said Kailar.

A few moments later the firstlings clustered around the two men, who bore bows and quivers, at one end of the courtyard. At the other stood the target, a man-shaped cut-out of wood, with a circle marking the heart. At the centre of the circle was a round spot the diameter of a gold piece.

Nimarl loosed his arrow first. The bolt slammed into the heart, and the nearest boy ran to look. "Two finger's breadths from the centre!" he shouted, and the firstlings cheered.

Nimarl turned to Kailar smugly. "Your shot, sir bard."

Kailar made no reply, but put arrow to string, drew, and released in one smooth motion. The dart shuddered into the wood an inch and a half from Nimarl's arrow—precisely in the centre of the heart.

The firstlings gaped at each other. Nimarl flushed, then bowed stiffly to Kailar. "Well shot. Spearwork is next."

The spear-throw went as had the archery contest. Kailar's spear hung in the centre; Nimarl's was a good hand's breadth away. A sound suspiciously like muffled laughter ran through the gathered firstlings, but it died in a hurry when Nimarl glared around at the boys. The master did not congratulate Kailar this time, but said only, "Spear-and-shield is next, bard."

The two men took blunted wooden staffs and round wooden shields and faced off. The contest was brief, wicked, and decisive. Almost before the firstlings knew what had happened, Nimarl was down, doubled over by a blow from the blunt tip of Kailar's shaft. This time the laughter wasn't muted at all.

Nimarl said nothing to the bard, but stalked into the War Hall. When he returned, he carried not the wooden swords and shields used by the firstlings, but the razor-sharp and deadly war-weapons that hung in the hall. He flung shield and sword before Kailar, and Telar paled. He had never seen Nimarl so angry—he had never seen *anyone* that angry.

"Bard," Nimarl said between clenched teeth, "you are not a bard at all. You are obviously a warrior—a warrior brought into this court by Telar to humiliate me before the firstlings. But no more! I Challenge you!"

The firstlings gasped. Those words meant a duel—probably to the death. Telar looked at Kailar's white face and realized he had not anticipated this. "Master Nimarl," he protested, "this is not what I sought! Believe me, I am not here to shame you, but only to show you that there are true men who are not warriors. Don't make me fight you."

"I have Challenged you!" Nimarl shouted. "You must fight—or I will kill you where you stand!"

The colour flooded back into Kailar's face; he stiffened. "As you wish," he said coldly.

"In the King's name, Kailar—" Telar burst out.

The bard turned to him. "Did I not tell you sometimes evil

cannot be avoided? But wait and see—some good may yet come of it." He turned back to Nimarl. "I am ready."

Nimarl pointed at the weapons in the dirt before him. "Arm yourself!"

Kailar hefted the sword and shield for a moment, then saluted Nimarl with his blade. Nimarl did not salute: he attacked.

His first stroke, blocked by Kailar's shield, drove the bard almost to his knees. Telar cried out, certain Kailar would fall. But he did not. Instead he threw his shield to one side, knocking Nimarl's sword-arm away, and drove in with the point of his blade—but not at Nimarl's vitals. Telar, with a thrill of fear, realized Kailar fought not to kill, but only to disable—to end the contest with no loss of life.

Nimarl realized it as well, and as he blocked the thrust with savage glee, cried, "Do you show me mercy, bard-who-is-no-bard? I'll have none for you!" A slash of his sword came within a hair's breadth of cutting Kailar in two, but the bard sprang back. With his own sword he blocked the return stroke, and smashed his shield down on Nimarl's with such force the master dropped to one knee. Nimarl tried to thrust up, under Kailar's shield, but Kailar brought the shield's edge down on the blade and it flew from Nimarl's grasp.

A cry rose from the watching firstlings. Nimarl was doomed!

The firstling master paled. He raised his shield in a hopeless attempt to block his death blow.

But it did not fall. Kailar stepped back. "Noble Nimarl," he panted, "I declare myself victor in the Challenge, but I decline blood-right."

Nimarl lowered his shield in amazement. "But you disarmed me—I insulted you—are you not going to take revenge?"

Kailar shook his head. "Master Nimarl, I sing songs. Someday I will sing one about today, and revenge does not make a sweet song."

Nimarl stared at him, bewildered, sweat streaking the dust on his face.

Telar ran to Kailar's side. "Kailar, are you all right?

Kailar laughed, a little shakily. "Not a scratch."

"And did you mean what you said? About making me your apprentice?"

The bard looked down at him. "There is a condition."

"Anything!"

"I will teach you the war-arts."

Telar stepped back a pace. "But—but—"

"Did you think I did all this—" he tossed his sword and shield into the dust—"only for these?" He gestured at the silent, watching firstlings. "Didn't you learn anything? It's possible to be both strong and peaceable. Sometimes you have to be strong and willing to fight in order to *remain* peaceable. But the rest of you—" he raised his voice then, and turned slowly, looking from face to face. "Know there is more to life than war! I take no joy in what I have done." He held out his hand, and hesitantly, Nimarl took it, and let the bard help him to his feet. "None at all," Kailar finished in a low voice.

"I—I don't understand," said Telar.

"Well, never mind. There'll be a long time to explain it." He kept his eyes on Nimarl. "Right?"

Nimarl inclined his head a fraction of an inch. "I do not understand you, bard; nor do I understand Telar. But I am no longer shamed. Bard or warrior, I would we had had a hundred like you in the Guard! I will tell Annuin you would be a worthy master for his son."

"Thank you, master Nimarl." Kailar bowed, then looked at Telar. "Shall we go, apprentice?"

"With pleasure, master—if."

"If?"

"If you will tell me what the song is you said would be partially finished today." Telar planted his feet. "That is my condition."

Kailar laughed. "Why, that's *your* song, Telar. The one you write day to day. You've just finished a major part of it. Now you get to move on to a whole new verse."

Telar frowned. "I'll never understand you, master."

Kailar led the way to the courtyard gate. "Perhaps someday, lad. Perhaps someday." And as they walked back to Telar's home, he sang:

> And so I play, and so I sing,
> To bring my wintry soul its spring,
> And new souls, too, my legacy
> To pass forever—on."

MEMORY JAM

nother (slightly creepy) unpublished story. I don't remember what prompted it, but I've always liked it. I just could never figure out who to sell it to...

~

JIMMY CONKLIN SAT at Granny Noggin's kitchen table, right hand wrapped around a water-beaded glass of milk, left hand holding a CD-sized chocolate-chip cookie. More cookies covered a blue china plate on the red-and-white-checked tablecloth. Slivers of rainbow, whittled from the sunlight by a silver-and-crystal spider-web sun-catcher in the window above the sink, splashed every surface in the kitchen with splotches of brilliant colour.

"I love your kitchen, Granny Noggin," Jimmy said.

Granny Noggin poured tea into a gold-rimmed pink china cup and brought it over the table. She sat down across from Jimmy. "I love it, too, Jimmy."

"It's my favourite place in the whole world!" Jimmy took a bite of cookie. "I could stay here forever," he mumbled with his mouth full.

"When you're here visiting me, it's my favourite place, too," Granny said. She sipped her tea.

Jimmy polished off the cookie in two more big bites. "I don't have any grandmas of my own, you know," he said as he picked up another one. "They both died when I was little. But they couldn't have been as nice as you."

Granny clucked her tongue. "Now, then, Jimmy, I knew your grandmothers. They were wonderful women."

"I didn't say they weren't." Jimmy took a drink of milk. "I just said I bet you're nicer."

Granny smiled. "Well, it's very kind of you to say so, Jimmy." The doorbell rang. "Excuse me."

Jimmy nodded, wiping milk off his mouth with the back of his hand.

Granny got up and went into the hallway. Jimmy amused himself trying to find all the rainbows in the kitchen. The ones on the floor were easy, but the ones hiding on the walls were harder, because Granny had lots of other stuff on her walls. Most of one wall was covered with ribbons from the Creelmore Agricultural Fair. All blue ribbons, and all for things like "Best Traditional Chocolate Cake with Home-Made Icing" and "Best Low-Fat Carrot Muffin" and "Best Whole-Wheat Bread" and even "Best Beet Pickles." *Yuck*, Jimmy thought.

One whole row of ribbons was for jams and preserves, all from the same year. "Swept the competition," Jimmy murmured, and took a big bite of cookie.

He heard voices in the hallway, but didn't pay much attention. "...it's just that I've been very depressed lately, Granny, and I was wondering if maybe some of your Sunny-Day Jam...Hazel Jardin recommended it..."

"Of course, dear." That was Granny's voice. "I could use a birthday..."

"A birthday?" A long pause. "All right..."

I could use a birthday, too, Jimmy thought. *I'll be nine!*

It seemed a very old age to him, although he knew that grown-ups were many times that old. His gaze slid across the wall to a picture of Granny Noggin. He didn't know when it had been taken, but she hadn't changed much: same round face and round figure, same apple cheeks, same white hair drawn up in a bun. She even had on the same kind of clothes he always saw her wearing: a dress in a bright flowery pattern and a frilly checked apron. The same pair of round spectacles perched on her button nose.

I wonder how old Granny Noggin is?

Granny bustled back in. "Mrs. Islington was just here, Jimmy," she said. "She'd like some of my extra-special Sunny Day Jam. Would you like to help me find a jar?"

"You bet!" Jimmy said. He jumped up, but took a moment to take another big swig of milk before following Granny down the rickety wooden stairs that led from a door in the kitchen into the basement.

At the bottom of the stairs, the only natural light came from three small windows set at ground level, so grimed with dirt and cobwebs that they turned the sunniest day into apparent gloom. But that was okay; what Jimmy liked in the basement was the *other* light.

It poured like rich, thick paint down the walls and over the floor from the rows and rows of jam jars on the shelves that lined every wall of the basement, except for the corner where the furnace and water heater lurked like sulking dragons. The light came in every colour the slivers of rainbow in the kitchen could boast, and then some. Some jars shone with the deep blue-green of the ocean in a *When Sharks Attack* video. Others glowed as yellow-orange as a campfire, or as purple as the bug-zapper outside the Take-a-Lickin' ice cream stand downtown.

Inside some jars something roiled and churned like tornado clouds, grey and threatening, spitting out occasional blue-white flashes. But the ones Granny went to, filling a whole shelf, gleamed pure white, like bottled sunshine. "Now, let's see," she murmured. "For Mrs. Islington, something from 1954, I think...I know I have one here somewhere..."

She rummaged about on the shelf, momentarily leaving Jimmy to fend for himself.

He trailed his fingers idly along the shelves, reading labels. "Beach Fun" had three distinct layers, one sunny, one sand-coloured, one blue and white. "Starry Night" was a deep, dark blue, scattered with glittering pinpricks of light. "Well-Met by Moonlight" glowed a faint silver, and "First Kiss" a delicate pink. And then there was another, called "Naughty but Nice," which was almost black, but gave Jimmy a funny feeling in his insides when his finger trailed across it.

"1947...1973..." he heard Granny Noggin muttering to herself. "Heavens to Betsy, I know I have one. I must have mis-shelved it."

Jimmy's aimless wandering had taken him back to the furthest corner of the basement, the dark one behind the water heater. For the first time he noticed a cabinet back there, tucked almost out of sight. He opened it, revealing three shelves of rather ordinary-looking jars, each glowing a pale yellow. Jimmy like their looks at once. He picked one off the shelf and looked at its label.

"Jimmy Jam," he read out loud.

He laughed with delight, and went running back to Granny Noggin, who was leaning over and reaching to the very back of a shelf of miscellaneous jars. "You named a jam after me!" he said, holding up the "Jimmy Jam" jar.

Granny straightened so suddenly she banged her head on one of the copper pipes that hung from the ceiling. She rubbed the bumped place with her hand. "You mustn't play with that!"

"But it's got my name on it!" Jimmy said, disappointed.

"That doesn't mean you can play with it." She held out her hand. "Give it to me, please." She sounded more stern than Jimmy had ever heard her before.

He stuck out his lower lip, but he handed over the jar. Quick as a flash, Granny tucked it out of sight in her apron. "Now," she said, "see if you can get that jar at the very back of the shelf for me. I'm not as limber as I used to be..."

Jimmy pulled out the jar she wanted, labeled "Sunny Day Jam, July 20, 1954," after which she bustled him back up the stairs. "Now how about *Monopoly*?" she said.

They played *Monopoly*, then *Scrabble*, then *Sorry* (even though Jimmy thought he was getting a little old for *Sorry*). One of the things Jimmy loved about Granny Noggin was that she always had time to play games with him. Late in the afternoon he said, "I'd better be going. Mom'll be wondering where I am." He frowned. "I can't remember when she told me to be home," he admitted.

"It's all right," Granny said. "I called to tell her you were staying for supper. They're going out tonight anyway, so there's no hurry."

"Great!" Jimmy said, and then it was card games and more *Sorry* until it was dark outside and he was yawning. "Aren't Mom and Dad home yet?"

Granny smiled sympathetically. "Why don't you lie down on the couch? You can nap there until they come for you."

"I'm not sleepy," Jimmy said automatically, but within twenty minutes he found he couldn't keep his eyes open any longer,And and willingly stretched out on Granny's overstuffed, red-and-yellow floral-print couch.

"I'm sure your parents will be here any minute," Granny said to him, sitting on the arm of his couch and stroking his forehead.

Jimmy nodded, and yawned hugely. His eyes closed, opened, closed again and stayed closed; within minutes he was breathing heavily.

~

Granny Noggin went into the kitchen and climbed on a chair to open the door of a cabinet high above the stove, still well out of Jimmy's reach, though barely—he was getting very tall.

She took down a polished rod of pale wood and a clean Mason jar, and took both into the living room. For a moment she looked fondly and a little sadly at the young man stretched out on her couch. She wouldn't be able to keep him much longer; one of these days he was bound to notice he wasn't nine years old any more, and once that happened he'd be no good to her.

She raised the wand and passed it over Jimmy's head a few times, her lips moving silently, then put the point of the jar into the mason jar. Instantly, the bottom inch or so of the jar filled with jam, jam that glowed a clear pale yellow—the same colour as the inside of her kitchen on a sunny morning. She reached her finger to the bottom of the jar, swirled it around in the jam a moment, then lifted it to her mouth and sucked.

She could almost feel her plumpness getting plumper, her eyes twinkling, her cheeks reddening, her grey hair fluffing and shining like fine silver. She smiled, and knew her teeth were straighter and whiter than a moment before.

It would indeed be a pity when Jimmy had to go. She loved Jimmy Jam. But she was sure she would love Madeline Marmalade or Peter Preserves or whatever took its place just as much.

She took the jar of Jimmy Jam down to the hidden shelf behind the water heater, and put it with all the rest. Tucked even further out of sight were three or four unlabeled jars containing an unappetizing brown mess, the memories of everyone who had known Jimmy before he had ridden his bicycle past her door one morning four years ago, and answered her call to come inside for cookies. She'd never eat or sell that jam, of course, but it kept the secular authorities from her door, searching for a missing child. Jimmy had not disappeared; he had simply been forgotten, and now when people caught a glimpse of him at her house, they thought he was a grandson come for a visit. She never introduced him, and the people who visited her, like Mrs. Islington, knew better than to ask questions.

After all, her prices were really very reasonable. Mrs. Islington would give up one day's worth of birthday memories for a new memory of a perfect sunny day, distilled from the sunny-day memories of half a dozen donors, to help her through her current depression; Mr. Franken, who had no happy birthday memories, would receive a jar of Happy Birthday Jam, distilled from the birthday memories of Mrs. Islington and others. No one was harmed, everyone was happy.

But everyone knew Granny could set her prices much, much higher if she wanted to. Sam Soroka had broken into her house and tried to steal a jar of Naughty but Nice. Sam Soroka was currently in the Tatagwa Mental Health Facility re-learning the finer points of dressing himself.

Granny smiled at the thought.

She went back up the stairs to the kitchen, and then took another look at Jimmy's long, lanky form, stretched out on her couch. She sighed. Puberty was such a nuisance. Jimmy might last another six weeks, if she was lucky. But there was no use putting it off 'til the last minute; she'd better begin planning now for the transition.

At least next spring should be a good year in the garden, she consoled herself. *Reward for all that digging...*

Jimmy Conklin sat at Granny Noggins's kitchen table, an untouched glass of milk by his right hand, an untouched plate of cookies on the table in front of him. He frowned at his left arm. Where had all that black hair come from? He rubbed his upper lip. It felt fuzzy. *What's going on?*

The sun-catcher over the kitchen sink spiked his eye with a

rainbow flash, and he blinked irritably. "I hate this kitchen," he muttered, then felt guilty as he heard the front door open and close—Granny coming back from an errand. He looked around to greet her—and froze with his mouth open.

"I love your kitchen, Granny Noggin," said the little girl in blue jeans and a frilly yellow top who was holding Granny's hand.

"I love it, too." Granny smiled down at the girl, then looked at Jimmy, her smile fading. "This is Alyssa," she said. "She's come to visit me for a while...just like you."

THE RESCUE

his is another early story, my second (after "The Minstrel") to be published in JAM *Magazine. All of my early stories were aimed at teen readers, because I was barely out of that age group myself!*

⁓

THEY WERE CRASHING AGAIN. Alicia knew with sick certainty everything that was about to happen, but that did not lessen the terror.

She could hear the braking rockets thundering and the atmosphere screaming around the falling lifecraft, she could feel the terrible heat, and she knew that something was wrong, that it wasn't supposed to be like this...

Then the pilot screamed over the intercom, "I can't hold her! Brace for impact!" and the lifecraft rang as though struck by a mighty hammer. The hull split open. Cold water burst into the passenger compartment, and for frantic seconds Alicia struggled with the safety belts, dazed by the impact, feeling the craft sinking under her. Then she was bobbing on the surface in her life jacket, the ghostly fingers of a current tugging at her, and she screamed as she slipped away from the outstretched hand of her father.

"Alicia!" her mother cried, over and over, so that she heard it long after the wretched survivors clinging to the still-floating forward half of the lifecraft disappeared into the mist. But finally even her mother's voice faded away, and she drifted, alone and helpless, in an endless ocean on an alien world.

～

Alicia gasped and jerked awake, then shivered, unable for a moment to remember where she was or why she was so cold. Slowly her eyes focused on a dimly lit wall of rough stone only a few inches from her face. She rolled over, and memory flooded back.

She lay in the cave where she had crawled after being washed ashore on the rocky beach. From her shelter she could see down to the ocean, rolling in slow, sullen swells onto the red stones. The grey, watery light, filtered through a thin mist, turned the sea the colour of old pewter.

Somewhere out there drifted her parents and the other survivors of the colony ship *Appalachia*; somewhere above circled the ship itself, an airless tomb for 142 other colonists, killed by the explosion that had ripped open the ship's hull as it entered orbit around Azgar.

Unless Alicia could find help for the survivors at sea, they would join their comrades as casualties. She had to get moving.

She crawled out onto the beach, stood, and winced, every muscle bruised from the crash and stiffened by her night in the cold, dank cavern. Her stomach cramped with hunger, and she longed for a drink of water.

But none of that mattered. She glanced at her left wrist; a tiny red light pulsed there in the centre of a black disk. Every survivor wore one of the homing devices, part of the emergency equipment on board the lifecraft. As long as that red light burned, she could find the floating wreckage again. But she needed help to reach it.

Help. She looked up and down the stony shoreline. Somewhere on Azgar was an Aaln colony, the colony the humans had come to join. It was to be the first joint venture for two races which had often competed, sometimes bloodily, for real estate.

The Aaln would help, if she could find them. They must be searching for survivors already; they would have heard the distress calls from the *Appalachia*.

But a planet was an awfully big place to search—for the Aaln, and for a young girl on her own. "Who never wanted to come in the first place," Alicia muttered, then flushed, ashamed. It sounded too much like "I told you so." She was here; there had been a disaster. She had to do what she could.

She turned left and started walking. *One direction is as good as another*, she thought. But the flashing red light on her wrist reminded her constantly of the penalty for failure.

Several hours later she stopped to rest where a stream flowed into the sea. Stunted bushes grew nearby, laden with berries she thought the colonists' training tapes had said were edible. The bushes were the first life she had seen, apart from some brown, grass-like tufts among the rocks and stringy green strands in the ocean shallows. And the mist had never lifted. Azgar was altogether a dismal world.

She drank thirstily from the stream, then picked as many berries as she could, sat on a large rock, and started eating. They tasted so bitter that despite her hunger she wanted to spit them out, but instead she forced them down and then picked more. She had no way of knowing when she would find more food.

She had yet to see any sign of the Aaln, and her spirits were low. Her feet hurt from her journey along the beach; the loose, flat rocks that covered it threatened her with a sprained ankle at every step. But high cliffs barred the way inland, and anyway, she knew the colony was fairly close to the ocean. If she kept following the shore, she would eventually find it.

Except she didn't have time to walk all the way around the continent.

Occupied with her aching arches and her gloomy thoughts, Alicia failed to notice the Aaln aircar approaching along her path until it swept overhead, the blast of its jets flattening the ocean and tearing at her clothes. She jumped to her feet, but before she could wave or shout, a soft blue light enveloped her.

Unconscious, she dropped to the rocks.

Alicia slumped on her bed in the small cell where the Aaln had locked her. She knew the aliens had only been on Azgar for six months, but the cell looked centuries old. Its walls of grey stone were broken only by a small, steel-barred window and a heavy iron door, and green slime grew in the corners. The pervasive cold and damp made it even more inhospitable.

Very soon now, she knew, the Aaln would come and demand that she lead them to the surviving humans. They knew the mechanism on her wrist was a homing device, but they didn't know how to operate it; for that they needed her.

Alicia had set out along the beach hoping to find the Aaln and lead them to her friends and family, but she was no longer eager to do so. She wasn't sure what was going on in the colony, but from the way they had treated her so far she didn't think the Aaln exactly planned to *rescue* the survivors.

She closed her eyes and summoned what she knew about the Aaln. They were reasonably humanoid in shape, but they weren't mammals: they were warm-blooded, scaled amphibians. Not reptiles, she reminded herself, but it didn't help. They looked like lizards to her, and she hated snakes and lizards and things like that. It was one reason she hadn't wanted to come to this colony...but for her parents the opportunity had been a dream come true, so what could she do?

Beyond the physical appearance of the Aaln, humans knew little about them. The two races could communicate, with an artificial language called Galactic (rather ambitiously, Alicia thought), but both were cautious about what they said.

However, some of that caution had recently eased on the part of the Aaln. The aliens had initiated the negotiations which led to the creation of the joint colony. The humans had learned during those talks that the Aaln had a semi-feudal culture based on a network of clans, each of which sent representatives to a Clan Council. A complex system of honour and privilege, combined with a measure of democracy, determined which clan held power and thus initiated and implemented policy.

For many years the governing clan had been a powerful and conservative one that feared and distrusted humans, but recently it had been replaced by a new clan, the Or'Karr, which wanted to increase the contact between the two cultures.

The humans had been eager to take advantage of the change. No one knew how stable the Aaln political system was; another clan could displace the Or'Karr at any time, and there were some clans that were very anti-human, especially one called the Ak'Lann.

Alicia opened her eyes very wide and sat up slowly. The name had only now surfaced in her conscious mind from her memory, but she had already heard it once that day. When she had revived from the stun blast she had been taken before the colony's governor for questioning—and the governor's name had been Arniss Ilkar Ak'Lann.

She shuddered as she remembered. Two powerful guards had held her before him. She still felt slimy where their hands had gripped her arms, though their scaly skin had been perfectly dry. But perhaps that feeling had been as much from the gaze of the governor as the touch of his guards; her first thought had been of a hungry snake eyeing a frog. Yet at the time she had still hoped he might help her.

"So one, at least, survives," the governor said in Galactic. "Are there others?"

"They're holding on to what's left of the lifecraft, out at sea," Alicia told him. "Please, you have to rescue them!"

The governor leaned forward. "How do we find them?"

"I can lead you. But we have to hurry. I don't know how much longer they can hang on."

"In good time, you shall indeed lead us. I am most eager to personally 'greet' all the humans." He motioned to the guards. "*Akkarsin, risskh!*"

They had dragged her away and dumped her in this cell, where she had since had plenty of time to regret telling the governor she could lead him to the others. She wriggled her shoulders uncomfortably; a spot on her back itched where a guard had slapped her as he shoved her through the door. "Lizards," she muttered.

"Sssssss." A snake-like hiss echoed in the room. Alicia snatched her feet off the floor and pressed her back to the wall, anxiously searching the cell's dim corners for the source.

"Sssssssssss!" Longer and louder—and it wasn't in the room, it was outside. She got up from the bed and turned to look at the window high above it.

The barred opening framed the fanged face of a young Aaln male, the crest on his head erect with excitement. "At last!" he whispered in Galactic. "I am here to rescue you. Watch through the door in case someone comes."

Sorely puzzled but not about to argue with any rescuer, however strange, Alicia did as he told her. The corridor outside remained empty as faint hissing noises sounded behind her. The smell of ozone bit at her nose, then the Aaln whispered, "All right."

She turned. The bars in the window were gone, and the young Aaln motioned for her to join him. She hurried across the floor and stood on the bed, but even so could barely get her fingertips over the sill.

The Aaln gripped her wrists and she flinched, though his hands were warm, dry, and strong. He pulled her up easily, and helped her scramble through the window, guiding her feet to the rungs of the ladder he had climbed to her cell. They descended into the dark street below, an alley between two of the few permanent buildings in the colony.

"Who are you?" she demanded then.

"My name is Nnikor Annil Or'Karr," he said, and she felt some relief at hearing that clan name instead of Ak'Lann... though she wondered if he were telling the truth.

"But why—"

"No more questions. Not now. We must go!"

"Where?"

He answered by setting off, away from the centre of the colony, toward the hills—*and the sea*, Alicia thought. She followed him as he slipped out from between the buildings and darted across an open space to the bushes beyond. He moved incredibly fast; *like any other lizard*, Alicia thought, then felt a little ashamed. After all, this lizard was saving her life.

But why? She still didn't know that, and she wasn't sure she trusted this sudden display of Aaln generosity. She wished they could stop long enough for her to get answers to a few questions.

Any possibility of that vanished, though, as they neared the crest of the ridge overlooking the colony. A bell rang shrilly behind them, and Nnikor hissed an angry word. "I had hoped they would not miss you for a much longer time," he said over his shoulder, continuing to climb. "Now we must move as fast as we can, all the way to the sea."

"And then what?" Alicia asked, panting.

"Then we go to rescue your friends, of course. What else?"

"You've never said," she pointed out. They reached the top and Alicia stopped and glanced back, hearing shouts. Lights moved out from the colony, and somewhere an aircar roared to life. "Why are you rescuing me?" she asked again.

Nnikor pointed down at the colony. "Do you really want to stop here long enough for me to tell you, or do you want to start running?"

Alicia looked down at the hornet's nest they had stirred. The answer was really quite obvious. "Run!"

They did.

Alicia felt trapped again in a nightmare she'd once had. She ran through the ghostly dark, eerily lit by the two mist-shrouded moons rising behind her, pursued by monsters. The only difference between the nightmare and the reality was that in reality one of the monsters was helping her—maybe. She still had doubts about Nnikor, but they didn't stop her from following him. What choice did she have?

The bushes had needles instead of leaves on their spiny branches, stones covered the ground, and there seemed to be no flat ground between the colony and the sea. Alicia's breath soon came in aching gasps, and despite the dampness, her mouth dried out until she could hardly swallow, and then only painfully. She heard herself moaning with each breath, but still she plunged after the dark shadow that was the tireless Nnikor.

Mist and sweat soaked her clothing and mingled and ran into her eyes, half-blinding her. She fell twice, banging her knees painfully on the rocks, but each time she struggled back to her feet and ran on.

At last they reached the cliff above the beach. Nnikor seized Alicia's arms just in time to keep her from plunging over the brink. "There is a way down here," he said. He was breathing only slightly harder than usual.

Alicia, practically blind, unable to speak, nodded mutely while taking long, shuddering breaths. She followed Nnikor slowly along the cliff edge, grateful for the rest, however temporary. By the time the Aaln found what he was looking for, her breathing, while not back to normal, at least no longer hurt.

"Here," Nnikor said at last, and halted. "The colony leaders don't know about this trail; they will look for us much further up the beach." He turned his pale, slit-pupilled eyes toward her. "Are you a good climber?"

No, she wanted to say, *I've never done any climbing in my life*, but she knew it wouldn't make any difference. "I'll have to be, won't I?"

Nnikor took something from the pouch-covered belt that was his only clothing. "Here," he said, and startled her by reaching his hands around her. When he drew back a loop of very thin rope hung around her waist. He tied another loop around his own narrow hips. "Go first. I'll follow. If you fall, I may be able to hold on."

That didn't encourage Alicia very much; it sounded like Nnikor expected her to fall. But then, she expected it herself. She took a deep breath and lowered herself over the edge.

She realized at once why this spot had been chosen. Instead of a sheer, perpendicular cliff, here there was a bit of an outward slope, broken and terraced so that in daylight she thought she would have had little trouble climbing up or down.

At night it was different. The mist-dimmed moonlight did little but cast confusing shadows on the cliff-face. She couldn't see where she put her feet or hands, and never knew when the rock she had chosen to trust might crumble away instead. When that finally happened for real, she did not fall—quite—but for a long time after she couldn't bring herself to move. Instead she clung to the rock, trembling, until Nnikor's urging from above finally persuaded her to take the next tentative step.

When at last she stepped down and felt firm, rocky ground beneath her feet, her shaky legs folded under her and she sat down hard. A moment later Nnikor joined her. "Can you walk?"

Alicia took a deep breath and tried standing again. Though her knees still trembled, they held her. "Yes."

"Then let's do so." Nnikor unfastened the rope from both of them, coiled it and stored it in its pouch again. "We are still being pursued." He strode away, and Alicia stumbled after him.

The walk to the water was blessedly short. They were right where they were supposed to be: above a small cove, where a fifty-foot boat rode at anchor. A small powered dinghy was beached on the shore. Alicia climbed into it and enjoyed the sensation of sitting still while Nnikor pushed off, splashing in the shallows, then clambered in himself.

They boarded the larger boat without incident. A simple craft, it had a cabin above-decks and enough cargo space below to hold all the humans. In the cabin were the controls, some equipment lockers, and two cots. Alicia sat on one of the latter while Nnikor started the engines and headed out onto the dark sea.

She had a hundred questions to ask, but somehow she never got them out; almost instantly she fell fast asleep.

Alicia woke, and gasped to see Nnikor's scaled, fanged face just centimetres from her face. He straightened at once. "It is almost dawn. You must guide me now."

"Dawn?" Alicia wiped sleep from her eyes, then swung her feet over the edge of the cot. "But we must have been travelling for hours. Why didn't you wake me sooner?"

"I only moved us far enough out so that we could not be seen from shore," Nnikor said. "We have held position since then. We must have daylight to make the rescue, and it is fast approaching. So if you will guide..."

Alicia shook her head. "No. Not yet."

"Your friends—"

"Can wait a few minutes longer. As long as this thing on my

wrist is flashing I can find them. But I want to know what's going on before I lead you or anyone else to them."

Nnikor hissed softly, then said, "All right. I have told you my name. If you know anything of the Aaln, you know my clan holds power, and that we support increased contact with humans.

"But in order to get Council approval for this colony, we had to award the governorship to the Ak'Lann Clan. We required them to first swear to follow our orders and set aside their anti-human feelings. That oath seemed to bind them—until now.

"They may not have had anything to do with the explosion on your ship—but then again, they may. They were certainly quick to take advantage of it. They began searching for survivors at once, and found you. They wanted you to lead them to the others so they could kill you all at once."

"Kill us?" Alicia swallowed. She'd suspected as much, but—

"Of course, kill you. They have already summoned one of their clan ships to remove your vessel from orbit. With no proof you ever arrived at Azgar, they can claim you humans broke the treaty and the planet is ours by default." His eyes narrowed to glittering slits. "There may even be more to the plan. They may deliberately leak the truth to the humans. Our two peoples have skirmished before. This could lead to all-out war—and war would please the Ak'Lann."

"But if the colony is governed by the Ak'Lann, how did you—"

Nnikor made a coughing sound that alarmed Alicia, until she recognized Aaln laughter. "There are many among the colonists who are of my clan or our supporting clans, but the Ak'Lann do not know it. My father saw to it they would not have the free hand they sought. They think we are all from clans that support them."

"Your father?"

Nnikor drew himself up proudly, crest erect. "My father is Tyssak Llin Or'Karr."

For a moment the name meant nothing to Alicia; then it regis-tered from the briefing tapes. "Clan leader!"

"Yes. This colony was his idea."

"But what happens when we rescue the others? The colony is the only place we can take them. They'll need food, medical atten-tion...if the Ak'Lann are still in control there—"

"My orders were to rescue you and the others," Nnikor said. "Others have received different orders. I cannot tell you more. You must trust me."

Alicia gazed at him reflectively; he looked squarely back at her. The story could have been an elaborate lie, but she didn't want to believe that. And even if it was, the odds were still better than they would have been if she'd led the governor and all his guards out there.

"All right," she said, standing. "Let's quit wasting time."

The sun came up shortly afterward. Alicia gnawed on a nutri-tive bar that tasted like dried seaweed (and probably was), and watched the mist turn from black to grey and suddenly to gold. For a few moments the sea was almost beautiful; then the colour faded away until only the familiar white mist and lead-coloured ocean remained.

"Doesn't the sun ever shine?" Alicia asked Nnikor.

"This is mid-winter," he said. "In the summer it is sometimes clear."

"I'll have to see it to believe it," Alicia said, but hoped silently she wouldn't be there to see it.

When her homing device indicated they were very close to the lifecraft, she had Nnikor slow the boat. They slipped forward until she could no longer indicate any direction at all, and Nnikor cut the engines.

Alicia peered anxiously into the silent mist. "Where are they?" she demanded, gripping the rail so tightly her fingers ached.

"Listen!" Nnikor whispered. Alicia looked at him, then dashed to the other side of the boat as she heard it, too—low voices.

Human voices. "There!" Nnikor cried, triumphant. Alicia followed his pointing claw, and as he started the engines again spotted the dark bulk of the lifecraft through a thin place in the mist—

—and at the same time heard the throbbing of other engines, deeper and more powerful than their own.

She spun, and to her horror saw a ship much larger than theirs nosing through the fog. Armed Aaln lined the railings, and the governor himself stood on the glassed-in bridge above the deckhouse.

"Traitor!" Alicia screamed at Nnikor.

He ignored her. He pushed the throttle forward and started for the lifecraft, but then killed the engines instantly as a bright red beam slashed across the bow, raising blisters on the tough plastic. Momentum carried the boat close to the lifecraft, though, and the pale, frightened survivors. Nnikor stormed out of the cabin and onto the deck, glaring at the governor's ship.

The governor's amplified voice roared across the water. "He is not the traitor, young human. In a way, you are. We had planned for you to escape anyway; we planted a microtransmitter on you." Alicia gasped, remembering the odd itching between her shoulders. "Your Aaln accomplice only forced us to act earlier than we intended." The governor's ship loomed very close to them now, turned broadside so they were looking into the barrels of the powerful beam rifles of the Aaln on its deck.

Alicia looked over her shoulder at the lifecraft, hidden from the governor's ship by their own, and saw three of the survivors easing hand-beamers out of holsters.

"Enough of this foolishness!" Nnikor shouted suddenly. He faced the governor, his webbed, clawed hands planted firmly on the railing. "Do you know me, governor?"

"Of course I know you." The governor sounded annoyed. "You are Nnikor Allin Yn'Tikk, and I will have you flayed for your part in this."

"Wrong!" Nnikor's lips drew back from his teeth—and it

wasn't in a smile. "The clan is Or'Karr, governor. Not Yn'tikk—Or'Karr!"

The governor hissed.

"I am the son of Tyssak Llin Or'Karr! Will you shoot me, governor? Because if you plan to kill the humans behind me, you must kill me, too. How will you explain the murder of a rival's son to the Council? Political intrigue is expected, but the old methods of terror are no longer lawful." He gestured at the mist-enshrouded sea. "Perhaps the Council will give you this planet you seem to love so much, Ak'Lann—all to yourself, as your place of permanent exile!"

A long silence ensued, broken only by the lap of water against the hulls of the ships and the lifecraft. Alicia could see an agitated conference underway on the other ship's bridge. Nnikor stood stolidly.

"Alicia!" someone whispered urgently behind her. She turned and looked down. One of the survivors on the highest part of the wreckage was aiming his hand beamer straight at her. "Get down!" he said in Terran. "I have a clear shot at that monster over there if you'll only get out of the way!"

She started to duck, but suddenly realized what such a shot would mean. "No! Father, stop him!"

"Alicia!" the man said, shocked.

"Why?" her father called up.

"Haven't you been listening? Nnikor is saving your skins right now by risking his own! But if you shoot the governor or any other Aaln, nothing can save you or me or him—and you'll start the very war that Ak'Lann governor over there is hoping for!"

"You'd trust that snake friend of yours to *save* us?" the man with the gun said angrily. "Get down, girl! I can still do it!"

"No!" Alicia cried. "Father—"

Her father struggled across the slippery lifecraft to the other man's side. "She's right, Hawkins. Don't—"

Hawkins swore and squeezed the firing stud, but at the same

instant Alicia's father slammed the weapon against the lifecraft hull. The beam shot harmlessly into the water, raising a cloud of steam, then cut off as it slid from its owner's numbed hand, splashed into the sea and vanished. "I should throw you in after it!" Alicia's father growled.

His daughter didn't hear him; her ears were full of the sound of her own pounding heart. It had skipped when the gun fired, but at least it still beat. She took a deep, shaking breath, and gripped the railing to steady herself.

None of the Aaln had noticed the incident; the humans had spoken only in their own language and the beam had been hidden by the boat. Nnikor still glared at the governor's ship.

The loudspeaker finally crackled to life again. "*Asskirr, nnikor-riss gan'slin...*"

"Speak Galactic, Ak'Lann," Nnikor broke in. "I will have nothing hidden from our fellow colonists!"

"All right, Nnikor, you win," the governor snarled. "For now. But you cannot stop me from doing what I want when I get you back on shore. You can't defeat me alone and you can't hide from me—and you can't support yourself and all those humans without the resources of the colony. The final victory will still be Ak'Lann's!"

Nnikor grinned, showing his impressive teeth. "I suggest you call the colony right now and see about that, governor." He reached back inside the cabin and turned on the boat's communicator. "I think I'll listen in."

"*Sslisskarr'akkil, Nnikor!*"

"Galactic, remember, governor? Though that particular phrase would be hard to translate..."

The communicator crackled. Alicia saw her father staring up at her, and tried to give him a reassuring smile. She must have failed; he continued to look worried. She gave up and instead turned to listen to the conversation.

"This is governor Arniss Ilka Ak'Lann, calling colony communications central," the governor said.

"Governor who?" a voice replied.

Nnikor laughed and Alicia stared at him. "What—"

He hushed her. "Listen."

"*Governor Ak'Lann, ur hisskan garrin—*" The governor dropped out of Galactic again.

"I think perhaps you have the wrong colony, sir, whoever you are," the voice interrupted him. "There are no Ak'Lann in charge here. This is the joint human-Aaln colony, and as of half an hour ago, all the Aaln—all the ones who are still free, of course—seem to have turned into Or'Karr supporters. *Well-armed* supporters."

Nnikor switched off the communicator, but Alicia could still hear the string of Aaln curses coming from the bridge of the other boat. "I think we will find everything as it should be when we get your friends back to shore," Nnikor said to her, with an expression remarkably less bloodthirsty than the one he had shown the governor. "Shall we start loading?"

Alicia mutely stepped forward and held out her hand. Nnikor looked puzzled, not understanding the custom, but took it. "Thank you," Alicia said simply, and for the first time, felt no revulsion at the touch of an Aaln.

DEVIL'S ARCHITECT

wo words: "programmable afterlife." Need I say more? (Apparently I do: here are 3,500 previously unpublished words inspired by that phrase.)

~

TERRANCE WALKEDEN KNEW WEALTH when he saw it, and the woman who had just entered the showroom of the Pearly Gate exuded it like an exotic perfume. Money practically dripped from the vat-grown mink draped around her shoulders, from the glittering micrograv gold spheres she wore as earrings, from the sleek black silk of her dress, and from the never-marred-by-the-sun porcelain perfection of her skin.

Peripherally, Walkeden saw Gerald Peters, his assistant manager, starting toward the new customer, but Walkeden stopped him with a hand on his arm. "I'll take care of her myself."

"Of course, sir!" Peters smiled, bowed, and turned away.

Walkeden molded his face into his best expression of sympathy and approached the woman, who waited by the showroom's silver sarcophagus centrepiece, one spike-heeled shoe tapping the marble floor impatiently. Walkeden held out his hand. "I'm Terrance Walkeden, proprietor and chief afterlife architect of The Pearly Gate," he said softly. "How may I help you?"

She squeezed his hand perfunctorily with bejewelled fingers and met his gaze with sapphire eyes. "May we talk—in private?" she said in a voice like velvety gravel.

"Of course. Come into my office, Ms....?"

"Mrs. Mrs. Helen Cavinaugh."

"This way, Mrs. Cavinaugh."

He escorted her past the afterlife-display holoprojectors built into the Grecian pillars of the showroom (and past Peters's amused gaze), into his ebony-panelled office. He closed the door, then turned to find Mrs. Cavinaugh gazing at him with disconcerting directness. "Won't you sit..." he began, but she cut him off. The velvet was gone from her voice and the gravel now had sharp edges.

"Never mind the false sympathy, Mr. Walkeden."

He blinked. "I'm afraid I don't understand."

"You will. Sit down."

Walkeden dealt with all kinds of people in his business; he simply nodded and sat behind his desk. Mrs. Cavinaugh took the seat across from him, and crossed one shapely leg over the other. "My husband is about to die," she said matter-of-factly.

"I'm very sorry to hear that."

Mrs. Cavinaugh laughed. "No, you're not. And neither am I. Thomas Cavinaugh, Mr. Walkeden, is a two-faced, two-timing, penny-pinching rat. Charming when I first met him, but the charm vanished long ago." She shrugged. "However, I won't have to put up with him much longer."

"A terminal disease?"

"Something like that."

"I see." Walkeden thought he did. Quite clearly. He cleared his throat. "Well, then, Mrs. Cavinaugh, I presume you have come to The Pearly Gate in search of a suitable afterlife environment for your—um, soon-to-be-late husband." He reached into his desk drawer, took out the latest catalogue, and slid it, face-up, across the desk. "Perhaps you'd care to browse..."

She kept her cold blue eyes on him. "I want a custom design."

Walkeden pulled his hand back from the catalogue, leaving it in place. "Are you sure, Mrs. Cavinaugh? You just described your husband as 'penny-pinching.' Custom design costs—"

"My husband is very wealthy, Mr. Walkeden, and while he has spent little enough of it on me while alive, I will inherit that wealth when he dies."

Somehow, Walkeden had guessed as much. "Very well, madam. But I would still suggest you look through the catalogue. It may be that we will be able to meet your needs simply by modifying something already in stock. No other firm has as wide a selection of nirvanas, heavens, utopias, and paradises as The Pearly Gate, and we are currently the only company offering Oneness-With-The-All—"

"You don't stock what I want. No one does."

"Indeed? What do you have in mind?"

If her eyes had been sapphires before, now they were blue Arctic ice. "Hell, Mr. Walkeden."

Walkeden sat very still. He already knew she was planning to kill her husband—none of his business. That being the case, he should have guessed she'd hardly want to install him in a paradise. He cleared his throat. "We offer a special discount on oblivion..."

"Not oblivion, Mr. Walkeden. Hell."

"But, madam, that's quite impossible. There are strict laws—"

"Not laws, Mr. Walkeden. Professional ethics, is all." She took a debit card from her slim black purse. "How expensive are your ethics, Mr. Walkeden?"

"Mrs. Cavinaugh!"

"A quarter of a million? Half?"

Walkeden couldn't take his eyes off that thin piece of plastic. The woman had done her homework; there was no law against what she was asking. The Supreme Court had decided three years before, in the landmark case of *Simon vs. City of Gold*, that while the religious were free to believe in the continuance of human identity after the death of the body via the soul, what afterlife architects placed into their computer-generated worlds were only computer simulations of the dead personalities they were based on, not the personalities themselves: that the artificial afterlives were, in effect, no more real than the worlds of computer games.

But the North American Society of Afterlife Architects had its own professional code, which prohibited unpleasant afterlives. Even Valhalla, with its eternal cycle of feasting and fighting, was against the rules. He could lose his license...

"If you turn me down, Mr. Walkeden, I'm sure you have competitors who will not," Mrs. Cavinaugh said.

He looked back from the outstretched debit card to her face. "Why choose me in the first place?"

"A mutual acquaintance recommended you."

"But who—"

"I need an answer, Mr. Walkeden."

Walkeden looked at the debit card again. The Pearly Gate did good business, but there was a high overhead. All that posh and glitter... Other afterlife architects had gone out of business—some of them because of him. He still wasn't as secure as he would have liked. The kind of money she offered would help—a lot.

"If NASAA found out..."

"Do you really think I am likely to tell them?"

She's planning to murder her husband. She won't tell anyone. And for the same reason, she can't blackmail me later.

It was, really, the perfect business arrangement.

Abruptly he made up his mind. "Very well, Mrs. Cavinaugh. I'll do it."

"Good." She started to slide the debit card into the slot on Walkeden's desk, but he stopped her with his hand on hers, her skin cool beneath his fingers.

"But not for a quarter of a million, or even a half. One million dollars, Mrs. Cavinaugh. Or it's no deal—and I report your request to NASAA and my...suspicions...to the police."

Her cool expression never changed; she just inclined her head slightly. "Agreed," she said. Walkeden pulled back his hand. Mrs. Cavinaugh finished inserting her card, then keyed in her security code and some figures. "$250,000 now, the rest when the job is done to my satisfaction. I'll give you a month."

Walkeden's satisfaction at the credit transaction gave way to outrage. "A *month*? For a whole new afterlife?"

"My husband only has a month left to live, Mr. Walkeden."

"But you haven't even told me what you want!"

The woman reached into her purse and pulled out a folded slip of paper. "This should give you ample detail."

He took it without opening it. "What about the preliminaries? I'll need a complete brain digitization—and a continuous persona recording from now until he dies." Reflexively he rubbed his own recorder, a tiny chip affixed to the skin behind his right ear, where he could show it to customers reluctant to have the inner workings of their minds stored in The Pearly Gate's computer. "A month simply isn't long enough for a good persona simulation."

Mrs. Cavinaugh smiled. Her perfect white teeth weren't pointed, but they still reminded Walkeden of a shark's. "The brain digitization is already in your computer, Mr. Walkeden, and the persona recorder has been in place for several weeks."

"Awfully sure of yourself, aren't you?"

"Oh, yes, Mr. Walkeden, I am." Her predatory smile vanished. "I'll check on your progress in exactly two weeks. In four weeks I'll want to give your work final approval."

"I trust your husband's condition doesn't kill him earlier than you anticipate."

"Oh, there's no fear of that. Goodbye, Mr. Walkeden." Mrs. Cavinaugh exited, and Walkeden caught a brief glimpse of Peters staring toward the office as the door opened and closed.

At once he turned to his terminal to check his personal account—and found it $250,000 richer.

A second check revealed a digitized replica of Thomas Cavinaugh's brain in place in the computer's memory. "It seems I am committed," Walkeden muttered.

But committed to what? He picked up the piece of paper Mrs. Cavinaugh had left.

It bore only two words. "Hieronymus Bosch."

Someone tapped on the door. "Enter," Walkeden said.

Peters stuck in his head. "Is there anything I should be doing for that woman who just left, sir? She didn't give us any instructions—"

"No, Gerald, I've dealt with it." Walkeden turned off the terminal. "Gerald, I've decided to take a month's vacation. I'm leaving you in charge."

Peters smiled and inclined your head. "Thank you very much indeed, sir. I shall endeavour to validate your trust."

Walkeden felt a familiar flash of irritation at his assistant's unctuousness, but brushed it off. Peters had been with him for three years, joining The Pearly Gate shortly after his own afterlife business had failed. Although Walkeden didn't like him much, he had to admit the man was a hard worker. It was time to give him his chance to show what he could do. And there was no way he could spend time at work creating hell without Peters getting suspicious. He'd have to work at home.

He spent the next hour sanitizing the computer records of any trace of Mrs. Cavinaugh's visit, then turned over the security codes to Peters and left.

For the next month Walkeden sequestered himself in his apartment. He spent part of his advance payment on upgrading his VR design equipment; he hadn't used his home rig much since giving up his freelance career to found his own company, and technology had marched on. Now, for a fraction of what he had originally spent setting up the Pearly Gate's system, he could create a home system that matched and, in some ways even surpassed it, in resolution.

Of course, the transfer of the persona simulation into the afterlife would have to be done using The Pearly Gate's specialized software and hardware, but Walkeden knew that computer inside and out. No one would ever stumble on the private hell he would build for Helen Cavinaugh's husband. Only he and she would ever be able to view it and watch Thomas Cavinaugh's simulated suffering.

And what a hell Cavinaugh's persona was condemned to! The note Mrs. Cavinaugh had given him carried far more information than he'd first thought. Heironymous Bosch was one of the most fascinating and bizarre painters of the late 15th and early 16th centuries. His most famous work was a triptych, "The Garden of Earthly Delights." The left panel showed the birth of Eve in the Garden of Eden. The central panel swarmed with naked men and women engaged in licentious revelry.

The right panel was "Hell."

A month was practically no time at all for the complex process of turning a two-dimensional painting into a full-sensory virtual reality. Walkeden spent every waking hour on it. He slept too little, ate too little, and drank too much coffee, while the fantastic images of Bosch's painted nightmare carried over into his dreams.

But, to his surprise, he found a grim satisfaction in the work. *I've been living behind a facade*, he thought. *I've been nothing but a glorified salesman, slipping on a mask of sympathy to make a sale. But I used to be an artist: and this proves that I still am.* Head encased in his VR helmet, he looked around at the frozen scenes of horror he'd been crafting. *Bosch's masterpiece—and mine, too.*

True to her word, Mrs. Cavinaugh called exactly two weeks after she had come to The Pearly Gate, and Walkeden, keeping the video off so she wouldn't see his bloodshot eyes and scraggly beard, assured her the deadline would be met.

But her call reminded him of the outside world, and so after she hung up he phoned The Pearly Gate. "Any problems?" he asked Peters.

"Nothing I haven't been able to handle, sir," Peters said. "You'll find all in order when you return."

"Two more weeks," Walkeden replied. "Enjoy yourself. Maybe someday I'll put you in charge for good."

"Thank you, sir."

Why not *give it all up?* Walkeden thought as he turned back to his work. *Concentrate on art, instead...serious VR work, none of this commercial stuff.* With a million dollars in the bank, he could afford to take the risk: and he wouldn't have to deal with Peters or Helen Cavinaugh—or their ilk—ever again.

"You look like hell," Helen Cavinaugh greeted him two weeks later as he opened the door of his apartment.

"Appropriate, don't you think?" Walkeden stifled a yawn, then made a grand gesture. "Please come in."

She stalked in and looked around the cluttered living room with distaste. Fast-food cartons, hardcopy, beer bottles and datasticks competed for space on the coffee table.

Walkeden followed her gaze and shrugged. "I've been too busy on our little project to clean house."

"It *is* finished, I trust?"

"Pretty well. I'd like to fine-tune it if I have time, but..." He led her into his study, even more cluttered than the living room, with trash teetering precariously on every flat surface. "Have a seat."

Mrs. Cavinaugh sat gingerly in the swivel chair in front of the terminal. Walkeden handed her the VR helmet. "Of course, even the best VR interface can't capture all the nuances that the simulated persona finds in a well-designed afterlife—for one thing, it engages all five of the persona's senses—but this should give you a pretty good idea..."

He booted up Hell and turned it loose.

Mrs. Cavinaugh stiffened. Her head turned this way and that, avidly, like a hawk searching for prey. Finally she laughed and sat back. "I've seen enough, Mr. Walkeden."

He stopped the program.

Mrs. Cavinaugh pulled off the helmet and tossed black hair out of her face. Her eyes glinted fiercely as she turned to look at him. "Impressive work, Mr. Walkeden."

"Well, of course, what you've seen is only the background," Walkeden said, pleased despite himself. "When your husband's simulated persona is added, the program will focus on him as he moves about the afterlife environment."

"Afterlife environment?" Mrs. Cavinaugh laughed. "Your occupation is as full of euphemisms as a mortician's, Mr. Walkeden. Call it what it is—hell." She stood abruptly. "My husband is not expected to last the night. I will bring his persona recorder to The Pearly Gate at 2 a.m. for the final transfer."

"Tonight?" Walkeden blinked. "I'd hoped—a few more details—"

"Tonight, Mr. Walkeden. Your work is quite satisfactory as is."

He would have protested, but a yawn seized him, and when it had passed, he just shrugged. "Tonight, then."

"I'll see myself out."

After she had gone Walkeden looked at the computer for a moment, thinking he might still try to smooth out a rough spot or two, but another yawn took him and he turned away. *If she likes it, so do I*, he thought, stumbling into his bedroom.

So exhausted even nightmares couldn't trouble him, he slept.

∼

At 2 a.m. Walkeden waited, cold and wet, at the back door of The Pearly Gate for his patron's arrival. Fresh sleep and icy rain had filled him with second thoughts, though it was far too late to back out. Still, one thought troubled him.

He knew why the ASAA prohibited unpleasant afterlives. The lawyers for the plaintiff in the Supreme Court decision, a deeply Catholic individual who has been horrified to find that his wife had chosen a particularly sensual afterlife for herself featuring multiple sexual partners, had made much of the fact that the simulated persona of a *living* person had never been successfully transferred into an engineered afterlife. The simulation always crashed, as though some essential bit of code were missing.

The plaintiff's lawyers had noted that many religious leaders believed that "missing code" was the soul, which, breaking free of a dying body, was attracted to the computer's copy of its former home, and thus gave the simulation "life."

The Pope, most imams, and assorted others thus condemned afterlife architecture in general, claiming that the computers hosting simulated personae were reservoirs of ghosts, man-made Purgatories preventing the souls trapped within them from proceeding to the true, eternal afterlife.

Walkeden had always said he didn't believe it. The Supreme Court had dismissed the notion as unscientific.

But...

Always before he had transferred people into pleasant, happy afterlives, for the comfort of survivors, who could look into their computers and see and hear their loved ones rejoicing in heaven or Neverland or wherever.

But this time...if soul transfer were anything more than a myth...

A car turned into the alley and Walkeden pushed the thought from his mind. *All I'm going to do*, he told himself, *is insert one complex computer simulation into another. The only pleasure or pain it will give is to those who look into it—and for Mrs. Cavinaugh, it's clear, it will be pleasure. And the money she'll pay will be pleasure for me.*

The car stopped beside him. Mrs. Cavinaugh got out. "My husband died just a few minutes ago," she said calmly. "I've brought you the persona recorder."

"I'm sorry for your loss," Walkeden said. He unlocked the door, then led her through a dark corridor and into the computer room, gently aglow with green status lights. He turned on the overhead LEDs. "No one can see in here from outside," he told Mrs. Cavinaugh.

"Please get on with it. I have to get back."

"Of course." Walkeden went to the circuit printer, booted it up, and then opened an airtight compartment above it and took out the smooth silvery wafer of a blank superchip. He slid it into place in the printer, then took "Hell" from its padded container in his pocket and placed it in one of the originator slots. Before he turned around Mrs. Cavinaugh was at his side, her husband's persona recorder in one outstretched white hand. She stared intently over his shoulder as he slid it into another originator slot, then turned to the circuit printer keyboard and called up Thomas Cavinaugh's brain digitization. He looked over the screen display to make sure everything was in order, then activated the merger program.

As the circuit printer hummed to life, he glanced at Mrs. Cavinaugh, thinking she looked very calm and relaxed for someone who had just murdered her husband. Could he have misread her?

"How did he die?" he asked.

She gave him a cold stare. "Suddenly."

"Of course." He turned to check the readouts on the screen.

"How long?" Mrs. Cavinaugh asked.

"A few minutes." Those minutes passed in silence. Walkeden watched the computer; Mrs. Cavinaugh watched him. He was uncomfortably aware of her gaze, and of her strange half-smile.

The figures streaming across the screen became zeros, then ended. A green light flashed.

"Your husband is in hell," Walkeden said without looking at Mrs. Cavinaugh. He reached for the new superchip.

A voice from the doorway stopped him. "Leave it, Walkeden. We're not quite finished with it yet."

Walkeden turned irritably. "Peters, what—"

He stopped when he saw the gun.

Mrs. Cavinaugh crossed to Peters and kissed him deliberately on the cheek, then turned to face Walkeden, her shark-like smile back full-force. "It's a sweet deal, Mr. Walkeden. My husband's money, your business, each other—and no witnesses."

Walkeden's mouth was very dry. "Peters! Why do you need my business with her money?"

"I don't. But I had my own business once, Mr. Walkeden. Until The Pearly Gate stole all my customers. Now you're the one who's out of business." He aimed the gun at Walkeden's head. "Permanently."

"Peters, wait—!"

"Good-bye, boss."

The gunshot was incredibly loud.

The lurid light of the burning city on the horizon reflects off the low and boiling clouds, turning the jagged landscape the colour of blood.

Walkeden crouches naked beneath an overturned table, blood from its red-soaked surface dripping onto his back. He wraps his arms tightly around his legs, trying to make himself as small as possible.

His eyes flick wildly from place to place; he cannot bear to focus on any one horror too long, but the images remain in his mind even when he closes his eyes—a hog wearing a nun's habit raping a naked woman; a giant hare carrying the trussed, headless bodies of a man and woman slung from a pole; a creature with the body of a man and the head of a bird ripping dripping strings of intestine from someone whose blood-soaked legs still kick the air feebly.

Screams rend the air, and searing winds waft the stench of burning sulphur and human excrement across the hot, barren rocks.

Walkeden hears a chitinous clicking behind him—but the worst horror of all is that he already knows what is about to take him in its curved, crablike claws.

He remembers programming it.

MOON BABY

This story appeared in the Summer 2000 issue of the moon-focused Artemis Magazine. *The genesis was simple: what would it be like, I wondered, to be the first human born on another world...?*

THE MOONQUAKE WASN'T MUCH, as such things went; back in Apollo City it wasn't felt at all, though of course it registered clearly on the hordes of seismographs that recorded every twitch of the moon's thick, cold crust. But here, near the epicentre, it was enough: enough to send Scott Morgan reeling across the rock-strewn plain like a drunk; enough to make Pamela Ash gasp and then say a most un-ladylike word as she staggered and fell on her moonsuited rear; enough to raise a thin miasma of dust that hung above the surface like mist over an Earthside swamp; and enough to topple a half-dozen medium-to-large chunks of basalt that had probably stood balanced on the crater's rim since before there was life on Earth. While Scott watched in horror, they tumbled down the towering crater wall in dust-shrouded slow motion and slammed soundlessly into the transporter, tipping it almost gently onto its side, where it lay like a dying cockroach, half-buried in rubble.

Then it was over. "Scott, what's going on?" Pamela cried.

"Shut up," he said, eyes on the transporter. "Tour One, Scott here. Do you read?" He paused. Pamela bounded toward him with giant steps, and he snapped, "Pamela, you idiot, you want to hole your suit?"

She pulled up, slipped, and fell on her rear again. He turned back toward the transporter. "Jack? Al?" Nothing.

"What's wrong?" Pamela picked herself up, trying to brush the dust off her suit, but it clung as if glued there. Her voice wavered. "Why don't they answer?"

Scott stared at her. Dust was still slowly settling on the overturned transporter, and she asked what was wrong? "Earthers!" he muttered.

"Earthers!" Scott growled in disgust as he watched the twenty-four tourists disembark from the Lunar Shuttle. They squealed and bounced up and down in the one-sixth gravity as though the moon had been put there just so they wouldn't have to buy a trampoline. You'd think after three days in zero-G and two days in slow-spinning Gorbachev Station, the novelty of low gravity would have worn off, Scott thought sourly. And most of them were old enough to be his parents. Or his grandparents.

Just like everyone else in Apollo City.

Scott shook his head and walked toward the tour group with the graceful, low-energy shuffle that marked a true Lunite. Jack Porter and Al Donovan, a hydroponics tech and an assistant geologist who had been pressed into service as tour guides, were doing their best to calm the Earthers down before one of them bounced a little too high and cracked his or her greying head on the ceiling. Then they'd be ushering them off to the "Apollo Hilton," just another pre-fab underground hut, dressed up to only slightly higher standards than the colonists' own quarters. Nothing like a real Earth hotel, Scott had been told, but then, nobody expected that; they'd paid the extraordinarily high ticket prices just to be on the moon.

He didn't understand why they'd want to. Nor did he understand why he'd been pulled away from the observatory to meet—he checked his wristcomp—Miss Pamela Ash. But he could guess. She was probably some old biddy who'd been a Scott Morgan groupie since the days when he was headline news on Earth. "BOUNCING BABY BOY BORN ON MOON" and "MOON TODDLER TAKES FIRST LOW-GRAVITY STEPS" and all that crap. She'd probably asked specially to see him, and Luna Agency, never one to miss a PR bet, had not only agreed, they'd ordered him to spend the entire tour with the dried-up old—

"You must be Scott," said a voice. A very young voice. He blinked and refocused his eyes from the group of aging tourists to someone who had come up on his left. A girl about his own age held out her hand. "I'm Pamela Ash."

"Come on!" Scott headed across the crater floor to the crippled transporter. If the hull had been breached—Scott hadn't grown up on the moon without being thoroughly indoctrinated about the effects of explosive decompression. He'd heard the stories from those who had returned from the futile rescue mission to Far Side Outpost after it had abruptly ceased transmission. He'd never seen a decomp victim himself—and after hearing those stories, he didn't want to.

"Has anybody been hurt? What about my parents? Are my parents all right?" Pamela sounded close to panic. She bounded after him, wasting energy and oxygen.

"How should I know?" *Can't she* see? he thought furiously. *Doesn't she* realize? If the transporter was holed, everyone inside without a suit was dead. Even if the hull was intact, the transporter had toppled onto its airlock. The people inside couldn't get out and he and Pamela, the only ones still outside, couldn't get in. He didn't know how much oxygen Pamela had left, but he knew how much *he* did—and it wasn't much. Not much at all. Yet she kept wasting what little she had with useless jabber and useless bouncing around and—useless. That's what she was. Useless. Like all Earthers.

As he led her after the others toward the Hilton, she kept up an endless string of prattle about Earthside entertainers and Tri-V programs and school friends and the two weeks she'd just finished "back home in Montana" riding horses and rock-climbing and how she'd been looking forward to coming to the moon for two years and how it was going to be hard to go back to high school after this—and she kept bouncing, bouncing, bouncing, as if she couldn't believe that a world existed where she weighed only one-sixth of what she was used to and she had to prove it to herself with every step. Scott grimaced, and wished he was back in the observatory comparing starplates, doing something useful instead of wasting his time with this...this *girl*.

He glanced over his shoulder at her as she paused by one of Apollo's few windows, this one showing the view out over the Sea of Tranquility. The three-quarter Earth hung in the sky like it did in the famous Apollo 8 photograph that decorated one full wall of the dining room. Pamela quit talking for a few seconds, and just for those few seconds, Scott couldn't help admiring the way the Earthlight reflected in her blue eyes and lit a few stray strands of her long, light-brown hair—and then she spoiled it by saying, "Isn't Earth beautiful? Have you ever been there?"

Scott turned away abruptly. "Hurry up. We've got to catch up with the others."

She hurried after him. "You didn't answer my question."

He said nothing.

"You've *never* been to Earth?"

Scott clenched his left fist, the one she couldn't see. "No," he said, in a tone that should have meant, "Leave it alone."

Apparently it didn't. "I know you were born here, but I just assumed—"

How much of this did he have to put up with? Scott clenched his fist a little tighter, his nails, short-bitten though they were, digging painfully into his palm. "You assumed wrong. Now drop it."

They were close behind the rest of the tour group now, just approaching the "lobby" of the Hilton, and his final words must have come out a little louder than he intended, because a couple near the back of the group, not quite as old as some of the others, looked around, frowning. "Hey, Mom, Dad," Pamela called cheerfully. "Isn't this *great*?"

"Wonderful," said the woman, smiling at Pamela, but then she gave Scott a look somewhere between "uncertain" and "unfriendly" before turning back to catch something Al Donovan was saying.

"How come you're not telling me all the stuff the other two guys are telling the old folks?" Pamela asked. She didn't seem to have been put off by his brusque answer one bit, but at least she had changed the subject.

"It's just a lot of crap about how Apollo City was built. If you'd done your homework before you came up here, you'd know all that."

"Oh, you mean stuff like, first permanent base established 2031, first year-round workers here in 2040, four years later, first baby born off-Earth—"

Scott's face burned. "Stop it."

"But you said—"

Scott looked ahead, saw the last of the tour group disappearing through the pressure door into the Hilton, turned and grabbed Pamela's arm and pushed her up against the wall. "Let's get something straight," he snarled. "The only reason I'm here and not doing something useful is that this is what I was assigned, and I don't have any choice. *Why* I was assigned this particularly unpleasant job I have no idea. It must be a punishment for something. I've got no use for lazy, wasteful Earthers. I've got better things to do than show a spoiled rich kid around Apollo City. I'm going to do it because up here, unlike Earthside, everybody has to work and sometimes they have to do things they don't want to. But I don't have to like it, and I won't be happy again until you and your parents and the rest of you rich wasters who could afford to blow money on something as useless as a trip to the moon are back on Earth where you belong. Got it?"

Pamela easily jerked her arm free. "You won't be happy 'again'? With an attitude like that, it's hard to imagine you ever have been." Then she smiled at him sweetly. "Now would you mind showing me where everyone else has gone? We wouldn't want my parents to start thinking we're trying to sneak off alone together. They might get the wrong idea." She bounded off down the hall, and Scott, after banging his hand hard once against the ceramic wall, glided after her, not nearly as smoothly as before.

Up close, the damage to the transporter looked superficial. The sides were dented, but not holed that he could see; he was glad the Earthside Lunar Agency idiot who had been pressing for big windows in the transporter just for the tourists had been properly ignored. But there was still no answer to his repeated requests for radio response, even from Pamela, who had fallen uncharacteristically silent. *About time*, Scott thought.

He slid around to the nose of the vehicle. The drivers' windows were buried in dust and small rocks, but he thought he could dig through the debris—in three or four hours. He glanced at the instrument panel on his left suit cuff: a little over two hours' worth of air left.

Something on the edge of the rubble covering the transporter's nose caught his eye. He bent down and, with a little effort, tugged it free.

Pamela leaped over to him. "What is it?"

"Main antenna." He tossed it aside. "That's why they're not hearing us." For the first time he said what he feared out loud. "If they're alive."

"If they're alive?" He could feel Pamela's horrified stare, though her expression was hidden behind her reflective faceplate. "But Mom and Dad are—we've got to do something!"

"We can't get in," Scott said. "And we can't see in. I don't—" He stopped suddenly. "Grab a rock."

"What?"

"A rock! Oh, never mind." He found a likely looking specimen nearby, knelt by the transporter, touched his helmet to the hull and began banging for all he was worth, the sound ringing as clear in his ears as he hoped it would ring inside the transporter—if there were still air in there.

Pamela dropped to her knees beside him and touched her helmet to the metal, too, her quiet, "Please, God..." almost lost in the clanging of stone on metal.

Following orders grimly, Scott spent two days showing Pamela everything—the hydroponics farm, the fusion reactor, life support, Base Central, living quarters, the recreation dome, laboratories—everything that made up Apollo City, home to 120 researchers and support personnel on one-year shifts, eight permanent residents, including his parents, and one native: him.

Pamela took it all in with wide eyes and that same upbeat approach that had annoyed him from the start. After meeting his parents, Drs. Arnold and Elizabeth Morgan, noted physiologist and honoured sociologist, respectively, she introduced him to her own: her father, Lloyd Ash, president of a company specializing in temperature-regulating sporting outfits, and her mother, Mary Anne Ash, who wrote historical romances set in the 1960s. They were a pleasant couple who obviously weren't at all sure what to make of Scott. "Guess you're glad to finally have someone your own age around, eh, son?" Mr. Ash said with bluff heartiness as they ate lunch together in the main dining room.

Scott, who had been as pleasantly neutral as he knew how to be during the meal, flushed, temper rising. It was what his own parents had said after he had come home from his first encounter with Pamela and the rest of the useless Earthers. They'd practically grilled him on what he'd thought of her, as if he should have fallen in love at first sight or something. He kept his voice under careful control as he answered Mr. Ash. "I don't mind being the youngest here. I do my full share of work."

Mrs. Ash laughed. "I'm sure you do, Scott, but haven't you ever had anyone to play with?"

Play with? What did they think Apollo City was, a resort? *Yeah*, Scott answered himself bitterly. *They probably do.* "No," he said.

"Oh, you poor boy!" said Mrs. Ash, and that was as much as Scott could take.

He stood up, chair skittering backward. "Excuse me. I have work to do." Then he left the table without looking back.

He went straight to the gym. Pamela found him there an hour later, "lifting weights"—though the resistance on the bar he was curling was actually created by a magnetic field. Sweat poured down his bare back and chest as he did a dozen repetitions at a higher "weight" than he normally used. "Very impressive," she said, coming around the machine to face him. "This is what was so important you were rude to my parents?"

"I have to work out every day," Scott grunted, continuing to lift.

"Have to?"

"Have to." He finished the reps and released the bar, then leaned on it. He didn't look at Pamela as he reached for a towel and wiped away sweat. "I'm sorry if I was rude. But your parents were rude first."

"All they did was ask a question—"

"Yeah? Well, what business is it of theirs?" Scott tossed the towel away and began readjusting the machine for bench presses. "I had enough of nosy Earthers prying into my life when I was a kid. I don't need it anymore."

"They were trying to be friendly."

Scott lay on his back and adjusted his grip on the bar. "I don't need Earther friends." He began lifting.

"Oh, right, you've got so many here on the moon." Pamela shook her head. "I can't figure you. So you're the first and so far the only person ever born on the moon. Big deal. You can't make a life out of that. But you're trying, aren't you? It's like you're part of the machinery here, not a real person at all. I've watched you: you're always alone, except when you're ordered to be with somebody, like me. You don't want Earther friends, and you don't have any Lunite friends. Far as I can tell, all you've got is yourself."

"Good enough," Scott said between clenched teeth.

"Yeah? I've seen *clams* with less shell than you." Pamela turned away. "I can tell this bus trip tomorrow is going to be a real joy."

Scott quit banging and waited, holding his breath. No answer. Beside him Pamela shifted position, and as her faceplate fell into shadow he was able to see her eyes, wide and frightened, in the light of her helmet instruments. He lifted the rock and banged again. Still nothing. Scott swore and lifted his head. "They're not—"

"I heard something!" Pamela cried.

Scott pressed his helmet against the hull again. Was that a faint click? It came again. *Yes!* He tapped back, wishing someone had thought to make Morse code required learning on the Moon for just such emergencies. They could communicate nothing except their presence, but whoever was inside kept tapping frantically, over and over...

At last Scott banged again, twice, by way of good-bye, and got to his feet. "At least we know they're alive."

"We've got to get help!" Pamela said frantically. "Can't you call Apollo City on your suit radio?"

Idiot! Scott thought. "Not enough range," he said. "What we've got to do is set up the transporter's emergency transmitter—it sends out a distress signal. But it has to go through the Lunar Communications Satellite, and it's low on the horizon from here. I've got to get it out of this crater."

"Back the way we drove in?"

"Too long. I've only got a couple of hours' worth of air left. What about you?"

"I don't—"

They shouldn't even let Earthers on the moon! "Left arm. Third readout."

Pamela looked. "3:07?"

"Three hours, seven minutes. Estimated from your rate of usage so far. Take it easy, you could have more. But it's still not enough to get out of the crater the way we came in." He tilted his head back and looked up the crater wall to the high rim from which the rocks burying the transporter had fallen. "I'm going to have to climb up there."

~

At supper, Scott's parents quizzed him again about his day with the Earthers. "So you had lunch with the Ashes," his mother said pleasantly as his father placed steaming dishes on the table. "How nice."

"No, it wasn't." Scott ladled potatoes onto his plate. "All they wanted was to ask nosy questions."

"What kind of questions?"

"The usual Moon Baby crap. 'Didn't you miss having kids to play with?' That kind of thing." Scott poured a glass of Pepsi-Coke. "What business is it of theirs? I get enough of that around here." He had the glass halfway to his lips before something suddenly registered on him. He set the glass down carefully. "Wait a minute. I didn't tell you I had lunch with the Ashes."

His parents exchanged glances. "Someone mentioned it—"

"You've had the cameras on me again, haven't you? *Haven't you?*"

"Now, son, the cameras are on all the time, you know that," his father said reasonably. "They're not aimed at anyone in particular—"

"But you were using them to watch me, weren't you? A laboratory rat gets more privacy than I do!"

"Dear, you have to understand, you're a unique—"

"I know all about how unique I am. My nose is rubbed in it every day, isn't it? Everybody is urged to work out, but I'm the only one who has to do it religiously, because I haven't quite developed properly, have I? Not enough gravity up here. Everyone has medical checkups on a regular basis, but I'm the only one who has to see the doctor every week and have a complete physical every month. And it all goes into the computer, doesn't it?

Wonder how puberty is affecting Moon Baby? Check the computer. Moon Baby's latest IQ scores? All in the computer. But you'd think I could at least eat lunch without being spied on by my own parents!" For the second time that day, Scott walked out on a meal.

Until that moment he'd been trying to think of a way to avoid the "bus tour," as Pamela had called it, a two-day trip out and back to a special dome set up at the Apollo 11 landing site, with a couple of stops in "scenic" locations where the tourists were suited up and carefully shepherded outside for a few minutes of "basking in the Earthlight beneath the unwinking stars," as the purple prose of the tourism brochure put it. Scott had hated the whole useless exercise, but now it appealed to him. Maybe it meant close quarters with Pamela and the other Earthers for a couple of days, but it also meant escape from Apollo City, from "safety" cameras and from his parents, who he sometimes thought had conceived him simply as a physiological and sociological experiment, though they claimed he was an "accident."

Either way, once his mother was pregnant, his parents had fought for three months with Luna Agency for the right for him to be born on the moon. The Agency had finally agreed, but had stipulated that no other moon-born children would be allowed until this "experimental" child had proved to develop normally.

So Scott had grown up surrounded only by adults, in a harsh environment, subjected to an unending barrage of tests and evaluations and, for his first few years, to an equal barrage of publicity. Finally the novelty wore off and the Moon Baby was allowed to slip into relative obscurity—until tourists started coming to the Moon. Then Luna Agency had made him one of their drawing cards. *See the Moon Baby in its natural habitat!*

Only this time, for the first time, they'd ordered him to accompany a single individual instead of just putting in an appearance, and as he mulled that over while getting together his gear for the tour, Scott suddenly realized the truth: it was all another experiment. Thrust the Moon Baby, now the first Moon Adolescent, into the company of an attractive young member of the opposite sex. See if he's grown up normal by the way he reacts.

"I might as well be on a treadmill!" Scott shouted, and just in case there was a hidden camera in his bedroom—and at that moment he wouldn't have been surprised—he made an obscene gesture to empty air, added a couple of choice swear words he'd picked up from the newest workers from the stations, then stormed out of the apartment. No, two days with Earthers didn't look bad at all.

Scott brushed away dirt from an equipment hatch at the rear of the transporter while Pamela watched, silent again. For a moment, as he tugged at the hatch, he feared it had jammed, but finally it jerked open, revealing the featureless white box of the emergency transmitter. He hauled it out and checked to make sure the green power light glowed at its base. Then he glanced at his wrist again. 1:41. He looked up at the sheer crater wall. He thought he could make it up and activate the transmitter. But they were still an hour from the Apollo 11 dome, a full day from Apollo City. The crew at the dome would set out at once, but by the time they reached the accident site...

His heart pounded in his chest and sweat ran off his face. Too bad his parents didn't have a monitor on him, he thought numbly. They could learn a lot: Moon Baby suffers abject terror. Moon Baby undergoes oxygen deprivation. Moon Baby suffocates. Poor Moon Baby.

He was wasting time. He started toward the cliff face, then pulled up short as Pamela bounded past, turned and faced him. "I'll lead," she said.

"Don't be stupid!" He didn't have time for this! "You're an Earther!"

"And you're a stuck-up Lunite with a chip on your shoulder the size of Alaska and a swelled head to match," Pamela said pleasantly. "You ever done any rock climbing?"

Scott hesitated. "No," he admitted finally.

"I have."

Scott blinked at her. Bouncy little Pamela, a rock climber? Under full gravity? He vaguely remembered her chattering about it the day she arrived, but...On the other hand, he remembered much more clearly the way she had so easily shrugged off his grip. And her body, as he couldn't help noticing when he saw her in the one-piece form-fitting undersuit in the transporter airlock as they'd suited up, was lithe, strong, and supple. But still...

"That was on Earth."

"Yeah, on Earth. Under one full gravity. On full-size mountains." She waited.

The moon is different, he wanted to say. *A hundred different things can kill you here besides falling. You could hole your suit, bump a control and never know it until the oxygen mix went bad, freeze your feet or fingers, go blind from looking into the sun...*

"I've got more oxygen than you do," Pamela continued relentlessly. "It's going to take help a while to get here even after the transmitter is turned on, isn't it? We're going to have to share."

Share? Share a suit pack? Scott had heard of it being done—once. If anyone else had tried it, they hadn't survived to talk about it. You risked losing all the air in both suits.

Which is what happens anyway if you don't get going, an inner voice taunted him. *What's the matter, Morgan—afraid Earthers aren't so useless after all? Afraid the Moon Baby isn't as wonderful and special as you'd like to think? Afraid she'll show you up?*

"All right," he snapped. "Let's climb."

The EVA went smoothly at first. Before they had left Apollo City everyone had donned undersuits. Now they slipped into the moonsuits themselves, with help from the Lunite guides. Scott helped Pamela into hers, finding himself momentarily nose to nose with her as he zipped up her suit and connected and checked the suitpack. She grinned at him and he found himself smiling back, and for a moment he wanted to stay that close to her, and maybe get a little closer...

He stepped back quickly, angry at his body's reaction. So she was young, and female. So what? She was a spoiled rich-kid Earther and his parents had set things up just to check how he reacted. He'd breathe vacuum before he gave them the satisfaction.

Pamela had reinforced his disdain of her out on the crater floor, when she ignored the call to return to the transporter and instead bounded half a klick away to investigate an oddly coloured outcropping of rock. He'd been forced to go after her; by the time he'd gotten them both headed back to the transporter, everyone else was already inside.

Then the moon had shrugged.

Pamela knew what she was doing, Scott had to grudgingly acknowledge. She'd insisted they use a piece of the webbing that had held stores on the outside of the transporter as a short rope, and now she toiled above him, testing each handhold and foothold, never moving until she was sure of her next step, yet even so, climbing steadily, twice as fast as he could have managed on his own—if he could have managed at all. The airless shadows were so black it was almost impossible to judge the rock they hid, but Pamela never seemed to put a foot or finger wrong.

Scott's own feet, fingers, legs, and arms ached abominably after fifteen minutes, were pure torture after half an hour. Maybe it was the pain—maybe it was their increasing height above the transporter and the jagged rocks that covered it—but as they neared the top, Scott reached for a rock he had seen Pamela pass over a moment before, and pulled himself up on it.

It crumbled away like cake and he fell.

Their makeshift rope brought him up with a jerk, a gentle jerk in the light gravity, but enough to set him swinging. He barely saw the sharp tooth of stone in time to throw up his arm and fend it off. Instead of smashing his faceplate, it rang against the side of his helmet. He grabbed at it frantically and clung to it, breathing hard, all-too-aware of how close he had come to finding out first-hand what explosive decompression was like.

"You all right?"

Pamela's voice was a little higher-pitched than usual, but steadier than his own was as he said, "Yes."

"All right, then. Reach up and put your hand where you see my left foot..." Step by step she talked him back onto safe rock, and she kept talking to him until, only a few minutes later, she abruptly disappeared. Another couple of metres and Scott reached the top himself, to find Pamela standing, arms spread, slowly turning a circle as she absorbed the view. "I wish I had a flag to plant!" she cried. *She's not even breathing hard*, he thought. He was, and—he checked—he had less than an hour of oxygen left. Not enough time for rescue to reach them from Tranquility Base.

He shook his head, refusing to think about it yet. First things first. He planted the transmitter firmly in the gritty soil, opened a small panel at its base, and pressed a switch. The device unfolded like a butterfly emerging from its cocoon, extended antennae, and let out a piercing electronic shriek that told everyone within receiving range that there was TROUBLE at this LOCATION and they'd better SEND HELP FAST! Scott knew it transmitted on every commonly used Moon frequency; he quickly reset his own radio to an unaffected one and then grabbed Pamela, who was staring at the transmitter with her hands uselessly over her ears, and reset her radio, too.

155

After that there was nothing to do but wait—wait for help to arrive, or for Scott's air to run out. There was little doubt which would happen first.

At first they sat in silence, then finally Scott asked, "You really are a good climber."

"Thanks. It's a big sport in Montana."

"Montana," Scott said. "I've seen pictures. It's very beautiful."

"Pictures! Pictures don't do it justice. You should come see it for yourself."

Scott stiffened. "I wish you'd quit saying things like that."

"Oh, come on. You can't be planning to spend your whole life on this rock."

His whole life? All thirty-two minutes of it? He shook his head. She still didn't understand about the air. Not really. *How can she?* Scott thought, half bitterly, half sadly. *In Montana there's lots of air.* "This is my home," was all he said out loud.

"I'm sorry. And it's very beautiful. But it's not—natural. It's not Earth."

"I'm not natural either. I'm the Moon Baby."

"And I'm a Montana Baby. It doesn't—"

"Don't you get it? I'm special. I'm unique. I'm an experiment. If I left the moon, went back to Earth—it would spoil the experiment." He paused. "And there's something else," he finally went on. He didn't like to talk about it, but what difference could it make now? "My parents—the other doctors—they think maybe I can never go to Earth."

"What?" They were sitting on the ground by the transmitter, back to back; he felt Pamela shift, sensed she had turned her head toward him. "Why?"

"Gravity. They're afraid of what might happen to me under full gravity."

"But they don't really *know.*"

"No. Some of them say, a couple of weeks in bed, some gentle exercise for a few more weeks, I'd be able to adjust. But some of them—" He shrugged, though he doubted she could sense it. "Some of them think I'd be risking permanent damage—I could be crippled. Or worse."

"That's why you work out so much!"

"Yes. And that's not all." He told her about all the other things being the Moon Baby had meant—the examinations, the lack of privacy, all the rest, the words starting slow and then flooding out of him, until he was talking about those things as he had never talked to anyone about them before.

When he had finished, Pamela was silent for a minute. Finally she said, "You mean, even arranging for you to spend time with me while I was here was just part of an experiment?"

"Yeah."

"That sucks."

Scott shrugged. "I'm used to it."

"But how can your parents—"

"I don't really blame them." Scott was surprised to find he meant it. "I mean, I understand it. This is the Moon. Apollo City is both a research station and a kind of frontier colony. Everything has to serve a purpose; most things have to serve two or three purposes. I might have been an accident, but once I was born, they couldn't waste me. So I became an experiment. Lunites—we tend to view everything that way. It has to be useful, has to accomplish something, or else it's just wasting space, wasting air, wasting time, all resources in short supply up here. If they hadn't learned from me, they'd have been wasting me. It's not that they don't love me, they're just—"

"Using you."

"That's not—"

"Sounds fair to me." Pamela sighed. "Look, Scott, believe it or not, I know what it feels like. My parents—they're busy all the time, you know? Dad's business keeps him away a lot, and Mom's always either off on publicity tours or locked in her office with a DO NOT DISTURB sign on the door. They try to make up for it by buying me stuff and letting me do whatever I want to. This trip was my idea. They weren't wild about it, but they felt so guilty about 'neglecting' me they went along with it."

"I don't see—"

"My parents are there, I guess, you know, in the house with me, but they're not *there*, not all the time. I figure the sooner I'm able to look after myself, make my own decisions, the better off we'll all be. Sounds to me like you're in the same boat. It's about time you started looking after yourself. Forget this Moon Baby crap and start thinking of Scott Morgan. What does *he* want?"

What does he want? Scott thought. *To be* useful *on the Moon as a walking guinea pig? Or to take a chance on the Earth?* It might be painful—even impossible. But shouldn't he at least try?

If he lived. The thought hit like a blow. He'd forgotten his situation. Amazing how the brain refused to accept, even believe in, its own impending end. He looked at his wrist, saw with bleak fascination he was down to five minutes of oxygen. He probably had a couple of minutes' leeway after that, breathing the air in his suit, but that would grow stale in a hurry, and then...

...then...

Then he wouldn't have to worry about what Scott Morgan wanted, because Scott Morgan wouldn't want anything at all.

If they were going to try to share suitpacks, they'd have to try soon, Scott thought, before lack of oxygen made him sluggish. But if they bungled it, when the transporter arrived it would find not one but two stiffening corpses beside the transmitter.

Even if they succeeded, that might be what the rescuers would find. Pamela had about an hour's air left. That should be enough for the Tranquility Base transporter to find them. But if they shared air, after the inevitable loss involved in the transfer they might each have only about twenty minutes—and that might not be enough. They could share air and *still* die together.

Pamela doesn't deserve that, Scott thought. The Moon was *his* home. He'd always known something could go wrong and the Moon would prove that old saying about it being a harsh mistress. If he died...well, it would be fitting, wouldn't it? First native born on the Moon, first native to die on the Moon. But Pamela...he'd wanted her to understand the Moon's harsh realities, but not that way. Cheery little Pamela deserved to go back to her Montana horses and her school friends and her rock climbing, to laugh under the Earth's blue skies, where she belonged and he never could.

And so he said nothing, only sat there in morbid silence and watched his wrist gauge count down his life; watched it reach zero, and heard the faint hiss inside his suit die away.

Light swept over his face, vanished. The ground vibrated. *Moonquake!* he thought sluggishly. *Aftershock*...the thought dribbled away into darkness.

More light. Voices. Air! He gasped air, rich air, unbelievably sweet air, and his eyes fluttered open. A woman loomed over him. He blinked her into focus. "He's coming around," she said, and vanished.

"Scott?" Pamela's worried face swam into his field of vision.

"Wha—?" His voice was dry as moondust.

"The transporter came—fifteen minutes after you passed out. They'd left Tranquility Base right after the quake, before they heard the transmitter, because they tried to contact the tour bus and couldn't. But they said they would have missed us completely if the transmitter hadn't been activated." Pamela sounded both happy and furious. "You idiot! I told you I'd share. You could have died!"

"Sharing—trying to—could have killed both of us." Scott coughed raggedly.

"But it didn't, did it?"

For a moment that didn't register on Scott's still-sluggish brain. "What? You mean you..."

Pamela grinned. "It wasn't that hard. I'd watched you connect all the hoses when we suited up, so I knew what went where." Her smile faded. "It was close, though," she admitted. "I figured we had about five minutes apiece left when the transporter showed up. If it hadn't left early..."

"I knew—not enough," Scott croaked. "That's why—didn't try it. Figured—you deserved air. Climbing—you saved everybody."

"*I* saved everybody? I was running around in circles chasing my own tail down below. I wouldn't have known how to set up the emergency transmitter—I didn't even know there *was* an emergency transmitter. *You're* the hero."

Scott shook his head vigorously.

Pamela grinned again. "Tell you what. We shared air, we'll share glory, too. But you have to make me a promise."

Scott managed a small smile. "Name it."

"You have to come rock-climbing with me again." Her eyes locked on his face. "In Montana."

Scott thought about what his parents would say; what Luna Agency would say, especially when he refused any publicity; what the doctors would say. He thought about what Pamela's parents would say when they found out their daughter was meeting that strange boy from the Moon in the wilds of Montana. But he didn't think about any of it very long. None of it mattered.

He'd almost died. Moon Baby *had* died. From now on, he was just Scott Morgan—not unique, not a hero, just a boy. Still a Lunite, and always a Lunite—but more than willing to give other parts of the Solar System a chance. Even Earth.

Even Earthers.

He met Pamela's gaze. "It's a deal."

THE DAYDARK

This was a very early story of mine, but it remained
unpublished until the fall of 2002, when it appeared in
Gateway S-F Magazine, *which focused on Christian science fiction. I*
grew up in the church of Christ, attending services three times a week.
My father was a preacher, teacher, deacon, and eventually elder in the
church. I graduated from both a Christian high school and a Christian
university. It's therefore not at all surprising that religion makes a
frequent appearance in my work, as it does in this story, albeit in a
low-key way.

THE THREE-WHEELED GROUNDCAR FISHTAILED around
every curve in the rutted cart track, spraying dust and pebbles
into the purple roadside weeds. The alien hobbling down the
middle of the road didn't even glance at it. Only metres away
from her, it skidded to a shuddering, reluctant stop.

Peter Campbell tossed back the canopy. "Out of the way!" he
shouted. The Altorian turned dim eyes on him. White tinged the

blue fur of her muzzle, above once-sharp teeth now yellowed and dull. "You're blocking the path, old one! Move!"

The Altorian's long, feathery-furred tail twitched, but she edged to one side. Peter accelerated past her, spewing dust in his wake, and instantly forgot her. His mind boiled with his latest argument with his father.

"I didn't ask you to bring me here, and I'm not going to spend the rest of my life here!" he'd shouted. "I'm going to be a spacer and that means off-planet school. I'm taking the next ship and you can't stop me. I'm sixteen. In the Commonwealth that makes me an adult!"

His father hadn't even raised his voice. "Your mother and I believe young people should remain with their parents. Commonwealth law cannot dictate how we raise our son. Nor does it apply to this planet. Here our law is molded by our faith." His eyes, startling blue, locked on Peter's. "Ask yourself, Peter—is it education you want, or the imaginary pleasures of far-off worlds? Remember the prodigal son."

Peter had shouted himself hoarse, but his father had remained implacably, infuriatingly calm. "You will not leave until we think you are ready. And no ship will take you without our permission; not while I am governor."

Peter swore and braked the ground car hard, skidding to a halt at the end of the cart track. Before him rose Shield Mountain.

Keltor emerged from his grandmother's hut into air still full of dust. His grandmother, coughing, hobbled up the track, and he ran to her and took her arm. She patted his hand. "Where does that one go in such a hurry?" he asked, muzzle wrinkled.

"I do not know or very much care," replied his grandmother, whose talk-name was Lia. "Though I suppose I should be pleased he ordered me off the road, instead of just running me down."

Keltor's tail lashed. "He ordered you, an elder of the People, off our road?"

"What does he care about the People? He did not even speak our language to me, but used his own harsh tongue."

"May the Shield fail him!" Keltor snarled.

Quick as thought, Lia's claws stung his arm. "You will never again say such a thing about anyone—even Peter Campbell!"

Keltor hung his head. "Yes, grandmother."

"That's better." She took his arm gently again. "The other Earthers are not like that one," she mused. "I wonder what made him thus...his father is a good man."

The waning growl of the ground-car ceased abruptly. Keltor glared down the cart-track. "If he comes back—" he began threateningly, then stopped. "Where is the fool going?"

"What do you see?"

"He is climbing Shield Mountain!" Keltor cried. "But today is Daydark!"

Lia released him. "His parents—"

"Too far!" Keltor started running, hearing his grandmother's cry of fear behind him—a cry that echoed silently in his own throat.

It took Peter an hour to reach the broad plateau atop the mountain. Breathing hard, he looked west. Mountains rolled away from him like frozen waves of stone, piling higher and higher until they broke on the mighty Worldwall two hundred kilometres distant.

But today black clouds hid that incredible granite cliff. Rushing toward him, they swallowed the snow-covered peaks rank by rank. Lightning flickered in the darkness.

Peter turned, knowing he should leave the mountain before the storm arrived, but eastward at the colony sun still glinted off the nose of the ship he had hoped to take off-planet, and he spun back to face the onrushing clouds. He had climbed Shield Mountain to get as far away from his father as possible, and also because his father forbade it, honouring some foolish taboo of the Altorians.

They can take me away from my friends and drag me to this planet, they can even make me stay here, but they can't make me obey their stupid rules, Peter thought. But there would be little defiance in slinking back with his tail between his legs before anyone even noticed what he'd done. He cast about for shelter, and spotted a dark hole in an upthrust, tumbled mass of rock roughly centred on the plateau. *Perfect*, he thought, and set out across the barren ground.

As Peter disappeared from view upslope, Keltor swallowed the shout he had been about to make. "Fool," he muttered. He resumed climbing, praying the Daydark held off.

By the time Peter reached the cave the clouds covered a quarter of the sky. A grey curtain of rain hung beneath them, only two valleys away. Lightning stabbed downward. Peter winced as an icy blast stung his face with flying grit, and plunged into the cavern.

Keltor, just reaching the plateau, saw the human disappear. "No!" he shouted in Terran, but the rising wind tore the word away.

He looked westward. It would be a race between him and the Daydark—a race he wasn't sure he could win. He remembered his grandmother, coughing in the humans' dust, ordered into the ditch like a servant—but with a curse, he dashed into the ever-rising wind. The human might be a barbarian, but Keltor was of the People. He had to try to save him.

Otherwise his grandmother would never forgive him.

Peter followed a narrow passageway down into a broad, hemispherical chamber. He'd reached for the glowrod on his belt as he entered, but he didn't need it. At the entrance to the chamber he stopped, open-mouthed and staring.

Huge, radiant eight-sided crystals lined the walls, filling the cavern with light. They brightened as he watched, and he backed up a step, but then the madly howling wind thrust a bit of itself down the passage, and thunder shook the rocks, and he stumbled forward into the heart of the chamber.

Awed, he watched the light wax until he had to close his eyes—and then someone smashed into him from behind, drove him to his knees, seized him by the waist and began dragging him back up the passage.

Peter struggled madly in the Altorian's viselike grip, but managed only to bang his shoulder painfully against a rock. The alien burst out into the open and started to drag Peter toward a nearby gully. But the wind screamed as though it had been waiting for them, and slapped them to the ground like an angry giant. Tumbling helplessly, they rolled in a tangle into the ravine.

Protected but bruised and deafened, they cowered there together. Squinting his eyes against the wind-blown grit, Peter poked his head up, wondering if he could crawl back into the cave —and gasped.

Brilliant light streamed from the cave entrance into the gloom. Lightning struck the far side of the plateau, then only a hundred metres distant, then fifty, and then—

Like the sun come to earth, energy arced from the clouds to the cave, ancillary bolts lancing from point to point of the rock formation. Peter felt his hair stirring. Muscles twitched in his face. The Altorian's fur stood on end. Tingling filled Peter's bones–

And then the bolt vanished.

Air rushed into the vacuum. Thunder rocked the mountain like an earthquake. Shrieking winds tore at the peak, sucking rocks and dirt into cyclonic funnels. Peter screamed involuntarily and buried his head in his arms, trying to block the sight and sound of what seemed the end of the world.

But the world survived, and so did he. The wind still howled, but it no longer deafened. Rain began, became a downpour. Lightning flashed, but the bolts seemed only harmless sparks after the vanished fury. Peter stared at the alien. Mud streaked the Altorian's blue fur, plastered flat by the rain. "What—"

"The *crraich*—the Daydark," the Altorian said in halting Terran.

Keltor's throat ached with the harsh alien sounds, but he wanted this incredibly foolish human to understand what had just happened—and what *could* have happened. What *should* have happened. Praise the One they still breathed!

"The Daydark—every three years comes. Your people not see yet. But we tell you, climb not mountain. Why you climb?"

"I—I wanted to get away from home."

Keltor didn't understand. Surely this whole planet was away from home, for the humans! He wanted to ask why they had left Earth to trouble *his* home, but couldn't frame the words. Instead he said roughly, "Almost you go far, far from home—we die, almost."

"Yeah, close call, wasn't it?" The human wiped rain from his eyes. "But I still don't understand. What was that beam of light? And what happened to the storm? The...Daydark. It's nothing like what it was."

"My people make cave—long, long ago. Turns *crraich* from death, to life. No kill—make grow." Abruptly Keltor spat an oath and gave up on the throat-tearing Terran. Let Peter do the struggling. "Ask the real question, hairless one!" he growled in true-speech. "Ask why you live! Ask why you deserve to! You insult my people. You treat us like animals. You despise my planet—my home. You break our laws. Ask, then, why I almost died to save you!"

Keltor broke off suddenly. Why *had* he climbed the mountain? Because his grandmother would be angry with him? That had been his answer earlier, but he knew it wasn't entirely true. He had saved the human because failing to try would have made him no better than the human. He had done it because People helped People—and the humans, however strange, however unlovable, however ugly, were still People—of a sort.

He stood, combing the worst of the mud from his arms with his claws. "We have a saying, Peter Campbell. Treat others as you wish them to treat you. I am sorry your race has not learned that lesson." He started toward the slope. He had upheld the honour of the People; he had saved Peter Campbell.

That didn't mean he had to like humans.

Peter did not follow for a long time. He sat in the rain, under a sky no longer midnight-black, but only grey and sodden. Not until true night approached did he get stiffly to his feet and hobble down the mountain.

Lia took the empty clay bowl from the table before her grandson knocked it to the floor. Keltor, head cradled in his arms, slept soundly amidst the remains of supper.

Rain pattered on the roof, falling from an overcast sky barely lit by the last of the hidden sun. Lia looked out at the dark bulk of Shield Mountain, then lit a candle. It would not need to burn long. Once she had cleared the table, both she and Keltor could go to bed.

She did not know Peter was near until he spoke from the doorway behind her. "Peace to this house," he said in heavily accented Altorian.

Lia dropped the bowl, then picked it up and turned, having smoothed the astonishment from her expression. "Peace to you," she said neutrally. "How may I serve?"

"I bring gift, respected one." From behind his back, Peter brought out a bouquet of flowers. Their petals glowed bright red in the candlelight. "From Shield Mountain."

Lia took them with wonder. "Beautiful!" She breathed deeply of their sweet scent. "But why...?"

She could not read human expressions well. What did that unlovely flush mean? "I...wish apologize. To you. For—on road. Dust?" He swept his hand through the air and made a growling noise. Lia backed up a step, then realized he was imitating a groundcar. She laughed, and at the strange sound the human also backed away. Quickly she swallowed her mirth, and bowed gravely instead.

"Apology accepted. And my thanks for the gift."

Peter's flush deepened. He hesitated in the doorway for a moment, looking at the sleeping Keltor, then said, "Walk in peace!" and almost ran away.

Lia glanced at her grandson. As the saying went, in the hands of the One, all things could be molded to beauty. She put the flowers in a bowl and returned to clearing the table.

Outside, the rain fell gently.

THE WIND

've always enjoyed ghost stories, but this is the only one I've ever written. (Don't tell anyone, but I actually wrote this on my employer's time while on a short-term contract filling in for the head of the advertorial department at the Regina Leader-Post, *who was on adoption leave. Some days, there just wasn't that much to do.) "The Wind" was published in* The Book of Dark Wisdom *in 2007.*

THE WIND ROSE IN THE NIGHT.

Carl Seitz woke to the moaning of the eaves and sleepily reached for the other side of the bed—only to come suddenly awake when all his reaching fingers touched was the smooth, cool flatness of an empty sheet. He'd slept alone for a month, but still, every night, the realization twisted his gut into a painful knot.

The window rattled, shuddering in its frame under the onslaught of the wind, as though something outside very much wanted to get in. Jennifer loved to listen to the wind, Carl thought. He could picture her lying beside him, could hear her rich alto. "Listen to it, Carl," she said. "It sounds so free, so alive...doesn't it make you want to just pack your bags and follow it, follow it wherever it goes?"

He rolled over and closed his eyes, but the dull ache of grief and the wind's rising howl would not let him sleep. He sat up and looked at the clock radio for the time, but its bright-red digits had vanished...and hadn't he left the radio playing?

The power must be out, he thought. He reached for his watch. Its lighted dial told him what he didn't really want to know: 2:47 a.m. From experience, he knew he wouldn't get any more sleep that night...and night, in Saskatchewan in mid-December, would stretch on another six interminable hours.

The window shook again. Carl pulled the covers over the cold tip of his nose. A deep chill pervaded the room, far more than even the northwest wind sharpening its claws on the outside walls could account for. Had the furnace gone out?

He'd better get up and check. There wasn't much point in staying in bed anyway.

He rolled out of the bed and knelt on the shag carpet, feeling for his clothes. Shivering, he pulled on the blue-and-red sweater Jennifer had knitted him for their first Christmas together, five years ago now. "It will keep you safe from the wind," she'd said. He fingered the sweater's herringbone weave. Those had been good days. Too bad they hadn't lasted.

The power failed often on the isolated old farm, so Carl always kept a flashlight in a drawer in the night-table. He fumbled it out and switched it on, and instantly the wind screamed so loudly he almost dropped the heavy light.

Something moved in the darkness at the edge of his vision. Heart pounding, he jerked the light around, lighting up one of the rose-covered curtains and he'd insisted on over Jennifer's objections. It shifted slightly as he watched.

Carl frowned. He'd have to check the storm windows, too. But first things first: the furnace.

He felt his way cautiously down the creaking stairs to the

kitchen, gripping the banister all the way, and paused there in the darkness. The old Formica-topped table and green vinyl chairs he'd refused to let Jennifer replace had belonged to his parents and were the ones he'd grown up with, as was the old round-cornered refrigerator. They were as familiar to him as his own face in the mirror.

But lately, whenever he came down here, all he could think of was Jennifer, sitting at the table that last stormy afternoon, her half-finished cup of tea long since gone cold, listening to the crying of the wind. And tonight, without Jennifer, without the friendly green lights of the stove and the microwave, without even the usual faint orange glow from the yard light outside, everything seemed strange, almost threatening. The refrigerator, its constant rattling hum silenced, loomed in the corner, a half-seen, oddly unfriendly presence. Even when he shone the light on it, he could not escape the feeling that something lurked just beyond the innocent white circle of light on the smooth metal door.

"So I'll clean out the moldy stuff tomorrow," he muttered. Despite the wind, the air in the kitchen somehow felt as stifling and still as the air in the bedroom had been cold and draughty. His words sounded dull and lifeless to his own ears, and he clamped his mouth shut.

Too much imagination, he thought. I've always had too much imagination. Mama always said so. Too much imagination.

Especially where Jennifer was concerned. He'd always found it all too easy to imagine what Jennifer might be doing while he was away in Regina. She never wanted to come with him. He'd be sitting in the casino or a bar, surrounded by people laughing and enjoying themselves, but all he could think about was Jennifer, all alone in this old house...until finally he'd begun to think that maybe she wasn't alone. Maybe she stayed home because she knew she wouldn't be alone.

And now she was gone, and he was alone.

Maybe a time would come when her leaving would no longer

haunt him, but tonight, with the house trembling and creaking in the freezing embrace of the wind she'd loved so much, tonight was not that time.

Especially not when he still had to go down into the basement.

Maybe that was why the kitchen seemed threatening this evening. It wasn't really the kitchen he dreaded at all, but the basement. As a child, he'd had recurring nightmares about that basement, ever since the day his mother had sent him down to fetch a jar of saskatoon jam. He'd reached up to get it, brushed through a sticky web, and yanked back his hand to find a fat brown spider clinging to it, a spider that had run up his arm, into his hair...he shuddered even now, remembering. Ever since, the basement's water-stained concrete walls and floor, its musty smells, its root-ends and beetles and cockroaches, had given him the willies.

He and Jennifer had talked about renovating it, making it into a shiny, fully finished basement like new houses had, a basement that could be a cool retreat during the heat of summer and a private guest apartment at Christmas. But all they'd ever done was talk, and nothing had been done by the time their talking turned to arguing, and shortly after that they'd stopped talking at all, and shortly after that...after that, Jennifer was gone, and it was too late. He hadn't gone down in the basement since that last time they went down...together.

In any event, no one would be visiting Carl for Christmas; his parents were dead, his brothers and sister lived in Toronto and Vancouver and Edmonton and didn't much like him anyway, and Jennifer's parents couldn't bear to look at him, now that she was gone. He knew they blamed him for her disappearance, and maybe it was partly his fault, but it was Jennifer's fault, too, what had happened.

He shook his head. None of this was getting the furnace fixed. He was just delaying the inevitable.

He opened the basement door. The wind screamed, the

kitchen door rattled on its hinges, and cold air blasted through around his feet. Jeez, I'm going to have to get the back door fixed, too, he thought, and let his annoyance start him down the stairs.

He was halfway down when the basement door slammed shut with a sound like a shotgun blast. Startled, he snapped his head around. His bare foot slipped off the step, the hand holding the flashlight jerked up, the flashlight described a glittering arc, crashed against the cement floor below and went out, and he half-slid, half-tumbled after it. During the fall, which seemed to take both forever and no time at all, he heard a sound like green beans being snapped by Jennifer's fingers; then he lay on cold concrete in absolute darkness, his ears ringing.

Something warm trickled down his face; he tried to raise his left hand to it, but his arm didn't want to work; it felt numb and somehow...misshapen.

It's broken, Carl thought. Of all the stupid...

And I'm bleeding. The thought seemed to come from within a deep fog. Shock, he thought. I'm in shock. I've got to get upstairs. Call an ambulance.

He tried to stand, using his good arm to lever himself up, but a wave of nausea slammed him back to the concrete, and turning his head, he retched out the sour remnants of his late-night snack of microwave pizza. His head spun. There was no way he could stand, much less walk...but maybe, just maybe, he could crawl.

He tried getting to his hands and knees, almost fell on his face when his hand slipped in the still-warm slime of his own vomit—which made him retch again, spitting up foul-tasting bile—but finally, coughing and spitting, was able to crawl slowly toward the stairs...

...or where he thought the stairs should be. He should have touched them, or the wall, at once; instead, his reaching fingers felt nothing but the smooth concrete floor. Confused, he crawled on—and then touched something that made him snatch back his fingers.

Not a spider, this time, but something far worse...broken pieces of concrete the size of his fist, and beyond that, cold, damp earth, solid to the touch, earth that had been tamped down hard, as hard as repeated heavy blows from a shovel could make it.

The shock cleared Carl's head. He knew where he was now, all right: the farthest corner of the basement, right up against the outside wall, not far from the root cellar, a separate room with both a door into the basement and steps leading up to the outside.

Careful not to touch the packed earth again, Carl felt his way along the broken edge of the floor until he came to the wall. Then, reaching up with his right hand, he found an electrical cable, strung from through rusted metal hoops in the crumbling concrete. As he pulled himself upright, a breath of cold air against the back of his neck made goose bumps race down his body. Damn, he thought, in inane counterpoint to the growing, throbbing pain in his arm. There's even a draft down here. The old place is falling apart.

Now he felt along the wall for the door to the root cellar—and felt, first, something made of cloth, hung over the electrical cable. For a moment he twisted the cloth in his fingers, uncomprehending—then jerked his hand back, gasping, his heart suddenly pounding, each thumping beat stabbing agony through his arm.

Jennifer's—Jennifer's cotton dress—even in the dark he recognized the feel, from the last time—God, how could he ever forget the feel of her dress from the last time he'd touched her? But it couldn't be here, it couldn't, not when she was gone. Not when she'd been wearing the dress on the night she...he...

The breath of cold air came again, curling around the base of his neck, flowing under his chin, caressing his face like a hand...

...like Jennifer's hand, the last time she touched him, as she reached up, not to strike him, as he expected, but as if saying a sad, disappointed good-bye to all their hopes, all their dreams, all the happiness they'd once promised to bring to each other.

The wind howled. The cold touch of air somehow seemed to

slip inside his clothes, touching him gently, intimately, like a lover, like Jennifer...

...and then he screamed, as the caress suddenly became as cold and sharp as a knife. Pain slashed across his chest like fingernails, and terror followed after, as, in the absolute silence that followed his scream, a moment in which even the wind died away, a voice in the darkness said, clearly and coldly and utterly calm, "Carl." And the voice...the voice was Jennifer's.

He screamed again, a wordless howl, and, pain forgotten, scrabbled along the wall for the door to the root cellar. He found it, tugged at it, screamed curses at it when it wouldn't open, and then when it did, so suddenly he fell, crawled back toward it, sobbing and panting.

Inside, he pulled himself up, jars of pickles and preserves crashing heedlessly around him. More of Jennifer's work, those jars; those times he'd been gone, she'd always said she was making preserves, or knitting, or painting, or singing duets with the wind, but he'd never believed her—how could he believe her? She was too perfect, too beautiful, he knew how men looked at her—the same way he'd looked at her—knew, knew they had to be coming here when he was away, had pictured their hands on her, their lips, their naked bodies entwined with hers in their bed, his and Jennifer's bed, and he hadn't been able to stand it anymore. He'd had to put a stop to it—had to. And he had. And Jennifer had gone away.

Forever.

He stepped forward, and broken glass from one of the jars he'd pulled down stabbed his bare foot. Spilled brine and vinegar seared the wound and brought him to his knees, where more glass ripped through his jeans, cutting to the bone. But he crawled forward anyway on his knees and right hand, moaning and sobbing, because he had to get away, away from that dress, hung impossibly on the wall, away from that tamped-down earth in the corner of the basement, away from that ice-cold touch, away, most of all, from that voice, that voice he'd loved, cherished...and finally decided to make his, and no one else's, forever.

His lacerated hand found the wooden steps leading up to the outside cellar door at the same moment that the door leading into the basement slammed shut behind him.

The noise brought him back to his feet, his whole body now aflame with agony. He could feel blood running down his calves from his knees, could feel it sticky on his one usable hand, but it didn't matter. He was almost out of the house, now, almost up the steps and into the clean, cold wind. It called to him, promising to wash away these nightmares of his own making. Hallucinations, that's all, he told himself as he dizzily mounted the steps. Has to be. Hallucinations. Guilt. That's all. But I shouldn't feel guilty. I shouldn't. I didn't mean to do it. It was her fault. She should have come with me. She should have stayed with me all the time. That's what she promised at our wedding, didn't she? She shouldn't have stayed here, alone, waiting for her lovers. And then she lied to me. She lied...she never admitted it, not even at the end, not even when I was holding her down, not even when my hands were on her throat, when she reached up and touched my face. Maybe if she'd admitted it, I wouldn't have...but she was lying to me. I knew she was lying. And I couldn't stand it. Couldn't stand to hear that beautiful voice telling me lies...couldn't stand to know that even our lovemaking was a lie.

So he'd put an end to the lies. He'd put an end to it all. And he shouldn't feel guilty. He shouldn't...

He bumped his head on the cellar door. Almost out. Almost safe, in the clean wind...and then he'd leave. He'd sell the farm. Start a new life. Lose himself in the city, far away from this house, and the basement, and the tamped-down patch of earth in the corner. Jennifer wouldn't follow him to the city. She'd stay behind.

She always had.

The wind died away again outside. He found himself holding

his breath, listening. Of course it had all been his imagination, so he wouldn't hear...

"Stay with me," Jennifer whispered in the dark. "Don't leave me alone with the wind, Carl. Stay here with me. Stay...forever." And this time there could be no mistaking the ice-cold touch of her hand in the dark...

Terror seized his breath in an iron-like grip, holding it in his throat; then released it in a scream that boiled up from his guts and exploded out into the cold air. The wind, suddenly stronger than ever, echoed him.

He thrust desperately up at the heavy cellar door with his one good arm. As the door lifted, the wind caught it, flinging it open. Carl plunged upward, frantic to escape—and the wind swirled, seized the door as it bounced from the force of its opening, and threw it closed again. Carl had one brief, horrifying moment to realize what was about to happen, then the iron-bound oak slammed down, fracturing his skull, snapping his neck, and smashing him down into the darkness of the root cellar, where, impaled on the broken glass of Jennifer's last preserves, his blood mingled with vinegar, brine, and syrup.

The wind died. In the kitchen, the refrigerator came to life, rattling and humming as it had for 40 years. Upstairs, red lights glowed on the clock radio, and a voice spoke in the stillness.

"It's a beautiful winter's night, folks; cold, clear and not a breath of wind. It's a night made for lovers, so cuddle close. Maybe you can make it last forever..."

LOST IN TRANSLATION

Those familiar with my novels may recognize this title. Published in 1994 in the first issue of the late, lamented science-fiction magazine TransVersion, *this story became the basis for my novel of the same name, which, as I recounted earlier, was first published by Five Star in library-bound hardcover and then picked up by DAW Books in paperback, launching my career as a DAW author. So you can understand why I have a soft spot in my heart for this tale...*

KATY HELD ON TO MAMA WITH ONE HAND and clutched a chocolate ice cream cone with the other. Mama and Daddy talked and laughed and Katy smiled, feeling their laughter tickling her inside, with none of the ache she felt when they were unhappy. And around the laughter-tickle was the warm glow of love—lots and lots of love. That she could always feel.

Behind her waddled a fat little synthibear, piping, "Wait for me, Katy!", and Katy kept turning around and saying, "Hurry up, bear!", and laughing as its chubby stuffed legs churned away, though it never got any closer. Katy had won it at the fair, in a shooting gallery. Even though she hadn't hit a single hologram the woman had called her a winner and given it to her, and that had made the whole day perfect, because the one thing she had really, really wanted for her sixth birthday was a synthibear, and now she had it! And she had ridden all the rides and eaten cotton candy and popcorn and zipmud, and the stars were shining overhead and Hardluck IV's three moons were bright and full, and Katy knew she was the happiest girl in the galaxy.

But just as they left the fairground, the sky went all ripply and was suddenly full of big silvery things. Katy's father said a bad word and scooped her up and grabbed her mother's hand and started running, and Katy felt that her parents were scared and that scared her, too, and she started to cry, and behind her the synthibear kept squeaking, "Come back, Katy, come back, Katy, come back..." until she couldn't hear it anymore, and that made her cry even harder.

All around people shouted and screamed and ran every which way, and a siren wailed from Government House, and Katy heard her father praying, almost sobbing, and she got so scared she couldn't even cry any more.

They ran down their own street, toward their own house, but now other things filled the sky, black, with wings, and one came right over their heads, high up, except suddenly it wasn't, it got really big really fast, and it had red glittering eyes and big white teeth and it carried something long and thin in its claws, and now they were on their porch and Katy's father shoved her through the front door so hard she tumbled over and over and hit her head and started crying again, and she scrambled up to run back to her parents, only something flashed really bright just outside the door and her parents fell down funny and she couldn't feel their love any more—

≈

Kathryn jerked upright, gasping, and slapped on the lamp, and the winged shapes crowding around her vanished into the pale blue walls of her cabin on the Geneva. Still half caught in sleep, she staggered to her feet. How could she face a S'sinn? How could she Translate? Karak would have to see reason, find somebody else. She'd—

Halfway to her comp terminal, she remembered. She'd already made that call. She sank back onto the mattress. No other suitable Translator was close enough, Karak had said, and Commonwealth Central insisted negotiations must proceed now. He knew how she felt about the S'sinn, but this was an emergency. He was sorry, but nothing could be done.

Kathryn pulled her knees up to her chest. Of course, the Fairholm/Kisradik situation was critical. Several bloody incidents had left the humans, the S'sinn, and their respective allies angry and nervous. Commonwealth Central had worked a miracle just getting the two sides to talk. "You must do your best, for the Guild, and for the Commonwealth," Karak had said, his beaked, tentacle-encircled face unreadable to her and the light years between them precluding the empathic link they would normally have shared. Then he had broken the connection.

There's no choice, she thought bleakly. No choice but another war. Remember what the last one cost. Remember what it cost you.

Katy sat, every day, in exactly the same place in the big upstairs playroom of the orphanage. She ate, and went to the bathroom, and dressed herself; but she never spoke, never played, never cried, even after the bad dreams. She just stared out the window at Earth's strange blue sky.

She saw the black van pull up to the curb and settle to the ground. She saw the alien emerge in its blue suit and shiny silver backpack and helmet. Any other child would have run to tell the others. But Katy didn't move, even when the stairs to the playroom creaked and Mrs. Spencer said, "Katy? There's some—someone here to see you."

Katy looked back at the sky. Mrs. Spencer had said once she was waiting for her parents, but Katy knew they would never come back, because there was a hole in her heart where their love had been, a hole that could never be filled, a hole into which her mind kept swirling aimlessly, like water going down a black drain. She stared out the window because nothing mattered any more.

The floorboards groaned, and a heavy hand touched her head. "Mrs. Spencer," said a thick, bubbly voice, "this child is suffering bondcut."

"Nonsense! She's perfectly healthy."

"Bondcut is not a disease; it is the trauma empaths suffer when someone with whom they were closely linked dies abruptly."

"Empaths? Katy's not—"

"This child must come with me. You have seen my authorization."

"But she's not well! She needs—"

"What she needs, Mrs. Spencer, is the company of fellow empaths, in the Guild of Translators. The Commonwealth Treaty allows us to draft any—"

"You mean kidnap!"

"—any individual who shows possibility as a Translator. If you will be so good as to pack her things—"

As they left, Mrs. Spencer remarked loudly to Mr. Piwarski that if Katy hadn't been happy in the orphanage with other children, she certainly wouldn't be happy God-knew-where with only monsters for company...

But Katy went quietly with the alien. She wasn't brave; she just didn't care. About anything.

∼

The Guild of Translators changed that. It healed the wound left by her parent's death. It became her family. And it gave her a purpose: to serve the Commonwealth, a bizarre association of disparate races held together only a love of profitable trade. Those races had ended the Earth-S'sinn war when it began to disrupt commerce, and brought Earth into the Commonwealth; but in time-honoured human fashion, one war had sown the seeds of another. The reptilian Hasshingu-Issk and the fiery, bird-like "elves" of Orris had themselves suffered at the claws of the S'sinn in ages past, and sided with Earth in the current dispute over who had first claim to newly discovered (and resource-rich) Fairholm/Kisradik. The Aza—or at least two of their principal Swarms—sided with the S'sinn, as did the water-breathers of Ithkar, Karak's homeworld. Only the slow-moving, slug-like dwellers of the planet humans called Swampworld remained neutral; no doubt they were merely waiting to see how things fell out before choosing sides.

No outside force would end this war, if war came; the Commonwealth would die, and with dimspace leaps allowing surprise attacks on any planet at any time, all seven civilizations might die with it.

Fear of such an unwinnable war, historians held, was all that made the Commonwealth possible. Yet still the Seven Races drifted toward conflict—or maybe, in the case of humans and S'sinn, sought it. These negotiations would decide the future. Full Translation was essential.

If Kathryn could bring herself to provide it.

She went into the bathroom and splashed cold water on her face. She might as well start what would be a very long day, the day she arrived at the place she least wanted to be in all the galaxy: the home of the race that had killed her parents.

~

The humans' footsteps on the polished marble echoed back from walls so far away they could only be dimly guessed at. Spidery silver columns soared from the floor to the haze-hidden roof, and S'sinn were everywhere—hanging from struts, perched on platforms, gliding from balcony to balcony on black leathery wings. A thousand gleaming red eyes watched the humans approach the dais at the vast hall's centre. And it was cold. Kathryn, arms bare in her blue Translator's uniform, shivered as goose bumps raced over her body. She clutched the small metal case in her right hand a little tighter, remembering the last time the S'sinn had darkened her sky.

"These negotiations were to be private!" Ambassador Matthews complained.

"They are," Kathryn said. The vast weight of hostility she sensed from the gathered S'sinn made her head ache, and the dais seemed no closer. "A white-noise curtain will ensure no one overhears."

"But all these—people—will be watching." Matthews gestured distastefully at the hall. "I don't call that private."

"The S'sinn have no concept of visual privacy." Kathryn had only met the Ambassador three hours before, when her shuttle landed, and she detested him already. Slim, fiftyish, with carefully combed steel-grey hair, he was the very model of a modern elder statesman—and apparently a complete fool. Hadn't he done any homework? Surely the man sent by Earth to prevent a war could have spent a few hours QuickLearning!

Unless Earth wanted another war...and if Earth had chosen Matthews with that in mind, what if they'd also chosen her? Could they know about her fear and loathing of the S'sinn, know that that would be the first thing the S'sinn Translator would feel when they Linked? Did they hope that in itself might derail the negotiations?

She rubbed the back of her neck. Paranoia! The Guild didn't work for Earth, it worked for the Commonwealth—for all Seven

Races. Its reputation depended on its neutrality, its pledge—her pledge—that Translation would be objective, that every shade of meaning, every emotional nuance, would be perfectly and impartially reproduced. "I renounce all ties to my home planet and species," the Oath ran. "I am no longer human, but Translator. I belong to no race, but am kin to all..."

"...and I serve the good of all, without bias or prejudice. I surrender my will freely, that others may speak through me. I make this Oath in the presence of Seven Races, by all the Races hold holy. May they judge me if I prove false." Kathryn had never been religious, but that last phrase seemed to echo in her mind, underscoring the seriousness of her commitment—that and the lead-like blanket of solemnity pressing down on her mind from the Seven Witnesses surrounding her in the Guildhall.

Karak's round, dead-black eyes peered at her through the heavy glass of his huge aquarium, his tentacles weaving a slow pattern. A Swampworlder pulsated dreamily in thicker, darker liquid in the tank next to him. Ten metres away, but still too close, a brown-furred S'sinn rested on a padded wooden rack. Beside him hovered a single Aza drone, wings humming, its four golden eyes sharing all with the Swarm. On her left stood three more winged figures, humanoid, but beaked and feathered, a mated trio of Orrisian elves. Behind her...but she didn't want to look at Jim Ornawka just then. Instead she focused on the final two Witnesses, the Hasshingu-Issk. One wore the bright green armband of a Master, vivid against his black scales; the other wore Medic's blue. While the Master watched with unblinking, slit-pupilled yellow eyes, the Medic wheeled forward a metal container. Opening it released a sharp, salty smell that mingled with his own sulphurous scent, stinging Kathryn's nostrils.

She knew what she would see, but still she flinched: the slowly writhing ropy grey mass nestled in the pink nutrient fluid pushed ancient primate "snake!" buttons. But mere squeamishness wouldn't keep her from this climax of ten years of training. At the Medic's nod, she lowered her hand into the case.

At first nothing happened. But slowly tingling spread through her hand, which grew peculiarly heavy; and, as the minutes passed, the squirming tissue in the case diminished. The tingling moved up her arm, into her shoulder, like an internal itch she could not scratch, but she held perfectly still, though silent tears ran down her cheeks. The Witnesses watched impassively.

Just when she thought she couldn't stand the horrible crawling under her skin one minute longer, it stopped.

The container was empty.

Sound rumbled around the room as each Witness confirmed that Kathryn had freely accepted what the humans called The Beast. Behind her, Jim said, "Amen."

Kathryn felt vaguely disappointed. She had just allowed into her body a genetically engineered artificial life form, a universal nervous system interface designed to augment her own natural empathic powers by allowing her to connect directly with the nervous system of any of the Seven Races, and all she had felt was an unscratchable itch.

But now the Master came forward. He opened a small case of bluish metal, revealing two very different syringes and a coil of silvery cord. The Master took out the smaller syringe and proffered it to Kathryn, who took it from his claws, embarrassed by her trembling fingers. Then the Master took out the other syringe, and plunged its dagger-sized needle into his thigh, his eyes never wavering from Kathryn's face. Kathryn, only too aware of the fear she was broadcasting to the Witnesses, put her own syringe against her bare upper arm and pulled the trigger.

The liquid hissed into her bloodstream. She felt only a slight sting and a faint warmth, but she knew that inside her chemicals were programming The Beast, preparing her for—

This. The Master uncoiled the silvery cord and touched one end to a matching patch behind his barely visible ear. It clung there as he held out the other end to her.

Kathryn knew some Guild trainees backed out even at this point. Many served faithfully in non-Translation duties. To withdraw would not shame her; it would simply prove she wasn't suited to be a Translator. You needed utter confidence in yourself to survive First Translation unscathed. Doubt could be fatal...

Breathing a prayer to One she wasn't even sure she believed in, Kathryn took the cord and touched it to the surgically implanted interface behind her own ear.

Humans talked of sex as the joining of two people. The night before...the young man behind her...but that union had been nothing compared to this!

She had never been to the Hasshingu-Issk homeworld, but in an instant, it surrounded her in all its sun-drenched beauty. She rolled on a baking-hot rock with her mate, fought in the Arena of God for the glory of the Toothed One, ripped out the throat of an issi'ki she had chased for kilometres across a lava plain. She knew the names of the Five Moons and the Cities of the Dead; she shed her skin and burrowed in ecstasy in the cooling mud; she understood why imperfect hatchlings had to be eaten and knew that she could explain that custom to the weakling Races that called it barbaric, if only she could...

...could...

...if only she could remember how! She panicked, her mind thrashing in the welter of overwhelming alien images. She was not Hasshingu-Issk, she was human, and she was lost, lost, lost...

...then she felt the Master lifting her dolphin-like out of the swirling depths, helping her shed him like he shed his skin, until they were linked, but separate; one, but two; a single organism with two minds, two mouths—two languages.

Kathryn opened her eyes and looked around at Jim for the first time. Those sweaty, exciting moments they had shared meant nothing now. This was what she had lived for, trained for, longed for.

The hole in her heart had been boarded over by a decade of empathic help; Jim had made her forget it for the briefest moment; but now, in this glorious union with her Hasshingu-Issk comrade/friend/lover, that hole was filled.

~

Kathryn strove to keep her walk steady, her face impassive. She had since Translated with Ava, Orrisian, Ithkarite and Swampworlder. Each time had been even better, even more soul-healing. But now...

...now she had to join with a S'sinn.

The Translation case wasn't the only baggage she carried to the dais.

The round platform bore a table and chairs for the humans and a chest- high podium and resting racks for the S'sinn. Kathryn stepped up onto the platform and waited while Matthews and his two aides took their places at the table. One S'sinn, already in her rack, watched them in silence. Three others stood just behind her.

Each S'sinn wore only a broad metal collar, embossed with a sign. The female on the rack, with the spiral crossed by a lightning bolt, was the Flight Leader—Matthews's opposite number. The other two, male and female, would be aides/bodyguards. Their collars bore spirals without the lightning bolt and they stood with their bat-like wings outstretched to show the insignia repeated in gold leaf on the black, leathery membrane. The fourth S'sinn's wings remained folded. His collar bore a triangle inside a circle inside a square—the same symbol Kathryn wore over her left breast.

Her head throbbed as she blocked the S'sinn Translator's attempt to establish a preliminary empathic link. By Guild etiquette that was unforgivably rude, but he'd learn soon enough what was in her mind. She stepped to the centre of the dais, set her case on the floor, opened it and took out the injector. Her hands trembled as much as they had at her First Translation.

The S'sinn Translator joined her with his own case. His scent, warm and musky, sent her mind flashing back to that horrible moment when the S'sinn warrior had stooped out of the sky above her parents. The warrior's scent had been rank, stronger, but at base the same alien, predatory smell.

Silently reciting the Oath, "I belong to no race, but am kin to all," she met the S'sinn's ruby-red gaze. The syringe in his clawed hand was empty. His eyes slid down to the still-full injector she held, then back to her face. Mouth so dry she couldn't even swallow, she pressed the injector to her shoulder.

Her hand still trembled as she returned the injector to its case. Behind her Matthews stirred and muttered something, but Kathryn kept her eyes on the S'sinn, her heart pounding painfully. The Programming meant nothing without the Link. She could still turn around, tell Matthews she couldn't do it, tell him he'd have to delay the negotiations, wait for another Translator...

The S'sinn lifted the cord from his case. He proffered her one end, and she took it hesitantly. With his eyes locked on hers, he touched his end of the cord to the tiny silvery patch beneath his sharply pointed left ear. Then he waited.

If she accepted the Link, there'd be no more hiding how she felt...

Matthews cleared his throat. "Translator Bircher—"

"Quiet!" she snapped. The Guild had no need to suffer fools, even important fools. Impelled by irritation, she firmly touched the cord to the patch under her own ear, and—

—Linked.

∾

Air lifted Jarrikk over the jagged peaks, twin hearts pounding. Behind him the humans rode the winds clumsily on black plastic wings, driven by raucous, smoking engines, graceless, ugly—but gaining, gaining all the time. He could hear their braying laughter. Desperately he sideslipped, then dove toward the thin white ribbon of river below him. Towering rock walls seemed to leap upward at him.

The humans' laughter changed to angry shouts. A beam slashed by on his left, another on his right. He was almost safe, almost into the gorge where the clumsy humans could never hope to—

Agony lanced his left wing. The stench of burning hair and flesh filled his nostrils, then his wing collapsed, the membrane ripping. He flailed out of control, fluttering down and down until he hit the river in a geyser of spray and pain...

Kathryn twisted her mind, fighting for self, as the S'sinn's deep-seated trauma threatened to overpower her. She could smell burning flesh and feel pain in body parts she didn't even have.

Her control firmed at last, and so did Jarrikk's. He had absorbed her nightmare, as she had absorbed his—and the Link had held. They opened their eyes, and after one look at each other, turned to their respective delegates.

"Begin," they said in unison.

The S'sinn reeled off a long list of grievances dating back to the War. Their words, inflections and body language Kathryn heard, saw and understood through Jarrikk's eyes, and Translated through her human flesh. She faced the humans with a sneer in her voice and a challenge in her stance, the closest human equivalents to the S'sinn's haughty contempt.

The humans responded with their own list, from the original S'sinn attack which they claimed had triggered the War (they didn't mention the half-dozen curious young S'sinn shot out of the sky before that by humans unaware they were sentient) to "this most recent outrage—landing colonists on a world already inhabited by humans" (they didn't mention that the two colonization attempts occurred simultaneously).

Charge and counter-charge flew, perfectly communicated by Kathryn and Jarrikk, formed by the Link into a flesh-and-blood computer with no concern about the belligerent content of the translated messages. At the end of four bitter hours, in the middle of one of Matthews's harangues, the timed-release antidote to the Programming severed the Link. Kathryn staggered as she lost contact with Jarrikk, feeling for a moment as if half of herself had suddenly died. She took a deep breath, pulled the Link cord free and stopped Matthews in mid-shout. "I'm sorry, Mr. Ambassador, but this session is ended."

Matthews glared at her, glared at the S'sinn, then bowed stiffly, gathered his papers and led his aides off the platform and out of the hall, footsteps clattering. The S'sinn stalked off in the other direction, showing their contempt by staying on the ground, although Kathryn knew Matthews would never realize it unless she told him. She shivered, chilled through and bone weary, and rubbed her throbbing temples. "I love being a Translator," she muttered.

Jarrikk cocked his head at her. Though the Link was gone, her inborn empathic ability remained, and she felt his own weariness and a concern that warmed her. "Sleep well, friend," she signed to him in guildtalk. "Until tomorrow."

"Tomorrow," he signed back. "Fly safely in this night's dreams." He closed and locked his case and trudged after the other delegates—and Kathryn knew that he stayed on the ground not from contempt, but because of that tragic boyhood contact with humans.

She picked up her case and turned to go—and stopped, feeling the red gaze of the hundreds of watching S'sinn. Instinct urged her to run for the distant exit; but mindful of the Guild's reputation, she walked slowly and deliberately across the marble floor.

In the human quarters, Matthews greeted her coldly. No surprise; Translators' own species often could not separate them from the message they conveyed so perfectly. Matthews undoubtedly thought of her as a near-traitor; but then, she thought of him as an absolute idiot, so they were more than even. He didn't even realize their windowless rooms were another deliberate insult; only the S'sinn's most contemptible criminals were locked up without a view of the sky.

She gladly retired right after supper and settled into bed. But sleep eluded her; what she had seen in Jarrikk's mind kept replaying in her head.

He had been a child on the planet where the War began. Linked, experiencing his memories, she had shared his horror at the humans' brutal murder of his friends, his joy when the monsters were driven away and the Supreme Flight Leader called for war, his fierce pleasure at the news of each subsequent victory—including the destruction of the colony on the planet humans called Hardluck IV. With him, she had agonized as the humans struck back—and then shared his shame and anger when the Commonwealth stepped in, and his fury when the humans were allowed to return to his own planet, making it the only jointly inhabited world. In youthful defiance, he had sneaked across the heavily patrolled border—and suffered for it. The humans would have killed him if a S'sinn border patrol hadn't seen the incident and demanded his return under the Commonwealth treaty.

If the Guild had not discovered his empathic talent and taken him for their own, he still would have died—at his own hand. The S'sinn expected no less of the flightless. He had as much reason to hate humans as Kathryn had to hate the S'sinn. Today, both had Linked, for the first time, with the creatures of their nightmares— and overcome those nightmares to work together, proof, if only those they were Translating for could see it, that humans and S'sinn need not be enemies.

But the blind fools couldn't see it. To the S'sinn the humans were brutal child-killers and to the humans the S'sinn were hideous bat-like monsters, and neither could wait to rid the galaxy of the other.

Kathryn's nightmare that night was Jarrikk's.

∼

As she severed the Link at the end of the following day's acrimonious session, Kathryn felt sick, knowing that the next morning there would be only one thing to Translate: the declaration of war —war, which had slain her parents and crippled Jarrikk. And they could do nothing; nothing but Translate—

Or could they? Kathryn's mouth went dry. The idea that had just come to her, unbidden, would violate her Oath. It could mean expulsion from the Guild, the loss of a second family...

...but it just might stop a war. She touched Jarrikk's wing before he could leave the dais. He turned his ruby eyes on her, and she sensed his puzzlement. "We need private talk," she signed. "Where...?"

For a moment he regarded her, puzzlement growing; then he opened and closed his wings, a gesture equivalent to a human shrug, and signed, "Follow."

As they crossed the floor the hostility of the gathered S'sinn increased tenfold. Kathryn felt like a mouse at an owl convention, but kept her even pace. Jarrikk could move no faster in any event.

He led her through a ten-meter-high arch into a long hall with smaller arches leading off at three levels. They passed through the third ground-floor portal on the right into a high-ceilinged, airy room with enormous, glassless windows opening onto the gardens outside the Hall of the Flock. Rough-woven tapestries hung from the other three walls above padded resting-racks of polished, multicoloured woods, and fragrant bluish vapour rose from a censer over the comp terminal. "Your home?" Kathryn signed.

"Yes."

"Beautiful."

"Thank you." Jarrikk hesitated, then signed, "You need not use guildtalk. Here, no one will overhear, and I understand your tongue."

"You do? But how—" Kathryn stopped as Jarrikk's boyhood memories welled up in her. He had learned the humans' throat-hurting language to spy on them. He could not speak it, but he understood it very well indeed.

That would make her task simpler. Guildtalk was marvellously flexible, as it had to be to serve all four semi-humanoid Races, but it had never been intended to convey the idea she had in mind.

Jarrikk watched her with the natural stillness of a waiting predator. What if he reported her to the Guild, had her removed?

Then war would come anyway, and she would have lost nothing. The Guild would die with the Commonwealth.

Hesitantly she began. "We work well together."

"Agreed," he signed.

"Our negotiators do not."

She felt his grim amusement. "No."

"They do not want peace." That was her first dangerous statement; such speculation was against Guild rules. She waited for Jarrikk's reaction.

"Agreed," he signed after a moment. She sensed wariness.

"Both sides must want peace if we are to avoid war."

Self-evident, but Jarrikk replied slowly. "Agreed."

"So—we need new negotiators."

No hesitation this time—complete denial. "We have no say. Governments choose."

"Perhaps they chose badly." Suddenly she could no longer read his emotion: he was blocking. She rushed on. "We serve the Guild.

The Guild serves the Commonwealth. War will destroy Commonwealth and Guild. Our loyalty to the Guild demands we prevent that."

A long pause. "We can do nothing."

"We can!" she insisted. Then she hesitated, suddenly afraid to make the final statement. In guildtalk it would have been impossible; even saying it felt—wrong. "We can fake the Link."

Jarrikk's red eyes widened and he backed away from her, growling. "No!" He let her feel his denial full-force.

"We must!" She countered with determination. "We must negotiate for them. We must find the compromise they will not. We must—"

"Lie! Break Oath! Dishonour Guild! Dishonour selves! Ruin everything!"

"War will destroy the Guild, destroy honour, destroy everything!" Kathryn moved after him. "War killed my parents." She pointed to his scarred, useless wing. "War made you walk!"

Backed into the corner, Jarrikk turned his head away, looked out through the window. A dozen S'sinn soared past. He watched them out of sight, then signed, very slowly, "Dangerous. You cannot know what will happen. Without Programming..."

"I know what will happen if war comes. And so do you."

Jarrikk looked at his crippled left wing, then at her. She felt his bitter agreement. "Yes," he signed. "Yes."

Kathryn blocked him then, trying too late to hide her sudden surge of fear. She felt Jarrikk's agreement waver. Hurriedly she said, "I'll prepare a proposal and send it to you before the morning session," and turned toward the door, barely catching his farewell message from the corner of her eye:

"May the Hunter of Worlds preserve us."

Back in her own quarters, Kathryn sat at the computer, trying to compose her thoughts, to recall all she had learned of Commonwealth law and treaty and the current dispute. They would need a truly workable compromise to pull this off, and she had only a few hours...

Yet her mind kept going back to the discussion with Jarrikk, and to another argument very much like it she'd had with Jim Ornawka, just before she left on the mission that had been aborted to send her here. Jim had come into her room while she was packing. No surprise there; he had persistently pursued her since that night before First Translation. She'd told him that she wanted to concentrate on being a Translator, that sex was part of her old self. It hadn't stopped him.

But the approach Jim had used that last time had been... different. "I just thought you might want something human to remember before spending six months alone with aliens," he'd said, running his finger down her arm.

Kathryn pulled away. "The Oath says—"

"I know, I know. 'I renounce all species ties...' Don't be too quick to take those words to heart, Katy. 'Species ties' are going to be pretty important if this Fairholm business blows up."

Shocked, she could only stare at him.

"Oh, don't get holier-than-thou." He looked hard into her eyes. "If war comes, will you side with aliens against your own kin?"

"They're our kin, too!"

"Even S'sinn?"

She tried desperately to read his emotions, then, and failed; he was blocking. Somehow, though, she knew her own reaction was nakedly obvious.

"Thought so," Jim had said, and left her, shaken and shamed. She'd slammed her suitcase shut and stalked out of the room that had been her home for half her life without even looking back. *I'm better than that,* she remembered thinking. *I meant my Oath.*

And now that same determination to treat aliens as her kin, as the Oath demanded, was leading her to break that Oath.

She wondered what Jim would have said.

She turned back to her computer, but she'd only been working for an hour when her terminal beeped, announcing a message. She punched "receive."

Words scrolled by. "Researched matter. Found following: 'Attempts to Link without Programming produce severe pain; one Orrisian volunteer suffered respiratory and circulatory arrest and narrowly escaped death. In all cases the Translator symbiote died, and volunteers required long periods of convalescence due to immune-system rejection of the symbiote dead tissue. All recovered, but were no longer able to function as Translators; their bodies rejected all attempts to introduce a new symbiote. Native empathic abilities survived, but augmentation became impossible.' Jarrikk."

Kathryn blanked the screen, then stared blindly at the windowless wall. Pain she could face—had faced, over and over—but the rest... "No longer able to function as Translators." It would be like bondcut all over again. A part of her would die.

But millions of other would die—fully—if she didn't take the risk. And Jarrikk didn't say where he'd gotten the information. Maybe he was having second thoughts, and was just trying to frighten her out of her scheme.

Well, he'd frightened her, all right—but not enough to make her quit. To prove to herself she meant that, she got up, took an empty Programming vial, filled it with distilled water, then coloured the liquid pale pink with a drop of blood from her finger. She placed it in her Translator's case, but stared at it a long time before slowly closing and latching the case and returning to her terminal.

Near dawn, when sleep could no longer be denied, she felt she had barely begun—but she could do no better. She had the computer translate the proposal and transmit it to Jarrikk, then fell fully clothed into bed and instant sleep.

Only seconds later, it seemed, someone knocked. "Duty calls, Translator Bircher," Matthews said through the door. "One hour. We're all anxious to conclude this."

I'll bet you are, Kathryn thought savagely. She splashed cold water on her face, surveyed herself in the mirror, shuddered, then returned to the computer to review her creation. Jarrikk had sent it back with a few eminently sensible changes. We make a good team, she thought as she read them—but if the information Jarrikk had sent her were true, she'd never Link with him, or anyone, again.

She cleared the computer and picked up her case. If Matthews had done the work she had just attempted, she would have held to her Oath. But from his actions she could almost believe war had been intended from the moment Earth colonized Fairholm/Kisradik.

At the door, she paused. If that were true, she was about to throw away her career, maybe her life, uselessly. Why should Earth accept a compromise if it truly wanted war?

Because Earth depends on its allies, she told herself, and they'll accept anything reasonable that preserves the Commonwealth. Even Matthews is enough of a diplomat to understand that.

She hoped.

The anger of the S'sinn packed into every recess of the Great Hall beat down on Kathryn like desert heat as she followed Matthews to the dais, but the air only felt colder. Jarrikk met her, and ritualistically they made their preparations. But when Kathryn pressed the injector to her arm, she felt nothing. The Beast inside her slumbered on. She took her end of the Link —and froze.

She could feel the ravenous attention of S'sinn and humans, could almost hear them saying, "Do it! Link! Give us war!"

She could. She could make some excuse, return to her quarters, inject the real Programming, and Translate perfectly, as her Oath demanded. War would come, but she would still be a Translator, still have that wonderful union with other races, the only thing that could fill the void left by her parents' deaths.

Her parents...they'd left Earth for Hardluck IV, dreaming of building a new and better world, only to have their dreams snuffed out by war. What she was about to do would destroy her dream just as surely—but maybe, just maybe, it would ensure that millions of others could keep theirs.

She pictured her father standing in her place, and her hesitation vanished. She touched the cord to the patch behind her ear.

Agony ripped her open, screamed through every nerve, as The Beast woke to alien, untranslatable signals. Kathryn's vision greyed and the world spun around her, roaring, but she clung grimly to consciousness, fighting for control, fighting to hide her suffering from Matthews, and gradually, oh-so-gradually, the pain subsided, leaving her nauseated but functioning—and, abruptly, terrified. She'd gone empathy-blind! She could sense nothing, not the hostility of the assembled S'sinn, not the worry of her Translation partner, not the impatience of Matthews. The symbiote inside her had died, and her own abilities with it!

Feeling blind, deaf and desperate, she nodded tersely to Jarrikk, and the S'sinn delegation began.

Kathryn heard only growling gibberish, but she began talking. "Upon consideration, the First Flight of S'sinndikk has realized that our mutual recriminations have been of little benefit to ourselves or to our allies. In the hope that these negotiations may yet produce a fruitful and lasting accommodation between us concerning the planet Fairholm/Kisradik, we propose the following compromise..."

Matthews heard her out, expressionless. Her inability to perceive his emotions unnerved her. How did non-empaths communicate? She might as well be talking to herself.

The S'sinn stopped, and hastily she concluded, "Do you have a response at this time?"

Matthews whispered to one of his aides, then said, "We will study your remarks and make a counter-proposal at our next session. Tomorrow morning?"

Jarrikk began speaking, and Kathryn held her breath. If he

Translated truly, as his Oath demanded, there would only be confusion on the part of the S'sinn—confusion and, very shortly, suspicion; suspicion that the human Translator had, unthinkably, lied. And the mere fact a Translator had lied could destroy the Guild and Commonwealth as thoroughly as any war...

Matthews frowned as the translation of his simple remark went on for an inordinate amount of time, but there had been similar differences before. Besides, Kathryn thought, what could he possibly suspect? Translators don't lie. Everyone knows that.

Another thought struck her, and she groaned inwardly. What would happen at the "next session" if she couldn't Translate?

One thing at a time. There might not even be another session. And if the S'sinn did agree to it, how was she to know, maimed as she was?

Jarrikk found a way. As the S'sinn finished speaking, he nodded—a human gesture meaningless to his own people. "Agreed," she told Matthews.

The delegates departed, and the galleries buzzed as the news spread among the S'sinn that negotiations would continue. Kathryn's knees buckled unexpectedly and she would have fallen if Jarrikk hadn't caught her. He gently tugged the Link free and she leaned against his broad, furry chest for a moment. "Thanks," she murmured, then, wary of how the crowd might react, straightened hurriedly. She knew Jarrikk wouldn't take it amiss; after two full sessions of Translation, they knew each other as well as anyone ever could know another person, better than she had ever known another human—certainly better than she had known Jim, whose image came to her unbidden, standing in her room, suggesting she might break her Oath...

Which she had. She shook her head, confused. "I'm blind," she told Jarrikk. He would know how she meant it.

"Very brave human," he signed. "Tomorrow both sides will present modifications to proposal, but I expect success."

"How?" Kathryn cried. "I can't Translate." A lump in her throat choked her; she swallowed angrily. She would not cry, not in self-pity; never!

"Please come to quarters?" Jarrikk cocked his head to one side, watching her.

Kathryn blinked. "Why?"

"Please. All will be explained."

How? she thought, but, "All right," she said.

In a way it was a relief not to feel the crowd's hostility as she walked with Jarrikk back to his sunny room. But when he ushered her through the arch, she stopped so suddenly he ran into her.

Karak's face looked out from the screen of Jarrikk's comp terminal.

"What—"

"Translator Bircher," said Karak. "I can hear you, but you are not in the visual pickup field."

She stayed put. "What's going on?"

"Translator Bircher, Translator Annette Mathieu is en route to S'sinndikk and will take your place in the morning session."

"Annette—" Kathryn stared at Karak, then suddenly turned furiously on Jarrikk. "You told him!"

He made no denial; simply stood, with inhuman stillness. She spun to face the terminal and strode into pickup range. "You said there were no other Translators near enough—"

"I said no suitable Translator was close enough. You were the ideal choice, therefore neither Translator Mathieu nor Translator Ornawka were suitable." Karak ignored Kathryn's glare. "The Council of Masters felt that if you and Jarrikk could overcome your mutual mistrust and successfully Link, it would demonstrate graphically the possibility—and need—of humans and S'sinn working together." He circled one tentacle. "It worked."

"It worked because I broke my Oath!"

"All unfolded as anticipated."

"Anticipated!" Kathryn's face flamed. "You expected me to break my Oath?"

"You did not break it," Karak said. "You upheld it. Your Oath states that all races are your kin. You kept your kin from destroying each other."

"But Translators can't lie. If the Seven Races knew—"

"Please see they do not find out."

"I need to sit down." Kathryn's stomach churned and a hot steel band seemed clamped around her forehead. She looked around, but of course there was no place to sit in Jarrikk's chambers; she had to settle for leaning on one of the padded wooden racks. Jarrikk moved close beside her. "Why me? Why didn't you send Jim?" Did Karak know what Jim had said to her before she left? she wondered, suddenly worried for him.

"Translator Ornawka was not suitable, but he was very helpful. He helped us ascertain the depth of your commitment to the Oath."

Kathryn straightened. "That argument was staged?"

"Translator Ornawka was very helpful," Karak repeated.

Kathryn shook her aching head and coughed. Jarrikk placed one clawed hand on her shoulder and she leaned gratefully back against his warm bulk. "Guess I misjudged Jim," she said softly. "But I'm still going to kill him next time I see him." She raised her voice. "There's something else. I'm empathy-blind. I'm—I'm not a Translator anymore."

"True," Karak said simply, and Kathryn closed her eyes. She'd hoped even yet that Jarrikk's information had been wrong; a child's hope. "However," Karak continued, "your natural empathy will slowly recover."

Kathryn's eyes flew open. "Truth?"

"Translators do not lie."

Kathryn grimaced. "So what happens now?"

"I see you are already feeling ill. This will provide the perfect excuse for you to withdraw. The ship delivering Translator Mathieu has an unusually well-equipped medical bay. Its personnel will take care of you."

Jarrikk moved around in front of her, blocking her view. "Until then, I take care of you," he signed.

She wished she could read him; at least he could read her. She let her gratitude flood her. He reached out his hand and patted her knee clumsily, and she laughed, knowing he had drawn the gesture from her memories. He moved around behind her again. Karak watched them with no visible change of expression. "So it all worked out the way you predicted," she said to him, almost angrily. "But you couldn't know that I'd—do what I did. I almost didn't. I almost backed out. The thought of no longer being a Translator..." Her throat closed on the words.

"We didn't know," Karak said. "One can never know. Nor did we know what Jarrikk would do—until we registered his library search for information on the effects of Linking without Programming. Such information is normally restricted, but I personally informed him of the risk you were both about to take. The decision, however, was entirely yours—and his."

"Both?" Kathryn twisted around to stare at Jarrikk.

"Both," Jarrikk signed.

"Why? There was no need..."

"Was. S'sinn would be shamed if human took risk, S'sinn did not. Such shame could poison relations."

"But they'll never know!"

"I would know. Someday they may, too." He touched her forehead gently. "Very brave human. Could not let you risk what I would not."

"But if you didn't Program..."

"As of today, two fewer Translators," said Karak solemnly. "Two new names in Hall of Honour. And new hope of peace."

Kathryn didn't take her eyes off Jarrikk. Crippled by the humans, his only worth in S'sinn society was as a Translator—and he had thrown that away for the sake of her wild scheme, trusting her completely...she laid her hand on the soft fur of his chest. "Very brave S'sinn." All this time she'd thought he could still read her, he'd really been as blind as she was. But he had still comforted her. "Very kind S'sinn," she whispered.

Jarrikk touched her forehead again. "Very good friend," he signed.

"Yes," she said. "Oh, yes." Without turning around, she asked Karak, "What use are we to the Guild now?"

"When your natural abilities return, you will still be able to seek out new human and S'sinn Translators. We will now need many more."

Kathryn remembered the day Karak took her from the orphanage. "I'd like that. I'd like that very much."

But Jarrikk signed sharply, "No. S'sinn will not accept such judgment from flightless one."

"Then what..." Kathryn stopped, appalled, as the answer crashed in on her from Jarrikk's memories. Flightless, no longer a Translator, Jarrikk would do what he would have done had he never become one—he would die, and S'sinndikk would honour his name. That part of her that had been S'sinn warmed with pride at the glory of his sacrifice—but the human part of her went as cold as the depths of space. She wanted to scream at him, to reason with him, but, at war within herself, all she could manage was a choked, "No!"

"It is our way."

"Karak..." Kathryn turned pleadingly toward the terminal.

"It is the S'sinn way," Karak said, and his image vanished.

Kathryn faced Jarrikk again. "But I don't want you to die!" The words exploded out of her.

Jarrikk opened his scarred wing. "Only in Translation am I free of pain. I no longer have that freedom. Death is my friend."

"I would not sentence you to a life of pain," Kathryn whispered. "But I will not be free of pain. Not if you die."

Jarrikk touched her cheek. "You will remember me. You will remember my memories. In you, I will live on."

Kathryn had no more arguments to give him. She gazed

mutely at his face, the face she had thought horrible only a few days before, but that now seemed sadly beautiful.

Jarrikk gestured out the open windows. "We have a few hours. Are you well enough to see the glories of our city? We are artists as well as warriors. There are many beautiful things I would show you."

"You already have," Kathryn said; but she took his hand and walked with him out under the open sky. The old pain, or something like it, was back in her heart; but this time, it was there to stay.

TEXENTE TELA VENERIS

his is the newest story in the book...in a way. "Texente Tela Veneris" actually started life as a short play, which I wrote for On the Line: A Freefall Through New Work, *a program Globe Theatre (mentioned earlier in connection with "The Path of Souls") ran for a few years, in which a director and group of actors did staged readings of new fifteen-minute scripts. When I was approached to submit a story to* Planetary: Venus (Superversive Press), *edited by A. M. Freeman and L. Jagi Lamplighter, one of a series of planet-themed anthologies (the theme extending not only to the physical planet but to their mythological namesakes), I realized that what was then called "The Weaver" could be adapted into a story about the goddess Venus. And here's the result!*

THE STATUE GLEAMED IN THE LEAFY SHADOWS like a pearl on green velvet, its white stone, unmarred by uncounted years of rain and wind, glowing as though lit from within. No sharp-edged shadow or too-bright glint of sunlight marred its rounded contours, and Jennifer Trenholme, standing transfixed at the top of the long stone staircase that had brought her to its

205

forest setting, thought it the most beautiful thing she had ever seen.

Behind her, her husband Arthur grunted up the stairs, his heavy hiking boots thudding onto the worn granite as though to punish them for being so high and steep. "This had better be worth it, Jenny," he yelled up at her. "Three hundred and seventy-four steps in this heat had damn well better be worth it."

She said nothing, but moved forward, out of his sight, suddenly feeling a need to touch the statue, to prove to herself that something so beautiful existed outside her dreams.

The stone felt warm and velvety, like the skin of a child. She rested her cheek against it while her breath and heartbeat, racing from the climb, slowed and gentled. The light breeze died away, and with it the murmur of the leaves, and for a timeless instant the world held its breath.

Then Arthur reached the top of the stairs. "That's it? That's *it?*" His voice boomed across the glade like a cannon shot, shattering the silence. "For God's sake, Jenny, it's just another damn statue. A damn statue of an old woman at a loom. There's a pigeon on her head, for God's sake!"

"It's the Weaver, Arthur," Jennifer said, voice soft, pleading, willing with all her heart that, just this once, he would under-stand, that he would love a thing that she loved. "Venus's Weaver. *Texente Tela Veneris.* She's ancient. Unique. The guidebook says she was here before the town. She's the reason there *is* a town."

"So what? It's a shithole of a town." Arthur stumped over, unslinging his backpack as he came. He dropped the pack at the Weaver's feet and sat down on her pedestal, back to the statue. He fished out a beer, popped it open, and took a long draught. Then he belched, wiped his mouth with the back of his hand, and fixed his cold blue eyes on her. "Don't know why I let you talk me into coming here."

"But, listen!" Jennifer took off her own pack, and pulled out the island guidebook the hotel clerk had given her. She opened it to a dog-eared page. "*Texente Tela Veneris* is all that remains of what was once a large shrine, unique in the Roman Empire,'" she read. "'Most oddly, though the shrine was dedicated to Venus, the statue does not depict Venus, but a weaver at the loom. Also odd is the fact that the shrine honoured two seemingly contradictory aspects of the Goddess: Venus Verticordia, the changer of hearts, and Venus Libertina, the freedwoman...'"

Jennifer glanced at Arthur, hoping for a spark of interest. But he wasn't even looking at her: he was glaring at his iPhone. "Damn third-world countries," he said. He shoved the phone back in his pocket. "No service."

Jennifer's lips tightened. She looked back at the guidebook and resumed reading, in a loud voice. "'Each year, on April 1...'" She stopped. "That's today!"

"You better not be about to tell me that you made me haul my ass up here as an April Fool's joke," Arthur said.

Jennifer took a deep breath, and read on. "'Each year, on April 1, the festival of Veneralia celebrated Venus Verticordia's power to change people's hearts. Matrons would ask Venus for help in affairs of the heart, sex, betrothal, and marriage. Even though this island was far from the centre of the Empire, wealthy matrons sometimes made the long, hazardous journey here for the Veneralia, for it was said that here, through her Weaver, Venus displayed her power to change people's lives more powerfully and directly than anywhere else.'"

Arthur snorted. "Imagine risking your life traveling here just to beg some hunk of rock for relationship advice."

Jennifer rushed on. "'Locals said Venus, pleased by a magnificent tapestry woven for her by a woman of this island, made that Weaver immortal, and gave to her power over the interconnected strands of lovers' entangled lives. The Weaver, it is said, can knot or unknot them, sever them, even pull them apart so that it would be as though the two were never intertwined...which may be why, over time, a second aspect of Venus came to be celebrated here:

Venus Libertina, Venus the Freedwoman (although some scholars think that Libertina is really a corruption of the older Libitina, the goddess of death).'"

"I'm feeling close to death right now," Arthur snapped. "Death from boredom. Is there a point to all this?"

"I just want you to understand," Jennifer said, hearing the pleading note in her voice and hating herself for it, but she *did* want him to understand, wanted him to at least pretend to be interested in the things she was interested in, the way he had been when they'd first met...surely that hadn't all been an act. They'd been so happy in the early years, but recently... "We've come halfway around the world to experience a new culture. Don't you want to learn about it?"

Arthur rolled his eyes and drained the last of his beer. He pointed the empty can at her. "You've got one more minute, then I'm out of here, with or without you."

Jennifer felt a familiar tightness in her chest. Her voice sounded strained in her own ears as she continued. "'It is said no one ever found the Weaver on their own. Only a few select individuals, chosen by Venus, ever truly met her...'"

Arthur burped loudly. "Yeah? *You* found her easily enough." He turned and crushed his empty beer can against the Weaver's white knee. "Look, so did I." He tossed the can into the shadows of the surrounding trees.

Promising herself she'd pick up the can before they left the glade, Jennifer resumed reading. "'To those granted access to the Weaver, Venus sent a guide, who could take various guises, sometimes animal, sometimes human. If the Guide led you to the Weaver, she would show you the tapestry of your own life. You could ask her to change your life by altering that tapestry, but those attempts almost always ended badly. If you simply left the weaving to the Weaver, however, you might well find your life substantially improved.'"

Arthur snorted. "Superstitious horseshit." He struggled to his feet, the effort bringing forth another prodigious belch. "Time's up. We're out of here."

"Just a few more minutes, Arthur," Jennifer pleaded. "Look, I'm done reading." She shoved the guidebook back in her pack. "Can't we stay just a little longer?" She touched the statue, looking up into the old woman's sculpted eyes. Peering down at the loom, they also peered down at her: at her, and, she felt, into her. A slight chill made the hair on the back of her neck rise, though it was a hot day. "Think of all the people who came here on this same day, year after year for decades, maybe centuries, pleading for help from the Goddess. Think how old this thing is, yet it's still in perfect condition..."

Arthur snorted. "I'm not getting any younger myself, and I'm *not* in perfect condition. And it's not the same day—the calendar has changed since then." He took an impatient step toward the stairs, glancing back over his shoulder at her. "Come *on*, Jenny."

"Arthur—"

Arthur spun and grabbed her arm, his fingers digging into her bicep. He yanked her away from the statue. "*Now!*" He shoved her toward the stairs, then bent over to grab his pack from the statue's base. "We're heading to the casino. It looks like the only place in this godforsaken dump to have any fun."

"Happy Veneralia," said a man's voice. Arthur jerked upright, dropping the pack.

The new arrival stood at the edge of the woods, holding Arthur's empty beer can. Neither old nor young, with the olive skin of the locals, he wore a simple white shirt, loose-fitting grey pants, and sandals. In his pierced left earlobe a pearl gleamed, the same milky white as the statue.

"Where the hell did *you* come from?" Arthur demanded.

"I live here," said the man. His English had only a trace of an accent.

"Were you spying on us?"

The man smiled. "Spying? No. But I saw you here, and came to offer my services, as I have done for many visitors before." He tossed the beer can to Jennifer, who, though surprised, caught it out of the air. She pushed it into her pack as the man spread his hands. "I am a guide."

"I can find my own way to the casino," Arthur said.

The guide's smile widened, revealing teeth the same pearly white as his earring and the statue. "I would not be so certain. The island paths can be confusing. According to one local legend, they shift in the night,." He pointed at the steps. "Except these, which are always here."

"Really?" Jennifer blurted.

Arthur glared at her. "Don't be stupid, Jenny. It's just superstition. Like this Weaver thing."

The guide laughed. "Exactly like 'this Weaver thing.'" He stepped forward, then, and ran his fingers over the statue's smooth surface, as though caressing the skin of a lover. "My people would not be here if not for the Weaver—or, at least, those who weave. This island is renowned for its woven goods. I am told that in America one of our tapestries can fetch a very high price, but few have ever been taken there: our weavers' work remains largely undiscovered." He looked up at the statue's face. "I know a woman who, like this woman whom Venus honoured, is a master of the craft."

Jennifer saw Arthur's expression sharpen and shift, from irritation to keen interest. But the guide laughed and turned away from the statue. "I am sorry. Here I am boring you with stories of tapestries when you are interested in the casino. And it is true, to go there, you do not really need a guide." He pointed toward the stairs. "In fact, from the top of the steps you can just see its roof. You must go through the plaza and past the church with the—"

"Never mind that," Arthur interrupted. "Tell me: just how much *would* one of these tapestries fetch in America?"

The guide shrugged. "I know very little about such things."

Arthur's eyes narrowed. "Guess."

"Perhaps... several thousands of your dollars?" The guard turned his hands palms-up. "So I have heard."

Arthur's attention was now fixed on the guide like a cat's on a bird. "Perhaps you can help us after all, Mr....?"

"My name would be difficult for you to pronounce. Call me...Dux."

"I'm Arthur Trenholme, Dux, and this is my wife, Jennifer." Arthur held out his hand, but rather than take it, Dux bowed. Arthur frowned and drew his hand back.

"Is it really Veneralia today?" Jennifer asked. "I know it's April 1, but Arthur's right, the calendar changed..."

Dux smiled. "We go with the times. It is April 1 by the calendar we use today, so yes, it is Veneralia."

"But does anyone still..."

"Jenny," said Arthur, without looking at her, "Shut up." To Dux he said firmly, "Take me to this weaver you know. I'd like to see her work."

Dux raised an eyebrow. "Are you sure? It is a considerable distance, and you were complaining of being tired..."

"We're fine," Arthur said.

"But, Arthur," Jennifer ventured, "we have dinner reservations in—"

"Shut *up*, Jenny."

Dux looked from Arthur to Jennifer, then nodded slowly. "As you wish. If you will follow me..."

Arthur took a step, then stopped. "Wait a minute." His eyes narrowed. "What's this going to cost?"

Dux shrugged. "Nothing." He smiled at Jenny. "It is my gift to you. A Veneralia gift."

"You mean you get a cut of the sales," Arthur said.

Dux's smile vanished. "The Weaver does not sell what she weaves, though you may take it, if you wish. This way." He turned and walked toward the woods.

"It's free?" Arthur looked at Jennifer and grinned—the first time he'd looked happy all day. "Holy hell, Jenny, we're going to make a fortune!" He hurried after Dux.

Jennifer followed, more slowly. She knew she should be happy Arthur had suddenly taken an interest in local culture, even if it was entirely because he thought he could make money. But what Dux had said made no sense. The Weaver would *give* you a tapestry if you asked? How did she make a living?

I'll ask her, she thought. She quickened her pace. At least they weren't heading to the casino.

The breeze didn't penetrate the trees. After five minutes, Jennifer's whole body was damp. Up ahead, Dux looked as fresh as ever, slipping through the forest so skillfully he seemed to not even disturb the leaves. Arthur, on the other hand, sweat glistening on the back of his neck, ploughed through the undergrowth like a bulldozer, which at least left a clearer path for Jennifer.

After what seemed like at least half an hour, Jennifer glanced at her watch, only to see that it had stopped. Ahead, the trees thinned, and a few moments later they emerged into a clearing...with a white statue of a woman at a loom at its centre.

Arthur stared at it, then grabbed Dux's shoulder and spun him around. "What are you playing at?"

Dux stepped back, somehow freeing himself from Arthur's grip without even seeming to try. "The path is complex. You must trust me. We still have some distance to go." He touched the statue's cheek, then led them out of the glade again, in a different direction than before.

More trees, more leaves, more heat, more sweat. Again, they emerged into a glade; again, at its centre stood a white statue. *The* white statue. Arthur turned on Dux, fists clenched. "Do you think I'm an idiot?" he exploded. "It's the same damn glade for the third damn time. Or are you lost?"

"I do not get lost," Dux said.

Arthur snorted. "Yeah? I'd like to see you find your way around Chicago."

"I have never left this island. I never will."

That startled Arthur out of his anger. "You've never been off this rock?"

"This is my home. I have no need to leave it."

Arthur shook his head. "Place like this sucks all the energy and ambition out of a man. I should know, I grew up in the shittiest one-gopher town in Minnesota. Better to head for the bright lights. That's what I did. That's where the action is."

"Thus spake the moth drawn to the candle flame, to his brief but painful regret," said Dux. He touched the statue's knee. "Our island contains world enough for me. That is why the paths wind and twist. They have a very long way to go."

"A straight line is the shortest distance between two points."

"Is it?" Dux smiled. Something about that smile made the back of Jennifer's neck tingle; no warmth from it touched Dux's eyes, whose pupils, despite the sunlight, were as wide, black, and fathomless as a starless sky. "Our island is alive. Only things that have never lived have straight edges. What does that say about your Chicago? A large dead thing is still a dead thing, and is not made more pleasant by virtue of being large. Rather the opposite."

"I'd still rather live there than in this backwater," Arthur growled.

Dux looked up at the sky. Blue when they had set out, it was now overcast, a thin layer of cloud turning it pearl-white, like the statue, like his earring. "A backwater is a place for quiet contemplation, the home of beautiful plants and creatures that need solitude and silence. The world would be a poorer place without backwaters, Mr. Trenholme." He lowered his gaze. "Shall we proceed?"

"Yes, dammit," Arthur snapped. "But if you lead us in a circle again..."

"Arthur," Jennifer said. "You're the one who insisted—"

"Shut *up*, Jenny!"

Dux looked from one to the other without expression, then turned and led the way back into the woods, once more taking a different direction than before.

Jennifer trudged after the guide and her husband, the thick underbrush tugging at her legs as though trying to pull her down. She kept tripping over roots, and having to dodge branches Arthur pushed out of the way, then released to spring back in her face. He never looked back at her. The day grew hotter with every step, it seemed, and Jennifer was soaking wet and gasping like a grounded fish when, at last, another glen opened in front of them.

For a moment, she thought it was the *same* glen, yet again, for at its centre sat a woman in white: but then she realized this "statue" was alive, hands and feet moving as though working a loom—

—but there was no loom to be seen.

Arthur stopped so suddenly Jennifer bumped into his back. "What the hell is this?" he roared at the guide. "You dragged me around in circles on this damn hill in 100-degree heat to see a crazy woman pretending to work an invisible loom? Who are you going to take me to see next—Rumpelstiltskin?"

"Do not assume that because you cannot see a thing, it is not there," Dux said.

Jennifer's breath suddenly caught as, looking past the woman, she recognized a bush laden with white flowers. "This is the same glade!"

Dux's black eyes flicked to her. "Yes."

"But we walked miles!"

"It is always a long journey to this place."

"Then... where did the statue go?" Jennifer's heart was pounding. She stared at the woman, remembering what the guidebook had said: *To those granted access to the Weaver, Venus sent a guide...*

She turned suddenly wide eyes on Dux. "You're not *a* guide, you're *the* Guide..." she breathed.

214

"Shut up, Jenny," Arthur snapped. "He's a con artist, is what he is." He walked past Dux to the weaver. "Hey! Hey, lady, there's nothing there!" He waved his hand through the air where the loom would have been, had it really existed—and snatched it back. "Shit! Some damn thing bit me!" He sucked on his middle finger.

"The spindle is quite sharp," Dux said.

Arthur ignored him. He pulled his finger out of his mouth and looked at its wet, shining tip. "Must have been a mosquito. Hey, you got malaria around here? Zika?"

Through all of this, the Weaver wove on, undisturbed. She had not looked up when Arthur approached her. Jennifer, drawn to her, stepped closer, brushing past Arthur, ignoring his glare. "Hello?" Jennifer ventured.

The Weaver did not react. Jennifer glanced at Dux.

"She does not speak, but she knows you are here," said Dux. "The Goddess told her you would come. She is weaving for you even now." He turned to Arthur. "You wanted a tapestry, Mr. Trenholme. If you ask for it, she will give it to you. Free of charge."

Arthur snorted. "She will, huh? All right, I'll bite." He shoved past Dux and stared up into the Weaver's face. "Hey, weaver-lady, can I have my tapestry?" he said, his voice mocking, childish. "Pretty-please with sugar on top?"

The Weaver reached... somewhere. Though only a few feet away, Jennifer didn't quite see where the Weaver's hand went, but when it returned, it held a piece of woven cloth the size of a tea-towel. The Weaver handed the weaving to Arthur, though she never looked at him, then resumed working on her invisible loom.

Arthur held up the bit of cloth. Knotted and rough, it looked like a piece of gunny sack. Ugly colours, blue and black and muddy brown, ran through it in random streaks, like polluted rivers through an industrial wasteland. Arthur's face turned bright red. "This is *crap!*" he roared. "I could weave better than this using a couple of paperclips and a glue gun!"

Jennifer looked nervously at the Weaver. "Arthur, don't—"

Arthur strode over to Dux and shook the tapestry at him, inches from the tip of his nose. "What the hell is this?" he yelled, face purpling. Jennifer wondered if he were about to have a stroke. "Dragging me in circles through the forest, showing me a crazy woman, now trying to sell me this? Look at it! *Look at it!* I wouldn't use it to wipe my ass!"

The Weaver turned her head, and for the first time Jennifer saw her eyes clearly. They were white and opaque, the colour of the statue, the colour of the stud in Dux's ear, the colour of the sky. Despite the heat, Jennifer felt a chill, cold as Chicago's wintriest wind.

"Look at this!" Arthur bellowed. "This thread is barely even attached. And it's the only decent thing in the whole piece of crap." He grabbed a thread that glinted gold in the milk-white light. "I can yank it out like—"

Jennifer climbed the worn granite steps up the thickly forested hillside. Sunshine reached through the leaves to dapple her face; she smiled up at it, enjoying its pleasant warmth.

Ahead, she heard voices.

"I'm not paying you a cent!" a man yelled. He sounded upset; she stopped. She didn't want to ruin a perfect day by encountering an angry stranger.

"Mr. Trenholme, I have never asked for money," said another man. His voice, smooth as chocolate, held no rancour. Just hearing it made Jennifer feel calm and safe. She stayed put, listening. "I told you I would guide you to this place, and so I have. If it does not please you, you are as free to go as you were to come."

"Then I'm leaving!" the angry man shouted. "I'll get my wife and..." His voice trailed off. "Why did I say that?" he said after a moment.

"What, Mr. Trenholme?" said the other man.

"'I'll get my wife.' I don't have a wife. I've never been married."

He suddenly sounded much calmer, no longer so threatening, though sorely puzzled. Relieved, Jennifer resumed climbing. She dearly wanted to see the other man, the one with the soothing voice.

She had almost reached the top of the stairs when a big man, wearing a sweat-stained golf shirt, shorts, and expensive hiking boots, appeared above her and started down. They bumped arms as he passed. "Sorry," he muttered, without really looking at her, and continued down the steps.

Not bad looking, Jennifer thought, glancing after him, but something about the way he'd held his mouth had rubbed her the wrong way. *Not my type, though.* She put him out of her mind. Instead she continued up the stairs, and stepped into a forest glade.

At its centre, an old woman in a white shift sat on a stool, her hands and feet still, her blind eyes gazing at nothing. Suddenly she remembered: this woman was a weaver. She'd been promised a tapestry. And Dux, the man who stood by the old woman, had guided her here. *How did I forget that just now?* she wondered. "I... I guess I went for a bit of a walk," she said, and even as she said it, she remembered that that was exactly what she'd done. "Is it ready?"

Dux smiled at her. "There has been a slight delay," he said in that wonderful voice. "I'm afraid the Weaver will have to begin your tapestry all over again. It may take some time."

Jennifer smiled back. "I'm on vacation. I've got all the time in the world. I'll watch."

"An excellent idea," said Dux. "I, too, enjoy watching the weaver work, even after all this time." He reached down and plucked something from the grass at Jennifer's feet. "Your tapestry will begin with this thread." He stretched it out before her eyes. It glowed a soft, buttery gold in the sunlight. "It was pulled from another, for which it was entirely unsuited."

Jennifer had never seen anything so beautiful; she laughed and clapped her hands. "Perfect!" she cried. "But how much will I have to pay for this tapestry?"

"It is a gift," said Dux. "Happy Veneralia."

He handed the thread to the old woman. She took it, and began to weave.

LANDSCAPE WITH ALIEN

Although my degree from Harding University is in journalism, I minored in art (officially; unofficially, my minor—possibly my major—was Dungeons & Dragons). Art—along with music—pops up in my fiction quite often. This early story, though previously unpublished, won an honourable mention in a Saskatchewan Writers Guild's short fiction competition in the 1980s.

KAREEN ALDONA ADDED A WHITE HIGHLIGHT to the orange flank of a boulder, considered a moment, enlarged it a bit, then set her brush aside with a sigh. She had hoped to finish the painting that day, but shadows were lengthening in the canyon, and it would take her most of the two remaining hours of daylight to get back to the colony.

She stood, stretching, then moved back from the easel to compare her creation to the real thing. *Not bad*, she thought, *but the light still isn't quite right...*

She shook her head. The sun, slightly more orange than Earth's, had a subtle effect very difficult to capture. "Next time," she promised herself. She cleaned her brushes, then packed them, her palette, and her paints into her metal art case, which she stuffed into her backpack.

She stored the painting and easel inside the nearby cave she had discovered on her first visit to the canyon, then filled her canteen at the gurgling spring farther inside. When she returned to the cave's mouth, she saw the alien for the first time.

Though slim and no taller than she, its thick, black fur made it look much larger. Eyes of brilliant, liquid yellow gleamed from its long-muzzled face as it picked its way on broad, clawed feet through the rocks. It wore only a thin grey belt, from which hung a knife and a leather pouch. A slender rod of crystal glittered on a silver chain around its neck.

Kareen's breath froze in her throat, and at the same instant the creature looked up and saw her, and stopped. Even across the fifty metres separating them, she heard its low, menacing growl.

It can't be real! her mind kept insisting, despite the evidence of her eyes. *There's no intelligent life on this planet. Dad's the colony biologist, he should know, right? The survey showed nothing. No cities, no villages, not even cave dwellings!*

But the impossibility of the alien's presence didn't make it go away. It stood its ground, staring at her, the growl rising to a cat-like moan that made the hair on the back of her neck rise up.

Kareen wanted to turn and run, but had nowhere to go. The only way into or out of the canyon was the slippery, rock-strewn slope above the cave, and the thought of attempting it with the alien behind her was too terrifying to contemplate.

Never taking its eyes from her, the creature slowly sank cross-legged to the ground. It drew its knife and thrust it into the ground close by its side.

Kareen tried to swallow with a throat suddenly as dry as the canyon floor. The alien's message seemed obvious: "I'm armed. Come no closer."

Why doesn't it just attack? she wondered sickly. *I couldn't fight it. I don't even have a club.*

She sat down on a large rock before her trembling knees collapsed, wrapped her arms around her legs, and bleakly met the steady glare of the alien. *But it doesn't know that,* she thought suddenly. *It doesn't know what kind of weapons I've got. It doesn't realize I'm helpless...*

She tensed as the creature reached into its pouch and took out a transparent, glassy cylinder. Still staring intently at Kareen, it took the crystal rod from around its neck and touched it to the cylinder.

Light flashed and Kareen jumped to her feet. Now what? A gun? A grenade? *I have to convince it I'm dangerous, too!*

She struggled out of the straps of her backpack, and opened it to take out the art case. The alien hissed softly when it saw the silver box. "Same to you," Kareen whispered.

Holding the case on her lap, she took out a sketch pad and a pencil, carefully keeping the lid of the case between her and the alien, so it couldn't see exactly what she was doing. "This ought to puzzle it," she muttered. And at least she could leave a record of what killed her for the rest of the colonists...

...for her parents...

Blinking back sudden tears, she rummaged in the pack again and pulled out her binoculars, hoping to make out what the alien was doing with the cylinder and rod. She had the satisfaction of seeing the alien snatch up its knife as she pointed the binoculars in its direction, but even through them the cylinder was only a meaningless, light-filled tube.

The creature watched her a moment, then thrust the knife into the ground again—a little closer to hand, this time. *Good,* she thought. *Let* it *worry for a while.*

Taking an occasional look through the glasses to get the details right, she began to sketch, while the alien continued to work on the glowing cylinder Kareen was convinced was a weapon. She only hoped the alien believed her imaginary weapons were as real as its own.

When the alien became hard to see, slowly disappearing into the gathering purple haze of twilight, Kareen put her sketchpad away. After the first few minutes when her hand had been inclined to shake, she had drawn well, better than usual, capturing a good likeness of the alien, even forgetting her fear for minutes at a time...but somehow her artistic success didn't seem nearly as important as it usually did.

She had decided what to do. Though for all she knew the alien could see in the dark, she had to try to sneak out of the canyon in the night. She couldn't just sit there, fighting sleep, picturing the alien creeping closer and closer...

She put the sketchbook in an outside pocket of the backpack and took out her canteen, taking a much-needed drink of water. Her stomach growled, reminding her of her missed supper. Her parents would be beginning to worry. Within an hour or two they would be organizing a search party.

Too long, she thought, waiting for dusk to become full night, watching the constant flickering glow that marked the alien's location.

Abruptly the light vanished. Kareen gasped, then scrambled up, listening.

She heard nothing but the faint whisper of wind across the stones.

Now, she thought. Wiping sweaty palms on the front of her shirt, she began picking her way over the stone-strewn canyon floor toward the slope behind her.

Her progress was agonizingly slow. Every few seconds she froze, listening for the clicking of claws on the rocks or soft, hissing breathing. But hearing nothing did not calm her fears. When she couldn't hear the alien, it could be anywhere.

When at last she reached the canyon wall, the first part of the ascent proved no problem. The gentle slope at the base was no harder to traverse by darkness than by daylight.

But halfway up the slope steepened. Flat, slippery rocks shifted treacherously beneath her feet, and as they crashed down behind her, Kareen realized all hope of slipping out of the canyon unnoticed was gone.

Heart pounding with fear and exertion, she reached the last stretch of the climb, four metres of nearly vertical rock. She had climbed two metres when, as she reached for a new handhold, she heard rocks *she* had not dislodged crashing down into the canyon.

She jerked her head around to look, though there was nothing to see, and her feet slipped. For a moment she hung desperately by the fingers of one hand, scrabbling with the other, and then the rock gave way and she fell.

Agony stabbed her ankle as she hit the slate-strewn slope and rolled, gaining momentum, in a growing avalanche of rocks, down to the very bottom of the wall she had so torturously climbed.

As she lay dazed, bruised, and bleeding, the rocks gradually stopped shifting and silence returned...or near-silence. Then the sliding of the rocks resumed. Someone—or some *thing*—was coming down the slope.

Kareen rolled over and sat up, but when she touched her ankle, pain lanced through it, and she knew she couldn't run, couldn't even stand. Dust ground between her teeth, and she felt for her canteen, but the backpack that contained it had vanished, torn off somewhere during her headlong plunge.

Now she heard what she had only imagined before, the click of claws on rocks. The sound stopped. Light flickered up the slope as the alien bent over something wedged between two boulders...her backpack. She watched it paw through her belongings, sniffing the brushes and paints, paging through her sketchbook. It bent down and picked up the pack and the light went out again.

By the time it reached Kareen the pounding of her heart in her ears was as loud as its claws on the rocks. Finally it loomed above her, a blacker lump in the darkness. It tossed something at her and she almost screamed, but it was only her sketchpad. Light suddenly glowed from the crystal rod around the alien's neck, and Kareen saw the sketchpad was open to her drawing of the alien.

From its pouch the alien drew out the glassy cylinder that had so frightened her, and, kneeling beside her, touched it with the crystal rod. A soft glow suffused it, and Kareen gasped.

Her own figure appeared in three dimensions inside the cylinder's walls, rendered in perfect detail and colour, sitting on a rock with her art case open and a pencil in her hands.

The alien made a sound like a soft purr and set the cylinder on the ground beside the sketchpad. Then it took Kareen's canteen from the backpack and, supporting her head with its warm hand, trickled cold water between her lips.

JANITOR WORK

nother early story, which appeared in the 1984 edition of The Canadian Children's Annual. *You might see similarities with "Moon Baby." In both, you might see similarities with certain parts of Robert A. Heinlein's* Have Spacesuit, Will Travel. *Heinlein and Andre Norton were, I think, the two greatest influences on my early writing.*

DARRYL NORTON LOOKED GLUMLY at the dust-covered object before him. It seemed to him he had seen an inordinate number of dust-covered objects in his short life.

Yet he had been very pleased when his father had given him this job in the Lunar Survey and Exploration Corps. Although Apollo City offered many kinds of entertainment, it was still a very small community, isolated by the void of space and the desolate lunar surface. The Corps had seemed like the place to find some adventure.

Some adventure, Darryl thought. He reached for the vacuum

nozzle. It was his job to clean dust from equipment that had been used on the surface, like this seismic charge.

Of course, it hadn't actually been *used*. Someone had just set it on the surface and brought it back. But any equipment like that had to be cleaned—by Darryl.

At least it was the last item. Darryl finished going over it once and was starting to pry into some of the harder-to-reach places when his wristwatch alarm went off. He looked at it, startled. 1800 already? In just thirty minutes the Apollo City spinball team would be playing the L-5s for the off-Earth championship.

He quickly examined the charge. Any dust left on it wasn't visible; no one would notice. He grabbed it and spun away from the table.

As he turned, the charge slipped out of his hand. He had given it enough momentum to send it crashing hard against the metal floor, but when he picked it up, he could see no damage. He placed it with the rest of the clean equipment, logged "work completed" into the computer and left, whistling.

The next day Darryl's father, Philip Norton, surprised him by taking him to the crawler bay, where he and a geologist, Andy Davis, were getting ready for a two-day trip to set out seismo-graphic equipment. Then his father surprised him even more by telling him he was going to be the third crewmember.

As Darryl climbed in through the crawler's airlock he hoped he was done with janitor work for good.

A few hours later he stood at the bottom of a deep crater. The crawler, his father, and Davis were all out of sight beyond the crater wall. Darryl had finished setting up his segment of the instrument package, and was simply enjoying the solitude, soli-tude as complete as though he were alone on an alien planet in another solar system. The voices crackling in his helmet, after all, could be coming from the orbiting starship, where the captain awaited his report...

Abruptly the voices ceased. A cloud of dust spurted over the crater wall and rapidly settled. Frightened, Darryl scrambled out of the crater—and froze when he saw the crawler.

Something had torn a gaping hole in its side.

"Dad!" Darryl screamed, and ran toward the vehicle, awkward in his suit. If the hole was in the crew room, everyone inside without a suit was dead—and he could see no one outside. He called his father again, but only static answered.

He reached the crawler, slipping and falling as he tried to stop. He got clumsily to his feet and hammered the airlock control with his fist. Nothing happened.

He grabbed the wheel to open the lock manually and turned it. The door slid slowly open, and he scrambled through, closed the door behind him, and opened the valve that would fill the lock with air from inside the crawler—if any air remained.

With relief he felt a blast of wind against his glove, and the moment the pressures had equalized he swung open the inside door and burst through.

Smoke from shorting electrical equipment filled the room. A shattered suit life-support pack lay against one wall. Davis crouched on the floor, bent over...

"Dad!" Darryl tore off his helmet and crashed to his knees beside his father.

"I'll take care of him," Davis snapped. "You get a fire extinguisher and put out those electrical fires."

"But—"

"Move!"

Heartsick, Darryl did as he was told. As soon as possible he was back. "How is he?"

"Not good." Davis injected something into the injured man. "He was recharging that life support pack when the explosion happened. All the electrical systems shorted out, and the suit's

oxygen tank blew up. He took a heavy shock and he's cut up, too."
He looked up at Darryl. "I won't lie to you, kid…if he doesn't get
help, he'll die."

"But what happened?"

"A seismic charge must have exploded in storage and
ruptured one of the big, high-pressure oxygen tanks. That blew
out the side of the crawler and took the electrical systems with
it. But there's no reason a charge should just…What's the
matter?"

Darryl had gone white, and he felt sick. He could imagine only
too well what might have set off a seismic charge prematurely—if
the outer casing was cracked, and dust got into the mechanism.

Davis helped him to a chair. "Are you hurt, too?"

Darryl looked up at him with eyes that didn't see. "I caused the
explosion," he whispered.

"What?"

"I caused it!" Darryl cried. "I was cleaning a seismic charge
yesterday—I was in a hurry—it slipped and hit the floor—and I
didn't report it, or even check it closely. It must have been
damaged."

Davis, who had been bent over him in concern, straightened.
"You little fool!" he exploded. Darryl cringed, certain the geologist
would strike him. He didn't, quite. "I should toss you out the
airlock. But I guess there's no point, is there? You've killed yourself as well as your father and me!"

"Can't you radio for help?" Darryl said faintly.

"The radio's ruined. And since we just made our daily report,
we won't even be missed for twenty-four hours. Your father won't
last that long, and neither will we. We have exactly fifteen hours
before the emergency life support gives out." Davis turned away
from Darryl and slumped in another chair, his eyes closed.

Only fifteen hours… "There must be something we can do,"
Darryl said desperately. Then he saw his helmet where he had
dropped it. He got to his feet.

Davis opened his eyes. "What are you doing?" he demanded sharply.

Darryl fastened his suit and picked up the helmet. "I'm walking back to Apollo for help."

"You're crazy. We're four hours out by crawler; that's close to twelve, walking."

"My life support pack is less than an hour used and we've got one full one. Each one is good for six hours."

"That's not enough."

"That's *just* enough."

Davis jumped up and grabbed the helmet. "I won't let you! You'll just be killing yourself!"

With more strength than he knew he possessed, Darryl tore the helmet away. "I caused the explosion," he said grimly. "I'm responsible for Dad being hurt. I have to do something, and I'm the only one who *can* do anything. My suit is too small for you, and yours is damaged. If I don't try, we're all dead, so if I try and fail...it doesn't make any difference." But his heart pounded as he said it, and his palms were wet.

Davis looked at him, then down at Philip Norton. "I can't stop you, short of tying you up," he said at last. "So go ahead." He lay a heavy hand on Darryl's shoulder. "Forget what I said before. Those charges shouldn't damage that easily. It's not your fault."

"It's my fault for not doing my job," said Darryl, and clamped the helmet down.

At first he found the going easy, since the crawler had had to stick to level terrain. But as foot followed foot for mile after mile and the hours passed, the pace began to tell. His legs ached after the first hour; he had never walked more than a mile at a time in his life.

He rested briefly when he felt he had to, but after several hours there came a time when he felt he could walk no longer. The pain in his legs was too much, and he couldn't get his breath...couldn't get...

His air supply was running out! He fumbled with the pack, hit the cutoff and felt the flow of air cease. He would have to breathe the air in his suit while he made the change.

If only he hadn't waited so long! His hands were clumsy and his eyelids heavy. The new pack was almost too heavy to lift, despite the low gravity, and his tingling fingers fumbled the connections.

But finally cool, fresh air flooded his suit and lungs, and with it came new energy. He wondered how much of his fatigue had been due to his lack of oxygen. With renewed hope, he pressed on.

Now, though, he knew the feel of the death that awaited his father and Davis if he failed—and if his father lived even that long.

Tears blinded him, and he blinked them away angrily. Crying would do no good. He had only one way to make up for his stupidity: make it to Apollo and get help.

Time dragged on. His footprints, sharp and clear in the harsh sunlight, stretched endlessly behind him. The barren, blazing landscape seemed unchanging. Darryl took to calling Apollo City constantly on his suit radio, but never got an answer.

Breathing became hard again, but this time there was no fresh air to be had. He could only stagger on.

He tripped over a rock and discovered his eyes had been closed. He tottered to his feet again. Where were the crawler tracks? He'd lost the—no, there they were. *How did they get over there?* he wondered fuzzily, but stumbled back to them.

Radio. He should try the radio again. "Apollo City—anyone! Can you hear me?" His voice came out in a croak.

He tripped and fell again. His breath rasped in his ears as he struggled up. The crawler tracks had moved again…it didn't matter. He had failed. He had killed his father, and Davis, and now himself. *And I matter least of all*, he thought.

He sank to his hands and knees, chest heaving, futilely trying to strain more oxygen from his nearly-exhausted air.

"…and I tell you, I heard something!" The voice crackled in

Darryl's ears. He found he was lying down again, and was faintly surprised at the softness of the rocky soil.

A different voice said, "You said you heard heavy breathing and someone mumbling. I say you're nuts."

Darryl felt he was supposed to say something, something important. But what?

"I know what I heard," the first voice said stubbornly. "Hello? Come in, whoever you are. Do you need help?"

Help. That was it. The word triggered Darryl's sluggish brain. "Help," he tried saying. His voice was ragged and hoarse, but the sound encouraged him. "Help"! Help me..."

"There *is* someone! Close, too!"

"Over there—by those crawler tracks!"

A moment later Darryl felt himself being gently lifted. He opened his eyes, which had somehow sagged shut, and caught a glimpse of the skeletal frame of an unpressurized lunar sled. "Crawler...explosion..." he croaked.

"An explosion on a crawler? Where?"

The metallic sheen of a spacesuit faceplate floated in front of Darryl's eyes. "What?" he said, confused.

"Where is the crawler?" the man said urgently. The sled was underway. A bump knocked Darryl's head to one side, and he saw the lights of Apollo City, just over the ridge on which he had collapsed. "Where is it?" the man said again. "Come on, boy, you've got to tell us..."

Darryl made a supreme effort to make sense of the demand. Numbers...the man wanted numbers. The coordinates struggled to the surface of his mind and he whispered them before darkness swallowed him.

Darryl recovered quickly once air was restored to him, but for four days his father fought for life. The shuttle from the orbiting station had rescued him and Davis barely in time. Only when the doctors told Darryl his father was out of danger did he surrender completely to the rest they had prescribed for him.

When at last he was allowed to visit his father, he went into the room with mixed happiness and dread. How could he face seeing his father lying in a hospital bed when he was the one who had put him there?

His father looked pale and drawn, but he smiled when Darryl came in. "Was that enough adventure for you, son?"

Darryl couldn't smile back. "It was my fault," he blurted. "I dropped a charge, and didn't check it or report it. I could have killed you!"

His father quit smiling. "You saved my life," he said quietly.

"It wouldn't have been in danger except for me!"

"We'll never know that for sure, Darryl. A lot of things could have caused that explosion. You can't be sure it was the charge you dropped.

"But what else—"

"It doesn't matter," his father said firmly. "Come here."

Darryl went closer, and his father clasped his hand. "Now, listen to me. Not doing your job properly was irresponsible and stupid. You know that better than I do after what happened. And it may even have caused the accident as you say." He squeezed Darryl's hand hard. "But even if it did, you more than made up for it. I'm proud of you, son.

Darryl couldn't speak, but he returned the squeeze: and, strangely, he felt not as if he had just ended a long, adventurous journey, but as if he were beginning one.

THE STRANGE ONE

A previously unpublished story, prompted by something I read, while working at the Saskatchewan Science Centre, about the mechanism of hibernation in mammals.

IAN STUMBLED THROUGH KNEE-DEEP DRIFTS on numbing feet, the bone-chilling cold of the screaming wind creeping inexorably through his warmsuit, sapping his waning strength. He knew if he stopped he would freeze to death, but he had long since lost all sense of direction in the swirling snow.

"Ian Thorne calling Base," he croaked into his transmitter. Only static answered. "Ian Thorne calling Base. Somebody..."

Lightning ripped the sky and his earphones roared. *Hopeless,* he thought. *Well, kid, you're not stuck in that little dome now. How do you like it?*

I get enough sarcasm from my father, he told himself. *I don't need it from you.*

His father. In a couple of hours Ian Thorne Sr. would be back from his geological survey and learn his son and namesake had disappeared. How would he react?

He'll just be angry I left the base without permission. And tell my frozen body, "I told you so."

A gust hammered Ian to his knees. Gasping, he struggled back to his feet and pressed on. *If he cared about me he never would have dragged me to Aleutia. Newhope was just a stopover to him—but it was my home!*

Something loomed ahead, resolved into the black stone face of a cliff. For a moment Ian leaned against it, though it provided no shelter from the wind. *And then confining me to the base for my "own safety"...what did he expect me to do, twiddle my thumbs for two months?*

It didn't help Ian's mood that his present predicament pretty much proved his father right. Strength refuelled by anger, he pushed away from the cliff, fought his way another dozen steps through the snow—and fell into darkness.

Pain stabbed his right ankle as he hit rock, and he crashed forward, reflexes honed on the hoverball field barely enabling him to throw himself into a shock-absorbing roll before his face slammed into stone. Swearing, he sat up, pulled off his ice-caked face mask and glared around.

Curving stone walls surrounded him, forming an almost-circular cave. The man-sized hole through which he had fallen, three metres above, was the only opening. Snow sifting through it fell gently on his upturned face, but the rest of the cave was dry.

Ian tried to stand, but agony shot up his leg and he fell to his hands and knees, tears blinding him. He pressed his forehead against the icy rock until the pain subsided, then lifted his head and looked bleakly around at the barren walls. No one knew where he was, and he couldn't contact Base. He had no food or water. The cave, though sheltered, was ice-cold, and his warm-suit's batteries were low. It was a recipe for slow death.

He licked suddenly dry lips. *Think, Ian. Remember the survival briefing.*

Oh, he remembered, all right. "Never travel alone. Never leave Base without telling someone where you're going. Never go out without a survival kit." Three basic rules—and he'd broken them all.

The cold pinched his ears. He eased himself into a sitting position, then scooted on his rear end out from under the column of falling snow. He pulled up his hood; as he did so a message glowed red on the control band on his left wrist: BATTERY LOW.

He looked down and touched a small, flat, gold-coloured metal box hooked to his belt. The thought of using it filled him with horror—but so did the thought of freezing to death. Convulsively he pulled it free, then broke the seal and flipped back the lid.

Inside, a hypodermic glinted in a bed of black foam, next to a dull-silver disk with a single switch on its upward face. Ian lifted the disk out and flicked that switch, then jerked his hand to the control band to lower the volume as a powerful, frantic beeping exploded in his ears. That signal would lead rescuers to him...if they ever heard it. In Aleutia's peculiar electromagnetic environment, and underground as he was, the odds were against it.

He lifted out the hypo and stared at the ruby liquid inside it. Its primary ingredient was HIT, hibernation-induction trigger, a synthetic human version of the blood chemical that caused squirrels and chipmunks to go into their long winter sleeps. The dosage in the hypo would put him into hibernation for seventy-two hours, slowing his metabolism so his body could maintain itself at a much lower temperature. Somewhat insulated by the powerless warmsuit and sheltered from the wind as he was, the drug would keep him from freezing to death.

But unless someone found him and moved him somewhere warm during those seventy-two hours, he might never wake again.

Ian took a deep breath, then another—and then plunged the hypo into his arm.

Drowsiness gripped him and his eyelids and limbs seemed

weighted with lead. He yawned and lay on his side, curling into a fetal position. The sound of the beacon ushered him into oblivion.

~

Kerr'tok was not supposed to go up: no one was, while the Strange Ones wandered the planet, for there weren't enough Listeners to track them all.

But Kerr'tok felt like a trapped *nek* after five twelve-days stuck in the close confines of Northwest Tunnel. He longed to breathe the crisp, clean air of the surface.

So long before firstmeal he sneaked away into Dead Passage. No one would see him there; the adults had no reason to go, and the little ones believed monsters lived in its abandoned chambers. Kerr'tok was too old for such terrors, but as he passed gaping doorways, opening into chambers his glowbulb did nothing to illuminate, it occurred to him that if the Strange Ones had found the Mouth and entered Dead Passage, they could be hiding...anywhere. So cubbish though he knew it to be, he quickened his pace, anxious to see daylight.

Dead Passage ended at last in a small chamber hung with thick black ropes. Kerr'tok set his glowbulb in a wall niche, then leaped up to seize one of the lines. As he descended the far wall rose and fog rolled across the floor: the cold breath of the Mouth.

Kerr'tok tied the rope so the door would not close; the outer mechanism had been destroyed to secure it from the Strange Ones' prying. Then he stepped into the Mouth, grey-lit by the hole in the high ceiling—and hissed in shock.

Something dead lay curled in a ball on the floor.

Monster! Kerr'tok thought for an instant, but as his pounding heart slowed he realized what the creature had to be: one of the Strange Ones.

Muscles tight, ready to spring away—though the creature had

to be dead, half-covered with snow as it was—Kerr'tok crouched for a closer look.

He poked the creature's leg with a cautious claw, and realized what he had first taken for naked, orange-red skin was an artificial layer, like the *orthokk* furs the People sometimes donned for long surface trips. But the Strange One's pale, furless face remained exposed, its fleshy lips parted to reveal even, blunt teeth. Its nose protruded and its eyes were too round.

Kerr'tok glanced at the opening above. The creature must have fallen into the Mouth and been unable to climb or jump out. But others might search for it, and if they entered the Mouth, they might discover the hidden door into the Dead Passage—and Golden Seer had prophesied what would happen then.

"They would take our Destiny." Kerr'tok could see Golden Seer in his mind's eye, standing in the Gathering Hall before all the people, the red light of the Great Fire burnishing his pale fur. "Not from evil—we sense no great evil within them—but by leading us from the Path. We would no longer be the People, but poor, weak copies of the Strange Ones. They must not find us."

Golden Seer must be told, Kerr'tok thought. *And Secondfather Tok'arrth too,* his conscience added, though he shuddered to think what his mother's father, who ruled Northwest Tunnel with the Seer's advice, would have to say about his folly.

He would first drag the creature's body into the abandoned tunnels; that way if its fellows came searching for it they would have no cause to enter the Mouth.

First Kerr'tok gathered the belongings the Strange One had dropped: a mysterious box of golden metal, a glass tube with a sharp metal needle on one end, a silvery metal disk. He put them in one of the empty chambers, then returned for the dead alien.

It was limp, despite the cold, and heavy. Kerr'tok dragged it a step at a time across the floor and through the door. Then he untied the ropes and the rock slab slid noiselessly back into place.

But as he released the rope he froze.

The creature behind him had just taken a long, slow breath.

~

Ian had expected to wake, if he woke at all, in the clean white surroundings of the Base infirmary. But when his eyes fluttered open he saw nothing but blackness, and still felt rock beneath him.

He lay still for a moment, disoriented. If he hadn't been found and returned to the station, then seventy-two hours must have passed and the HIT had worn off. But he wasn't cold—the air was cool, but much warmer than it had been in the circular cavern; warm enough he wouldn't freeze.

Maybe warm enough to wake me, he thought, and felt for his watch. Its dim light showed him nothing of his surroundings, but confirmed his suspicion: only twenty-four hours had passed since he took the HIT.

He sat up and stared into the darkness. "Hello?" he croaked, and echoes told him he was in a much larger cavern than the one into which he had fallen. Though ravenously hungry, with a throat like sandpaper, he was alive—but not at Base. Which was impossible.

The hood of his warmsuit had been pulled back. As he tugged it on again he heard the steady beeping of the homing signal. Touching his throat mike, he called Base, but heard only the beeper in reply. Even the static had vanished, and buried alive as he seemed to be, he couldn't believe his transmission was going anywhere.

And neither am I, he thought. *I can't wander around in the dark. Someone brought me here—sooner or later they'll be back.*

Or maybe some *thing* had brought him there. He remembered survey-team tales of giant carnivorous bear-like creatures. What if one of them had brought him home as a midnight snack?

That uncomfortable thought had barely come to roost when

the darkness was relieved by a pale pink glow. He lay in a large, rough-hewn chamber; the growing light entered through a low arched doorway. A moment later its source came into view, borne by...something.

The thing looked roughly human, though smaller and more slender than Ian and covered in smooth grey fur. Three sharp black claws curved around the tiny globe that gave off the pink light. It wore no clothing, but carried a bulging leather pouch over one shoulder.

When it saw Ian sitting up it froze, its sharp ears flattening against its skull, then snarled, revealing sharp fangs. Its long tail lashed.

Ian raised both hands in what he hoped was a universal gesture of peace, while his mind reeled. *Intelligent life! But we haven't had a* hint...

His furry visitor took a step closer, then another. Ian didn't move, and finally it stood only a yard or two away, so near he could smell a hint of bitter musk, alien but not unpleasant. It stared at him with gleaming golden eyes, and he stared back.

Now what?

Kerr'tok clenched the glowbulb so tightly its light dimmed. His terror upon realizing he had brought a live Strange One into the Tunnels had driven him to Golden Seer. He had expected anger, but when he knelt before the golden-furred elder in his tapestry-hung chamber the Seer said only, "Our Destiny is in your claws, young Kerr'tok."

"But Golden One, what should I do? Should I kill the Strange One?"

"Could you?"

"I...I don't know. It is horrible...but it is hurt. I would rather heal it. But if it endangers the People..."

"There is always danger." The Seer paused. "You ask what you should do. I tell you, do what you think best." He slipped down from his stool and padded across the chamber to a table set against one wall, littered with parchments and writing-sticks and an assortment of colourful crystals. The Seer selected a bright green crystal, then pressed it to his forehead and closed his eyes. He held it there for a long moment, then sighed deeply, opened his eyes, and held out the crystal to Kerr'tok. "Return to the Strange One and give him this. Beyond that, you must decide."

Trembling, Kerr'tok had returned to the chamber where he had dragged the Strange One. The Seer had said the Destiny of the People rested in his claws, yet had given him no guidance, only a strange command. He considered going to his Secondfather; but his Secondfather would surely kill the Strange One. He could not let that happen until he had done as the Seer asked, however little he understood it.

He fervently wished he had stayed home that morning. Was a breath of surface air worth *this*?

Now he faced the terrifying Strange One. Its strange five-fingered hands were spread in a gesture Kerr'tok hoped was peaceful.

He reached out and put the crystal in one of them.

Ian instinctively closed his hand on the green crystal, then cried out and tried to drop it as it blazed with light—but his fingers wouldn't unclench.

Brighter and brighter it glowed, stabbing into his brain. His vision blurred and his head reeled, and for a moment he sensed a third person in the chamber, had an impression of age and immense wisdom—and then the crystal went dark and everything was as it had been.

He dropped the crystal as if it had burned him, and the alien snatched it out of the air with cat-like reflexes. "What happened?" Ian gasped, and the alien jumped back, fur bristling.

"You spoke!" it said.

Ian gaped. "I can understand you!" Then he clamped his mouth shut as he realized his words were not coming out in Unilingua, but in a vowel-heavy, moaning tongue.

"The Golden Seer has given you our language," the alien whispered.

"The Golden Seer?"

"The Old One..." Suddenly the alien straightened. "I am Kerr'-tok. Our meeting brings warmth."

"Uh—I'm Ian Thorne." His own name sounded strange in his hears. A thousand questions danced in his mind, but one overrode the others. "Where am I?"

"This is the Dead Passage of the Northwest Tunnel. I brought you here after finding you in the Mouth."

That meant nothing. "When?"

The alien closed his eyes for a moment. "The sun is now at zenith. I found you as it rose."

Ian struggled to his feet, wincing at the pain in his ankle. "Do you know where our base is? Can you lead me there? My people will want to meet you..." A considerable understatement. "And they'll be worried about me." Possibly an *overstatement*, at least in the case of his father.

Kerr'tok sprang back toward the door. "I will not let you destroy us!"

Ian stared. "Destroy you? We want to talk to you, learn about you, teach you about—"

"It is all the same! You would take us from the Path—the Seers have said!" His voice became a deep growl. "I will kill you if you try to leave!"

"You can't keep me prisoner! Let me go, or—"

"Or what, Strange One?"

Ian tensed, but the alien's gleaming fangs and claws made him hesitate. He was bigger and stronger, but also partially crippled and without those formidable natural weapons.

But what was Kerr'tok afraid of? "Why didn't you just kill me when you found me helpless?" he demanded. "Why bring me inside?"

Kerr'tok didn't relax. "I thought you were dead. I dragged you out of the Mouth so your people would not find you and perhaps stumble on us."

"But when you found out I was alive..." Ian took two limping steps toward him. "You didn't kill me because you don't kill if you can help it. You're peaceful."

"Come no closer!" Kerr'tok snarled.

Ian paused. "We're peaceful, too. We're no danger to you. *I'm* no danger to you. Let me go."

"I cannot! Golden Seer said I carry the Destiny of the People! If I let you return to your people, they will come here. They will find the hidden entrances, and the Path will be lost to us!"

Ian knew there was truth to what Kerr'tok said. Other non-technological sentients had lost their own cultures in the over-whelming galactic one, had been reduced to second-class members of a society they had not helped build and had no place in. He could imagine their anger and resentment—heck, he didn't have to imagine it; he had felt it himself when his father had taken him from *his* culture, Newhope, the only home he had ever known. He had struck back by disobeying his father and leaving the base—and had almost killed himself in the process.

Swallowing hard, he looked into Kerr'tok's blazing eyes. "I won't try to escape. I doubt I could, with this ankle." He lowered himself carefully to the floor, both to take the weight off his aching leg and to appear less threatening. "Tell me about your people. Maybe if I understood this Path of yours..."

Kerr'tok's ears perked, and his claws slipped back into their sheaths. "If you will tell me about yours! Though your Path is not ours, I admit I am curious about you Strange Ones." He slipped the pouch from his shoulder. "I have brought food and water for you..."

Ian grinned and gestured at the rock beside him. "Sit anywhere."

~

When Kerr'tok left the Strange One late in the afternoon his head whirled with all he had heard. Cities on a hundred planets, ships that sailed the stars, machines that thought...

The Tunnel seemed even more confining than before. *This whole planet is a prison*, he thought. *And we'll never be free of it if the Seers have their way.*

He stopped as though struck, frightened by his thoughts. The Seers were the guardians of the People. He had never before questioned their wisdom...had he already been led from the Path by the Strange One, in so short a time?

But isn't their way of life better than ours? something inside him argued stubbornly. What great Destiny could the People have except to dwindle away to nothing, a pale, fading remnant of a once-great civilization?

He came out of the Dead Passage into the Suncave. A green forest filled its vast expanse, lit and warmed by a giant, sun-bright glowbulb at the cavern's apex. Feathered flitters, blue and gold and red, mingled with yellow-furred furry gliders in the space above the trees, their chirping and chittering echoing off the cavern walls. Here, and in the other Suncaves, was all that remained of the once-teeming life of the surface, preserved by the Old Ones when they fled the encroaching ice.

Isn't that all we are doing? Preserving a dead way of life? Isn't it time we tried something new? What Destiny can possibly await us here except extinction?

He shook himself and followed a winding footpath down to the stream that meandered through the Suncave. He stretched out on its lush green bank and closed his eyes. He knew his family, especially his Secondfather, would be wondering where he was, but he couldn't return to them while such troubled thoughts filled his mind.

Music began in the distance, the rich harmonies of the Sunset Song drifting into the Suncave from the Passage of Ritual, marking the setting of the sun on the surface above and the slow dimming of the sunbulb. Kerr'tok heard the somber words as though for the first time:

> Beyond the mountains clad in ice
> The sun in blood goes down.
> The Dark of Death engulfs the land,
> The Shadowlord puts out his hand,
> And taking life as his due price
> Puts on his starry crown.
> But we who wander here below,
> Trapped in these caves of stone,
> Remember sunsets long gone by,
> And though black shadow fills the sky
> Our lives give night a golden glow
> As though the sun still shone.
> Through night and deadly day, storm-blown,
> We hear the future call.
> We tread the Path the Old Ones trace,
> Heads high, unbowed, a still-proud race,
> Our Destiny, our goal, unknown,
> But worthy of us all.

Kerr'tok opened his eyes and blinked at the sunbulb, no longer quite so bright, and taking on an orangey tint. No one knew their Destiny. No one knew the end of their Path. That meant it wasn't written in stone; it could be changed.

By him.

The Strange Ones could give us the Galaxy, and I want it, Kerr'tok thought. *But to have it I must surrender my people, too. What then of our struggle to survive and grow? It would mock our ancestors' courage.*

He got to his feet and climbed the slope back to the Dead Passage, his mind suddenly made up. Ian'thorne must not be allowed to betray them.

∾

Ian saw the approaching glow of Kerr'tok's glowbulb and thought, *Well, I'm ready for him.*

After Kerr'tok had left, he had thought long and hard about what the alien had told him about his race's tragic and proud history. All of that effort and sacrifice would be meaningless if the People were swallowed up in the greater galactic culture: their way of life would be relegated to a footnote in some dry textbook about extinct primitive civilizations.

Ian knew the People's Seers had real power—his ability to speak the People's language was proof of that. If they said contact between humans and the People would destroy the People, they were probably right. It had certainly destroyed other cultures.

Ian knew one other thing, something his father had told him: Aleutia, the planet of the People, was beginning to warm. The millennium-old ice age that gripped it had already eased. Within a few decades, the land above these caverns would be free of ice. The People could emerge and reclaim their planet...*if* it still belonged to them.

And so Ian had come to a decision. Both frightened and exhilarated, he watched Kerr'tok enter. "I have thought on our words," Kerr'tok said. "And I have decided—"

"I've thought about it, too," Ian interrupted, "and I've decided I can't go back." He took a deep breath. "I want to stay with the People."

Kerr'tok stared at him, fanged mouth gaping, and Ian laughed. "I hope that stunned look means you approve."

"It is a gift beyond hope," Kerr'tok breathed. He held out his clawed hand. "Come. I will take you to the Golden Seer, and then present you to my Secondfather, who rules this Tunnel."

"I would be honoured," Ian said. As he let Kerr'tok pull him to his feet he marvelled at how little emotion he felt. He had just written off his old life with a few simple words—and felt no regret. No doubt his father would grieve, or pretend to, for a few days. *After that,* Ian thought, *he'll probably be relieved to be free of me.*

He limped after Kerr'tok along the Dead Passage, anxious to see the fantastic underground civilization Kerr'tok had described, anxious to tell the Seer what he knew of the planet's future. Light glimmered faintly ahead. *The Suncave!* he thought with excitement, but Kerr'tok stopped suddenly and gripped Ian's arm so hard his claws pierced the warmsuit. "Hey—" Ian pulled away from him. "What's wrong?"

"Do you not smell it?" Kerr'tok hissed.

Ian smelled nothing but Kerr'tok. "Smell what?"

The light ahead grew stronger. "My people come!"

"So?"

Kerr'tok turned wide eyes toward him. His nostrils were flared and his breath came in short, rapid gasps. "They are in hunting heat—and the only prey in this passage is you, Ian'thorne!"

Ian didn't understand; but before he could respond a band of the People appeared down the tunnel—like Kerr'tok, but as large as Ian. They saw him and surged forward with a moaning howl that stirred the hairs on the back of Ian's neck.

"Stop, Secondfather!" Kerr'tok cried, thrusting Ian behind him and holding his glowbulb high. "There is no prey here!"

The lead alien slowed to a catlike prowl. "The Strange One is our prey," he growled. "Stand aside, second-son. Did you think we would not smell him? He is a threat. He must die!"

The aliens behind him howled their approval, and Ian's heart pounded in his chest.

"No!" Kerr'tok's scream was piercing and defiant. "The Golden Seer knows of the Strange One. He does not want him killed!"

"The Golden One advises, but I rule." The leader's tail lashed the air. "The Strange One must die and his body be found by the others, before we are uncovered in their search for him. Even now one of their crawling machines approaches the Mouth!"

Kerr'tok whirled to face Ian. "How?"

He paled. "The beeper must be getting through," he whispered. "The storm must have died. I couldn't turn it off..."

"Let us by, second-son!"

"No!" Kerr'tok howled again. Keeping himself between his elders and Ian, and not looking around, he asked, "What will make them go away?"

"They must find me, and the beeper."

"Dead?"

"No..." Ian stared at Kerr'tok's stiff back.

"You said you would stay rather than reveal us to your people, Ian'thorne. Would you protect us another way?"

Ian realized what was being offered. "Yes! If they find me with the beeper—they'll look no farther. We'll be gone for good in sixty days, and my father says there's nothing here to draw colonists...you'll be safe!"

"Then go!" Kerr'tok tossed his glowbulb back over his head and Ian caught it automatically. The alien kept his gaze on the now strangely silent mob. "To the very end of the passage. You will find the door back into the Mouth. Quickly!"

"But the others—"

"I will not let them pass," Kerr'tok said. "They cannot remove me without violence, and that is forbidden against another of the People." He raised his voice. "Or will you depart the Path to keep others on it, Secondfather?"

The older alien glared at him, ears twitching.

"Go, Ian'thorne," Kerr'tok repeated gently, finally looking back at him. "If I could, I would come see your marvels. But my people..."

Ian swallowed. "May warmth be yours, Kerr'tok." Then he turned and limped away as fast as he could, trying to ignore the pain in his ankle.

Behind him the mob howled, and again he heard Kerr'tok's piercing shriek of defiance, but he dared not look back. He ducked into the chamber where he had awakened and retrieved the beeper and his other gear, then limped on down the tunnel.

Only a few yards further along was another, smaller chamber. A simple system of ropes and pulleys connected to a sliding stone door. He hauled it up, then released the rope and dove through before the slab could descend again.

When he pulled up his hood his headphones were free of static, and outside the wind no longer howled. Above the sound of the beeper he heard a human voice. For a moment the words were unintelligible, then his brain switched gears and he recognized the Unilingua phrases. "Crawler Two calling Ian Thorne. Ian, can you hear us? Crawler Two calling—"

"Crawler Two, this is Ian. Come in!"

"Ian! You're alive!"

"Yes! Where are you?"

"Practically on top of your beeper, it sounds like. Where are *you?*" Ian explained briefly, and heard someone shout in the background. "We see it! We'll have you in five minutes."

"Is my father with you?"

Silence, for a moment. "Uh...he's back at base, Ian. He, uh, said he didn't see what use he'd be on a rescue mission."

Good old Dad, Ian thought bitterly.

"Hang in there, kid. You'll be home before you know it."

Home? Ian looked at the closed doorway behind him, and thought of the People. He would have been proud to be one of them...but could he really have joined them without destroying them in the process? His very presence had disturbed their civilization; led them from the Path, they would have said. If he had told them of their planet's warmer future...for all he knew, it might have destroyed them.

The People had their Destiny; he wondered if it weren't their unshakable purpose he had envied and wanted for his own life. "I guess I'll have to find it for myself," he murmured.

He only wished he could have met the Golden Seer...

Even as he thought that, another presence touched his mind, the wise old someone he had felt when the People's language was given to him. *Golden One?*

He heard no words, but warmth and gratitude flowed from the bodiless presence—then suddenly he was alone again, and, he realized with a trace of sadness, without any knowledge of the alien tongue.

Their Destiny is still their own, he thought. Outside he heard the crawler, and he smiled. *And so is mine.*

Kerr'tok's Secondfather finally pushed him out of the way. Ruffled but unhurt, he got back to his feet as the mob howled down the tunnel. He knew they would find nothing; he had felt the cold blast of air that meant Ian'thorne was safely gone.

He wondered what punishment he would face from his Secondfather. Severe, no doubt, but he would survive...as would their people. Ian'thorne would keep his word.

Briefly he thought of the shining civilization the Strange One had described, of the myriad worlds he would never see, the wonders he would never know.

But he pushed the thoughts away. *Ian'thorne has his Destiny, and I and my people have mine,* he thought.

For a moment felt the presence of the Golden Seer, warm with gratitude. "There's a thing or two I'd like to ask you, Golden One," he murmured, and turned toward the Suncave.

I COUNT THE LIGHTS

In 2016, Laksa Media released Strangers Among Us: Tales of the Underdogs and Outcasts, *edited by Lucas Law and Susan Forest, described thus: "Nineteen science fiction and fantasy authors tackle the division between mental health and mental illness; how the interplay between our minds' quirks and the diverse societies and cultures we live in can set us apart, or must be concealed, or become unlikely strengths." I was honoured to be one of the contributors to this anthology, a portion of the proceeds from which was donated to the Canadian Mental Health Association.* Strangers Among Us *went on to win an Alberta Book Award for Best Speculative Fiction and the Aurora Award for Best Related Work.*

~

SELVAN HORI, TERRAN AMBASSADOR TO PREVARIS, paused on the stairs that spiralled around the Tower of the Silent God and peered anxiously at the pool of shadow in front of him. One of the green lights that gleamed eerily every nine steps had just gone out, vanishing as he stepped away from the previous light, and between the darkness and the black stone, it looked disconcertingly like the next dozen or so steps had entirely vanished. Since he was currently some two hundred feet above the cobblestoned courtyard of the Temple complex that was not a comforting thought.

The air around him moaned with the constant song of the Tower, carved here and there with complicated openings that turned it into a giant organ pipe, played by the sea breeze by day and the land breeze by night, so that only in the stillness of dawn and sunset did it fall completely silent. The complex chord engendered awe and tranquility in Prevarians, apparently, but it contained enough subsonic frequencies that the dominant human response was faint terror.

The steps haven't gone anywhere, *he told himself.* The light has just gone out.

But he paused anyway, partly to gather his courage, partly to give his pounding heart a chance to slow and his breathing a chance to steady.

"I count the lights."

Alfred Kelvas, Head of Security for the Terran Diplomatic Mission to Prevaria, tapped the soundbud in his right ear and glanced at the flexible screen on the underside of his left wrist. The datalink status indicators glowed green. As far as the AI back in the Embassy was concerned, that had been an accurate translation of the short squeaking phrase the blue-skinned Prevarian monk hunched on the stone bench before him had just uttered.

Maybe the translation had been faulty in the *other* direction. Kelvas decided to try again.

"I'm sorry, I think the translator may have malfunctioned," he said, while the speaker concealed in the breastplate of the body armour he wore under his dark green uniform squeaked like a demented mouse. "I asked your name."

The monk splayed his three-fingered hands and turned them rapidly from side to side, the Prevarian equivalent of a vigorous nod. He squeaked again. "I count the lights."

Kelvas forced down his irritation. Two days ago, Ambassador Selvan Hori had fallen from the three-hundred-foot Tower of the Silent God, the central feature of both the Temple and the capital city of Prevaria. Support for the painstakingly negotiated trade agreement between Terra and Prevaria was plummeting as fast as the late ambassador had. Kelvas's superiors were demanding answers, the Prevarian Motivator, roughly equivalent to the Terran Prime Minister, faced revolt from the hard-core isolationists on her Council of Satraps, the Navy was making contingency plans for a complete withdrawal...and somewhere, the planetary pillagers who lurked in the shadows between the civilized stars were gathering their mercenary forces in anticipation of moving in and taking over. Prevaria stood on the brink of invasion, conquest, and environmental ruin, though its politicians didn't seem to grasp that reality.

All of that meant increasing pressure on Kelvas to find some answers. He didn't have *time* for malfunctioning translators.

Nor did he have time for the cheerful tri-tone bell that suddenly sounded in his earbud. "Excuse me," he said to the monk. "I have an incoming communication."

"I count the lights," the monk said...possibly.

Grimacing, Kelvas stepped off to one side. He tapped twice on his earbud to accept the call. "What is it, Simon?"

"I'm sorry to disturb you, sir," Simon's deep voice came back, "but Tyrone Boynton is in your outer office. He's been there since this morning. Five hours and counting."

Kelvas closed his eyes. "With Eve, I suppose?"

"No, sir," Simon said. "By himself."

Kelvas's eyes flew open again. *That* was new.

Eve Boynton had been after him for weeks to find a job for Tyrone in the Embassy. Kelvas liked Eve. He'd known her back on Earth; she'd come to their house in Bozeman for dinner once or twice, on weekend jaunts from the Diplomatic Corps Training Centre in Geneva, and his wife, Annie, had liked her, too. She'd barely mentioned her brother then—he and Annie had gathered Tyrone still lived with their parents, and was attending some kind of special school, but Eve hadn't said exactly what kind of school or why he needed to attend it.

But then, a few weeks ago, Tyrone Boynton had showed up *here*, on Prevaria, arriving on the regularly scheduled Navy supply ship, taking advantage of the rule that allowed family members to visit staff on station, at least in locations where nobody was shooting at each other. By the regulations, he was due to return to Terra on the next ship headed that way, in about a fortnight. But a week ago Eve had come to Kelvas, Tyrone in tow. They'd sat in his office, Eve stiff and upright in one of the leather-covered chairs in front of his desk, Tyrone in the other. No taller than Eve—and Eve was not a tall woman—he had an oddly unfinished look, his facial features soft and doughy. He'd sat with his eyes downcast, rocking slightly in his chair, his hands, too big for the rest of his body, gripping his knees tightly the entire time.

Eve had told Kelvas why Tyrone had come to Prevaria: the siblings' parents had died and she'd begged the authorities to send him to her. He couldn't live on his own, she'd explained. If he'd stayed on Earth—or if he returned there—he would be institutionalized. Eve, her voice breaking, had begged Kelvas to allow Tyrone to stay.

The trouble was, the Diplomatic Corps rules were clear: to live on Prevaria in the Embassy compound long-term—and draw a Diplomatic Corps paycheque—Tyrone had to have a job...of which there were none suitable to someone of his limited mental capacity. Kelvas had explained all that. Eve had begged. He'd finally gotten rid of her by agreeing to "see what he could do," but in fact he hadn't given it another thought—certainly it hadn't crossed his mind since the Ambassador's death.

He wouldn't have been particularly surprised to hear that Eve was waiting in his outside office, hoping to press her case further, but Tyrone by himself? That made no sense at all. The young man hadn't said a word when he'd been with his sister.

"What is he doing?" he asked Simon.

"Sitting. Staring at the Persons of Interest screen. Rocking back and forth," Simon said. "Special Agent Eston is the Officer of the Day. I could ask him to come take Tyrone away but...I think that would frighten him."

"Probably," Kelvas agreed. "I assume you've called Eve?"

"I've tried, sir, but she's on duty in the comm centre, and you know how crazy things are there since the...incident. She's out of touch for another couple of hours."

Kelvas sighed. "And I presume you've told Tyrone I won't be back for hours...if at all...today?"

"I tried, sir. I'm not...I'm not sure he understood."

Kelvas shook his head. He really did not have time for this. "Then let him sit there as long as he wants," he said, aware he'd let his irritation into his voice and not really caring, either. "Once Eve is off duty, have her come get him." *And then have her make sure he's on the first ship home,* he wanted to add, but didn't. *There's no place for someone like him here. Especially* now.

"Yes, sir."

"Anything else that needs my attention?"

"Mr. Kimblee would like to meet with you."

Kelvas sighed again. "Let me guess. He's champing at the bit to organize the withdrawal of the Embassy staff."

"He did indicate that contingency planning of that sort would be the purpose of the conversation," Simon said carefully.

John Kimblee, Kelvas's second-in-command, had never had a good word to say about Prevaria in Kelvas's hearing: he clearly resented being stationed on a primitive new-contact world without access to the many pleasures of the Core Worlds. He would have closed down the Embassy the second they'd heard about the Ambassador's death if it had been up to him.

Fortunately, it hadn't been.

"Tell Mr. Kimblee I will speak to him at my earliest convenience, and leave it at that," Kelvas said. "Anything else?"

"No, sir. Sorry to have bothered you."

"Just doing your job," Kelvas said. "No need to apologize." *But don't bother me again,* he wanted to say, and he suspected that, too, seeped into his tone of voice.

"Yes, sir," Simon said. "Simon out."

The tri-tone played again, in reverse order.

Kelvas took another look at the screen on the underside of his wrist. All datalinks remained green. He turned back to the waiting monk. "All right," he said. "Let's try this again. What's your name?"

Big-eyed like a lemur and with a snout like a dog, the monk looked up at the Tower of the Silent God, looming over the courtyard, and pointed with the longest, central finger of his left hand. "I count the lights!"

Ambassador Hori leaned against the black stone of the Tower, breathing deeply of the cool night air. He'd had no choice but to make this ascent. Prevarian tradition insisted that no treaty could be finalized until the negotiating satraps had ascended the Tower, both to meditate upon the agreement and to show their commitment to upholding it before the Silent God.

The climb was made along this staircase, bereft of any guardrail, which spiralled around the spire's exterior. Every nine steps glowed a dim green crystal lantern, set above a carved face, each face an Aspect of the God, each unique: some smiling, some frowning, some howling in rage or fear, some slack in sleep or death. Believers offered a silent prayer as they passed each Aspect. Ambassador Hori was not a believer in the Silent God, but he was a somewhat-lapsed Catholic, and now, as he waited to regain his breath, he offered a prayer of his own, to the Archangel Gabriel, patron saint of diplomats, that he could make it to the top of the tower without suffering a heart attack.

He dared not fail. To do so could well sabotage the trade agreement he had been working on for six long local years—almost eight Earth years.

He knew well enough there were plenty of Terrans for whom that would be the ideal outcome. For that reason, he was ordinarily accompanied everywhere he went by two bodyguards in constant contact with his head of security, Alfred Kelvas. But the High Deaconness who presided over the Temple Complex had made it clear that no weapons could be carried up the Tower, and since his bioengineered bodyguards were weapons in and of themselves, their presence on the Tower could and would have been seen as sacrilege, and used to derail the impending agreement. And so, over the strong objections of both his bodyguards and Kelvas, whom he had formally absolved of all responsibility for whatever might happen to him during the climb, he had left his men stationed at the foot of the steps, and ascended on his own.

His heart no longer pounded and his breathing came more easily now, and that in turn had lessened some of the sound-spawned disquiet. He was at least two-thirds of the way to the top—he could surely make it the rest of the way. There's life in the old man yet, *he told himself, smiling—it was something his wife liked to say to him. He took a fresh breath and, staying close to the Tower wall, stepped cautiously into the pool of darkness.*

Kelvas glared at the monk, still pointing uselessly at the Tower, and then spun away from him. He strode across the courtyard to where the High Deaconness stood with her handmaiden, a young Acolyte, in the shadow of the Tower, already lengthening as the sun sank toward the blue saw-toothed mountain range in the distant west.

"Is there a problem?" the High Deaconness said. Though her loincloth was the same plain white as the monk's, several jewelled gold bracelets on each arm and a gold circlet on her brow marked her rank as the highest non-secular authority on the planet.

"Yes, High Deaconness," Kelvas said, "I'm afraid there is. Your so-called 'witness' will only say one thing. 'I count the lights.'"

"I'm sorry," the Deaconess said. The translator rendered her squeaks as calm and slightly amused. "I thought I had made it clear that Brother Lodolo is one of the Holiest."

"Yes, I heard that," Kelvas snapped. He wondered if the translator would accurately render his irritation, and decided he hoped it did. "I thought that meant he would have special knowledge of the Tower. Why does he keep repeating that meaningless phrase?"

"But it is not meaningless," the Deaconess said, now sounding puzzled. "He is one of the Holiest. The Holiest are those closest to the Silent God, for their minds are uncluttered."

"Uncluttered?" Kelvas said blankly. Then he understood. "You mean...*empty?*" He glanced back at Brother Lodolo. "Oh, that's just wonderful," he snarled...under his breath, but of course the translator passed the phrase along.

"Is it not?" the Deaconess said. "To be able to concentrate on worship without the distraction of more mundane concerns...the Holiest are the most fortunate of the God's children."

Lodolo, clearly agitated, suddenly stood up and strode across the courtyard to Kelvas. He jabbed his finger upward at the Tower. "I count the lights!"

Kelvas's irritation swelled to the point he had to clench his jaw to keep from saying something so undiplomatic to the Deaconess it might provoke a worse crisis than the one in which they already found themselves. *Who am I kidding?* he thought sourly. *It couldn't get any worse.*

But he needed *answers.* He needed a *witness,* and he'd thought that was what he'd been promised. Instead, he'd been presented with the village idiot.

"Thank you," he said to Lodolo, though gratitude was the farthest thing from his mind. "I'm done."

He turned away.

Lodolo grabbed his arm. "I count the lights!" he cried. "I count the lights!"

Startled and annoyed, Kelvas pulled his arm free, so hard he tugged the monk off-balance. The little alien stumbled and fell onto his bare blue knees. Kelvas barely noticed. "Who else?" he demanded of the Deaconess.

The handmaiden had hurried forward to help Lodolo to his feet. Kelvas belatedly realized how badly he had just erred when he saw that the Deaconness's ears had flattened—as bad a sign in a Prevarian as in the dogs they vaguely resembled.

"You will talk to Lodolo, or you will talk to no one," the Deaconess said. Her squeaks had a sibilant hiss to them he didn't need the translator to interpret: he had deeply annoyed and offended her, and he couldn't afford that. If any answers were to be found, they would be found here, at the Tower of the Silent God, where the Ambassador had met his gruesome fate, so close to where Kelvas now stood that he would be walking in the man's blood if it hadn't been scrubbed from the stones.

The guards the Ambassador had left at the base of the stairs had heard the impact, halfway around the tower from them. They'd run to the scene. One had spent the next few minutes throwing up while the other, of stronger constitution, had frantically called Kelvas. Meanwhile the monks had also come running. As their religion demanded, they had immediately set about removing the Ambassador's scattered parts and ritually cleansing the place where he had died. By the time reinforcements had arrived from the Embassy, the Ambassador's remains had already been burned to ash in the furnace of the central altar, the smoke of his immolation rising up the chimney at the heart of the Tower, completing the ascent his body had fallen so fatally short of.

The fact the Prevarians had disposed of all evidence before the Terrans could even begin their investigation had not inclined the anti-trade forces among the Terrans toward granting the benefit of the doubt, and in turn their accusations of assassination were rapidly driving those few Prevarians still on the fence about the wisdom of trusting the Terrans toward their own anti-trade camp.

If any answers were to be found, it would have to be with the help of the High Deaconess; and so, though it grated on him like fingernails on steel, Kelvas forced himself to say, with as much sincerity as he could manage, "I apologize, High Deaconess." He looked at the monk, who stood hunched over, rubbing his knees. "Brother Lodolo." He turned back to the Deaconess. "I am feeling the stress and I allowed it to sharpen my tongue in a most undiplomatic way. Please forgive me."

The Deaconess's ears flattened further for a moment, and he thought he had ruined everything; but then they slowly rose. "Apology accepted," she said. "This is a difficult time for us all."

I doubt it's as difficult for you as it is for me, Kelvas thought sourly. *Although if the Navy withdraws and your precious Temple is flattened by scavengers* pour encourager les autres, *it will* be.

He turned back to the Brother Lodolo, who had straightened and folded his arms. He rocked from foot to foot. "I count the lights," he said, the translator giving his voice a pleading tone. "I count the lights. *I count the lights.*"

"I'm sorry," Kelvas said. He knew the apology sounded stiff, but he did the best he could. "I'm sorry, but I don't understand."

"Is your translation link broken?" the Deaconess said behind him.

"No," Kelvas said.

"Then how can you not understand? Lodolo counts the lights."

"But...why?" Kelvas turned back to her. The handmaiden who had helped Lodolo had taken up her eyes-downcast post at the Deaconess's left hand once more. "*Why* does he count the lights?" *And how the hell is that of any use?* he wanted to add, but didn't.

"I told you. He is Holiest. His mind is uncluttered, giving room for the presence of the Silent God. He counts the lights because that is how the Silent God has told him to worship."

This is going nowhere, Kelvas thought again. But diplomacy insisted he continue the charade a little longer. "But...what lights?"

"The lights of the Tower." The High Deaconess pointed up. "There are five hundred and sixty seven steps on the outside of the tower. Every nine steps, there is a light: sixty-three lights in all. Sixty-three is a holy number, for the holiest number is three, and sixty-three is three threes."

Three threes? Kelvas frowned for an instant, then understood: the Prevarians calculated in base four, in which the highest digit was three, because they were three-fingered. The numeral 333 in base four equaled 63 in base 10.

"Every night," the Deaconess continued, "Lodolo walks around and around the tower. He counts the lights, from bottom to top, then from top to bottom, then from bottom to top. He does this sixty-three times, one for each light. Then he ascends the Tower, counting again from bottom to top; and descends, counting from top to bottom. Thus does he worship the Silent God. And something he saw, as he performed this act of worship two nights ago —the night the Ambassador fell—has troubled him deeply. Offended him, I would judge."

But he can't communicate it, Kelvas thought. *Great. Perfect.*

Kelvas felt a cautious tug at the sleeve of his uniform. He looked around. Lodolo hastily stepped back, as though afraid Kelvas would knock him down again. *That was an accident*, Kelvas thought, but now that his irritation had subsided...slightly...he felt guilty. "It's all right," he said to the monk, keeping his voice as calm as he could. "What is it?"

Brother Lodolo, short even by the standards of his people, stood, child-like, only as tall as Kelvas's chest, which made it hard for Kelvas to remember that in fact—as the Deaconess had told him as she guided him to the monk—he was twice Kelvas's age. The Prevarians lived longer than humans, and Lodolo was elderly even so. He didn't repeat his single phrase this time: instead he pointed at Kelvas, then pointed up the Tower.

"I don't understand," Kelvas said, again. He was getting very tired of that phrase. He *hated* not understanding. It was his job to understand: to understand the ramifications of the deteriorating diplomatic situation, to understand the society of the planet on which he served, and when things went horribly awry—and nothing in his long career had gone as horribly awry as things had gone here with the Ambassador's death—to investigate *until* he understood. He glanced at the High Deaconness. "Do you know what he wants?"

"He wants you to Ascend the Tower with him," the High Deaconess said, the Translator rendering her as astonished. "It is a great honour. Without precedent."

A great honour? Kelvas thought. He looked up at the black stone spire. How many steps had she said? Five hundred and sixty-seven?

He sighed. Still, he followed Lodolo the short distance to the base of the Tower because, with the High Deaconess watching, what else could he do? *And anyway,* he thought sourly, *I could use a little divine favour right now.*

But as they approached the start of the long staircase that wound around and around the tower, Lodolo held up a three-fingered hand and then pointed to a bench built into the wall. "Now what?" Kelvas said, irritated all over again.

The High Deaconess and her handmaiden had followed them. "You cannot climb the Tower of the Silent God while the sun is above the horizon," she said, as if it were self-evident. "It is not a place one goes to see the sights of the world, but to see inside one's own soul. You must wait until twilight."

"I'm not—" *climbing it to worship your non-existent God,* Kelvas almost said, but fortunately thought better of it. Instead he paused, glanced at his watch, and said, "Very well."

Though the climate in the Prevarian capitol, tempered by the nearby ocean, varied little, the days still grew short in the winter, and the solstice was only a few tri-days away. Technically Kelvas could have returned to the Embassy for an hour, but that might have meant facing Eve and Tyrone Boynton or John Kimblee, and he didn't want *that*. So instead he sat on the bench next to Lodolo, who fortunately did not continue repeating "I count the lights" over and over again as Kelvas half-expected. Instead, the monk rocked silently.

The motion reminded Kelvas of Tyrone. He wondered if Eve's brother were still sitting in the outer office, staring at the Persons of Interest screen. The images and videos that cycled endlessly on that screen were of known troublemakers and terrorists and criminals. All Diplomatic Corps security headquarters were required to display the POI feed in prominent locations: the modern equivalent of a bulletin board covered with wanted posters. Kelvas had never heard of anyone being apprehended because someone had seen his or her image or video in the POI feed, but regulations were regulations.

Which reminded him again of Eve's request he bend those regulations for her brother. He sighed. Much as he sympathized with her plight, bending regulations risked an official reprimand, and that, in turn, risked a black mark on his record just before retirements—which could impact his pension.

Of course, failing to solve the murder of the Ambassador he was charged with protecting would be an even bigger black mark. He glanced at Lodolo. Was this rocking blue alien with the "uncluttered" mind really his only lead to what had happened?

Apparently, God help me. He glanced up at the Tower. Any *god*.

He turned over his wrist to expose the datascreen and spent the remaining time until sunset reading messages and sending several variations of, "The investigation is proceeding apace and a resolution is expected shortly," which was a flat-out lie, but at least bought time.

I'm chasing wild geese, he thought sourly as he sent the last message. He glanced at Lodolo, who had stopped rocking and now sat motionless, eyes closed. *And sooner or later those wild geese are going to turn into pigeons and come home to roost.* Despite everything, his mouth quirked. *I must be worried. I'd never have come up a mixed metaphor that ugly if I were thinking clearly.*

He sighed. He'd almost taken early retirement from Diplomatic Corps Security three years ago, and if he had, he and Annie would currently be fishing in the mountains of Montana and hoping against hope their daughter would find someone with whom to give them grandchildren. But the opportunity to be head of security at a major new embassy on a newly opened planet had seemed too good to pass up. The pay was very, *very* good. Though Annie hadn't made the trip out here with him, she'd visited a couple of times, courtesy of the free-transportation program that had also landed him with the Boynton problem.

I guess we can still go fishing after I'm cashiered out the service, he thought sourly. *In a much smaller boat. Wearing a disguise. Which will also be useful for panhandling for loose change on weekends.*

He sent a final note to Simon, updating his secretary on where he was and what he was doing. If he fell off the Tower like the Ambassador...well, it would end all hope of a trade agreement, for one thing, but what really concerned him was that he not simply vanish without Annie ever knowing what had happened.

Almost without his noticing, the sun had slipped behind the dome of the Temple. The lengthening shadows vanished completely a few moments later. In the deepening twilight Lodolo finally stirred, and looked up at the Tower. "I count the lights," he said helpfully.

"So I've heard," Kelvas said. He got heavily to his feet. "Let's get this over with."

The High Deaconess had left them during the hour they waited, but she reappeared now, striding across the stones of the courtyard on bare three-toed feet. "I will wait here for your return," she said. "To learn what you have found."

Or to make sure they clean up the blood promptly, Kelvas thought.

The eerie green bioluminescent lights of the Tower had come on as the light faded. As the evening land-breeze sprang up, the Temple had begun to emit a low organ-like chord that made the hairs on the back of Kelvas's arms stand up. He knew the Prevarians felt peace and awe when they heard it, but considering what had happened to the Ambassador, he thought the human fear-response might be more appropriate.

Lodolo began to climb. As they passed the first light he said, as Kelvas expected, "I count the lights"; but then, for the first time, he said something else. "One." Another nine steps. "I count the lights. Two." And again. "I count the lights. Three..."

They climbed onward. The steps, worn and slightly rounded, sometimes even sloped down, away from the tower. Kelvas kept as close to the wall as he could, trailing one hand along it. The last light slipped from the sky. Darkness surrounded the base of the Tower: all illumination in the Temple Complex was shielded to prevent it from spilling upward. Only outside the Complex wall did the ordinary bluish illumination favoured by the Prevarians appear, and even that was sparse: the Prevarians had better night-vision and what they considered brilliant illumination was more like what Kelvas associated with the kind of restaurant where the ambiance was more important than actually seeing what you were eating.

Lodolo strode confidently up the middle of the stairs, seemingly unconcerned by the ever-deepening abyss to his left. "I count the lights. Fourteen..."

Kelvas was fit for a man in his late 50s—he had to be, in his position—but he still found the climb wearing on him. The ambassador had *not* been particularly fit—he *hadn't* had to be, in *his* position—and Kelvas found himself impressed Hori had undertaken the climb at all. *He really believed in this trade agreement*, he thought. *He really cared about this planet and its...people.*

"I count the lights. Twenty-eight..."

Kelvas had never cared very much about any of the worlds on which he'd served. His heart was always back on Earth. He didn't *hate* the various aliens he'd met, and he'd done his level best to understand their societies, but not out of real interest: only so he could do his job and identify potential threats to the diplomats he was charged with protecting. He didn't think of them as people so much as *things* that he had to deal with efficiently in order to do his job.

"I count the lights. Thirty-two..."

Like this simpleminded monk. He gulped more air and kept climbing, trying to ignore the growing ache in his calves.

Around and around. And then...

Just like that, Lodolo stopped. He didn't say, "I count the lights." He didn't say...what number were they up to? Forty-six? Instead, he made a low, unhappy moan in his throat. He tugged at Kelvas's sleeve, and pointed. Kelvas, who had been climbing with his head down, concentrating on putting one foot after the other, looked up.

He couldn't see any reason for the delay. They stood two steps below one of the green lights, casting a paltry pool of illumination to his eyes, though no doubt beautifully bright to Lodolo. An Aspect of the God, smiling beatifically—although even that had a slightly demonic look to human eyes, given the strangeness of the Prevarian face—stared out from the wall below the light. The next light glowed some five metres away.

Kelvas looked at Lodolo. The monk, still moaning softly, had begun to rock back and forth again, for no reason Kelvas could see.

Kelvas resisted the urge to say. "I don't understand." He resisted the urge to say, "I count the lights. Forty-seven." But he couldn't just stand there all night, either. He took a step forward, and then another. The monk's moan deepened.

As then, as Kelvas passed the screaming Aspect of the Silent God, the next light, number forty-seven, went out.

To Kelvas's eyes, it was as if the steps disappeared completely, swallowed by the darkness. Their black stone barely showed even in the green light of the bioluminescent lamps. The stars glimmering overhead had no hope of reflection.

Lodolo plucked at Kelvas's sleeve, as though trying to stop him from advancing. But Kelvas pulled free, barely noticing, mind racing. Was this where the Ambassador died? Had Lodolo seen this interruption in the lights as he walked around the Tower, counting the lights?

But why had the light gone out? And what lurked in the darkness?

Kelvas turned and looked out over the city, trying to get his bearings. The Embassy glowed on the horizon, its Terran lights brighter and whiter than anything else in sight. The Ambassador had fallen from the side of the Tower facing the Embassy...a pointed fact that the anti-traders insisted pointed to a Prevarian murder plot.

It could have been right here.

It *had* to have been right here.

But how did that help him?

He couldn't send a forensics team up here to investigate: the Deaconess had made it clear that would not be allowed. The Prevarians lacked the technological know-how to even attempt to gather samples, and in any event, the steps were ritually washed every day, the only time anyone mounted the Tower while the sun shone.

If he were going to discover anything, it would have to be here and now. He took the flashlight from his belt and unfolded the collapsible framework that allowed him to attach it to his uniform cap so he could keep his hands free. With it firmly in place, he reached up and switched it on. Lodolo cried out in distress and flung his blue arm over his big eyes at flare of bright white light. "Sorry," Kelvas said. He started back up the steps, head down, studying each riser and runner in turn. A trip wire, perhaps? But no, not if the steps were washed daily: someone would have discovered it.

He looked up at the wall as he approached the spot where the next lamp should have gleamed. There it was, its crystal sides reflecting his torch, but devoid of even the slightest green glow itself. Below it, the Aspect of the Silent God: in this instant, in sharp contrast to the Aspect he'd just left, screaming in apparent terror, mouth wide, eyes bulging, the perfect embodiment, for a human, of the Tower's constant threatening moan.

He looked down at the steps again, and leaned forward to get a closer look at the step right in front of the burned-out lamp.

Just enough light came from the stars glittering above that Ambassador Hori could make out the shape of the dark lantern, and the indistinct Aspect of the God below it. He came abreast of it.

Something slammed into his side. He toppled left. The steps were only a metre wide, and sloped downward. His upper body fell into nothingness, and dragged his legs with it.

Prevarian gravity was very close to Earth's. Ambassador Hori had just over four seconds to stare up at the whirling stars above him before, for him, they were blotted out forever.

"I count the lights!" Lodolo shouted—*screamed*. Then the monk slammed into Kelvas from behind even as something else shot over his head, brushing against his shoulder. Kelvas thudded to the steps, gasping, then rolled over.

In the light from his torch he saw Lodolo struggling for balance on the very edge of the precipice, giant eyes enormously wide in terror, arms flailing. He started to fall backward...

Kelvas lurched forward and grabbed the monk's blue-skinned

ankle, jerking Lodolo back onto the steps even as he toppled. The monk slammed down on the black stone harder than Kelvas had, and lost his breath completely, gaping soundlessly as his face purpled in the light from Kelvas's headlamp.

Kelvas whipped around again, turning his head this way and that, searching frantically for their attacker. The circle of light slid over black stone. Nothing on the steps. Nothing on the—

No...there! A flicker of movement, in the gaping mouth of the Aspect of the God. He raised his light. A round black ball, contracting as he watched, settled silently into place. An instant later the darkened lamp glowed back to dim green life.

Kelvas got carefully to his feet and drew the weapon he wasn't supposed to be carrying on the Tower, a tiny personnel stunner. He jammed it into the opening and triggered its powerful electric jolt. The thing in the mouth of the carved face sizzled and popped and then dropped to the steps, which sloped downward enough it would have rolled off if Lodolo, recovered somewhat, hadn't shot out a three-fingered hand and grabbed it. "I count the lights!" he gasped out.

"Indeed you do," Kelvas said. "And you do a very good job of it." He picked up the ball to examine later. He held out his hand to the monk, who gripped Kelvas's five fingers in his three and let Kelvas help him to his feet. Kelvas took a deep breath. Adrenaline had left him feeling a little shaky. "Let's go down," he said.

But Lodolo, releasing his hand, tilted his head left then right then left again, head the Prevarian equivalent of a human head-shake. "I count the lights." He moved to the wall and touched the lamp, fully alight again. "Forty-six," he said. And then he turned away from Kelvas and resumed climbing. "I count the lights," he said nine steps farther along. "Forty-seven."

Kelvas hesitated. He looked at the black ball. Then he shoved it into his pocket and followed Lodolo, all the way to the top of the Tower of the Silent God.

Four Prevarian tri-days later, Kelvas sat in his office at the Embassy, his back to his desk, looking out over the city through the office's single large window. In the middle-distance, the Tower of the Silent God pointed at the sky. The sun had almost set, and already the green lights were beginning to glow along the five hundred and sixty-seven steps.

The black ball he had recovered had quickly revealed its secrets: triggered by the presence of a Terran, as had been the dousing of the light, but not by the presence of a Prevarian, it had been planted very specifically to kill the Ambassador...or any other human who happened to climb the Tower, but no other human ever had or had been expected to.

It was clearly not Prevarian technology, but tracing it to its human source might have proved impossible had a lead not have been forthcoming from a most unexpected source.

Hence the visitors whose arrival Kelvas was at this moment awaiting.

The tri-tone chimed in his earbud. He tapped it twice. "Yes, Simon?"

"Eve and Tyrone Boynton are here," Simon said.

"Send them in," Kelvas said. He turned around to face the door, and stood as Eve and her brother entered. He nodded to Eve, whose face bore an interesting expression of mingled hope and pride, but when he'd rounded the desk, he went straight to Tyrone. "Tyrone," he said. He held out his hand. Tyrone looked at it.

"Shake his hand, Tyrone," Eve said.

Tyrone looked at her, then back at Kelvas's hand. He held his hand out hesitantly. Kelvas took it and shook it firmly. "Thank you, Tyrone," he said. "Without your help, we never would have solved Ambassador Hori's murder."

"Mr. Kimblee...meet with bad man," Tyrone said in his high-pitched voice, soft and lilting as a child's. "I saw him." He pulled his hand back, and turned around and pointed at the office door. "Out there."

"I know you did," Kelvas said.

He had returned from his climb of the Tower to find Tyrone and Eve waiting for him in his outer office, under the watchful eye of Simon. Simon had leaped to his feet as he entered. "I'm sorry, sir," he'd said. "I called Eve as soon as she came off-duty, but she couldn't get Tyrone to leave, either."

"I'm sorry, Mr. Kelvas," Eve said, and he heard the fear in her voice, knew she was afraid Tyrone's strange stubbornness would convince Kelvas once and for all there was no place for her brother on Prevaria. "All he'll tell me is that he has to talk to you. Over and over again."

Over and over again, Kelvas thought. *Like Lodolo.* And so he had done what he would never have done before, and sat down next to Tyrone and asked the boy what he wanted to say.

And Tyrone had pointed at the POI screen and explained, in his halting fashion, that he had seen Mr. Kimblee talking to one of the people on that screen. He had pointed out the man when his face rolled around again: a certain Peter Legat, with known ties to one of the criminal syndicates bankrolling some of the more notorious of the planetary pillagers.

Tyrone, it turned out, liked to walk around the Embassy compound late at night. "He doesn't sleep well since Mom and Dad died," Eve had explained. "He walks to make himself tired."

I wonder if he counts the Embassy lights? Kelvas had thought in passing, while he busied himself with sending messages, and arranging an arrest detail. A little over half an hour after Kelvas's return from the Tower John Kimblee was in custody and under interrogation.

As Kelvas's second-in-command Kimblee had of course been fully aware of the Ambassador's plan to ascend the Tower of the Silent God. A thorough forensic audit of his assets had revealed that he had also been in the pay of Legat's syndicate. His enjoyment of the luxuries of the Core Worlds had not been feigned: he'd enjoyed them so much, during his last visit there, that he'd been massively in debt until he agreed to work with Legat to try to sabotage the Prevarian trade agreement.

Of course, although the murder device had been of human manufacture it had not been *placed* by a human: that had been the work of one of the *Prevarian* anti-trade factions: one whose own links to the waiting scavengers had been uncovered by the...*forceful*...investigations of the Prevarian government. The faction had made a deal to rule the planet on the scavengers' behalf once the trade deal was dead and the Terran Navy gone. The sacrilege of Prevarians actually daring to climb the Tower of the Silent God in order to commit murder had shaken Prevarian society to its core, just as the corruption revealed on the Terran side had shaken Earth—and destroyed several fortunes, reputations, and political careers.

The new Ambassador, Kuzue Akamatsa, even now awaited the descent of darkness so that she...and her entire staff...could ascend the Tower. Once that had been done, the trade agreement would, at last, be formalized. Kelvas had spent the day making the security arrangements for the signing ceremony to be held the next day in the Great Hall of the Prevarian People, out of sight on the other side of the Embassy from his office.

But that was for later. "You did a good job, Tyrone," he said. "A very good job. Would you like to work for the Diplomatic Corps permanently?"

He heard Eve's gasp, but he didn't look at her, only at Tyrone. Tyrone's brows pulled together. "Perm...permanently?"

"For good," Tyrone said. "Work, and stay here with your sister. For good. "

Tyrone's face split into an enormous grin. "Yes, Mr. Kelvas! Yes, please!"

Now Kelvas looked at Eve. "He'll work as a night watchman,"

he explained. "He'll walk the grounds just as he has been. He'll report anything out of the ordinary he sees." He turned back to Tyrone. "Can you do that? Watch carefully every night? Report anything you see that you think is strange?"

Tyrone nodded vigorously. "I see things," he said. "I see when things are different. That's how I saw Mr. Kimblee and the bad man. I can do that."

Kelvas held out his hand again. "Then welcome to the Terran Diplomatic Corps."

This time, Tyrone shook his hand without prompting.

Kelvas looked at Eve again. "Take him to HR and get the forms filled out," he said. "They're expecting you."

"I stay, Eve!" Tyrone cried to his sister. "I stay!"

Tears glistened on Eve's cheeks. She hugged Tyrone tightly. "You stay!" She smiled over his shoulder, rather wetly, at Kelvas. "Thank you, sir, thank you!"

"You're welcome," Kelvas said softly.

Eve led her brother out of the office, and Kelvas returned to his chair. He turned it to look out the window once more. Darkness had descended at last. The new ambassador would be beginning her ascent of the Tower of the Silent God.

Though he couldn't see all of them, Alfred Kelvas began to count the lights.

THE MOTHER'S KEEPERS

In 2017, Laksa Media followed up Strangers Among Us *with* The Sum of Us: Tales of the Bonded and Bound, *once again edited by Lucas K. Law and Susan Forest: "Twenty-three science fiction and fantasy authors capture the depth and breadth of caring and of giving. They find insight, joy, devastation, and heroism in grand sweeps and in tiny niches. And, like wasps made of stinging words, there is pain in giving, and in working one's way through to the light." Once again, a portion of proceeds went to the Canadian Mental Health Association, and once again, I was one of the included authors...*

I WAS TWELVE YEARS OLD when the Krollians invaded for the first time.

We heard of the attack the way we Keepers heard of all doings on the surface: as rumours, running through the corridors of the Mother's House like the rivulets of water that sometimes found their way through cracks in the walls despite our best efforts.

"Praella, did you hear? The Krollian monsters have attacked us," my best friend, Melka, whispered to me as we waited to carry our blocks of biosugar into the refining chamber. Her headruff, normally erect with the vibrant force of her bubbly personality, lay flat against her narrow skull, and her normally iridescent pre-pubescent scales had shifted to near-black. "I heard it from Pillory, who heard it from Fanella, who heard it directly from Slivian, who is her comfortmate."

I nodded. That made it authoritative indeed: Slivian was the Gatekeeper of the Public Courtyard, and she alone among all of us spoke regularly with the people on the surface.

"Do you think they will come here?" Melka said then, quieting her voice even more. Idle chatter was discouraged among all Keepers while on duty, but *especially* idle chatter that might undercut morale and hence reduce the efficiency of our service. "The Krollians? Into the Mother's House?"

"No," I said, and I said it with complete confidence, because I was twelve, and I had been born into the service of the Mother, and I believed in the sanctity of our mission and the wisdom of the Seniors absolutely and without reservation. "They will not."

Then we heard a warning hiss behind us and twisted around to see Senior Santilla giving us a look as cold as the cryocreche, and we spoke no more of it.

My faith seemed justified: within a day whispers ran through the halls that the Krollians had been repelled, and that only a few dozens of our warriors had been killed and returned to the Mother, and life went on as before in the Mother's House, as it had gone on for generations before my birth, and as I thought it would go on for my entire life and many generations more.

But I was only twelve.

I was nineteen years old during the Winter of Terror. The years since the Krollian invasion had seen an uneasy peace grow between their race and ours, and so a few Krollians had been permitted into our city. They were always under guard, peace or no peace, because they were so large and fearsome in appearance, and so bristling with natural weaponry, that had a single one run amok many lives might have been lost. Yet despite being closely watched, these tourists, we heard, had turned out to be terrorists, for in every public place which a Krollian had been permitted to visit, a bomb exploded. A thousand people died in the explosions and ensuing conflagrations, and the Mother herself lost several appendages, to the dismay and consternation of the Physicians, who rarely had to deal with extensive injury. We would have gone to war against the Krollians then and there if not for the fact that we had no means of doing so: our weapons had always been purely defensive, powerful at driving off invaders but stationary and useless for attack.

Or so I heard, again through rumours dribbling through our corridors, again finding their way to my ear through Melka, by then my comfortmate. We shared quarters just outside the waste treatment chamber on Level 6, where we were assigned. A nasty and smelly assignment it was, too, at least when the aging tubes failed and we had to clean up the Mother's untreated feces, but all young Keepers did a turn in waste management and we did not complain...at least, not where a Senior could hear us.

"I heard the Krollians had requested an opportunity to visit the Public Courtyard of the Mother's House," Melka whispered to me as we cuddled in our sleep pod. Both of us had shed our final childskins a year before, and our adult scales, so much softer than the protective ones of our immaturity, made a pleasant slithering sound as she shifted position against me. "If that had been permitted..."

I nuzzled her neck. "No bomb could have been planted in the House without the Seniors finding it," I murmured, very softly, for it was late and my mind was already drifting toward sleep. "You worry too much, Melka."

"And you don't worry enough, Praella," I thought she said, but I may have dreamed it, for my consciousness was already slipping away.

I was twenty-five years old when we finally attacked the Krollians. The warrior males had spent the intervening years building new weapons, studying maps, planning the assault. By the time I heard of the attack, it was long over, the wounded and our dead streaming back into the cities, returning to the nurturing arms of the Mother. A great victory, the males said, or so the rumours ran in our halls, and I, still young and trusting, accepted that. Melka did not, and we argued. We were arguing a lot, by then.

Though I accepted the claim of victory, I knew how the number of dead and wounded must have distressed the Mother, as she provided nourishment for those in recovery and digested those who did not—or whom the Physicians deemed would not—recover. We were worked off our feet for months, and *our* stress was but a pale reflection of the Mother's. How much that stress affected her I did not know, then, but I found out soon enough.

We all did.

I was thirty-three years old when the Mother became ill.

This time the news did not come to me through rippling rumour. By then Melka and I had had our inevitable final disagreement, and no longer shared sleeping quarters or anything else beyond cursory nods when our paths crossed in the corridors. Leaving Melka, some three years after the Winter of Terror, had helped me to focus on my work to the exclusion of all else, and now I was a Keeper of the First Tier, only one step below the Seniors, the youngest ever to achieve that rank. As a Keeper of the First Tier, I had the privilege of attending the Seniors' Council, though of course I was forbidden to speak during the meetings or to speak *of* the meetings to anyone outside the Council afterward. Santilla, who had frightened me into silence more than twenty years before, was now Eldest, and therefore the only one of the Keepers to whom the Mother spoke directly, and then only in fragments that had to be carefully interpreted before any proclamation of the Mother's will could be made.

But Santilla was unequivocal in *this* proclamation. 'The Mother is unwell," she told us. "The Physicians are examining her biological systems as we speak, but they have so far found nothing specifically wrong, nothing they can treat. They say she is suffering from a generalized stress disorder. Her tissues are deteriorating."

The other five Seniors on the Council exchanged glances, their bedraggled ruffs, patchy with age, flat against their brown-spotted skulls. "But...she is the Mother," one of them said at last. "She cannot be ill. What will become of our people if she is ill?"

"She is a living creature," Santilla said, her voice as cold and implacable as the glare with which she had so often frightened me when I was a child. "All living creatures are subject to the ills of the flesh. All living creatures eventually die."

"Die?" The whisper came from my right, not from the round table at the centre of the Council chamber, and I shot a horrified glance in that direction, at Astilla, the only other First Tier Keeper, some ten years my elder. Fortunately for her, the Seniors' age-occluded hearing masked her outburst. I pretended I had not heard, either, but I understood her shock. Was the Mother *dying*? *Could* the Mother die?

Of course she could. Of course she *would*. As Santilla had just said, all living creatures eventually die and though the Mother's House was filled with machines to support her vast, sprawling body, the Mother was still a living creature. But I had never imagined it could happen in my lifetime. The Mother had existed for centuries, and all of us Keepers were the fruit of her wombs, her parthenogenic offspring, born only to serve her needs, to care for her immense body and the support systems that aided its function, while on the surface, in the City that had grown around her House, her fruiting bodies and medical teats and a hundred other interfaces provided sustenance for the males and females who reproduced and lived and died in the ordinary way.

Without the Mother, the City would collapse. The population would have no choice but to flee, to set up some poor, scrabbling settlement like those our people had subsisted in for millennia before the creation of the Mother. And if the latest rumours were true, and the Krollians now surrounded us, there was nowhere to flee.

If the Mother died, if she even became too ill to provide for her surface children...then every one of our people might likewise die. Our race could cease to exist!

"What do we do?" asked Frenella, the youngest of the Seniors, only ascended to the council a half-year before. "Eldest? What would the Mother have us do?"

"The Mother has not spoken to me," Santilla said. "I have prayed night and day for a word, a single word, but have heard nothing." For the first time her façade of icy calm cracked a little, and with it her voice, as she added, "All we can do is our duty. All we can do is continue to care for the Mother, as we have been born to do."

We shuffled from the Council chamber, lost in our own thoughts.

The next day, I learned that Astilla had fled the House during the night, vanishing into the city throngs. As the only other Keeper of the First Tier, I became first in line for the Council of the Seniors, as soon as there was an opening: as soon, in other words, as a Senior died.

~

I became a member of the Council of Seniors two years later, when I was thirty-five years old, the way opened for me by the death of Santilla, who failed quickly after the fateful meeting where she told us of the Mother's illness, as though beneath her icy exterior her strength had melted away and poured out of her at having to deliver such devastating news.

The new Senior was named Quinla. The Mother did not speak to her, either.

~

I was fifty-seven years old when the last of the Keepers who were not on the Seniors' Council abandoned their service.

The Mother's condition had worsened, slowly but inexorably, in the years since Santilla first shocked us with her announcement. Whole levels shut down without warning. The appendages nourishing the City above withered and died and rotted. The smell of decay hung, a choking miasma, in our halls. We no longer heard much of anything from the world above, but more and more of our sisters fled there, fled the stench of rot and despair: Astilla had just been the first of many.

Among them: Melka. We had not spoken for years, but I still felt a pang, like an echo of an echo of an echo of loss, when I heard that she, too, had abandoned her sacred duties to try to save herself.

The departures became even more frequent as word trickled down to the Keepers that the Krollians had promised safe passage for anyone who wanted to flee the dying city. The tale now was that the Winter of Terror had in fact been engineered by a faction of warmongers among our own males as a pretext for a strike against the Krollians, whose wealth and resources they envied. With the defeat of our forces (for the "great victory" had been just the opposite), the truth had come out. Supposedly peace now reigned between our peoples, though some still wondered darkly if those who entered Krollian lands ever emerged beyond them.

Yet even those fears did little to convince our Keepers to stay with the Mother, and so we dwindled, and dwindled, and dwindled still.

Although, to be blunt, there was little enough for the few Keepers who remained during those final years to do. Duties unchanged for centuries simply ceased to matter: the careful trimming of tissue, the cleaning of conduits and cables, the oiling of exposed flesh. Dead tissue need not be trimmed, unused conduits need no longer be maintained, broken cables connecting two nodes that had both ceased to function need not be spliced, and wherever the Mother's flesh lay exposed, it seemed, it glistened with the iridescent slime of unchecked bacterial growth, rotting away from the surface as well as from beneath.

Yet the Mother still lived, and we continued to look after her remaining hearts and, in the most sacred and central chamber of all, her massive brain, untouched by decay but increasingly cut off from the outside world. What thoughts still flickered within that table-sized mass of grey matter none of us could tell, for the Mother had spoken to no one for years. Fanella had ascended to the position of Eldest five years after Quinla, and she, too, had no response to her prayers and pleading.

One by one, the remaining few Keepers who were not on the Senior Council slipped away, to throw themselves on the mercy of the Krollians. Five of us remained: only five, where once there had been five hundred.

When I was seventy-one years old, I became Eldest.

There were only two of us left by then: Fanella and I. The other Seniors had died; in two cases, taken their own lives. Fanella had been so sunk in dementia for three years by then that she could not even feed or clean herself, and so I cared for her as I still cared for the Mother, though my duties had dwindled to preparing the nutrient mixture that kept her brain and her last still-beating heart functional.

Like the Mother, the House had fallen into decay, and I rarely ventured into its dark, dank halls: I couldn't bear to see the corridors that once had thrummed with activity and life reduced to grim grey catacombs. I lived my life in a few central rooms, surviving on the same nutrients I gave the Mother and Fanella, mixed from the vast stocks that could have supplied our meagre needs for a hundred years.

One morning I went into Fanella's cell and found her lifeless in her bed, her filmed eyes wide and staring, her scales already beginning to fall from her emaciated body. I placed her into the digestive tank, and so she became the last of the Keepers to feed the Mother, the final sacred duty of a lifetime of duty.

I wondered, as I watched her body bubble and twist as it sank into the dark green fluid, if even Fanella would have remained to the very end, had she still been capable of independent thought or action these last few years; or would she, too, seeing the object of her devotion and duty slowly slipping away, have decided to steal a final few years for herself, and leave the Mother to her inevitable decline?

I also wondered, as I turned from the bubbling pool, why *I* had remained.

I picked up a fresh bladder of nutrient and made my way, far more slowly than I used to, for arthritis had me firmly in its fiery grip, up the long stairs to the Mother's brain chamber. Like so many others, I could have left years ago, while there were still people in the city above us. I doubted any now remained: I had had no word from the surface for years, but an exploration of the corridor leading to the Public Courtyard had ended a hundred yards shy of the exit when I encountered tons of rubble blocking my path, some of it clearly from the elaborately carved stones of the Courtyard walls.

I hoped that the Krollians had been true to their word and let my people pass safely through their lands. Perhaps the rubble choked the hall simply because, with my people gone, the Krollians had razed the city to build their own structures. Perhaps even now ten thousand Krollians lived their lives above me, unaware of my existence, or the Mother's slow dying.

Perhaps. Or perhaps the Krollians had murdered everyone, destroyed the City, and salted the earth upon which it had stood.

There were other passages to the surface, of course, through the winding halls where the Mother's appendages had once stretched their way, but I dared not risk the journey. If something happened to me, what would become of the Mother? I knew she was dying, knew there was nothing I could do to stop it, but I would not abandon her. I would not leave her to die alone. My life had been spent caring for her, and my life would end caring for her. To leave would have made my life a travesty; to stay gave it meaning.

I attached the nutrient bladder to the feeding tube, and sat silently, rubbing my aching knees, as slowly, so slowly, the Mother took the nutrients into what little of her remained.

My care of the Mother would not last much longer, I knew. Someday soon the Mother would finally die. Perhaps then I would make my way to the surface and see what was left of our world. But not before.

Not before.

It was clear the single nutrient bladder would last the Mother for hours yet. I made my slow, aching way back down the stairs to my hard, narrow cot.

When I was eighty-four years old, the Mother died.

I woke from troubled sleep. Someone had spoken to me.

I stared into the darkness. I now slept in the Mother's brain chamber, making my agonizing descent to the nutrient chamber no more than once a week, for the Mother took almost no food now. Nor did I: my limbs were frail, my fingers like matchsticks. Every night when I lay down I wondered if I would awake, if, after all this, I would fail in my charge, and, by dying before the Mother, leave her to die alone after all.

But someone had spoken to me. Someone had *spoken* to me.

Praella, the voice in my head said again, and I barely recognized the word as my name, I had not heard it in so long.

My mind has gone, I thought.

No, said the voice. *It has not.* It sounded amused, but also very, very tired.

"Mother?" I whispered out loud, in sudden fear and hope. I was Eldest, the Mother only spoke to the Eldest, but I had never thought, especially not *now*, so near the end...

My time is done, the Mother said.

"No," I protested, but it was a foolish thing to say, as if she did not understand the truth as well as I.

Are you trying to salve my feelings? the Mother's amused voice replied within my head. *There is no need. I have been dying for a very, very long time. It is a wearisome process, and I am glad to reach an end.*

I sat up, slowly and painfully, as I did everything, and looked at the Mother's brain. Her last heart still beat slowly, erratically, in the chamber beneath us, and I could see the vessels on the surface of the brain swell as each slow contraction drove blood through them. "Why have you not spoken to me until now?" I said out loud. I heard the peevishness in my own voice but did not try to soften it. "I have been caring for you, alone, for years. Alone."

Why? the Mother asked then.

I started to speak, stopped, reconsidered.

Why? the Mother asked again.

I waited a moment longer, the answer growing within me until

I was certain. "Because," I finally said, my voice hoarse, for even this little bit of speaking had tired it after years of non-use, "that is who I am. A Keeper of the Mother. Born of you, to care for you. I could not abandon that charge and remain who I am. I would become something else, something I do not know how to be, something I do not *want* to be.

"I am a Keeper. I am the Eldest. I am the last."

Then it is time, the Mother said within my head, and though I opened my mouth to ask, "Time for what?" I never uttered the words, for in that instant the Mother filled me: every corner of my mind, every corner of my body, a flood of knowledge and memory, power coursing through me such as I had never imagined. I could feel my body changing, feel my every cell being rewritten.

I gasped.

The Mother's brain quivered, then stilled.

The veins upon its surface no longer pulsed.

The Mother was dead, but I still lived...

...and the Mother lived in me.

I rose from my bed. I no longer ached. My scales were as smooth and soft as when I used to share a bed with Melka, my joints renewed, my eyes clear, my hearing unmuffled.

I no longer feared for my people. The Mother knew, had always known, where *all* of her children had gone. The Krollians had been true to their word. My people now lived in a valley five hundred miles to the east, a valley that opened into the sea. They had become fishers and farmers. A new settlement was already beginning to take shape, but it would always be a primitive place compared to what they had lost...unless they had a Mother.

I will make my way there, the last to leave the old city. I will rejoin my people, the Mother's children: my children, now. I will call the Keepers who still live, Melka and the rest, and though they once abandoned their charge, they will return to me. They will help build a new House for their new Mother using the knowledge I now carry within me, and once it is built, I will let the changes begin.

As the centuries slip past, I will grow to fill the House. I will feed and comfort the City and its inhabitants, and my offspring will care for me as I once cared for my Mother.

And someday, far into the future, I, too, will slip at last into the silent night of death...and a new Keeper will receive the ancient memories, and the cycle will begin again. I, Praella, will be just a memory of a memory by then...but not completely forgotten. *Never* completely forgotten.

There is no immortality. Everyone dies. But as long as our race survives, I will be remembered, by Mother, after Mother, after Mother: the Keeper who kept her promise, the caregiver faithful to her Mother to the end, and who in turn became the new Mother of a new world.

FAIRY TALE

In some ways, this previously unpublished tale may be the most subversive story I ever wrote: a counterpoint to portal fantasies. (Which I love, don't get me wrong. But real life and the real world can be as wonderful as any fairy tale or fantasy realm...)

ON A SPRING DAY SO MAGNIFICENT the cankerworms were bungee-jumping from the tops of the elms out of pure glee, Alexander Parker found a fairy.

He wouldn't have seen it at all if he hadn't decided that morning (for the umpteenth time) that he really should get more exercise. So, after he got home from dropping Mary off at work, he crossed the street, intending to walk around the park a couple of times before settling down at the computer for another thrilling day of writing technical manuals.

The leaves hung limp in the windless air, so the sight of a mosquito trap swinging wildly from its thin wire hanger brought him up short. Intrigued, Alex walked over to the trap and peered inside.

The trap looked like two small pizza boxes stapled together at the corners. A sticky substance covered a blue grid on the bottom, and trapped in it, along with innumerable dead mosquitoes, a feebly squirming wasp, and a couple of shiny black beetles, was something large and flapping.

At first Alex thought it must be one of the giant moths that had appeared from nowhere that year. Mary had glimpsed one fluttering around the porch light the night before and had let out a yelp that brought Alex running. Alex grinned at the memory. Mary, a city girl, hated moths, mice, spiders, grasshoppers, and most other things that crawled, scurried, hopped or just hung there. Although Alex had grown up on a farm, he found her squeamishness endearing. It gave him a chance to play Fearless Outdoorsman, and the look of gratitude in her eyes when he'd chased the Moth from Hell into the night had sent pleasurable chills down his spine.

The creature's wings fluttered again, and it squeaked. Alex frowned. Moths didn't squeak. A bat?

Too small. He moved in closer. Its wings glistened like...a dragonfly's, maybe? Still cautious, Alex picked up a twig, reached into the trap's dim interior, and gave the thing a poke.

"Ouch!" it squeaked, and Alex jumped back, tripped over his own feet and fell on his rear in the grass.

Feeling silly, he scrambled to his feet and brushed off his butt, hoping no one had seen him. Imagination, that's all it was. Nevertheless, his heart pounded as, holding his twig like a tiny sword, he advanced on the trap once more.

"Poke me with that thing again and I'll poke it back where the sun don't shine!" a tiny voice screeched.

Alex's heart went into triple time, but this time he stood his ground. *It's a trick,* he thought. *A publicity stunt...there's a camera somewhere...*

"No, nobody's videoing this," the voice snapped. "And you aren't crazy, and since I can tell just by looking you've always been a major nerd, I think you can also rule out a drug flashback."

"Bu—bu—but—" Alex didn't normally stammer, but this occasion seemed to call for it. "Who—what—"

The voice sighed. "It's easier to show you than explain. Stick your big ugly nose in here and take a good look. I don't sting."

Expecting at any minute to hear the theme music from *The Twilight Zone*, Alex did as he was told. What he saw made him wonder if someone had slipped PCP into his morning coffee at the Human Bean.

The creature had spread its glistening wings and now sat glaring at him. Its eyes were huge and blue, Japanese anime eyes, way out of proportion to its face. Aside from that, and pointed, Spock-like ears and eyebrows, it looked like a tiny man. A tiny man in a tiny green kilt.

"Satisfied?" it—he—said.

"You're a—a—" The word wouldn't come. Alex cleared his throat. "Fairy." He felt ridiculous just saying the word. But what else could you call a tiny man with wings?

"Well, these days the King would prefer that we be called 'people of magical heritage,' but, yeah, I'm a fairy. So how about helping me out of this roach motel? Despite what you may have heard, we fairies don't hang out with bugs on a social basis. Especially dead ones."

This is insane, Alex thought. *Or maybe I am.* He looked around again. Halfway across the park, a woman in a halter top walked a panting Afghan hound. A magpie scolded them both. A '74 Camaro rumbled by, bass pounding from the stereo. The sun burned Alex's face. Everything seemed perfectly normal...except for the fairy caught in the city mosquito trap.

The fairy sighed. "Look, buddy, what's your name?"

"Alex," Alex said, then immediately wondered if he should have. Weren't fairies supposed to be able to work magic on you if they knew your true name?

But the fairy didn't seem interested in casting a spell. He was massaging his tiny calf. "Cramp," he muttered. "So, your name is Alex. Great. Wonderful. You know what my name is, Alex? Dandelion. Don't ask me what my parents were thinking. But, hey, call me Dan. In fact, I insist on it." He grinned, and for the first time Alex saw he had long, sharp incisors, like a vampire's.

The grin vanished. "Look, Alex," Dan went on in the exact same tone of *faux bonhomie* a used car salesman might use to close a deal, "I don't care if you don't believe in me. But even if I'm just a figment of your imagination, so what? What've you got to lose by helping me out of here? And if I'm real, well, hey, you know the rule about helping out a fairy."

No, Alex didn't. But all the same, he had to admit the fairy had a point. Even if Dan were just the product of too much cell-phone radiation, or the milk two days past its best-before date he'd used on his cereal that morning, Alex couldn't walk away and leave him stuck in a mosquito trap. It wouldn't be right. "What do you want me to do?"

Dan shrugged his shoulders and winced. "It's these bloody wings. I was trying to barrel-roll through the trap—I know, I know, *bad* fairy, *stupid* fairy—and I got both tips stuck. If just one was stuck I could probably pull free, but I'm afraid if I try to pull too hard the way they are now I'll tear a wing, and nothing is sadder than a fairy with a torn wing—sitting on a damp spiderweb all day, begging for honeysuckle juice from passersby, you know how it is—so if you could just kind of gently peel up the tip of each wing..."

Feeling foolish, Alex reached in. The wings felt soft, even a little furry, not at all like dragonfly wings. "Watch it! Careful now, careful..." Dan's words ended in a squeak as Alex pried up his right wing tip.

Alex froze. "Are you OK?"

"Great, great, couldn't be better..." Dan waved one hand airily, but his tiny chest heaved. "Carry on, carry on..."

The second wing was stuck tighter, but with a fingernail, Alex finally peeled up one corner, and a moment later had the whole thing free, just like peeling a Post-It note from its pad.

Dan's kept his oversized eyes scrunched closed until Alex let go. "You did it?"

"I did it."

Dan opened his eyes, then spread his wings and looked from one to the other. He flapped them once, twice, whooped with delight—and vanished, with a sound like a finger snap.

Alex stared at the mosquito trap. Nothing moved inside it. Even the wasp had quit struggling.

"I've gone crazy," he said out loud.

Overhead a jet traced a white line, dragging its engine-roar behind it. A block away, a child laughed. In the park, an old man in a ragged coat picked slowly through a garbage can.

A perfectly ordinary day.

Alex crossed the street, went into his office, and stared at his computer for the rest of the day without writing a word.

That night, lying in bed, Alex debated telling Mary. The moment seemed inopportune: she'd become engrossed in *Martha Stewart's Living*. "So," he envisioned himself asking, "Martha have any suggestions on how to keep fairies out of mosquito traps?"

He'd already missed his best opening, Mary's usual "Anything interesting happen today?" as she came through the door. Through supper and an evening of TV, he hadn't managed to summon up the courage to broach the subject. And now...

Well, really, what was there to tell? He'd obviously been working too hard. Technical writing deadlines were always ridiculous, two or three weeks for an entire manual, if he was lucky. Recently, it had been more like two or three days.

He glanced at Mary again. Her long red hair hid her face, but he could envision her expression, intent, focused, the tip of her tongue just showing between her lips. He pictured her eyes widening, her smile melting into worry, and he knew he couldn't tell her. He couldn't bear to make her unhappy.

It wouldn't happen again, anyway. In two weeks they were off to Banff. He'd relax. No more seeing things...

The lamp by the bed abruptly dimmed. The clock beside it stopped ticking. A sudden chill made Alex shiver.

"The power's gone off—" Alex began, then his heart skipped a beat. Mary wasn't breathing! "Mary!" He grabbed her arm, but she might have been made of oiled marble: his fingers slipped away. "Mary!"

"She's fine," said a tiny voice in his ear, accompanied by a strange hum. "You're the one something has happened to."

Goosebumps raced over Alex's arms. He turned to see Dan hovering just off his left shoulder, his wings humming and blurring like a hummingbird's. "But...but you weren't real!"

Dan sighed. "Jeez, not again! Personally, I blame the education system, filling all your head with scientific claptrap...back in the eleventh century we never had this problem...well." He perched on Alex's shoulder. "There. Feel that? I'm real." And indeed, Alex could feel Dan's tiny buttocks resting on his shoulder, like two hot peas. "Sorry I was gone so long, but I had to report to the King, and you know how it is in Faerie—you can never be sure how time is passing outside. Frankly, I'm surprised it's not sometime next week."

"What have you done to Mary?"

"Weren't you listening? Nothing! I've done it to you, so we could talk in private. I've pulled you into the Borderspace between your world and Faerie. We can stay as long as we like, and when you go back, no time will have gone by at all." He grinned. "Cool, huh?"

Alex was pretty sure Einstein would have called it impossible, but Einstein never had never met a seven-centimetre-tall person of magical ancestry, either. "Why?"

"To give you your reward, of course."

"Reward?"

"You saved my life. The law is clear. I've got to give you a boon."

"A wish?"

"Do I *look* like a leprechaun? Not a *wish*. A *boon*—a favour. But my boon is just as good as a wish!" Dan looked smug. "I can give you what you've always wanted!"

"How would you know what I've always wanted?" Alex felt unnaturally calm. Shock, probably. Well, it beat screaming.

"I did some research. Time is pretty fluid for us. I can't go into the future, but I can observe the past. So I did." Dan shook his head. "You were a real loser in school, Alex. Never fit in, no friends, always reading those fantasy and science fiction novels, playing *Dungeons and Dragons*, always wishing you could have magic and adventure in your life instead of algebra and phys-ed. Well, guess what?" He spread his hands. "Ta-da! It's yours!"

"What's mine?"

"Magic. Adventure. Don't you get it, Alex? I can take you to Faerie." His voice dropped to a whisper. "Think of it. No more computer manuals. No more deadlines. No more noise, pollution, crime, poverty. Faerie is paradise, Alex. Just close your eyes. Close your eyes, and I'll show you..."

Alex's eyelids drooped, fell shut...but instead of darkness he saw fantastic images: endless forests, snow-capped mountains, crystalline lakes...cities of golden marble, scarlet flags snapping from the top of every tower...laughing people gathering for games, for dances, for feasts where the tables groaned under the weight of food...knights in glittering armour...

No sickness.

No death.

No children.

His eyes flew open. He snapped his head around so suddenly the fairy squeaked and shot halfway across the room. "Don't *do* that!" he scolded, zooming back.

But Alex's eyes weren't on Dan but on Mary, cold and still, her hand frozen in the moment of turning from "Twelve perfect paint shades for the nursery" to "Celebrate summer with light-hearted asparagus soufflé!"

The images of Faerie faded from Alex's mind like a dream. Dan zipped around in front of him. "But it's all you ever wanted! Alex, think of the adventure! The beauty! The wonder!"

Alex reached out and tried vainly once more to touch his wife. "I've already got adventure, and beauty, and wonder," he said softly. "You're too late, Dan."

Dan made tiny retching noises. "What is this, a *Hallmark Hall of Fame* presentation? Alex, Faerie is full of beautiful women. *Willing* women, if you get my drift."

"But no children."

"Children? Alex, people live forever, there'd be a horrendous population problem if every Tom, Dick and Fairy could have kids whenever..." His voice trailed off. "Oh." He studied Alex closely. "You're serious, aren't you?"

Alex nodded.

"Well, that's all very well for you, pal, but it leaves me up the proverbial creek." Dan flew in close and leaned on Alex's nose, forcing Alex to go cross-eyed. "First, I don't like leaving myself in your debt. 'Neither a borrower nor a lender be,' as that old scoundrel Robin Goodfellow dictated to Shakespeare. Good advice all around. But that's not the half of it. It's the King who worries me."

Alex felt confused. "What's the King got to do with me?"

"Well..." Dan looked uncomfortable. "Uh...he sort of—uh, ordered me to get you into Faerie. See, he'd just as soon not have any humans running around who know about us, not in this century."

"So your offer was just a trick!"

"No!" Dan sounded genuinely offended. "Faerie is everything you want...or used to want, anyway. That's why I thought getting you there would be a piece of cake. But..." He circled around to Alex's right side to whisper into that ear. "There's some in the King's court could be calling for an abduction scenario, if I come back without you. The Changeling Guard could be activated again —they used to steal children during that whole 'we need some kids around this place' phase the Queen went through a few centuries back—women! Anyway, they could take you against your will." He suddenly stopped and slapped his hand against his forehead. "Idiot! I've got it! That's what I can give you!"

"What?"

"Listen closely." Dan cleared his throat, then spoke loudly and formally. "Alexander Parker of Regina, I thank thee for thy kindness, and in gratitude for thy service, I, Dandelion Thistlehair of Faerie, do grant thee this boon: to live out thine appointed days within this world, to have children and grandchildren, to grow old and die. By the granting of this boon I pay my debt to thee in full. Dost thou agree?"

"But the Changeling Guard..." Alex said, confused.

"If I give this promise as my boon to you, there's nothing they can do," Dan said fiercely. "A fairy's word is sacred. Faerie itself would come crashing down if they took you after this. Of course, exactly how I'm going to explain myself to the King...well, I'll burn that bridge when I come to it." He flew in close and stared intently into Alex's eyes. "But be sure, buddy," he whispered. "Be very sure."

Alex's eyelids closed again. Faerie once more spread itself before him, full of music and laughter, of beauty and wonder and peace...but the image faded even as he tried to focus on it, replaced by another, more beautiful to him than anything else on Earth or off it: Mary, smiling at him.

He opened his eyes and found he was smiling, too. "I'm sure."

"Then it is done." The fairy stared at Alex a long time. "You know, in movies when something like this happens, the fairy or wizard or whatever usually tells the hero he won't remember any of it."

"Is that what you're going to tell me?"

"Sorry, buddy. This is real life. Can't do it. What I'm saying is, you'd better hope you made the right decision, 'cause for the rest of your life you're going to remember what might have been." Dan glanced at Mary. "She'd better be worth it."

"She is."

Dan shrugged. "Can't see it myself, but maybe I'll check back in a month or so—that'll probably be about thirty years, your time —and see if you still feel that way. Good-bye, buddy. And thanks again." With the sound of a finger-snap, he vanished.

The lights brightened. The clock ticked. And Mary, Alex saw with relief, finished turning the page...not away from the nursery story, but toward it. She brushed her hair back with one hand, and gazed at the pictures of cribs and toy boxes for a long time with a slight smile. Finally she seemed to feel his eyes on her, and looked up. "What?" she said, the smile widening into a grin.

"Just...thinking." Alex stroked her arm, the arm he hadn't been able to touch before. "Thinking how much I love you...more than all the world. Any world."

Mary laughed, tossed the magazine onto the floor, clicked off the lamp, and snuggled up to him, resting her head on his shoulder, her fiery hair cascading across his bare chest. "It's a good thing I love you too, then."

"It is," said Alex. "It's a very good thing."

He smiled in the dark, hugged her close, and slept.

JE ME SOUVIENS

"*Je* e me souviens" *means "I remember" in French. It's the slogan that appears on Quebec license plates. Originally published in the Summer 2002 issue of* Artemis Magazine, *"Je me souviens" was later reprinted by Tyche Books in its anthology* Ride the Moon. *It also received an honourable mention from Gardner Dozois in his annual* Year's Best Science Fiction *anthology. It's one of my personal favourites of all the things I've written...and it seems somehow fitting that it be the last story in this collection.*

THE HOPCAR SOARED OVER THE CRATER WALL and settled to the rock-strewn floor just a few metres away. Its bright-green metalwork, only slightly dulled by the dust its landing had raised, gleamed in the Earthshine.

Years of trudging across the crater floor from my habidome to the shrine had turned my own moonsuit the colour of old bones. Recently, my skin had begun to take on that same skeletal grey, as though, like the legendary chameleon of old Earth, I was beginning to blend in with my surroundings. Nevertheless, with both gloved hands I brushed away the fresh layer of dust the hopcar's arrival had deposited, wanting to look my best for my guest.

After all, it had been most of a decade since the last one.

The dust settled, and the hopcar's airlock slid open, revealing my visitor, her own moonsuit so spotlessly white that it glowed almost as bright as the smooth pearl-white globe of the Earth, hanging above us.

"Welcome, Ms. Chai," I said into my helmet microphone. "I am Brother Damon."

"Then you really do exist," a woman's voice came back in my ears. "I admit I half-expected I'd get out here and find the whole thing was an elaborate joke by my friends."

I didn't know how to respond to that; I didn't know what she meant, then. Instead I said, "If you'll follow me, Ms. Chai, I'll show you to the shrine."

"Lead on, Brother Damon. And call me Tia, please."

"Very well, Tia." I waited until she joined me, then led her across the crater floor toward the shadowed wall where the shrine is buried.

"I don't see anything," Tia said.

"Wait until we step into shadow," I said, which we did a moment later. "Now turn off your lamp and wait for your eyes to adjust."

Her lamp went out; I had never turned mine on. We waited in silence for one minute, two; then, "Oh!" she said.

From the darkness ahead of us emerged the ghostly image of a door, a simple, arched doorway outlined in faint, glowing silver. Words in a thousand ancient languages and alphabets surrounded it on all sides, always the same words, whatever the language, whatever the script. "*Je me souviens.*" "I remember." "*Ich mich erin-nern.*" "*Recuerdo.*" A faint path, outlined in the same luminescent silver, wound through tumbled rocks to the door.

"Now we will go in," I said.

The door swung outward at our approach, and then closed

behind us. We stood in a chamber walled and floored in smooth, black rock. Overhead, a single glowring, set in a golden sunburst, struck sparks of fiery light from thousands of tiny crystals embedded in the stone. For the short time we stood there, as the pumps filled the chamber with air, we might have been floating in space, surrounded by stars.

"Cool," said Tia.

The glowring changed colour from silver-white to a golden-yellow, and I removed my helmet. Tia followed suit, and shook out long black hair that proved to me she seldom visited airless worlds; those who often wear vacuum suits keep their hair cropped short, as I did, when I still had hair.

She smiled at me, dark eyes flashing in a heart-shaped, almond-coloured face. She was younger than I had anticipated; but then, perhaps I was older than she had anticipated, for the first thing she said was, "How long have you been here?"

"I have kept this shrine for almost fifty standard years," I said, aware, as I had not really been in a long time, of my own balding pate and lined face, thinning now toward gauntness. A part of my mind chided me for my vanity, while another part, forever young and foolish, lamented the fact this dark-haired beauty would never find me attractive. Until a few weeks ago, the chastity drugs had silenced that part, but the medirobot had stopped providing those drugs after my last physical examination.

I stepped forward and lightly touched the inner door, and it opened, admitting us into the shrine itself.

We might have been in one of the ancient churches of Earth, familiar to me from the archives of the Order. Carved from billion-year-old moonstone, the shrine is a long, high-ceilinged vault. Pillars march down both sides, carved in the shapes of trees, their branches blending smoothly into the gothic ribs of the ceiling, and twining across the walls in a profusion of stony leaves and twigs. Set among the branches, like strange fruit, are globes of red crystal, each containing an oil lamp. Their soft light spills like fresh blood across the polished grey floor, offering the only illumination apart from the silvery glow of the nave.

There stands a great basalt sphere, ten times the height of a man, the oceans and landmasses of old Earth molded in high relief upon it. Billions of photon emitters prick the surface, individually too tiny to be seen, one for each human being still living on the Earth when the great asteroid slammed into the North Atlantic, cracking the crust like an eggshell, boiling away the oceans, shrouding the dying world in steam and gas.

The light is siphoned down from the moon's surface through fibre-optic threads. As the featureless white Earth waxes and wanes, a translucent, sourceless glow likewise waxes and wanes across the basalt globe.

I waited for Tia's reaction. The last pilgrim, all those years ago, wept. Even though I visit the shrine every day, changing the oil in the lamps, sweeping the already spotless floor, polishing the globe, reciting the prayers that have been said every day in this place for most of three centuries, I occasionally find tears in my eyes, too.

After a long moment, Tia spoke. "I can't believe this is still here." Her voice was too loud for that silent place, yet she raised it even louder, as though trying to raise an echo.

There are no echoes in the shrine; reverberation suppressors built into the pillars ensure it.

"Where would it go?" I said.

"I guess what I really mean is, I can't believe you're here." She looked around. "For fifty years, you've been tending this place? For what?"

"For the Order."

"What's that?"

"Let's sit down. Even lunar gravity, I find, wears at a man my age." I was feeling every one of my years at that moment. I slid into a pew, and she slid in beside me. For a moment, I looked at the globe.

"Three hundred years ago," I said, my voice hoarse (except for the daily prayers, I spoke so little), "the Earth was destroyed. Yet, by the grace of God, humanity survived: here on the moon, on Mars, elsewhere in the solar system. Barely self-sufficient, the colonies struggled. Some failed. Many more people died. But humanity survived. And since then, we have conquered the stars themselves. Now there are a hundred worlds, where before there was only one."

"By the grace of God?" Tia gestured at the globe. "Eight billion dead. Where is God in such a calamity?"

"Had the asteroid hit a century before, when there were no self-sufficient colonies, humanity would have gone extinct," I said. "God gave us the time we needed to develop the technology we needed to survive...just as He gave Noah time to build the Ark."

"Even if that's true, why this shrine? What purpose does it serve?"

"If we are to remember the grace of God, we must remember the catastrophe from which we were spared—and the billions who were not," I said. "In the years after the destruction of Earth, my Order was formed, an Order dedicated to serving God, in remembrance and honour of all those who served God on Earth, in all the myriad religions humanity's God-given sense of the divine had spawned. With the support of all the colonies of the Solar System, we built this shrine, and we have kept it ever since, saying daily prayers for humanity's dead. Humanity's leaders came here to dedicate it. People from all over the solar system made pilgrimages to it. It inspired poetry and artwork and literature and music for decades. It inspired humanity itself—inspired it to a rebirth and rededication, focused its efforts on surviving and prospering."

"But...surely that would have happened anyway."

"Maybe. Maybe not." I looked at the globe. The Earth was near full, and all the globe's landmasses glowed with light. "This place reminds us of where we came from, and all those for whom our ancestral home became a grave. For the Order, it became a sacred trust. And though we serve God in many other ways throughout the Hundred Worlds, we have always kept a brother or sister here, to keep the shrine and greet the pilgrims who visit it."

Tia bit her lip for a moment, then burst out, "But...nobody really cares any more, do they?"

"You are proof that some do. You cared enough to make the journey here from...wherever you are from."

"Oskana," she said. She must have seen my incomprehension, for she added, "Alpha Centauri IV."

"An unusual name."

She shrugged. "I'm told it's a word from an ancient Earth language meaning 'the place where the bones are piled.' Oskana only has plant life now, but giant animals lived there millions of years ago. You can hardly take a step without tripping over a fossil."

"The place where the bones are piled." I nodded at the globe. "It would be a fitting name for Earth."

She looked at me in silence for a moment. I could tell she was troubled. I waited for her to speak.

"I didn't come because I care," she said at last. "I came on a bet."

It was not what I expected. I had no response.

"A friend bet me this place was real; he'd read about it in some old history," she hurried on. "I bet it was a myth. I was coming to Luna on business, so I decided to see for myself. And here I am."

My stomach churned; my heart fluttered. How could this holy shrine, meant to last forever, have become a myth in less than thirty decades?

I looked back at the globe to give myself time to gather my wits. *Perhaps she felt that way* before *she came*, I thought. But I could not believe that anyone could fail to be moved by the shrine. "And now that you have seen it?" I ventured at last.

She stared at it a long moment more. "It's smaller than I

imagined." She stood, and gave me a bright, insincere smile. "Thanks for the tour. I have to catch a ship, so I'd better be going."

I wanted to shout at her, argue with her, cajole her...but we have strict rules against proselytizing; those who come to us must come of their own free will. I could answer questions, as I had, but that was all my vows would allow.

Silent, I led her back to her hopcar. I didn't watch her leave; instead, I turned away and trudged across the crater floor to my habidome.

In the main room, between the dining table and my narrow bed, the medirobot's casket-like diagnostic chamber still yawned open, just as I had left it after the checkup two weeks ago that had changed everything.

I sat at the table and stared at the chamber.

For fifty years, the medirobot had found nothing wrong with me beyond the usual ravages of time. My heart was strong; my bones, after so many years at low gravity, were not, but there were effective treatments for that, once I returned to a planetary environment.

The results of my last physical had been...different.

Perhaps I had missed a scheduled check-up; it seemed likely. I passed my time in ritual and work, each day the same as the one before. And my days, governed by Earth's rotational period, bore no relationship to the alternating sunlight and darkness that crept across the eternal lunar landscape. I might well have misplaced a month; perhaps even a year.

And perhaps the habidome's shielding was not what it should have been; perhaps it had not stopped as much of fifty years of sleeting radiation as it should have.

Whatever the reason, I had gone from being healthy on my second-last checkup to anything but on my last one. This time, the nanoprobes that searched every nook and cranny of my body, like the spies the children of Israel sent into the promised land, brought back reports of giants: an explosively metastasizing cancer that had already colonized much of my body.

It meant the end of my time at the shrine. Within 24 hours, the automated hopcar that brought me supplies would arrive, and I would ride it back to Apollo City, to see what modern medicine could do for me. Perhaps nanotechnology or gene therapy or some new treatment could keep me alive for many more years, even decades. Perhaps not. Either way, my time here was done.

In a way, I felt relieved. I did not regret joining the Order; I did not regret the hermitic life; I did not doubt my decision to serve God. But I had wondered, in the years since the last pilgrim had visited, if perhaps I could have served God better on my own world, perhaps in the monastery whose white walls, looming above our farm, had so fascinated me as a child.

Tia's visit made me question my devotion to the shrine even more. If most of humanity no longer knew the shrine existed, or cared, why should I?

I took off the gold-trimmed, dark green vestments I had donned for Tia's visit, and climbed into the medirobot's chamber. The robot stabbed me in the arm, dispensing a little of the pain medicine that helped me sleep. I climbed stiffly out, dimmed the lights, lay down on my bed, and slept.

In the morning, for what I thought would be the last time, I followed my usual routine. After a simple breakfast of reconstituted cheese, bread, and fruit, I donned my moonsuit and made the trek across the crater floor to the shrine. The Earth had reached full, and its perfect white ball threw my shadow in sharp relief across the crater floor, even though the sun itself was out of sight beyond the wall. I wondered who would take my place; what brother or sister, young and idealistic as I had once been, would make this trek next.

That thought stayed with me as I swept the shrine free of the dust Tia and I had tracked in, refilled the red lamps with oil, in the hope they would burn until my replacement arrived, and then opened the stone chest before the globe where I kept the holy symbols of Earth's religion, swathed in black velvet.

I began the two-hour litany of prayers.

Once I had had to refer to the red-bound book that also lay within the chest for the words of the prayers, for instructions on how to spin the prayer wheels and burn the incense. But the litany had long since become second nature, a calming ritual that seemed to take both no time at all and all the time in the world.

Today, though, I stumbled over the words, as the constant thought intruded: "This is the last time…"

Relief mingled with my sadness when I finished. I packed away the holy items, bowed to the shining globe, donned my dust-stained moonsuit, and went out through the black stone airlock.

A silver hopcar waited near the habidome.

Its profile looked odd. As I got closer, I realized the hopcar did not carry the usual crates of supplies. Instead, there was only a small black octagonal chest, a light in its lid blinking green: a message capsule from the Order.

Puzzled by the absence of supplies, but not overly concerned, since I intended to leave the shrine anyway, I took the message capsule inside. It contained a small silver datachip nestled in thick red padding. I removed the chip and slipped it into my computer.

"Greetings in the One whom all humanity serves," began the message, which appeared only in text, without voice or vid. "I write to tell you that your long and worthy service has come to an end. The Order has decided that the Shrine to Home, which you have tended for so many years with such faithfulness, is to be abandoned. It seems clear to us that humanity no longer feels the need of worship or meditation in that once-holy spot. Our resources are limited, and constantly shrinking, as human spirituality fragments among the Hundred Worlds; and so we feel it best to close the shrine.

"This car will remain at your disposal until you are ready to leave, then will return you to Apollo City. We have arranged passage back to your homeworld of Manor, where you are to report to the monastery at your convenience. In the Service of the One, Henri Michaud, First Secretary."

I sat and stared at the message for a long time. Here was official permission to do the very thing I was preparing to do: leave the shrine and return to the mainstream of humanity. But it had never crossed my mind that the shrine would be abandoned, that I would be its final keeper.

I should have been excited, happy, ready to drop everything and seek out the medical attention that might prolong my life. But instead, brought face to face with the impending closure of the shrine, my thoughts did not turn to the length of my life, but to its purpose.

For fifty years, I had lived to tend the shrine. Abandoning that purpose to save my own life would make those fifty years, the greater part of my life, meaningless. It would mean Tia had been right, and this place no longer mattered—not to the vast crowd of humanity spread among the Hundred Worlds, not to me... perhaps not even to God.

And who even knew if my life could be saved? The medirobot was not optimistic, and it was a long journey to any place that would have the latest medical technology; certainly Apollo City, an interstellar backwater now, did not. I could be dead before any ship I might board could reach any place that might have a hope of saving me.

I put on my moonsuit and stepped out into the crater; but instead of going to the shrine, I stood just outside the habidome, looking up at the pure white pearl of the Earth.

The asteroid that slammed into humanity's home had been unexpected, devastating, and fatal. But humanity lived, through God's grace; and in a way, the Earth, too, lived on, in images, words, thoughts, beliefs—and in this shrine to its memory.

My cancer was just as unexpected, just as devastating, and just as fatal. But if the shrine closed, nothing of me would live on beyond my death; my years in service here would be forgotten, a footnote in the Order's archives, nothing more.

I could do nothing to make the Order keep the shrine open; but I could, perhaps, reach beyond my death to those who might someday come here after me, just as the shrine was meant to do.

I sent the hopcar back with a reply acknowledging the message from the Order, announcing my resignation, and letting them know I would not be returning to Manor.

Then I began my final vigil.

For days now the pain has been constant. I will no longer let the medirobot dispense the drugs that could ease the discomfort. The pain will end soon enough, and in this place of mourning, pain is appropriate.

I no longer follow my ritual of cleaning and prayer. Instead, I spend most of my time in the shrine, gazing at the globe. I let its silvery light wash over me like water, light from eight billion fitful ghosts...soon to be joined by one more.

The last oil has burned in the blood-red lamps, so the shrine is darker now. Soon, the last of the food will be gone, or the water will run out...or perhaps the pain in my cancer-ravaged body will become too much for me to bear. And then, my waiting will cease.

I have programmed the computer that controls the shrine's functions to open the inner and outer doors together on my voice signal. When the time comes, very soon, I will enter the shrine, hang my moonsuit by the door and make my way to the altar. I will surround myself with the holy items of a hundred faiths, open the red-bound book and place it on the floor, then prostrate myself before it. And then I will command the airlock to open.

Open to vacuum, sheltered in the crater wall, the shrine may last a million years or more. The fibre optics that cause Earthlight to play across the basalt globe may fail, but the globe itself may endure long after humanity has vanished from the galaxy.

But if, someday, humans, or whatever humans have become, return to the Moon and find the shrine, they will also find, prostrate before the globe, one faithful man, still honouring the billions who, unable to flee into space, died on humanity's ancestral home—and honouring the grace of God, through which a remnant of the human race survived.

Each of us must find the purpose for our own life.

This is mine.

ABOUT THE AUTHOR

Edward Willett is the author of more than
60 books of science fiction, fantasy, and
non-fiction for adults, young adults, and
children. *Marseguro* (DAW Books) won
the Aurora Award (honouring the best in
Canadian science fiction and fantasy) for
Best Long-Form Work in English in 2009,
and the second book in the *Double Helix*
duology, *Terra Insegura*, was short-listed
the following year. His young adult fantasy *Spirit Singer* (Tyche
Books) won the Regina Book Award at the 2002 Saskatchewan
Book Awards. Several other of his books have been shortlisted for
both the Aurora and the Saskatchewan Book Awards.

Willett's eighth novel for DAW, *The Cityborn*, came out in July
2017; his ninth, *Worldshaper*, launches a new fantasy/science
fiction series for DAW in September 2018. Other recent titles
include the *Masks of Aygrima* trilogy for DAW (written as E.C.
Blake), the two-book *Peregrine Rising* far-future science fiction
duology for Bundoran Press, and the five-book *Shards of Excalibur*
YA fantasy series for Coteau Books. His non-fiction runs the
gamut from science books to biographies to history.

Born in Silver City, New Mexico, Ed moved to Saskatchewan
with his parents from Texas when he was eight years old, and
grew up in Weyburn, where his father taught at Western Christian College. He earned a B.A. in journalism from Harding
University in Searcy, Arkansas, and returned to Weyburn to being

his career at the weekly *Weyburn Review*, first as a reporter/photographer (and columnist and cartoonist), and eventually as news editor. He moved to Regina in 1988 to become communications officer for the then-fledgling Saskatchewan Science Centre, and became a full-time freelance writer in 1993.

For two decades Ed wrote a weekly science column that appeared in the *Regina Leader Post* and assorted other newspapers; an audio version also ran weekly on CBC Radio's *Afternoon Edition* in Regina for seventeen of those years. He has also appeared on CBC TV nationally to talk about science topics.

In addition to writing, Ed is a professional actor and singer who has performed in numerous plays, musicals, and operas, as well as singing with various choirs, including the Canadian Chamber Choir, and, currently, the Prairie Chamber Choir. He lives in Regina with his wife, Margaret Anne Hodges, P. Eng., a past president of the Association of Professional Engineers and Geoscientists of Saskatchewan, and their teenaged daughter, Alice.

You can find Ed online at www.edwardwillett.com.

facebook.com/edward.willett

twitter.com/ewillett

instagram.com/ecwillett